A Rendezvous in the Duke's Bedchamber . . .

"Would you like a drink?" he asked.

"Yes, I'd like whatever you're having," Juliet said, trying to cover her apprehension.

"You can be sure we'll enjoy the same pleasures tonight, Juliet."

"That sounds ominous. I came here to settle things between us."

"You're nervous?"

"What a silly question. Of course I'm nervous," Juliet said, recalling the wager she had no intention of losing. "I've never been ravished."

"Do you like it?" he asked.

"The idea of being ravished?"

"Nay, the liquor . . . the Dram Buidheach. And I promise to ravish you quite thoroughly. You'll like that too." He tipped his glass toward her. "Taste it."

The thick liquor spread over her tongue and dissolved like marzipan candy. "It's very good."

"Take small sips, Juliet. It's very potent."

Feeling brazen, she said, "Like you?"

"Oh, I'm much more potent. The liquor will warm your belly, but I'll set you on fire . . ."

"An exciting new writer who should not be missed."

—*Affaire de Coeur*

For orders other than by individual consumers, Pocket Books grants a discount on the purchase of 10 or more copies of single titles for special markets or premium use. For further details, please write to the Vice-President of Special Markets, Pocket Books, 1633 Broadway, New York, NY 10019-6785 8th Floor.

For information on how individual consumers can place orders, please write to Mail Order Department, Simon & Schuster, Inc., 200 Old Tappan Road, Old Tappan, NJ 07675.

Highland Rogue

Arnette Lamb

POCKET BOOKS

New York   London   Toronto   Sydney   Tokyo   Singapore

For Ron Dinn

A Hoosier by birth.
A Texan by choice.
A nice guy by nature.

An *Original* Publication of POCKET BOOKS

POCKET BOOKS, a division of Simon & Schuster Inc.
1230 Avenue of the Americas, New York, NY 10020

ISBN: 0-671-73001-0

First Pocket Books printing July 1991

10 9 8 7 6 5

POCKET and colophon are registered trademarks of
Simon & Schuster Inc.

Cover art by Nick Caruso

Printed in the U.S.A.

Special and heartfelt thanks to Barbara Dawson Smith, for teaching me how to be a mother. To Susan Wiggs, for showing me how to be a teacher. To Joyce Bell, for keeping a straight face throughout.

Chapter 1

Apprehension skittered up her spine. The feeling found no purchase in senses numbed by weeks of exposure to the biting Highland wind. She shivered from both cold and fear. In a matter of moments she would meet the nobleman who held in his hands the fate of her secret mission.

Her footsteps echoing in the great hall, Juliet White stared at the knot of jet black hair perched on the crown of her escort's head. But her mind focused on putting one foot in front of the other. A peat fire smoldered in the massive hearth. The earthy aroma wafted to her nose and teased her frozen limbs with the promise of warmth. Servants milled about the finely furnished hall, their rustic clothing reminiscent of costumes she'd seen in the Harvest Play in Williamsburg.

Wistful images carried the threat of homesickness. Resolutely, Juliet put Virginia from her mind and glanced at the ancient walls of Kinbairn Castle. She had crossed an ocean and journeyed through the hills of Scotland. She would not lose courage now, when she was about to meet the duke of Ross.

Her imagination conjured a picture of this wealthy peer of the English realm. He would sport a powdered wig, of course, decorated with birds and bows, and soaring toward the rough-hewn beams of the ceiling. His clothes would be satin, no doubt, cut from a bolt of some nauseating shade of puce or daffodil, tucked and tailored here, padded and bejeweled there, all to cleverly hide a blue-blooded body gone to fat and dissipation.

Her spirits lifted; she chuckled inside. She would

1

curtsy nicely. He would afford her no more than a passing glance, then hold out a gloved hand, ripe with the scent of sandalwood and beringed with some heraldic signet. She wouldn't kiss it, though. Or would she? What if the milksoppish lord insisted? Could she risk failure for the sake of pride? No. Nothing would prevent her from finding the information she so desperately needed.

"You'll find His Grace in the scullery." Her escort pointed an ink-stained hand toward a door.

Baffled, Juliet stared at the closed portal. The iron handle was worn smooth. Beneath a dusting of flour, kitchen grime clung to the aged wood. "The scullery?"

"Aye, 'tis where he sums the accounts and scolds the maids."

Puzzled by the woman's mischievous smile and concealing her own surprise that the duke would be found in such a lowly room, Juliet approached the door. Fabric rustled as the escort departed. With the slightest pressure the portal slowly and silently opened.

Smells assaulted her nose. Barrels of smoked fish and kegs of ale blocked the entrance. Herbs, spices, and ripening birds hung from the rafters. Gazing between two vessels, Juliet searched for the duke. She spied a man, an arm's length away, yet shielded by the wall of supplies. Shocked and confused, she shrank into the shadows and peered through a gap in the casks.

Behind her, the distant peal of childish laughter echoed in the halls. The innocent sound lent an unreal quality to the erotic scene before her.

Her back went rigid; her icy hands suddenly thawed and gripped the edge of a barrel. He wasn't summing accounts or scolding maids. He was seducing a servant! And where was the powdered-up duke? Surely this country-clad ruffian couldn't be the lord of the keep.

He sat in a chair, his thickly muscled arms dangling at rest, a writing quill in his hand, a woman on his lap. His chestnut hair, oddly braided at the temples and worn long enough to touch his shoulders, shone in the soft candlelight.

"I've work to do, Cozy," he insisted, his voice thick

with the musical burr of the Highlands, his expression stern with repressed merriment at their lusty game.

From her perch on his lap, her skirts hiked above her knees, her blouse bunched at her waist, the maid wriggled her hips and smiled confidently. "Aye, you do." She boldly cupped a naked breast and leaned forward, offering a taste of herself.

Juliet tried to move, but her feet seemed rooted to the rough stone floor. Her horrified gaze stayed trained on the space between the kegs.

His gaze dropped to a puckered nipple. In profile, his distinctive brow and long, slender nose were aristocratic, out of place with that wild mane of hair. "You're courting trouble, lass, and keeping your laird from his duties."

"Aye, Your Grace. I am."

A flush crept up Juliet's neck and cheeks, warming skin that moments before had been aching with cold. This rogue *was* the duke of Ross!

The maid slipped a hand between them and caressed his groin. "And what about *his* duties?" she asked meaningfully. "Seems he's got a mind of his own today and like to bust yer buttons, don't I help him out o' there."

The quill drifted to the floor. The duke groaned; his head fell back against the chair. The ropy tendons of his neck stood out in sharp relief. He swallowed visibly; then a slow, rakish smile spread across his face, revealing perfect white teeth and crinkled lines at the corners of his eyes.

Having released the buttons, the maid reached for one of his braids and began to pull him toward her. Her lips parted in readiness. She whispered a suggestion that curled Juliet's toes.

Juliet came to her senses. Cozy and the duke might enjoy dallying away their time, but that didn't mean she had to witness it. Assuming a businesslike mien, she stepped into their line of vision and cleared her throat.

The maid turned. Sitting bolt upright, her hands covering her bare breasts, she gasped. "Who are you?"

"I'm Juliet White."

The duke rolled his head toward her. His smile faded.

3

With the care of a plantation owner eyeing a slave at market, he let his dark blue gaze rake Juliet from her disheveled pale hair, over the wilted lace at her bodice, past her travel-stained dress to the scuffed and wet toes of her boots. He looked up and focused on her face.

Her mouth went dry. Her legs grew weak as a spring fawn's.

He concluded the frank inspection with a naughty grin. Infuriated by his insulting appraisal and angry at her girlish reaction to it, she knotted her fists and tried to calm her heartbeat.

"What do you here, Juliet White?"

The casual question in his voice took her by surprise. He wasn't bothered in the least that a stranger had caught him fondling a servant.

Drawing herself up, she said, "I've come from Edinburgh to apply for the position of governess."

He frowned. The maid guffawed.

"Off with you, Cozy," he declared, grasping her waist and depositing her on the floor. In an indignant huff, she righted her clothes and sashayed around the barrels. Glaring at Juliet, Cozy stomped out. The duke pushed himself to his feet and casually began to button the placket of his leather breeches.

Mortified that her eyes kept straying below his waist, Juliet looked away.

He chuckled softly, knowingly. "Are you experienced, Mistress White?"

Shocked, she whipped her eyes back to his. "Experienced?" she choked out.

His grin broadened. "In the art of governessing, Mistress White. What else?"

A steely calmness spread through her. If he thought to intimidate her with his lecherous behavior, he could think again, for she had come too far and given up too much to forfeit her mission now. Schooling her features into blandness, she unclenched her hands. "Of course I'm experienced."

"We'll see."

As he worked at the buttons, she was haunted by the silly picture she had formed of him. Much taller than she'd expected, and leaner than he'd appeared when seated in the chair, the duke of Ross was no polished dandy. The finely woven shirt of pale blue wool hung open to his waist, exposing a massive chest covered with glossy hair and decorated with a necklet of hammered gold and glittering amulets. A tooled leather belt, as wide as the length of her hand, rested on narrow hips and accented devilishly long legs. He emanated power, alien yet alluring. Juliet had an outrageous desire to touch the hair on his chest and warm her fingers against his skin.

She fought a blush as he slipped the last button into place. With unexpected grace, he bent to retrieve the quill. She spied his signet ring and took grim satisfaction that she'd been correct about one aspect of him.

As he straightened, those deep blue eyes, a shade darker than the ocean she'd just crossed, watched her carefully.

"White," he mused, his hands toying with the grouse feather. "And your given name is Juliet?"

He spoke her name in the French fashion, the first syllable a breath of air, a lover's kiss blown across a crowded room. She wanted to look away, but could not. *"Oui,"* she managed to reply.

"A fitting name for one so fair. But what's in a name?"

Fair? She was as plain as Cogburn's brown horse. "Thank you."

"Who showed you here?"

"I don't know her name—a thin woman with black hair and ink-stained hands."

"I might have guessed. Gallie's up to her usual tricks. I don't suppose she offered you ale or the warmth of the fire."

Gallie. The name conjured visions of success. The smug older woman kept the Book of MacCoinnichs! Excitement raced through Juliet. "No, she . . . ah . . . brought me here straightaway."

With a flick of his wrist, he tossed the quill on the table. "Then we shall refresh ourselves," he announced, cupping a hand beneath her elbow and escorting her out the door, "and you can tell me how you acquired that unusual accent in Edinburgh."

Alarmed that he was so astute, Juliet tipped her head back and saw his eyes searching hers as if looking for something she had yet to reveal. Her heart pounded madly. But how could the duke of Ross, a wealthy and notorious nobleman, have any notion about why she'd come to Scotland? The problem lay with her, she decided, for soon would start the lies. Forcing a smile, she said, "Edinburgh? You think I'm from Scotland?"

Confusion softened his features. "Well . . . nay. But from where, then, Juliet White, do you hail?"

Her heart tripped faster at the caress he made of her name. "From Virginia, sir," she said truthfully.

"The American Colonies." He released her arm and waved her ahead of him into a narrow hallway. " 'Tis a fair pace to the solar. Are you up to it?"

"Sir, I've come halfway across the world over rough winter seas. Another jaunt in your castle won't tire me."

Light from a dozen oil lamps danced on the stone walls and floors. Smells from the kitchen faded, replaced by the clean scent of wax and bathing soap. His soap.

"Why would you come to Scotland?"

Now that he wasn't looking at her, she could recite the tale she'd practiced. But then his warm hand touched her neck. The lie stalled in her throat.

"This way." He splayed his fingers and steered her toward another hallway.

Fighting back a wave of guilt and ignoring the pleasant feel of his touch, she said, "To work for the gentry."

"Ah. Then you're ambitious."

"No. Not precisely. I'd merely like the same chance as others." A spark of truth, fueled by bitterness, tinged her words. "At home, I would always be passed over in favor of an imported tutor."

"An exported Colonial tutor," he said with a smile in his voice. "Who seems to enjoy walking."

She felt his eyes on her back and grew self-conscious of her disheveled appearance. How else could she look after days of riding in an unsprung and uncovered cart?

Her stubborn pride surfaced. "I'm as well trained and capable as any male tutor from England."

"And much bonnier. You're shivering. Are you cold?"

Unprepared for solicitude from such a womanizer, Juliet searched for an answer. Weary from the journey and doubtful that she could ever pull off this ridiculous ruse, she found the strength to nod.

"Well, don't be thinking I'll pull you into my arms to warm you, lass. I wouldn't dare give you the wrong impression of a member of the 'gentry.' "

She went stock-still. He bumped into her. His hands grasped her upper arms. Against her back she felt the muscled contours of his chest and the hard trunks of his legs. He radiated warmth and strength, two things she was sorely missing.

"Don't get too comfy, lass. We're not in the scullery."

Her back went stiff with indignation. She shook him off and continued walking. "I'm no prude, Your Grace. What you do to your maids, and where you choose to do it, is your affair."

"True," he said crisply. "But you've mixed your words. Cozy was doing to me, not the other way 'round. Were you truly experienced, Juliet White, you would know that."

Had he been the victim? A willing victim, she decided. What difference did that make? She was here for one reason, and his immoral practices had nothing to do with her. "I stand corrected, then."

" 'Tis glad I am to hear that, lassie. I wouldn't want to spoil my reputation."

"But in Edinburgh, they said you—" Juliet whirled around.

His eyes danced with merry challenge. "Said what? Don't stop now."

She couldn't believe her ears. The most notorious rake in Scotland was making a jest of his ill-gotten fame! He seemed proud of the gossip. "You care not what they say about you?"

He tossed his head back and roared with laughter.

The sound echoed off the ancient walls, warming the air and lightening her mood. "What a strange man he is."

Chuckling, he wiped his eyes. "Not so strange, lass. Just uninterested in the conversations of people with too much money and too little imagination."

Aghast that she had spoken her thoughts out loud, she felt a blush creep up her neck.

"No need to be embarrassed. I like a woman who speaks her mind." Before she could reply, he added, "But do you speak Scottish?"

At ease for reasons she did not understand, Juliet began walking again. "If you mean Gaelic, no, I don't speak it."

"In Scotland," he murmured, "we call our language *Scottish*. No matter, though." His voice dropped and sounded genuinely remorseful. " 'Twas nice of you to come, but you'd never suit."

Juliet's heart lurched. He couldn't refuse her. Not before she had spoken to the woman named Gallie, not when her goal lay so tantalizingly close. Desperate to change his mind, she turned around. And found herself staring at an amber stone carved in the shape of a stag and nestled in the mat of red-gold hair on his chest. Unable to meet his eyes, she said, "You mean because I don't speak Gaelic?"

"Scottish," he corrected.

She hadn't anticipated this complication. Looking up, she expected to see that stern, watchful gaze. Instead, a grin played about his mouth. "Scottish," he insisted.

"Scottish," she conceded.

He chuckled. The braids danced about his shoulders, and the stag shimmered in the lamplight. "So you can converse as civilized people do, my dear, and teach my children."

"On the contrary." With all the bravado she could muster, she insisted, "Your children will learn more quickly if they speak English, and I'm very good with languages. They can teach me Scottish." Hesitantly, she added, "They do speak . . . uh . . . some English, don't they?"

He folded his arms over his massive chest. "Aye,

8

they speak the king's tongue, and a wee bit of French."
Smiling indulgently, he added, "And too many words
they shouldn't know. But not your Virginia English."

His light banter and fatherly reply charmed Juliet. "In
America, Your Grace, we call our language *American*."

His eyes twinkled; a grin teased his handsome mouth.
"Touché. The solar's through that door."

Hoping she was making headway, she turned again and
followed his direction. Her spirits soared when she spied
Gallie standing at attention near the hearth in the solar.
The woman curtsied and murmured, "Your Grace."

Although shorter than Juliet by several inches, she
carried her small frame in queenly fashion. She'd
washed her hands and donned a fresh apron of faded
saffron cotton. The springlike color complemented fair
skin with fewer wrinkles than one would expect for a
woman of her years. Studying those dark eyes, alight
with a youthful gleam, Juliet wondered if she had misjudged Gallie's age.

But none of that mattered; Gallie had the answers
Juliet sought. King George himself could not keep her
from finding the truth and locating the man who had
betrayed her sister and left her to die.

The duke picked up a chair and moved it near the
fire. "You'll be warmer here."

Her limbs aching, she carefully lowered herself into
the chair.

"Bring ale for our guest, Gallie," he said, "and *Dram
Buidheach* for me."

Gallie screwed up her face. "What am I to do for that
foul-mouthed mugger she brought with her? Draw him
a steaming bath?"

The duke shot Juliet a questioning glance. "Is he your
man?"

"My man?" she asked blankly.

"Your husband," he said slowly, as if she were dim-
witted.

Gallie clasped her hands together. "You're married?"
she squealed much like a maiden. "Saint Ninian's
blessed us this time!" Turning to the duke, she said, "Did
you hear that, Lachlan? A married governess."

"Haud yer wheesht, Gallie."

"No!" Juliet put in. She'd expected to lie often while at Kinbairn Castle, but on this topic she could tell the truth. "Gallie refers to Cogburn Pitt. He traveled with me from Virginia." The real reason Cogburn had come with her was none of their affair.

The duke ensconced himself on a thronelike chair. "Is he your servant, then?"

Startled, Juliet replied, "I'm hardly the type to employ servants, Your Grace."

He sighed as if impatient. "Then why is he traveling with you? Is he your lover?"

Flabbergasted, she blurted, "Neither am I the type to have a lover. I couldn't have come so far alone." Her discomfort rose. "I'm here to apply for a respectable position, and I resent your implication that I would bring along a lov— a paramour on my journey. Or that I would have a paramour at all."

Looking incredulous and oddly discomfited, he said, "How was I to know? You could be a duchess under those wrinkled clothes."

Her desperate mission momentarily forgotten, she laughed out loud. "Are duchesses synonymous with lovers?"

Gallie cackled. "Aye, and the duke has a way with both." She rolled her eyes. "Ah, Lachlan, the Colonial's out of reach. She brought her own man."

"Haud yer wheesht!" he roared again.

She clucked her tongue. "You'd best hire her now, before she and her fine man get away."

"And you'd best mind your tongue, Gallie MacKenzie. I won't tell you again. Fetch the drinks; then be about your business."

Gallie exited the room, gales of mirth trailing down the hall.

MacKenzie. Gallie was a MacKenzie. Did everyone in Ross bear that name? And when on God's green earth would she meet the person named *MacCoinnich?* She edged her damp boots closer to the hearth. Suddenly aware of how cold she had been, she held her hands out to the fire. Steam rose from the hem of her skirt. As the chill left her, she gazed about the unusual chamber.

Compared to elegant Mabry House and the tumble-down orphanage she'd grown up in, Kinbairn Castle seemed unique, ancient. Battle-axes and broadswords adorned the walls. Between the weapons hung embroidered tapestries and gilt-framed images of haughty noblewomen and stern-faced men.

Her imagination took flight. She pictured soldiers heavily laden with armor, wisps of colorful silk tied about their mail-clad arms. She envisioned the duke of Ross astride a snorting, prancing destrier, and preparing to lead his army into battle. He'd raise his arm and swing his claymore in a circle—

"Are you getting warm?"

His voice interrupted her romantic musings. He lounged in the carved chair, his long legs crossed at the ankles, his folded hands resting where the maid had caressed him. Juliet felt a flush of renewed embarrassment. She moved away from the fire. "Overwarm, actually," she murmured.

" 'Tis not the best time to travel about the Highlands. You should have waited till spring. The weather's bonnie then, and the yellow's in the broom."

She couldn't have waited until spring, but she had no intention of telling him that. From the web of lies and deceptions she had woven, she drew upon the few truths she could unravel. "I was told you needed a governess, and I haven't the means to sojourn in Edinburgh until the weather turns fair."

Moving his hands from his lap, he rested them on the arms of the chair. She couldn't help herself; her eyes stayed fixed on the placket of buttons; her mind stayed focused on what lay beneath them.

"Why would you choose the Highlands? A dainty lass like you would feel more at home in Edinburgh or the Court of St. James."

With effort, she cleared her throat and turned her gaze to the fire. The lie slipped easily from her lips. "Yours was the first open post I found."

"That's not unusual. 'Twas a bold move, coming to Scotland. Were you unhappy in Virginia?"

"Not at all."

"Are you running away from someone?"

"Of course not. I never run away from anything."

"You understand that I'm only surprised. You're the first Colonial governess to apply for the job. Why?"

She shrugged and forced a laugh. "Perhaps one of my ancestors was a Scotsman with the wanderlust. Perhaps he passed it on to me."

"You don't look Scots," he drawled, giving evidence of his easy way with women. "Mayhap Baltic with your fair hair and doelike eyes, but not Scots."

"I wouldn't know, sir." As she had so many times in her life, Juliet ignored the pain of being abandoned by careless and selfish people who couldn't be bothered with another daughter.

His brows shot up. "You were orphaned?"

Pride lifted her chin; determination fueled her words. "Yes. But if you think to pity me, sir, don't trouble yourself. I've made a fine life for myself." She'd made a place for herself in the world by hard work and strength of character. "I love my work. I enjoy children, and they take easily to me."

A flicker of admiration shone in his eyes. "And how came you to be a governess?"

"As a child I was hired out to a scholar of Latin in Richmond. I swept the stoop, whittled his quills, and dusted his books. Eventually he taught me to read and write. He died when I was twelve."

"How old are you now, Juliet White?"

Would she never become accustomed to the sound of her name on his lips? Pushing the disquieting notion aside, she fluffed out her drying skirts. "Two and twenty, Your Grace."

"You appear . . . ah"—he gazed at her breasts—"more mature."

Because of her bosom? As a connoisseur of women, he would find nothing of interest in her. She was plain; she was dowdy; she was unremarkable. Lillian had been the beauty. Lillian, with spun gold hair and laughing brown eyes. Lillian, the loving sister who had shielded Juliet from the cruel tricks of the older orphans. "I'm quite practical, sir. I've worked too hard to be frivolous about life."

"My apologies. 'Twas not my intention to offend."

She willed the bittersweet memories away. "I was not offended," she said, and meant it. Now was not the time for maudlin thoughts about the past . . . and Lillian.

"What did you do after the scholar died?"

"I indentured myself to the Mabry family of Williamsburg."

"By the rood, lass!" He leaned forward and drilled her with those piercing blue eyes. "How could you make that decision? You were but a child."

He was wrong, absolutely wrong; her struggle to survive had driven every childlike characteristic from her. Summoning the bravado that had enabled her to make this journey, she laughed. "Oh, but I was lucky indeed, Your Grace. While most indentured servants were emptying chamber pots, tending tobacco fields, or worse, I was learning French and geometry. By the time the Mabry children were old enough to need a governess, I was ready to teach them."

"You've a challenge here, then," he mumbled ominously.

Juliet tasted victory. "I'm very accomplished, Your Grace."

"Know you astronomy?"

She nodded.

"Name the brightest star in Orion's belt."

So. He thought to test her, did he? "The belt stars are bright, Your Grace, but the red star, Betelgeuse, is Orion's brightest."

He frowned, the expression bringing a stern look to his overtly handsome features. "Aye, in the sword."

"Nay," she declared, "at the shoulder." He could think her bold, but she would not demur, not when he challenged her mind.

His mouth twitched with humor. "Know you deportment and finesse, Juliet?"

Contentment spread through her. She could sit for

hours in this ancient castle and speak of the things no other adult had cared to hear. Her gaze caught his. Yes, she would enjoy exchanging ripostes with the duke of Ross. She didn't hold back the smile, couldn't stifle the urge to copy his burr. "Aye, Your Grace, *department* and finesse."

He laughed at her mimicry.

She rose and walked to the grouping of portraits. "Who is this gentleman?" She indicated a stern-faced man with a plaid draped over his shoulder.

"He's Colin MacKenzie, the first duke of Ross."

Turning, she found herself nose to chest with the current duke. "Are you the second in the line?" She managed to raise her head.

"Nay," he said gravely, though laughter glimmered in his eyes. "I'd be over a hundred and fifty years old, were I that."

"Oh," she stammered, feeling foolish. "I didn't know. I mean, well, I merely thought . . ."

"Thought what?"

Slipping deeper into the trap of her own ignorance, and becoming fascinated again by the amber stag in his necklet, she turned back to the painting. "You favor him, Your Grace."

"Colin?"

"To me you do."

"Nay, lass, for Colin was a wee man, hardly bigger than you. 'Twas the fourth duke, Kenneth." His hand appeared over her shoulder as he pointed to another portrait. "He gave me my height."

Oh, yes, she thought, this burly Highland lord had manliness to spare. "Have you a name and number, too?"

"Aye, Lachlan, and the sixth." He lowered his arm until it touched her shoulder. "Are you suitably impressed?"

"Of course," she quickly replied, while her mind made a slow exploration of his hand, his wrist, the weave of his shirt. "Have you a shawl, like his?"

"Shawl?" He choked out the word. " 'Tis a tartan,

not a shawl, and nay, I've not one. The English forbid it."

Surprised that he would allow anyone to forbid him anything, she spun around. His face was pulled into a frown. "How dreadful. Can't you do something?"

His arm fell to his side. "Oh, aye," he drawled sarcastically, "I could wear my tartan and be hanged by the English." His expression turned sad. "If I had a tartan."

Outrage boiled inside her. "I hate the English. They tax the Colonies unmercifully; they control our trade. Mr. Mabry has no say in the price his crops yield. His tobacco factor in London pays him just when it's convenient."

His arm propped casually on the fireplace mantel, his brows lifted in surprise, the duke seemed all attention.

Self-conscious, and surprised by her own vehemence, she waited for him to voice his disapproval.

"Have you references?"

Relief spread through her. He *was* considering her for the post. "Yes. From the Mabrys, the vicar, and Sir Axel Beverly, a scholar at the College of William and Mary."

"I would have a look at them later."

"Of course, Your Grace. They're in my satchel."

Gallie trudged into the room, a tray in her hands. She looked from the duke to Juliet, then smiled. "You've won him over, I see. He's stubborn as the church on Sunday when it comes to the lassies. Spoils and coddles—"

"Bite your meddling tongue, Gallie, and fetch them."

He took Juliet's arm and guided her to a chair. Then he seated himself.

Tipping her nose in the air, Gallie put down the tray and picked up the glass. She bowed at his feet. "Your pardon, my lord duke. I lost my wits." She held out the drink. "Toast yer laird or lose yer head."

His eyes narrowed. "You'll lose more than that, I trow. Take your superstitions with you, and leave us be."

She got to her feet and strolled out the door. Smothering a chuckle, Juliet poured herself a tankard of warmed ale. "To the duke of Ross," she ventured boldly.

He held up his glass. "You're a quick one, Juliet White," he said with good humor. "But don't be encouraging Gallie. She needs no help from you to make mischief."

Certain she had a chance at the position, and praying Gallie's book would tell her what she needed to know, Juliet sipped the strong ale. Although different from the yeasty brew of Edinburgh, the drink suited her palate. For reasons she could not explain, a calmness settled over her. She felt comfortable, as if she were sitting in the Mabrys' schoolroom instead of an ancient Scottish castle an ocean away from home.

Remembering the names of the people she'd met during her journey, Juliet said, "It seems everyone's a Mac-Kenzie. Are they all relatives? Do you have a large family, Your Grace?" And where were the blasted MacCoinnichs?

"Clan," he corrected. "Aye, we're more potent even than the Diamaird Camerons or the MacDonalds of Skye."

"How do you remember them all?" She held her breath; the right answer would put her a step closer to her goal.

His expression grew tender. "I don't suppose you'd know about keeping track of one's kin, would you, Mistress White?"

Why hadn't he called her Juliet? The wistful thought vanished when he added, " 'Tis Gallie's job to keep up the Book of the MacKenzies."

Success sang in her veins. If she could find this Book of MacKenzies, surely the Book of MacCoinnichs would be close by. "You've a record of all your kin? How wonderful."

He strolled to the sideboard and refilled his glass. Fascinated at the graceful way he moved, she could not stop staring. Without a sag or a pucker, the breeches hugged his narrow hips and flanks. The fine stitchery at the seams outlined his muscular calves; the carved buttons at the placket accented his masculinity.

The decanter clanked against the tray; Juliet came to her senses. She had not come to Scotland to gawk at some skirt-chasing duke; she had come for a purpose.

She sipped the ale. When he had seated himself once more, she asked, "Did the first duke of Ross have a chronicler like Gallie to keep the Book of MacKenzies?"

He rolled the glass between his palms, making a clink-clinking sound as his ring struck the crystal. "The book?" His hands moved faster. "I had thought you interested in buttons, Mistress White. 'Tis a pastime of the English king, you know, carving buttons."

Mortified, she wanted to slither under the chair. Did this Scottish womanizer miss nothing? She juggled the tankard, nearly spilling the contents. "Any monarch who styles himself 'a most miserable sinner' and proceeds to trespass against his Colonial subjects is bound to display odd behavior."

The clinking stopped; the duke's brows shot up. "Bless Saint Ninian," he declared. "I've met a lady patriot. How long have you been in revolt, Mistress White?"

The gleam in his eyes fired her defenses. "Not as long as your family's been keeping a record of its people." There. She'd steered the conversation where she wanted it.

He lifted the glass her way. Her heart beat faster at the coyness of his salute.

"Gallie must be quite busy, keeping up with your clan."

"Aye, she is."

Juliet stared into the tankard and counted the rings of foam, marking each sip she'd taken. "What's in the book—that keeps her so busy?"

He shrugged. "Births and deaths. Handfast marriages and hell-wrought hangings."

Pretending to pick a speck from the tankard, she said, "Like when a MacKenzie marries a MacCoinnich?"

"We're very careful about a match like that."

Were the MacKenzies and the MacCoinnichs enemies? Oh, dear, she hadn't considered such a complication. Looking up at him, she blinked and asked, "Why?"

"Enough about the book; the topic is forbidden."

"Like your tartan shawl?"

Humor flashed in his eyes. "The penalty's much worse."

"Oh?"

"Aye." He seemed to be enjoying himself. "Speak you again of the blasted book and I'll have your tongue cut out and fed to MacBride's hounds."

Laughter bubbled up inside her. "You'll do no such thing, my lord of Ross; you're merely trying to frighten me." Once she had the position, she'd learn the answers for herself. "How old are your children?"

He seemed to relax. "About six."

"Oh, just one? But I thought Gallie said—" She stopped; things were going too well. One child, or twins, it made no difference. After years with the Mabry boys and girls, the duke's offspring would be a welcome delight. "Have you a daughter?"

"Lass," he corrected, stern-faced.

She rested her hands primly in her lap. "Ah, yes. That would be Scottish for 'girl.' "

" 'Heathen' on occasion, some would swear," he grumbled, but beneath the gruff words his love shone clear.

A long-forgotten dream, unbidden and unwelcome, crept into her mind. A dream of frilly dresses, decked-out ponies, and loving parents.

The tramping of small feet and the titter of girlish laughter echoed in the hallway, drawing Juliet from her reverie. She sat upright and put the mug aside. Would the girl be a hoyden? Absolutely, considering the amount of noise emanating from beyond the doorway. No matter. She would manage this child.

Smiling confidently, she slid a glance at the duke. He watched her closely, but his attention was clearly focused on the child about to enter the room.

Juliet, too, marked the approaching footfalls. Would the child's hair be the rich chestnut shade of her father's? Or would she be fair and delicate? Was she shy or bold? Would her eyes dance with merry light or challenge with stubborn pride?

Chapter 2

Papa!"

Running on spry legs encased in leather breeches, golden braids swaying from her temples, the girl bounded into the room and landed in front of the duke.

He smiled and tugged her braids. "Hello, poppet."

Reaching up, she grasped his thicker braids and demanded, "Hug me, Papa."

He held out his arms. The sprite leapt into his embrace. Closing his eyes, he grunted in satisfaction as he rocked her from side to side.

Juliet felt a burst of joy at the unfeigned show of affection. The duke made a lie of the tale about nobility ignoring their children. Hope blossomed inside her; surely a man who cared so deeply for his own child would understand and support her reasons for coming to Scotland. Should she tell him?

Movement in the doorway caught her eye. She glanced up just as a second girl, of an age with the sprite, marched into the room. So, they *were* twins, she thought. How charming.

Wearing a flour-streaked smock and a smug expression, the dark-haired girl plopped down on the arm of the duke's throne. Tenderly, he wiped a smudge from her nose, then pulled her onto his lap. She bussed his cheek and wiggled free. Her eyes, the exact shade of his, flicked to Juliet. "Who's she?"

"I'm Juliet White. Who are you?"

The sprite unwound her arms from her father's neck and turned around, staring. She squared her shoulders and lifted her chin, which set her braids to swaying. Before she could speak, the dark-haired girl said, "She's Agnes, and I'm Lottie."

Agnes glowered at her sister. The expression was a babyish rendition of the duke's scowl.

19

Looking from one daughter to the other, he said, "Mistress White has come a long way to meet you, but I haven't decided whether to keep her yet."

"If you scold her she'll stay," said Agnes.

Lottie sighed dramatically. "Cozy said we couldn't have cider, Papa," she lisped through the space where her front teeth had been. "I told her you'd take her to the scullery and scold her again if she didn't get off her bum and fetch us a quaff. She said you could take your scolding to the Orkneys 'cause she wasn't havin' none of it."

Juliet knew better; the maid had been eager for the duke's brand of punishment.

A grin played about his mouth at the mention of his assignation with the maid. "Cozy has a tart tongue, lassie. I'd not have you learning her bad habits."

"Aye." The girl nodded gravely. " 'Tis why you scolded her twice today."

"Aye, 'tis."

He obviously wouldn't know a scruple if a parson braided one into his hair. Affection for these twin daughters seemed his only redeeming quality, but did it excuse him for being a profligate rake? No, not in Juliet's mind.

Her sensibilities in shreds, her body exhausted from the long journey, she bristled. "Scolding, Your Grace?"

Beaming with arrogance, he said, "Are you worried I'll scold you?"

"Dinna fash yourself over that," Agnes said. "He don't usually scold visitors. Except there was that Lady Addington . . ."

"Can we please have cider?"

"Aye, Lottie," he said. "As soon as Thomas has a keg brought from the cellar."

Eager to win the affection of these girls, Juliet said, "The blacksmith's wife back home had twins. But they're boys and look very much alike."

"We ain't twins," Lottie announced.

"Agnes?" a girlish voice called from the hall. "Agnes, where are you? Why didn't you wait for me? Lottie said—" Another girl stepped into the room, her hair the chestnut shade of the duke's, her eyes a wintry shade of hazel. Her chubby body was swathed in a tentlike creation with bulging pockets and a tear at the hem.

Juliet stared in surprise. She had read in the *Virginia Gazette* of the oddity of triplets, but she had never expected to see a set.

"That's Mary," Lottie volunteered. "She pinches sweets from the pantry when Cook's not looking. And she don't wash her teeth if she ain't made to."

"That's codswallop, Lottie MacKenzie. You're just vexed 'cause you lost your teeth." Mary turned an imploring look to her father. "Gallie promised me a shortbread if I'd fill her lamp. I did, Papa, and I didn't spill even a dot of oil."

"She still don't wash her teeth."

Mary whirled. "Agnes don't either, and she's the only one that's still got her front teeth."

"That's enough, lassies." The duke looked from one to the other. "I'd have you all remember our guest and your manners."

"Her?" Mary pointed at Juliet.

"Lottie don't have manners," grumbled Agnes.

"She don't have the look of the guest," Lottie said. "She's mucky as Mrs. Percy's Sunday wig."

"Lottie!" The duke slammed a fist on the arm of his throne.

Mary chortled; Agnes fought the urge and lost, dissolving into gales of laughter.

The duke leaned close to whisper in Agnes's ear. As he spoke, her brown eyes darted here and there. She nodded. He winked and gave one of her braids a tug. Her face aglow with purpose, she scrambled off his lap and darted into the hall. A moment later she returned, leading yet another child. As fair and delicate as Mrs. Mabry's cameo, this fourth girl seemed a study in quiet obedience and angelic beauty. She clutched a tattered book to her chest.

"That's Sarah," Lottie said. "She's forever readin' the books in Papa's library."

"Lottie . . ." the duke warned.

Immediately contrite, she stepped to Sarah's side. "She's the pretty one, ain't she? She's nice, too, but she's shy as Gallie's mouser cat. You mustn't ever yell at her."

Her mind in an absolute boggle, Juliet stared at the four girls, now standing in a row. These were not stair-step children. Hadn't the duke said his children were about six? Although as different as cotton and tobacco in appearance, they favored one another in subtle ways.

Juliet glanced at him, then back at his daughters. The noses and the eyes. Ah, yes, the similarities lay there. Agnes and Mary had been blessed with a smaller version of that finely sculptured nose. Lottie and Sarah possessed his eyes. Juliet tried to picture the woman who could have borne so many children at once. No wonder the duke was a widower; no woman could have accomplished such a feat and lived. Or did she live? If so, did she sanction the duke's dalliances?

Juliet braved another glance at him. Those watchful eyes were still trained on her, but now they glittered with challenge. Hoping to thaw his frosty look, she said, "Your children favor you, Your Grace."

"You needn't be an Edinburgh scholar to see that, Mistress White."

"An Edinburgh scholar could see that," Agnes echoed.

The girls formed a circle around his throne, each touching him in some fashion: Agnes, casually resting an arm on one of his broad shoulders, her direct gaze reflecting inner confidence; Lottie, a flour-smudged hand atop his sun-browned wrist, a watchful expression in her dark blue eyes; Mary, her plump hip nudging his bent knee, an inquisitive expression accentuating her country-fresh complexion; and Sarah, tentative as a bird, her book held tightly in one hand, the other tucked securely under the collar of his shirt.

Juliet's throat grew thick at the harmonious picture they made. He seemed a giant oak sheltering his precious seedlings. Loneliness blossomed inside; she valiantly suppressed the emotion. If she could win their approval, she, too, might experience a measure of that familial joy.

"I should be grateful for the opportunity to meet the duchess of Ross," she said.

The duke's brows shot up; the girls frowned at one another in confusion.

"There's no duchess," Lottie chirped. "There ain't never been a duchess here. We was all born without a blanket."

"No, we wasn't," snapped Agnes. "We was born on the *wrong side* of our blankets, you wiggle-head. You always fankle it up."

Juliet ceased to listen. Bastards! Not an oddity of birth. The stories about the duke's reputation were more than true. She searched his face for some show of emotion, some sign of how she should proceed. She found only a bland, handsome stare.

Past the point of good manners, she asked, "They have different mothers? All of them?"

His earlier protectiveness paled when compared to the fierce expression he shot her. "The lassies are sisters, and my daughters." His voice dropped to an ominous rumble. " 'Tis all that matters to you, Mistress White— and to everyone else. You may take that news back to Edinburgh and spread it like the plague."

Knowing anything else she said on the subject could work against her, Juliet looked at Lottie. "Tell me the meaning of 'fankle.' "

A sheen of tears glistened in the child's eyes.

The duke leaned forward; Agnes and Sarah moved with him. "Lottie said nothing wrong." He spoke slowly, distinctly. " 'Tis but a Scottish expression meaning she was mistaken."

He'd misconstrued her meaning. "Of course she didn't say anything wrong," Juliet said. "I merely asked about the meaning of the word. 'Fankle' is not a word used in Virginia."

"Where's that?" Mary asked.

"In the American Colonies," Juliet answered, her eyes on the girl, but her senses attuned to the duke. "Do you know of them?"

Lottie's vulnerability seemed to have passed. "Sarah knows. Sarah knows everything."

Deliberately avoiding the duke's gaze, Juliet looked at Sarah. "Do you know about the Colonies?"

The girl turned beet red, ducked her chin, and peeked at her father. He turned to her, pride dancing in his eyes. "Do you, Sarah lass?"

Her nod was nearly imperceptible.

In a voice softer than Juliet expected, he coaxed, "Then tell Mistress White what you know about her home."

She bowed her head. Lamplight sparkled in the strands of her golden hair. " 'Tis across the Atlantic Ocean," she began in a voice as light and soft as swansdown. "They grow tobacco there . . . for Papa's pipe."

"Aye, they do, Sarah," he said. "What else do you know of Virginia?"

The child cleared her throat. "Between the thirty-sixth and thirty-ninth parallels, the colony was founded by the Virginia Company in sixteen-seven." She paused to draw breath and momentum. "Under the command of Captain Christopher Newport, the flagship *Sarah Constant*, the *Godspeed,* and the *Discovery* sailed up the James River and founded a settlement at Jamestown."

"I told you she knew," Lottie chirped.

Mary jerked her head around. "Why don't we grow tobacco, Papa?"

The duke straightened in the chair. "Because the auld sod won't bear it, Mary. 'Tis lucky we are to harvest a bushel or two of oats from our rocky Highland soil."

The girl turned back to Juliet. "Is it fun to grow tobacco? What color are the flowers? Is it as pretty as heather?"

"Tobacco is grown for money, Mary, not for fun," Juliet said, grasping the opening. "As for the blossoms being like heather, I wouldn't know, for I've never seen heather. But I'd like to."

Four small faces expressed disbelief. The duke's mouth twitched with laughter, giving Juliet another glimpse of the rogue she knew him to be. He cleared his throat. "Mistress White is interested in becoming your governess."

The girls responded by examining Juliet in their own peculiar ways: Agnes looked condescendingly critical,

Lottie extremely skeptical, Mary overtly curious, and Sarah inordinately pleased.

As five pairs of eyes scrutinized her, Juliet's palms grew damp and her traveling stays pinched the tender skin beneath her breasts. She hadn't lied when she said she was good with children. She hadn't boasted, either. So why did she feel uncomfortable? Why did the duke insist on discussing the matter in the presence of his children?

Determined to keep her composure, she stiffened her back. "Your Grace," she began hesitantly, "perhaps we should conduct this interview in private."

"There is no privacy at Kinbairn Castle," he retorted. "Surely you've deduced that, Mistress White."

"Except when you're scolding," Lottie said. "You always do that in private."

"Until today," he mumbled.

"Why can't we have a Scottish governess?" Agnes demanded.

"You could, lass," he replied, his tone noncommittal, "in spring, when the weather turns fair, but why don't you want Mistress White?"

"She's not pretty."

"That's rude, child, as well as incorrect. You know better than that."

"I'm sorry, Papa." Nervously she twirled one of her braids. "I do know better than that."

"Aye, you all do."

Sarah's face glowed; Juliet rejoiced, for she had an ally in the shy girl.

Lottie declared, "We've had twelve Scottish governesses and two Sassenachs."

Amused, Juliet asked, "What's a Sassenach?"

"The heathen English," answered Agnes with great importance.

Sensing a chink in their armor, Juliet said, "Well, I'm certainly not English, and I would like to be governess number fifteen."

"Can you speak Scottish?" Mary demanded. "Do you know the story of our bonnie prince?"

"Of course I know the story of Charles Stuart; everyone in the Colonies knows.'' Leaning forward, she lowered her voice and added, ''I also know the story of Pocahontas.''

Lottie stepped forward. ''What's a poka huntath?''

Juliet said, ''You don't know about Pocahontas?'' In turn, she looked at each of the girls. When none spoke, she said, ''Why, she was the bravest Indian princess who ever lived. I thought all children knew about Pocahontas.''

''Was she, Papa?'' Mary asked, tugging on his sleeve. ''You never told us about her. Was she the most important princess?''

''I trow she was, Mary,'' he said, a note of humor in his voice. ''John Smith thought so.''

Mary swung back to Juliet. ''Will you tell us the tale in Scottish?''

Juliet's confidence sagged. ''No. In French, perhaps, or Latin or English.''

''Oho!'' proclaimed the duke, steepling his hands beneath his chin. ''Have you forgotten your American tongue so quickly?''

Juliet blushed. This Highland rakehell was too quick by half, but if he wanted to match words, she would oblige. ''Of course not, Your Grace. I seem to have *fankled* it up. I meant, of course, to say 'American.' ''

The girls gaped; the duke pointed a finger at Juliet. ''Touché again, Juliet.''

Her mind swirled with the lilting echo of his informal address.

''What's American?'' Mary asked.

''The language I've been speaking,'' Juliet replied. ''A language without the 'hubba-hubba' of the 'hoity-toity' Sassenachs.''

The room came alive with the titter of girlish laughter and the deep rumbling of the duke's humor.

''Miss Witherspoon was hoity-toity,'' Lottie said.

''And she said 'hubba-hubba' all the time,'' blurted Sarah.

Catching the duke's eye, Juliet baldly said, ''Did your father scold her?''

His mouth fell open; Juliet felt a gush of delight.

"Nay." Lottie drew out the word. "Gallie said no decent man would ever scold Miss Witherspoon."

Sarah took a step forward, but her hand still gripped the duke's shirt. "Will you teach us American?"

"Certainly. Will you teach me Scottish?"

Her gap-toothed grin lit up the room. "Aye."

"Do you allow whispering in the schoolroom?" asked Agnes.

"Of course," Juliet replied. "Unless it's about me."

Leaving her post at the duke's side, Agnes began pacing like a field general addressing troops. "Can we have animals in the nursery?"

"Well, I see no problem with pets, unless, of course, you happen to have an elephant or a bear."

The duke laughed again. "You needn't encourage them, but if you persist, you'll pay the price."

The pleasant sound of his voice wrapped around Juliet and warmed her to her toes. She was struck again by the sheer handsomeness of his features. The sturdy planes of his rugged face could embellish a coin from any shore. No wonder the mothers of these four girls had loved him and borne his children. But where were the women now?

Again, Agnes was on the prowl. "Do you ride bareback?"

"If it's like riding in a cart across Scotland, thank you, no. I wouldn't care to ride bareback."

"I always ride my pony bareback," boasted Agnes. "Papa does, too."

"Papa don't ride a *pony,*" said Lottie, rolling her eyes.

Mary moved closer to Juliet. "Must we practice sums and letters?"

"An illiterate woman is no better than a brood mare. Yes, you must," she insisted.

"Nay," declared Agnes, swiping the air with her small hand. "I won't do it. Writing letters all day is silly, 'cause we got no one to post a letter to."

"What of your relatives? Surely your mothers—"

"Mistress White," the duke cut in, his voice cold as

27

the wind outside, "some things *will* be discussed in private."

Knowing she had crossed into dangerous waters, Juliet tried a different tack. "What, then, of the day you rule a household, Agnes?" she challenged. "How will you know your overseer is honest?"

Mary butted in, "What's an overseer?"

Juliet turned to the duke for help.

"Steward," he offered smoothly, "but in Scotland, our servants are free."

His reply triggered thoughts of the costly bargain she'd made in exchange for this journey to Scotland. Saddened by the thought of ten more years of bonded service, she was grateful when Agnes proclaimed, *"I'll* employ a churchman to do my ciphering. I don't need your book-learning."

Surprised that a child should be allowed to speak so boldly to her elders, Juliet said, "You'll hold your tongue and learn your lessons."

The duke shifted in his chair. "I haven't engaged your services yet, Mistress White."

"You need them, Your Grace."

He raised his eyebrows. "Perhaps we *should* speak in private, since you seem to know my needs so well."

Mary stepped forward. "Are you going to scold her, Papa?"

His eyes locked with Juliet's; her breath lodged in her throat. "Perhaps I will, Mary." Once again, he examined Juliet, but this time she felt as if he could see through her clothing. His gaze rested on her breasts. "When she's earned a scolding."

Now Juliet knew why they'd gone through so many governesses, but neither this lusty duke nor his bad-mannered children would put her off. If he wanted his daughters spoiled, she could easily oblige him. As soon as he'd given her the job and she'd located the information she sought, His Grace would be looking for governess number sixteen. And her conscience would be clear. Right? Suddenly she wasn't sure.

"If you don't learn your letters now," she reasoned,

"how will you write to your father after you marry and move away?"

Mary looked mortified. "We're never leaving Papa!"

Sarah gasped, "Nay, never."

Lottie drew herself up. "And we don't need a governess."

Agnes moved close to her father. Absently, he toyed with one of her braids. "Do we have to practice making our curtsies?" she demanded.

Juliet pictured Agnes dressed in satin and bows, her dark blond hair in a wild tangle except for the braids at her temples. No doubt she'd take a beating rather than forgo those braids. Challenged by the task of turning stubborn Agnes into a proper nobleman's daughter, Juliet said, "Your father's an important man. Do you wish to make him proud of you or will you shame him?"

Four pairs of eyes looked to the duke. He propped an elbow on the arm of his throne and rested his chin in his palm. His slow, lazy smile taunted her. "Before we discuss teaching my lassies manners, I'd see your own. Curtsy for me, Mistress White."

Although softly spoken, the words constituted a command. Caught in a trap of her own setting, Juliet knew she must obey or risk failure. Still, the idea rankled her American pride. Instructing these Scottish girls within the privacy of the schoolroom was one thing; making obeisance to another adult simply because of his parentage was quite another.

"We await your curtsy, Mistress White." He uncoiled his hand and waved it at the floor.

She ground her teeth. This overblown blue-blooded Scotsman thought to put her in her place, did he? She smiled sweetly. "I'm not dressed for a proper curtsy, Your Grace. I should bathe and don a fresh frock to make myself worthy to bow before such majesty as yourself."

One eyebrow rose. "Oh, but I find your rustic garb enchanting. And as your prospective employer, I must insist on examining your deportment." The command rolled off his tongue like a Highland waterfall.

She ached to tell him exactly what she thought about

his despotic ways. Instead, she knotted her fists in the folds of her stiff skirts. Momentarily tucking away her pride, she bowed her head and sank to the floor. She counted to five, then started up again.

"I don't recall giving you permission to rise."

Much to Lachlan's delight, she stopped, and lowered herself to the floor again in a curtsy the duchess of Argyll would have envied. She thrust up her chin proudly. What was it about this bold American that made him long to bring her up by his own hand? Those brown eyes, trained on him, sparkled with resentment. He'd pull his spies out of Easter Ross to know why she was here. He couldn't think of one logical reason for Juliet White to be in the Highlands in the dead of winter. And more, he couldn't think of one logical reason why he wanted her so.

A hand tapped his shoulder—Sarah. Her delicate features, so like her mother's, reflected an inner sadness that touched his heart.

"Can she bide a wee, Papa?"

The quiet purr in her voice turned his insides to warm porridge. He could count on one hand the number of times this shy child had taken the initiative.

He turned to Juliet White. Those lovely brown eyes glowed with anticipation. In that instant he glimpsed a vulnerability about her. Before he could examine the look, it was gone. But now he glimpsed something else in her eyes—an elusive quality that begged to be explored.

Desire flared in his loins.

Good judgment told him to send her away. Her story about seeking to better herself in the Highlands was as weak as a Lowlander's beer. Any truly ambitious governess would have curtsied to him in the scullery, Cozy or no. If Juliet White's motives were true, she'd be shouldering up to the nobles in Edinburgh, not scheming her way into the household of a Highland duke.

"Can she, Papa?"

His heart told him to do this one thing to make Sarah happy.

30

"Aye, lassie." He took the child's angel-soft cheek in his hand. "She can stay awhile."

Sarah smiled the smile that would one day drive men to madness. Agnes, Lottie, and Mary might get more attention now, but one day he'd be wielding his claymore to keep the wrong man from Sarah.

"Papa says she can stay," Lottie blurted. "Sarah likes her."

Sarah shyly dropped her chin. Agnes and Mary stared at Juliet White. Graceful as a swan, she effortlessly held the curtsy. Those whiskey-colored eyes reflected the same elation he'd seen in Sarah's. Why was she so pleased that he'd said yes? Why was *he* so pleased?

Mary tugged on his sleeve. "Is she our new governess? Are you going to make her curtsy till supper?"

Tried patience flickered in the governess's eyes. "With your permission, Your Grace, I would rise."

He nodded. In one fluid motion, she gained her feet. The glow of the hearth fire illuminated her face. Not pink and flawless like those of the beauties of the day, Juliet White would be a late-blooming beauty. She'd be bonnie indeed at twenty-five, bonnier at thirty. Behind that budding loveliness and innate grace shone a bright mind, a mind he intended to explore, a body he intended to survey. He'd find out why she'd come to Scotland, and if she thought to win herself a Highland lord and the title of duchess, he'd put a stop to that. But first he had to know how far she would go. His mouth grew dry at the thought; he licked his lips.

"He's going to scold her," Lottie said.

Stifling his manly urges, Lachlan turned his thoughts to the welfare of his children. "Not tonight, Lottie. The new governess is fair exhausted. That's no cause for a scolding."

Reason told him they needed the guidance Juliet White could provide. He'd examine her references. Whatever her misfortune, he stood to gain from it.

Holding his arms wide, he said, "Come, lassies."

They scurried for a spot on his lap. Wrapping his arms around them, he shot the Colonial a cold stare. "You're not to cane these bairns, nor may you send them to bed hungry. If you're cruel or indifferent to my children, I'll send you packing before the snow melts. You're to teach them their letters, their numbers, and the graceful ways of a lady. I'll have them raised up proper. Can you do that, Juliet White?"

In a clear voice, flavored with that enchanting Virginia drawl, she said, "Aye, Your Grace. You won't regret your decision."

Would he? He chuckled. He was not some bonnet farmer desperate for a woman to warm his bed and bear his sons. He had plenty of the former and years to find the latter.

"Sarah will show you to your room. You have my permission to sleep in on the morrow. Later in the day we'll discuss your salary and your other duties." And he'd decide when to test the extent of her ambitions.

Triumph glittered in her eyes. "Thank you, Your Grace."

She wanted something from him, Lachlan knew that. He intended to find out what it was.

Chapter 3

I told you she wouldn't snore. She don't even sleep with her mouth open. You lose, Agnes. Give over your red ribbons."

"Nay, Mary; she'll snore. Governesses always snore."

"Let's go back to our room."

"Nay, Sarah. The wager's on till she stirs. I say she'll snore louder than dreepy ol' Miss Witherspoon."

Smothered laughter.

"Haud yer wheesht!"

"Let's go back to our room."

"Shush."

Pretending sleep, Juliet stole a peek through slitted eyes.

Poised at the foot of the bed, the three waited like

kittens ready to pounce on a ball of yarn, Agnes in the same breeches and shirt she'd worn the night before, Mary and Sarah in their bedclothes.

Mary rolled her eyes. On an exasperated sigh she whined, "She'll be abed all day. Papa gave her permission."

Footsteps sounded in the hall. Agnes whipped her head toward the door. A braid slapped against her cheek. "Someone's coming. Hide under the bed."

Before the three had a chance to move, the door swung open. Lottie marched in, her finger pointed at her half sisters, her nose in the air. "I told you they was here," she whispered to a sour-faced Gallie, who stood in the doorway.

In her haste to reach the others, Lottie tripped on the hem of her nightgown. Mary laughed. Agnes fumed. Sarah reddened.

"You're a pack of heathens and wicked enough to shame even the sheriff of Easter Ross," hissed Gallie. " 'Tis the devil's work, watching a body whilst she sleeps."

"That's superstitious blather," Agnes snapped. "The only bad luck is havin' Lottie for a sister."

Gallie's eyes narrowed. "Out! You foosty scunners."

When Agnes didn't move, Gallie grabbed the girl's braid. "You'll wish you'd been born Irish when His Grace hears about this, Agnes MacKenzie."

"I'll tell him." Lottie headed for the door.

"You tell Papa, you prissy besom," Agnes called after her, "and I'll toss your petticoats down the privy shaft."

Juliet held back her laughter until the door closed behind them. Then she buried her head in the pillow to muffle the sound.

The jingling of harnesses and the rumbling of wheels drew her attention. Noisy shouts echoed from the courtyard.

Cold reality settled over her. Dear Lord, what had she gotten herself into? Shivering, she burrowed deeper into the down-filled mattress. Nervously she glanced about the unfamiliar room. Sunlight glistened on the diamond-paned window. Like the frost that coated the wavy glass, raw fear clouded her thoughts.

Since the summer of 1762, when she'd received the letter from Lillian, Juliet had dreamed and planned for this journey. But her naive expectations bore little resemblance to this cozy room in a Highland castle. What other surprises would she encounter before she found the man named MacCoinnich?

Her eyes filling with tears, Juliet succumbed to the pain tearing at her heart. The pillow that had muffled her laughter moments before now absorbed her heart-wrenching sobs.

After bargaining away the next ten years of her life, she had packed her bags and sailed to Scotland, dreaming of being reunited with her older sister. But that dream had died a month ago when she knelt at Lillian's lonely grave in a cemetery in Edinburgh. From the director of Saint Columba's hospice, she'd learned that Lillian had died in childbirth just days after posting the letter. But the baby girl had lived. A man named Mac-Coinnich had paid for the funeral and taken the child. Now Juliet must search the records of his clan and find this MacCoinnich. To do that, she'd willingly bound herself to a rakehell Scottish duke and his unruly daughters. All for the price of a glimpse at the Book of Mac-Coinnichs.

Did the book exist, or had the duke told her some stitched-up tale? Even when she found the book and learned the man's whereabouts, she would have to contrive another role and travel to some other part of Scotland. When could she begin the long journey home?

What a naive fool she had been.

Determination followed on the heels of her dark mirth. She would find the scoundrel named MacCoinnich, no matter what. Then she'd take her niece and return to Virginia and the security of Mabry House.

Her courage restored and her tears dried, Juliet bounded from the bed. She gasped when her feet touched the icy stone floor. Hurrying to the blackened fireplace, she added kindling to the coals. Grimacing, she picked up a wedge of peat and tossed it on the fire.

By the time she'd chipped the skin of ice from the water in the basin, washed herself, and dressed, the heavy aroma of coal-laced earth filled the air. As she twisted her unruly hair into place and secured it with wooden combs, she chided herself for not taking the time to braid it last night. But weariness and the hot bath the duke provided had sapped her will to perform even the most elementary tasks.

Remembering the way she been awakened, she smiled. Surely the duke wouldn't punish the girls.

But he had, she surmised. Curious, she stopped in the doorway of the dining hall to gaze at them across the cavernous room. Agnes and Lottie sulked; Sarah looked conscience-stricken; Mary appeared smug, a chubby hand proudly patting her head where she'd pinned the red ribbons she'd won from Agnes.

Unnoticed by the dismal group, Juliet stepped onto the thick carpet and approached the long table. The duke did his best to appear casual, but she saw through the facade. His jaw was clamped shut as he sawed viciously at his food. A governess might scold her charges and go on about her business, but a parent invariably suffered as the guilty victim of his own punishment.

He lifted a tankard to his lips. Over the rim he scanned the mulish occupants of the table. Then he spied Juliet. For an instant, relief and welcome glittered in his eyes. She felt an unexpected wave of contentment.

"Good morrow, Mistress White," he said.

"Good morrow to you, Your Grace, and ladies," she said, reaching for a chair at the opposite end of the table.

"Governesses don't sit there!" Lottie exclaimed. "Papa said—"

"*You,*" he snapped, "are to mind your tattling tongue, Lottie MacKenzie. *That* is exactly what I said."

Lottie gasped and shrank back; Juliet's respect for the duke trebled.

Rising, he said, "Please sit here." He indicated the

empty chair to his right, "so you can shield me from these recalcitrant children."

Although gruffness underscored his tone, the glint in his eyes and the set of his mouth told her he was teasing. At ease, she took the chair and reached for her napkin. "Thank you, Your Grace."

"There's honeyed milk and watered wine." He pointed a fork toward a group of pewter pitchers surrounded by plates of food. "And small beer if you're so disposed."

"After a fortnight in that rickety cart and fare poorer than sea rations," she said wryly, "I'm disposed to eat one of those shaggy-haired cattle of yours."

The girls giggled; the duke toasted her with his mug. "I shall remember your preference for beef, Mistress White, but today we have kippers, a halesome parritch, and scones."

"Thank you, it all looks tasty, and I'm glad you didn't offer haggis," she answered, and reached for the kippers. "That's all the carter seemed to like."

The duke laughed. Lottie almost choked.

Agnes declared, "I like haggis."

"But not of a morning," whined Lottie. "Even Papa don't take haggis then."

As Juliet poured milk into her mug, she stole a glance at him. Dressed in a gray linen shirt and waistcoat of dark nubby wool, he might have been a country gentleman from Virginia—except for that thick mane of hair and those distinctive braids at his temples. Replacing the pitcher, she sipped the cold milk from her mug, her senses still firmly fixed on the duke of Ross.

"You slept well?" he asked. "Your bed was soft and warm enough, and the linens didn't chafe?"

The woodsy aroma of his shaving soap drifted to her nose. Did he shave and dress himself or did he have a valet? Who plaited his hair? Discomfited that she would even care, she answered, "Thank you. The accommodations are most generous and to my liking." Why should she wonder how this rogue began his day? For all she knew, the buxom Cozy played groom to him. Juliet White had more important things to ponder than this rakehell duke—such as finding the Book of the MacCoinnichs.

He studied her closely. "You washed your hair," he said. " 'Tis fair as toasted corn."

Startled that he would speak of such a personal matter at the table, Juliet searched for a proper answer. His heated scrutiny, his lazy smile, drained the words from her.

Mary reached for another scone and slathered it with butter and honey. Juliet snatched it up. "How very sweet of you to share." The girl was too pudgy by far.

"Well done, Mistress White," the duke whispered. Louder, he said, "When we're through with breakfast, I'll show you about the castle."

Maybe she'd find out where Gallie kept those books. Tamping down her excitement, she asked, "How many rooms are in the castle?"

"I never counted."

"How many halls?" she asked.

"Four, counting the servants', and one scullery."

The devil tossed mischief in her mind. "The cozy one?"

He stared straight ahead. His jawline softened as he smiled. "Ah, yes, the cozy scullery. Would you like to see it again?"

"No. Tell me of the other rooms."

His eyebrows shot up. "We could begin with the bedrooms, but you need be concerning yourself with only one." His rolling burr enhanced the suggestive quality of the remark.

"I meant to say," she began, uncomfortable with the come-hither look in his eyes, "that I'm curious about your home—your castle. I've never seen one before, except in picture journals."

"Sarah knows all about Kinbairn Castle," volunteered Lottie.

Sarah shot to her feet and took a deep breath. "Commissioned in sixteen-thirteen by the first duke of Ross, Kinbairn Castle conforms to the practical yet elegant architecture of the period. The stair tower and gable-ended turrets corbel out at the northeast and northwest corners."

"Thank you," the duke cut in. "You're a treasure, Sarah lass, but I insist on showing her myself."

Juliet pushed aside the unease she felt at the thought of being alone with him.

"Like you the winter frost and snow, Mistress White?" He leaned back in the chair and rested the mug on his leg. His waistcoat fell open, revealing leather breeches, glove-soft and skintight. A drop of water trickled down the side of the mug and onto his pant leg. The liquid slithered across the taut fabric and ran down the inside of his leg.

Her own leg itched unbearably. She took another drink of the sweetened milk. He wanted to discuss the weather and all she could think of was the cut of his clothes.

"Mistress White?"

"What? Oh . . . the weather. Yes, I suppose I do," she managed, serving herself from the porridge bowl, "although it never gets so cold in Virginia."

"Does it snow there?" asked Mary.

"Occasionally, and on those days the cook makes molly-tops from the new snow."

"What's a molly-tops?" Mary lisped.

Juliet sweetened her porridge with honey. "A drink made with snow, vanilla, and sugar."

Mary turned to Lottie. "Do we have vanilla?"

"A wee bit, but Cook won't let us waste it on snow."

Mary looked imploringly to her father. "Papa, can we?"

"Nay," he cut her off. "We'll get no more vanilla or other spices until the tinker comes."

"But—"

"But when he does come, we'll consider it."

"But we might not have any snow then."

"Please mind your manners at the table or take your meal in the kitchen."

Mary looked crestfallen. Her half sisters began to squirm.

"You are all excused to the schoolroom. Set it to rights so Mistress White can begin your lessons."

Juliet expected complaints. Instead, Agnes bolted

from her chair. "Lottie," she commanded, "you get the broom and the rags. Sarah, you get the feather duster and wood wax." Hands on her hips, she continued, "Mary, tell Cozy to fetch a bucket of water—hot water."

Mary stuffed a scone in each pocket and headed toward the kitchen. Agnes called after her, "An' tell Cozy if it ain't hot, Papa'll scold her good."

To keep from laughing at the little chief and her band of obedient Indians, Juliet covered her mouth with her napkin.

"Amused, Mistress White?"

The irony in his voice quelled her humor. Still, she felt comfortable because she would soon slip into a familiar role. "How could I not be amused, Your Grace?" She allowed her eyes to meet his. "Agnes is a mirror of you."

He glanced at the departing girls. "Aye, that she is," he mused.

Juliet was again struck by the timeless beauty of his masculine profile. A notorious rake he might be, and wealthy to the point of extravagance, but this Scottish duke did not disguise his affection for his bastard offspring.

"In more than looks," Juliet added. "She strives to emulate you in every gesture and nuance."

He looked at her sternly. " 'Tis your job to change her hoydenish ways. I would have her be a lady."

"Trouble yourself no more on that, Your Grace. I'm really quite good."

"You're also bonnier than I thought last night."

Absurdly pleased, Juliet said, "It's kind of you to flatter me, but I would prefer you did not."

"You presume to tell me what to say and what to do? I'll have you remember that my preferences are my own."

"You've obviously had many." The words slipped out before she could stop them.

His eyes gleamed. "Does that disturb you, Mistress White?"

"Of course not. I merely wondered what happened to the girls' mothers."

His amusement abruptly vanished. "None of your affair," he stated flatly, his eyes as dark as a night storm. "You're here to teach, not to pry. I may have given you the position, but I did not give you leave to meddle."

His anger disconcerted Juliet. She had been curious, and perhaps that was wrong, but he had no right to treat her like an ill-bred servant. Shrugging her shoulders, she said, "You gave yourself leave to speak of my toilet, so I assumed you enjoyed discussing personal matters at the table."

"Oh, I do," he said. "You are only forbidden to meddle with my lassies' past. All else is fair game."

"I wasn't meddling. I merely thought if Agnes had someone to write to, she'd be eager to learn her letters. I am no backstairs gossip, Your Grace."

He toyed with one of his braids; the casual gesture belied his serious expression as he studied her face. "I accept your apology. How my lassies came to be is history. Their future is your concern."

She longed to call him a pompous blue blood. She'd said nothing to apologize for! She started to rise. "If you'll excuse me, Your Grace, I must tell Cogburn we'll be staying."

The duke rose, too. "I've seen to that, but I'll take you to him. Perhaps a stroll about the castle yard will cool your hot temper."

She turned so quickly she bumped her hip on the table. Wincing, she rubbed the spot. "You are mistaken, sir," she said through clenched teeth. "I have never possessed a temper."

"Nay?" He grinned. "Then why are those dainty nostrils flaring? And why do I see fire in your eyes, Juliet White?" His gaze drifted below her waist. "Because you hurt yourself? I'll be glad to see to that bruise."

She jerked her hand away. "That won't be necessary."

Laughing as if at some private joke, he sauntered toward the door. "Then come. I've a dozen people waiting to see me, and twice that many estates to manage. But I can spare you a few moments."

"Don't put your royal self out," she muttered.

He turned, one eyebrow arched. "What was that?"
"I'd be delighted."

Bundled in her warm cloak, a woolen scarf knotted
about her head, she stepped gingerly on the snow-covered ground and gritted her teeth against the biting wind.
Beside her, his head bare, the duke seemed unaffected
by the cold. He hadn't even donned a coat. Snowflakes
settled in his chestnut mane and on his burnished eyelashes. Juliet shivered.

"Cold?" he asked, a smile in his voice.

She willed herself to stop shaking and start concentrat-
ing on her purpose. By the time the snow melted, she'd
have found this MacCoinnich and claimed Lillian's
child. Then she would make haste for home. Thoughts
of a sultry Virginia summer warmed her. "Only a bit."
She kept her voice light.

" 'Tis but a wee promenade to the stables, and Ian'll
have a fire going, I trow."

"Trow," she repeated. "That means you know he
will—have a fire."

"Aye, and you're doing a fair job of trying to impress
me with your Scottish."

The spring house door flew open. Wings flapping,
their necks extended, a pair of geese scurried out. "And
are you impressed?" she asked.

"Hum." His eyes roamed her face and neck. "Most
favorably impressed. Are you?"

Warmth fled up her cheeks, but she had to strain to
keep her teeth from chattering. "I haven't decided yet."

"Having second thoughts about taking the post, are
you?"

Hoping to play on his sympathy, she said, "Of course
not . . . unless you don't want me."

His gaze settled on her breasts. "Oh, I want you,
lass, and make no mistake. But I wouldn't want you to
think my expectations too high, this being your first day
and all."

Her skin prickled. No man of importance had ever
looked at her that way, let alone flirted so outrageously
with her.

A laundry maid dashed past them, her basket overflowing. "Oh, excuse me, Your Grace." Flustered, she shifted the load, curtsied, and moved on.

"You were going to talk to me about my other duties."

"So I was. And your wages, too."

They passed beneath a tree, barren except for a few shriveled berries. He snapped off a limb and rolled it between his flattened palms. He'd held his glass that way last night. The action signaled that he was deep in thought. About what?

"In Edinburgh," she began tentatively, "I heard that the post paid fifty pounds a year."

He plucked off a berry and tossed it to a goose. "The earl of Moncrief pays his governess thirty pounds a year," he said.

Was he merely making conversation or earnestly haggling over the wage? Fifty pounds a year wouldn't buy his tobacco. But it would be a nest egg for Lillian's child. "Does this earl have four children?" she asked.

"Not that he claims." He pitched the last berry at the honking goose and began snapping the limb into twigs. Her fingers felt numb. His were strong and surprisingly graceful. He was so easy to admire when he denounced men who discarded their children. How different her life would have been had her father possessed a grain of the duke's loyalty.

" 'Twould seem the Edinburgh gossips were correct," he began, "on this one matter. I'll agree to the fifty pounds, but you've other duties, too."

She'd agree to any task as long as it meant she could search for the Book of MacCoinnichs. "Yes, Your Grace."

"The lassies are your first concern. I'll expect you to report to me daily on their progress. You can come to the library after they're abed."

"Yes, Your Grace." The library! She'd find out tonight if he kept the crucial books there.

"Have you any questions about them?"

"Not at present, but if I do before tonight, I'm sure Gallie will oblige me. You're a busy man, and I wouldn't want to disturb you."

He looked down at her, and the message in his eyes spoke of quiet moments before a cozy fire. "You disturb me right enough, lass, and I wonder . . ." He stopped, leaving her hanging on his words. What had he been about to say?

A dog howled in the distance. A wagon rumbled past. She saw her reflection in his dark eyes. The image of a prim governess, the perfect disguise for a woman with a purpose. Or did he see through her?

He tossed aside the twigs and his serious thoughts with them, for his eyes crinkled with mirth. "Gallie is a moon person. You'll be taking your life in your hands if you wake her before sunset."

How odd. And inconvenient. But Juliet wasn't about to let Gallie's sleeping habits deter her. She'd just find another way. "Thank you for warning me. I doubt Agnes would have."

He chuckled at that. "That one would have the servants calling her 'Your Majesty,' if she could."

Juliet caught the contagious humor. "I wonder where she learned that."

" 'Tis a mystery to me, lass."

So coy. So charming. And why not? He'd had plenty of practice.

A gust of icy wind whistled through the trees and across the fallow kitchen garden. Juliet pushed her hands deeper into her pockets. "You spoke of other duties."

"You'll supervise the preparation of meals and, in my absence, greet any visitors."

Was he leaving? The prospect filled her with ambivalence. But if he absented himself regularly . . . "Certainly," she murmured, watching the crows and sparrows peck through the snow-covered ground.

"You'll oversee the housemaids and the seamstresses."

"Of course." When would he go? How long would he be gone? Long enough, she hoped, for her to find the Book of MacCoinnichs.

"You'll sweep the stoop and oversee the scullery."

His words yanked her attention to him. "What?" She batted snowflakes from her nose.

A facetious glimmer shone in his eyes. "Are you always so inattentive?" He guided her around a puddle crusted with ice. A milkmaid scurried past, followed by a cat with a crooked tail.

Are you always so direct? she wanted to ask. "No, Your Grace. I assure you I am not usually inattentive."

" 'Tis good to know. Where was I?" He stared at the distant hills. "Ah, yes. You'll oversee the scullery, but don't be scolding the maids."

"I wouldn't dream of it."

"You could watch me scold them."

Outrage boiled inside her. *"Haud yer wheesht!"* she shouted.

He stopped. The castle loomed behind him. Like skeletal fingers reaching for the turrets, withered vines clung to the ancient stone.

"Me?"

Anger loosened her tongue. "Yes, you! I won't be the brunt of your vulgar humor, even if you are a duke. I'm an intelligent governess, not your Cozy." The truth of that statement fired her confidence. Through hard work and dedication Juliet White had earned the respect of her social betters. "You have no right to speak to me so. I'll oversee your kitchen and the seamstresses, but I will not set foot in that scullery. Ever. Nor do I see why you find the notion humorous."

"I see. And have you any other prudish eccentricities? Don't lie to me as you did about your temper."

Afraid she'd gone too far, she softened her voice. "No, Your Grace. I do not have any other prudish eccentricities. And I suppose I do have a temper after all."

"I'm glad that's settled," he said. "And as soon as you've seen this Cogburn Pitt, I'll be sure to give you that tour of the halls. And the bedrooms."

That twinkle still lingered in his eyes. Would he never stop toying with her? "Will you please change the subject?"

"Have a spat with this Pitt fellow, did you? Don't want to discuss him?"

"I meant the bedroo—" She choked on the word.

He stopped. "Oh, I'll take you there, lassie, and straightaway."

Gathering the shreds of her dignity, she said, "I meant, I don't want you to show me the sleeping quarters." His eyebrows shot up. Her patience fled. "I'm sure the girls will show me all I need to know."

"I could show you things you never imagined you wanted to know."

Ignore him, she told herself. He's just trying to turn you into one of his conquests.

They rounded the stair tower and headed into the castle yard proper. Sarah's description became a vivid reality. Horses and wagons, workmen and shouting children, milled about the inner bailey. Soldiers patrolled the high stone walls and guarded the open castle gates. With the portcullis raised, the opening resembled the mouth of a snaggle-toothed beast.

"Do you have many enemies?" she asked, eyeing the soldiers.

"Only one, and he's far away."

"Then why the patrols?"

"A show of strength gives my people confidence."

"They're like you in that, then."

"Me? Confident?" His eyes widened in a blatant attempt at an innocent expression.

Juliet looked away to keep from laughing. He had the most disarming way about him. No wonder he had so many illegitimate children.

At the base of the wall stood dozens of buildings and shops, each equipped with a chimney. In slender plumes, the smoke drifted skyward and filled the crisp air with the now familiar aroma of peat.

"A MacKenzie!" shouted one of the guards from his post up on the battlements.

The duke waved; the youthful soldier grinned and waved his crossbow.

Watching the exchange instead of where she was going, Juliet lost her footing and slipped. The duke caught her arm and drew her to his side. "Have a care, lass." He squeezed her gently. " 'Tis icy ground."

His breath frosted on the wind, but his body felt as

warm as a blazing fire. She had never, even in her child-hood fantasies, expected to meet a man like the duke of Ross. "Thank you," she stammered, drawing away.

"Be yer lairdship teachin' the lassie a Highland jig?" the youth yelled down. " 'Tis raw out today fer chasin' skirts, even fer you!"

"I'm never *that* cold, Jamie."

An ancient man herding a dozen fat sheep stopped to ask a question in what she recognized as Scottish.

Chuckling, the duke replied, "Nay, Rabby MacCoinnich, she's no light-skirts, but the lassies' new governess."

MacCoinnich. She stared at the shepherd. Was he a relative of the man she sought? Or could this old man actually be the one? Surely not, considering his advanced years. At the first opportunity, she would speak to the fellow.

The duke started walking again. "There's the falcon mews." He pointed toward a long, narrow building. Hammered into the ground near the entrance sat a grouping of inverted cone-shaped stones with icicles trailing down their sides. " 'Tis Agnes's favorite hiding place. You can often find her here."

The shepherd whistled. A dog bounded to his side.

"Do you have a favorite hiding place?" Juliet regretted the words instantly. Drat her wayward tongue.

"Aye." He grinned. "You can find me in the library, the scullery, or"—he paused dramatically—"in my sleeping quarters."

She quickened her step. How could she keep her mind on her purpose with this Scottish rogue embarrassing her at every turn? She hadn't counted on him being so captivating and so manly.

"This way." He guided her toward the largest of the buildings. "But not so fast or so inattentive. You might slip again; then we'd both go sprawling. Although, come to think of it, that might prove amusing."

She slowed her pace and ignored his innuendo. Behind her, in a mixture of Scottish and English, the shouts and urgings about the old shepherd continued. "MacCoinnich!" the men hooted. He was obviously well liked, she concluded, since the jests concerned his prowess with women, his capacity for whiskey, and his fierce Scottish temper. "Are your people always so open in their admiration?"

The duke pulled open the stable door. Warm, hay-scented air rushed out. "Pay them no mind. 'Tis harmless talk to pass a winter's day."

She stepped inside, loosened her scarf, and walked to a glowing brazier. Horses whinnied and kittens mewed in the dim room. "They think highly of him, don't they?" she said, thawing her hands by the fire.

He frowned. "Who?"

"MacCoinnich." Saying the name aloud gave her confidence. "They speak of him as an old friend."

He stared curiously at her, then shook his head. Melted snow dripped from his braids. "Aye, they think of the MacCoinnich as more than a friend."

Cogburn Pitt emerged from a stall. In his wake ambled the biggest horse she'd ever seen. Ten years her senior and once a bond servant in the stable, Cogburn had been her friend since she'd come to Mabry House. He'd agreed to pretend in this mission. A fun-loving sort, the industrious Cogburn could shake off the worst life had to offer. Only one thing bothered him: the cold.

"Frigid, godforsaken country," he grumbled, staring at the floor.

Compassion rose inside her. He wore a stocking cap pulled over his bushy eyebrows and a muffler tightly wound around his neck. His bulbous nose resembled a ripe persimmon.

"Come by the fire, Cogburn," she coaxed, "and tell me about that enormous beast."

"Juliet!" He dropped the reins and crossed the distance in three strides. Through chattering teeth, he said, "Need a dozen blankets to keep warm in this miserable land." He stamped his feet and rubbed his arms. "I'd trade my blooded mare for a bit of Virginia sun."

"Morning again, Pitt," said the duke.

Cogburn merely nodded; Juliet decided his lack of warmth toward the duke was a result of a lack of warmth in general. She wished he'd agreed to stay in

47

the castle rather than in the stables, but he'd said he preferred horses to blue-blooded noblemen.

The horse took a step forward, but stopped, holding a shaggy hoof off the ground. "He's got the hoof rot," said Cogburn.

The duke picked up the reins and spoke softly to the animal. Then he knelt, lifted the hoof, and sniffed. His head shot back. He winced and bent to check the other hooves.

Cogburn wrapped Juliet in his burly arms and urgently whispered, "We must talk. I've learned something about 'MacCoinnich.' "

Excitement raced in her veins. She clung to his shoulders. "Oh, Cogburn, how wonderful."

"Shush!" He glanced at the duke.

"Pitt!" the duke snapped over his shoulder. "Fetch Ian. Now. Tell him to bring his hoof tester and rake."

"Later," Cogburn muttered to Juliet, and rushed out of the stable.

After a gentle pat to the horse's withers, the duke plunged his hands into a bucket and began scrubbing them. "In the Highlands, a man's word is a commandment, so to speak," he said conversationally, although his expression seemed unduly serious. "I do not abide liars and poor mothers."

A philosopher, thought Juliet. "I agree, Your Grace, that honor is a commendable trait in any culture, for either sex."

"Oh, aye." He shook the water from his hands and walked toward her. "Why, then, did you lie about Pitt?"

She blinked in surprise. "What do you mean?"

"He *is* your lover. He called you Juliet and all but drove his hand up your skirts just then."

The insult sent her pride reeling. "Why, you gutter-thinking—" She gasped as he advanced on her. Suddenly alarmed by the cold gleam in his eyes, she backed away.

He followed. His long strides enabling him to take one menacing step to her three. "It seems I thought the truth, Juliet. Who is Cogburn Pitt to you?"

She kept retreating, but her eyes stayed trained on his. He wasn't teasing now. What would he do? "I told you. He's my friend."

"Friend? Not by any standards I know."

She burned to tell him what she thought of his standards, but that would get her dismissed. "What are you talking about?"

"Who else but a lover would bring such color to your face?"

She took another step back; he bore down on her. "Or set those marvelous eyes to dancing so?" He reached for her.

She jerked away. "I do not have marvelous eyes. Or marvelous anythings."

"Ah," he said. "So now you play the coy maiden? We'll see about that. You're not being original in trying to arouse my jealousy. But it's working."

Her temper was working, too. She held out her hand to ward him off. She needed to gather her wits. "Stay where you are."

The horses grew restless in their stalls. The kittens cried out in earnest. Juliet wanted to cry out, too.

He came closer. "I believe there's something you want to tell me, isn't there, Juliet?"

Fear bolted through her. Fear and confusion. She searched for an escape route. But he stood solidly between her and the door.

"Tell me the whole of it, and if you've come at the bidding of Neville Smithson, I advise you to confess it now."

Smithson? What was he babbling about? She side-stepped the salt lick and almost stepped on a wailing, spindly-legged kitten. 'I don't know anyone named Smithson. What's gotten into you?"

"You. You've gotten into me, Juliet. Your mouth is made for kissing," he whispered, his lips a breath away from hers.

She tried to twist away, but he cradled her face in his hands. His palms were damp and warm and smelled of the woods after a rain. He'd held Sarah's face just so. But now the hot message glowing in his eyes had nothing to do with fatherly love. "Don't pull away from me, lassie."

A braid touched her hair. Her eyes drifted shut. She felt as if she were standing on the edge of a crumbling cliff. Waiting. He wound his arm about her waist and pulled her against his chest. Her breath stalled in her throat. The cliff crumbled away. She grasped his arms. Why didn't he kiss her?

"You've brought me to full bloom, lassie. I'd have you harvest the crop. Now open your mouth and kiss me."

Soft fur touched her calf. Her eyes snapped open. Blue eyes, dark as sin and dangerously seductive, filled her vision. The cat was twirling itself around her leg. The duke was going to make love to her. Dear God! He intended to seduce her right here. Panting, she twisted free and ran.

"Juliet!"

As loud as a church bell on Sunday, his voice boomed through the stable. She stopped and looked around. She was in a stall! She spied a rake. With shaking hands, she grasped the handle and whirled around. "Leave me be or I'll scream!"

He stood an arm's length away. An intense light glittered in his eyes, and his chest heaved. "You lied," he said, his gaze open, honest. "Admit it." He snatched the rake from her hand. "I won't condemn you for why you came here. But I won't have my lassies used as pawns. Tell me who sent you and what Cogburn Pitt has to do with it."

How much had he guessed? Or had he? What if he was speaking of this Smithson fellow? The duke would see through her now if she lied. She searched for a truth. "Cogburn is the Mabrys' tobacco agent. I've known him since I came to Mabry House. And he is not my lover. I've never had a lover."

He sighed and looked away, as if gathering patience. "I know that, lass. Bless the great Bruce, you've never even been kissed!"

She felt as if she'd been slapped. She knew she wasn't pretty, but she had been admired by men. The baker's son had held her hand once. The tinker told her lavish stories about the goodness of her soul. Suddenly it seemed very important to let this lusty Scotsman know that her life hadn't been devoid of admirers. She drew a deep breath. "I most certainly have been kissed."

His eyes snapped back to hers. She felt his gaze penetrate the depths of her soul. He didn't believe her. Why did that bother her so?

"A popinjay in Richmond kissed me," she blurted. "And he limped for a week." There. Let him braid that news into his hair.

He put aside the rake and scooped up the mewling kitten.

Why didn't he say something? Determined to regain her composure, she raised her chin. "I did not come to Scotland to lose my virtue to a Highland rogue like you."

He closed the distance between them. The cat leapt from his arms. "Then why have you come to Scotland?" he gently demanded.

Mesmerized by his melodious voice and softly parted lips, she opened her mouth. She didn't have the slightest idea what to say.

The stable door crashed open. A wall of frosty air invaded the room, cooling senses that had been afire moments before.

"MacCoinnich!" yelled the intruder.

Trapped in a gloomy corner, the name ringing in her ears, she could not look away from the duke's piercing gaze.

"Are ye in here, MacCoinnich?" the voice demanded. "That Pitt fellow said—"

"Aye, I'm here, Ian," said the duke.

Juliet's heart jumped into her throat. "MacCoinnich?" she whispered in disbelief. "Why does he address you so? Your name is MacKenzie."

He smiled the patient smile she'd seen him bestow on his daughters. "Aye, 'tis, lass, but the old folks use the Scottish. That's why Ian calls me MacCoinnich."

A sharp pain pierced her breastbone. Her legs grew weak. MacCoinnich, MacKenzie. The names spun in her mind. The duke of Ross was also known as MacCoinnich.

He had four daughters, all the same age as Lillian's child would be.

Sweet, abiding Jesus. One of those girls could be her niece.

Chapter 4

But which one? Which girl was Juliet's only kin?

She grasped a rung of the smooth mahogany ladder and straightened. Darkness hovered in the corners of the library. The aroma of pipe tobacco hung in the air. Through tired eyes, she stared at the book-laden shelves that towered to the ceiling. Light from the petticoat lamp illuminated the titles within reach: songbooks. The bitter taste of failure mingled with the musty odors of aged leather and yellowed parchment. Sparing a mere glance at a volume of William Congreve, she sighed, gave the ladder a shove, and moved on. The lamp swayed on its hook, and the circle of light swung wildly. Other titles blinked in the light: husbandry tracts, farming, sheepshearing.

Where was the blasted Book of MacKenzies?

Which child was her niece?

For a week Juliet had grappled with the question. She'd studied each of the duke's daughters. She'd searched for some nuance, any resemblance to Lillian. Agnes, with her independent and spontaneous nature, brought memories to mind of Lillian facing the headmistress at the orphanage. Mary, with her constant and complex questions, created a striking parallel to Lillian. Lottie, with her mature awareness, seemed so like Lillian. Sarah, with her angelic face and golden beauty, appeared the image of Lillian. But Juliet had to admit that she might be thinking wishfully. Deep in her heart she still pictured Lillian as the fairest of women, but she hadn't seen Lillian in so many years.

Again she tried to remember the last time. The day had been warm, the quay crowded. Her neck had hurt from craning to look at the older sister who was going away. Lillian had worn her best straw bonnet, tied beneath her chin with a wide red ribbon. She'd donned her Sunday dress, too.

Juliet tightened her grip on the ladder, but instead of the hard wood against her palm, she felt the crisp folds of the cotton skirt she had clutched that day.

A gnawing ache ground away at her.

Bending down, Lillian had freed Juliet's hand. "I'll send for you," she had promised. 'I'll find a position in the fancy home of some titled gentleman." She cupped Juliet's tear-streaked cheeks. "You'll have a pony to ride. We'll deck him out in ribbons and gillyflowers. Oh, please don't cry."

Her heart breaking, she had stood on the dock from noon until dusk and watched the square rigger become a speck on the horizon. As night settled over the water, loneliness crept into Juliet's soul.

Three years later the letter had come. Lillian had fallen in love and would soon bear a child. Juliet would have a niece or nephew. Lillian would send for her sister once she and the child were settled.

As the years passed, Juliet made excuses for the broken promise. She no longer dashed to the house of the postmistress. The dreams faded, the images grew dim. As she matured, Juliet began to worry that ill had befallen her sister. And now, heartsore from the past and uncertain of the present, she struggled for control of her emotions.

Her confidence plummeted. Even if she continued to steal an hour a day, it would take weeks to search the duke's library. Thinking of the opposite wall, as crammed with books as this one, she looked over her shoulder.

And spied the duke of Ross standing in the doorway. Watching her.

Her throat clamped shut. She grew still as a stick. But her hand, now clutching the ladder in a death grip, began to tremble. How long had her employer been spying on her? Did he suspect her true purpose?

"Good evening, Your Grace."

"It is now."

Since that morning in the stable when she'd learned who he really was, she had tried to put the man from her mind and concentrate on her business. Even standing in the schoolroom and supervising the girls' penmanship lesson, she'd been haunted by the memory of being held in his arms. Had he caressed Lillian just so?

Appalled, Juliet stepped away from the ladder and lowered her gaze. Nervously she fluffed out her skirts. "You wanted to see me about the girls, I believe." She glanced needlessly at the lantern clock. "At nine o'clock."

He leaned against the door frame and crossed his arms over his chest. His gaze slid to the clock. "And I've kept you waiting."

He could have kept her waiting until the James River dried up and she wouldn't have cared. "I didn't mind." She flashed him a smile. "I enjoy perusing your library."

"I favor intelligence in my women." He grinned and started toward her. "In the beginning, that is. Later—"

"I am not one of your women," she blurted, stepping back.

"You did a fair imitation of it in the stable when I almost kissed you. Even if you are a virgin."

She gasped. He obviously thought every woman pined for his attention. But she knew him for what he was, for what he'd done. "I most certainly did not—do not pine for you. I mean, I'm a virgin— Oh, drat. That's none of your business."

His expression grew thoughtful. He tilted his head to the side; a braid brushed his shoulder. "How, I wonder, have you gone from innocence and passion to indifference and defiance, all in the course of one week?"

Because I found out you seduced my sister!

She swallowed back a knot of anguish. If she told him the truth, he would dismiss her. But heaven help her, she didn't want to be alone with him. Still, she had the advantage; she knew him for the rogue he was.

He strolled to the ladder and extinguished the petticoat lamp. "You were about to tell me why you've become so cold and so elusive."

Steadying her hands, she began lighting the brace of candles on the leather-topped table. The sharp scent of cinnamon drifted to her nose. "I'm very busy with your daughters and with my other duties. I've come to know the kitchen staff, but I can't supervise the housemaids properly until I can find my way around the castle."

"You're cold to me and warm to that fellow Pitt. Why?"

Her relationship with Cogburn was none of the duke's affair, but he expected an answer. "Cogburn is my friend and you are my employer." She blew out the taper.

"I do owe you an apology for assuming that you and Mr. Pitt were intimates."

Satisfaction rippled through her. "I accept, and since Cogburn will be leaving for Glasgow soon . . ." She didn't finish the thought.

"Will you miss him?" he asked, accusation plain in his voice.

Had she misread his apology? "Oh, please, Your Grace." She turned her palms up, her patience dwindling as quickly as the slender candles. "One moment you accuse me of playing the Jezebel, the next you apologize and swear you were mistaken. Which will you do next?"

He raised a hand to his mouth and with his thumb and forefinger, tugged on his bottom lip. His eyes drifted out of focus. "That depends on what you do next."

She counted to ten. He simply wasn't accustomed to her, and she was unfamiliar with nobility. As she would address a confused child, she said, "I'm your children's governess, and I hope that you will treat me as nothing more, nothing less."

His brows rose, and merriment twinkled in his eyes. "The last governess crawled into my bed and performed an interesting tutorial on my body."

Her good intentions fled. "Make no mistake," she ground out, "this governess won't go near your bed."

He chuckled. The golden necklace glittered in the light of the candle flames, but the glow was overshadowed by the glimmer in his eyes. "Are you challenging me, lassie?"

"No. I'm merely making my position clear."

"I'll warn you, I know many positions. And I do enjoy a merry courtship." He reached for her.

She jumped back. "Not with me, you don't. I had hoped you wanted to discuss your daughters' progress."

"Oh, I do." He sounded as earnest as a choirboy, but she knew better. Beneath that handsome exterior lurked a faithless scoundrel.

"You employed me to teach your children and supervise your household. I should like to get on with my report, if I may. I'm certain you'll want to keep abreast of the girls' studies."

His dark blue gaze locked on the bodice of her green muslin gown. She grew warm under his intense scrutiny. Had he looked at Lillian that way? Fury blazed through Juliet.

He murmured, "I most certainly await your . . . pleasure, Juliet."

He had the most winsome way of turning every response, every statement into a seductive innuendo. How could she, a Colonial and a virgin to boot, hope to outwit him, a peer of the English realm and a renowned rogue? She must. She had no choice.

She took the chair opposite him and said, "Where shall we begin?"

He picked a pipe from the rack on the side table, and from his pocket, he produced a leather pouch. After seating himself, he filled the pipe and used a candle to light the tobacco. Around the pipe stem, he said, "You're doing that again."

"Doing what?"

His gaze fixed on her. He pulled the pipe from his mouth, made a circle of his lips, and blew out a perfect ring of smoke. Like a feather on the wind, it floated lazily toward her. "A blacksmith couldn't pry your lips apart. You're sitting straight as a nun, your dainty hands folded primly in your lap. But your thoughts are anything but pure."

The smoke ring, now the size of a dinner plate, drifted closer. Had she not moved to one side, the ring would have circled her head. How could he read her thoughts?

He couldn't possibly know her so well. He was merely trying to goad her. She relaxed. "In future, Your Grace, I'll try not to annoy you with my behavior."

He put the pipe to his lips again. "On the right subject," he murmured, "you can behave as you please."

"Very well." She ignored the innuendo and chose a topic that was certain to put him in his place. "Cozy went on a rampage today and threw your bed linens and shaving soap down the privy shaft."

He sighed and raised his eyes to the ceiling. "We've ample linens, and the tinker brings my soap. Tell me of the lassies. Are they abed?"

He obviously didn't care what his mistress did. "They're sleeping like angels."

He almost spit out the pipe. "How did you manage that?"

"I told them a story and they fell asleep."

He slouched in the chair and rested his feet on the table. His boots were so highly polished that she could see the reflection of the candle flames in the leather.

"They'll expect you to read to them every night," he said.

Honesty came easily. "I don't mind." She smiled fondly. "It's interesting to see Agnes so attentive and . . . ah . . . so quiet."

His brows rose. "No mischief-making during your story? Agnes didn't make rude noises or pinch her sisters?"

"Nay, Your Grace. She was fascinated by the bravery of Pocahontas. Lottie, however, accused John Smith of cavorting with the heathen Indians."

"Hum. What sort of cavorting?"

"Sorry. I meant consorting."

His lips curled up in a knowing smile. "She's a bit of a prude on occasion, my Lottie is."

"Do you find fault with prudishness in a woman?"

"I can think of four I wish had been prudish," he muttered.

How like a man, to blame the woman for his lustful ways. Juliet wished Lillian had been more circumspect; if so, she would be alive today.

"What are you thinking," he demanded, "that distresses you so?"

Juliet's wary gaze caught his. "I'm not distressed. I was thinking of Lottie. She doesn't mean to be a prude. She's simply stating her opinions so that people will notice her."

"An interesting observation, Juliet. What did Mary and Sarah have to say about your story?"

"A great deal, as you can imagine. Mary asked a dozen questions about food, from how often the Indians feasted to what Pocahontas liked best to eat. Dear Sarah had done her homework."

"Oh?"

Juliet chuckled. "She recited the unfortunate circumstances of the death of Pocahontas."

"Tell me."

"She died while preparing to sail home to Virginia. Sarah cried and begged me to stay in Scotland because she fears that I might die, too, if I try to return to Virginia. Agnes said—" Laughter bubbled up inside Juliet.

"Come, now, share the jest."

"Agnes said she'd rather die than be buried at Gravesend, like Pocahontas."

"Oho!" His rich laughter filled the room. "She's as stubborn as a Lochiel Cameron, that one."

Juliet couldn't help but say, "They're lucky to have a father who loves them so much."

Pride glowed in his eyes. "I'm good at loving females."

"I'm certain you are. Have you other questions about your daughters?"

"Nay." He waved the pipe and said expansively, "I approve of your methods."

She wanted to tell him he could take his approval and stuff it in his pipe. She'd told him she was good with children. Would he never believe her?

The side door opened. Thomas, the steward, walked into the room and to the duke's side.

A tidy man, Thomas appeared to be about thirty years old. Although he spoke with the same burr as the duke, the similarity ended there. Thomas was dressed in trim black knee breeches, a gathered white shirt, and a cut-away coat. He wore white stockings and square-toed shoes with horn buckles. His straight black hair was neatly clubbed at the nape of his neck, and his side-whiskers were stylishly clipped. He reminded her of a stuffy undertaker.

"Your Grace, Mistress White. Forgive the intrusion, but we have visitors from—" He glanced sharply at Juliet. Then he leaned over and cupped his hand by the duke's ear. Rudely, he began to whisper.

The duke's feet slammed to the floor. He stiffened in the chair, and his teeth clamped down on the pipe stem. His hands balled into fists. The longer Thomas spoke, the angrier the duke became. His dark blue eyes narrowed, and his nostrils flared.

What dire news could the steward have brought?

Rage, as black and bottomless as the waters of Loch Liddle, surged through Lachlan. He slammed down the pipe, the taste of his favorite tobacco now bitter in his mouth. The governess jumped, and her enchanting eyes widened in fear. Slender hands, which had been primly folded in her lap, now gripped the arms of the chair. She was hiding something. He knew it. But he couldn't address her motives tonight.

In a matter of moments, his peaceful and enjoyable life had been ripped out by the bloody roots.

"By Saint Columba!" he swore. "I'll have Neville Smithson's balls on a platter."

"Your Grace, what shall I do with the MacKenzies?"

The urgency in Thomas's voice spurred Lachlan into motion. He pushed to his feet; the chair crashed to the floor. His frayed patience welcomed the violence. "How many are there?"

"Six. Counting the children."

The children. Helpless bairns trapped in the cruel jaws of adult warfare. "Leave them where they are for now, but go to Ian. Ask him to offer them shelter."

"Straightaway, sir." Thomas exited through the double doors leading to the main portion of the castle.

"Can I help?" asked Juliet.

"Stay out of this," he grumbled. Blind to all but the

trouble awaiting him in the next room, he stalked to the side door.

"Your Grace?"

Over the buzzing in his ears, he heard her soft Virginia drawl.

He whirled. "Aye?"

She jumped back. Fear widened her eyes.

He glared at her.

Haltingly she said, "May I stay here awhile?" She waved a delicate hand toward the wall of books. "Tomorrow's lessons . . . I'd like to prepare."

"Prepare a bletherin treatise if it pleases you!" He knew he was being unreasonable, but at the moment he couldn't control his anger.

Her lips clamped shut again. Her back ramrod straight, she walked to the ladder and picked up that silly lamp. He heard an infant wail in the next room. Rage thundered through him anew, but he wiped off the angry scowl and quietly opened the door to his study.

The scene was worse than he'd imagined.

Shoulders slumped, brow furrowed with strain, the man hovered about his children. Three stair-step lads, dressed in wrinkled but well-tailored clothing, their hair unkempt, fidgeted near the lassie.

Lachlan's heart turned over at the sight of her. He judged her age at seven. She clutched a crying child in her arms and in the English dialect of Easter Ross, whispered childish words to the babe. Where was the mother of this brood?

Lachlan closed the door.

Five pairs of eyes focused on him. The lads shuffled their feet and rubbed the cold from their arms. The man started forward. He wore his fair hair clipped short, as was the fashion in Easter Ross. Although considerably shorter than Lachlan, the visitor was thickly built with strong hands and an honest face.

The man bowed. "Your Grace. I'm Fergus MacKenzie, a cooper from Nigg. I would've waited until morn, but the farrier said you'd want to know about what the sheriff has done to us." He stopped and shook his head. Sorrow clouded his eyes.

Lachlan forced himself to smile. Any apprehension would add to the man's woes. "Never mind that weasel Smithson now. 'Tis glad I am you came, Fergus. And who be these fine bairns?"

The man blew out a nervous breath and, with callused hands, traced the edges of his lapels. "My lads and lassie, Your Grace." He turned to them. "Stand proper, now, and mind yourselves for the duke of Ross."

The lads bowed. The girl attempted a curtsy, but almost toppled over. The older lad steadied her. She glanced fearfully at her father. The infant cried on.

"They're bonnie ones," the man murmured, "considering . . ."

"And Mrs. MacKenzie?" Lachlan prayed for the right answer.

A weak smile ticked at the corners of Fergus's mouth. "In the wagon, sir, in the stable. She's been weak since the birth, and the journey was hard on her. She's resting. My eldest lassie is with her."

Relief washed over Lachlan. "When did she birth the bairn?"

Pride puffed out his chest. "Four months ago, Your Grace. The lad came out wailing, he did." He glanced fondly at the child. "Ain't stopped. We feared he wouldn't make the journey."

Lachlan beamed and clamped a hand on the man's shoulder. "Bless Saint Ninian! A lad. 'Tis a day to celebrate. You're a lucky man, Fergus. I've four lassies myself."

MacKenzie gazed lovingly at his family. "Aye, Your Grace. I just hope I can continue to feed them. I want to make a new start here."

"So you will. Pour yourself a dram." He indicated the spirits cabinet. "I'll be right back."

The infant needed attention and the poor lassie wanted rest. Lachlan thought of Juliet. He didn't stop to ponder his decision, but went back to the library. And suppressed a hoot of laughter at the sight of the Colonial governess.

She stood with her back to him, her hands on her hips, her eyes surveying the bookshelves as if they were a wild boar ready to charge. The pose accentuated her trim waist and gently flaring hips. Like a child in a fit of temper, she stomped her foot and spat Agnes's favorite swearword.

He closed the door behind him. "If you step in a pile of that, you'll soil your slippers."

Her head whipped around so fast the coiled braid atop her head wobbled. "Your Grace?" She pushed the crown of hair back into place, but it didn't stay. "I was just thinking of . . . oh, nothing of importance."

Grinning at her discomfiture, he said, "Now that you've done thinking unimportant things, I've need of your help. There's a bairn in the next room and a tired lassie who needs help. I'd like you to take them to the kitchen. Give the babe to Cozy and the lassie to Cook."

"Certainly." She hurried to the door, as if glad to leave the room. "Is the child ill?"

"Nay, he's merely tired and hungry."

"I'd heard the cries—"

He stopped her with a hand on her arm. "They're a troubled family and very important to me. I'd have you be kind, especially to the bairns."

Her chin jutted out. He'd trade the crop of spring lambs to hear what she was thinking.

"I think I can manage that, Your Grace." Sarcasm dripped from the words.

He felt guilty, but he didn't have time to explain. How could this Colonial understand the problems of Easter Ross? The cruelty and injustice of Neville Smithson? How could he admit his own sense of futility in the matter?

He couldn't. He ushered her through the door.

"Fergus MacKenzie, this is Mistress White, governess to my children."

The man shifted his weight from one foot to the other. "Mistress White," he mumbled.

"Mr. MacKenzie." But Juliet's attention was fixed on the weary lass, who clutched the crying babe tighter. She crossed to the girl and knelt.

"Hello. My name is Juliet. What's yours?"

The lass ducked her head. "Grace."

Juliet made a quiet speech and held out her hands. Grace glanced at her father, seeking his approval.

"She's a very proper governess," Lachlan said.

Fergus nodded. Wide Scottish blue eyes locked with Juliet's. The girl handed over the child.

Juliet lifted the blanket and leaned close to the child. "A boy?" She breathlessly asked, her face aglow with kindness. "What pretty red hair he has."

The lassie nodded her head. Gravely, she said, "He's four months old. My mother has red hair, too."

Lachlan stared, entranced, as Juliet cooed to the child in that soft drawl. The crying stopped. A tiny hand latched on to her wobbly braid. The infant jerked and the rope of hair tumbled free, falling past Juliet's waist.

She looked at Fergus. Laughingly, she said, "You might consider calling him Hercules. He certainly has the strength."

Fergus beamed. His bairns relaxed. "Thank you, ma'am," he said quietly. "He looks to be a braw one."

"Well, now." Juliet shifted the babe to the cradle of one arm and held out the other to the lass. "If you gentlemen will excuse us, Grace and I will see what we can do about feeding this braw fellow."

"Go on, lass," Fergus coaxed, "and have a care with yourself."

A small trembling hand slid into Juliet's. She gave it a little squeeze. "You'll be just fine, Grace."

As they approached the door, the eldest lad scurried over and opened it. Juliet allowed the girl to go first, then took the lead down the corridor and through the dining hall. The child began to fret again. Grace looked up, her heart-shaped face pinched with worry.

"I think he'd like some milk, don't you?" Juliet said.

She'd lost her front teeth, but new ones peeked from her gums. "Aye," she said gravely. "Then he'll go asleep."

Juliet's mind whirled with questions. Why had this family arrived in the middle of the night? What dire situation had brought them from that place called Easter Ross? Why had the event caused the duke so much distress? She shifted the child in her arms. He was still crying when she reached the kitchen.

Mrs. MacKenzie-the-cook jumped from her seat at the long wooden table. She set aside the paring knife and a turnip she held. The turnip rolled onto the floor. Quick as a rabbit, Grace scooped it up, dusted it off, and placed it among the pile of peelings.

Cook smiled, revealing a dimpled cheek and piggyback eye teeth. This blade-thin woman enjoyed a special relationship with the duke, for he treated her like a saint.

"What have you there, Mistress White?" Cook asked.

Juliet uncovered the child. Laughing, she said, "Two more MacKenzies, Mrs. MacKenzie. They're from Easter Ross."

"Oh, dear," said the cook with a sigh. "That bastard sheriff's got no business ruling Scots. When will he stop his madness?" As if she didn't expect an answer, she said. " 'Tis welcome you are."

Cozy looked up from her spot at the end of the table. Pouty lips drooped as she glared at young Grace. "If that's another of his lordship's bastards, tell her the nursery's full."

Anger ripped through Juliet. She wasn't about to put the child in Cozy's care. "Be quiet, Cozy, or go to your room."

"Yes, Your Highness," the maid sneered, and flounced off.

"Never mind her," Cook said, wiping her hands on her apron. "She wouldn't know kindness or charity if she met one of them in the lane."

"I'm afraid you're right. Will you warm some milk for this lad?"

Cook chucked the babe's chin. "Of course, and I think I have a biscuit for his sister." She turned to Grace. "Would you like that?"

The girl's smile was strained. "Aye, ma'am."

"Have a seat, dear."

Grace heaved a sigh and plopped down at the table. Juliet sat, too, but her mind lingered on the reasons behind this family's sudden arrival.

* * *

Lachlan poured himself a fortifying Dram Buidheach, then offered the bottle to Fergus. Thomas entered the room. After reciting fatherly instructions, Fergus told the boys to go with the steward.

Once alone with Fergus, Lachlan broached the subject of the man's departure from Easter Ross. "I've heard so many tales. What did Neville Smithson do to you?"

Lips curling in disgust, Fergus said, "The scunner brought a cooper up from Yorkshire. Smithson gave lumber to the Sassenach, and he fair gave away his barrels. I couldn't compete. I worked at carpentry and thatching roofs, but the sheriff wanted me and mine gone, same as he has the other MacKenzies in Easter Ross."

Fury clutched at Lachlan's insides. Smithson had a respectable position and a lovely wife. He should count his blessings. "Damn that miserable bastard!"

"Aye, he's a bastard true and true. No decent man would claim siring the likes of him."

"God! I'd like to run him out of Easter Ross strapped to a caber." But he couldn't do that.

"Begging your pardon, Your Grace, but has the king named you overlord of Easter Ross?"

Lachlan had paid a steep price for his father's error in judgment twenty-five years ago when he'd sided with Bonnie Prince Charlie. Everyone in Easter Ross continued to pay. "Nay. And damn the worthless Hanoverian. I can't set foot in Easter Ross."

Fergus shook his head sadly. "The king and the sheriff carry a grudge against the Scots. Ain't right, no MacKenzie ruling Easter Ross."

Lachlan rose and began to pace. Eleven years ago Neville Smithson had married Bridget MacLeod, daughter of the earl of Tain. The marriage had been troubled from the start. Three years later, Bridget had thrown Neville out. He'd gone to the English court and sought the sheriffdom of Easter Ross. He'd succeeded in gaining the position, then returned to Tain, the principal city in Easter Ross. Bridget had borne a child every year since the reconciliation. The Scotswoman had obviously settled her differences with her English husband. Why couldn't Neville solve his problem with the MacKenzies in Easter Ross?

Seemingly resigned, Fergus said, "Neville Smithson wants no MacKenzies in Easter Ross."

Family pride and good sense warred within Lachlan. At length, he said, "You're better off here. MacKenzie-the-brewer can always use a skilled cooper. His whiskey's all the rage."

Fergus drew himself up. " 'Tis glad I am to hear that. Thatching roofs is backbreaking work, and the pay won't feed a moorhen."

Lachlan chuckled. "There's a wee barren cottage an hour's ride away. The roof's fair crumbling, but the field's lain fallow these two years. You could grow your own food."

" 'Twill seem like a castle to me and mine." Staring at his hands, he said, "I'm grateful, Your Grace. They said you'd help us."

"They?"

The man's mouth quirked in a half grin. 'The Highlanders that blacken the face of Easter Ross."

It was a common saying and one that, years before, had warranted stiff punishment from Kenneth MacKenzie. Would that Lachlan wielded as much power as his forebear. He planned to petition the king again, but this time he would ask the duke of Argyll to intercede on his behalf. Once Lachlan won the title of overlord of Easter Ross, he would take on the job of righting seven years of Neville Smithson's wrongs.

Unwilling to ponder that challenge now, he finished off his drink. "Hie yourself to your family, Fergus. You've a roof to thatch on the morrow."

"What of the bairn and the lass?"

"We'll keep them here tonight."

Fergus bowed. "You won't regret taking us in, Your Grace."

Once alone, Lachlan picked up his quill to begin his letter to the duke of Argyll. An hour later he stared at a blank page. He went to the library to fetch his pipe.

And found the governess, the petticoat lamp held high as she scoured a shelf of books. She'd let down her hair, and it flowed in thick waves to her knees. She wore a green woolen robe belted snugly at her waist, a waist that looked to be a perfect fit for his hands.

He felt an instant's disappointment, for he'd thought Juliet White different from the others. He hadn't expected her to make herself available to him. Life was chock-full of disappointments. Who was he to question the methods that sent this woman into his arms? He needed her.

Lust rumbled in his gut. She was so absorbed in her task that she didn't notice his approach. Unable to resist the allure of all that shiny hair, he plunged a hand into the mass.

She froze in place. The lamp quivered in her hand. Her breath came in soft gasps. "Please let me go."

"How do you manage to hold up all this hair?" he asked, his fingers buried to the wrist in the thick strands. "You seem too slight for the weight."

"Please . . ." she whispered softly.

"By and by." With his free hand, he took the lamp and hooked it on the ladder. Then he turned her around and touched her cheek. She tried to move away, but with the bookcase behind her and him towering over her, she had nowhere to go. He liked that very much indeed. The tiny lamp flame spread a soft glow on her hair and brightened the blond strands to sunny yellow, the darker strands to molten gold. She smelled of lilacs on a balmy summer day.

Wide, wary brown eyes studied him. "I want a book, Your Grace. That's all I want."

Had he not played out this scene with half a dozen of her predecessors, he might have believed Juliet White, so forthright was the expression in her eyes. He liked her eyes and her hair and her petal-soft skin. She had even chosen a book. How quaint. She held it behind her back. The awkward position of her arm caused the robe to part, revealing a nightgown of sheer pink cotton, a border of delicately embroidered leaves at the neckline. With each breath, her breasts rose and fell.

"Of course. I'll give you what you want."

He leaned forward; she leaned back. Her shoulders

touched the bookcase. Those whiskey-colored eyes never left his. A slender hand eased up his chest and pushed against him. He gave her high marks for the maidenly gesture of protest. But a show was all it was; he'd seen this trap too many times before.

Cocking his head to one side, he lowered his mouth to hers.

She tasted of cider and clean, soft woman. But her lips weren't soft. He recognized the token resistance and chose a suitable response.

He moved a breath away and whispered, "Relax, lassie, and part your lips. Just one kiss." If he had a shilling for every time he'd said those words, he'd buy Virginia.

As expected, she acquiesced. She opened her mouth, and his lips settled firmly on hers, exploring, savoring, learning the shape of her mouth, tracing the slick pouting lower lip, mapping the sweet bow of the upper. As he moved in slow circles, their breath mingled, but he wanted more.

"Open wider and give me your tongue," he breathed against her mouth. She began to move against him, writhing in all the right places: the knot at her belt dragged back and forth over the swollen ridge of his manhood; a delicate knee slid between his legs. If this was resistance, he thought, she should bottle it and sell it in Drury Lane, for her manner was original. And seductive as hell.

But there was a difference in Juliet White. She seemed to hold a part of herself back, and if he hadn't known better, he'd have thought she was being coy. But he knew coy women, and he understood what they liked.

His hand wandered to her breast, and much to his delight, the mound filled his hand. His manhood jolted to full bloom, pulsing and stretching, aching to have her. With both hands he kneaded her lush breasts while his mind pictured her naked, wanting him, spreading her legs invitingly wide, and he imagined her pleading, rubbing her thighs and urging him to take her.

" 'Tis a crime, lassie," he rasped, "to hide such a bounty. Undress for me. Let me see you in the firelight. Let me love you till the moon and stars yield to the sun."

She stood stock-still. He pulled back. Her lips, dark and lushly wet, parted. Her breasts, full and gloriously aroused, heaved with every breath. But her eyes expressed loathing. "What is it?" he asked.

"I willingly gave you the kiss to keep you from taking it."

She needed a nudge, an opening. "Aye, and you wanted more." He held up his hand. "I'm inviting you to take what you want, lass."

She shook her head. Her hair spilled over her shoulders. "What I want you won't give freely."

"Oh? I'll give you a bower strewn with fragrant petals."

"That's not what I want."

"Then what?"

Her eyes narrowed. She drew her sleeve over her mouth as if to wipe away the taste of him. His pride stung; no woman had ever accepted his loving, then shunned him so convincingly. In the faint glow of the lamp, she appeared the righteous maiden unjustly accused.

"I don't want a cheap seduction. I want respect. And a book."

Before he could challenge her, she ducked under his arm and moved out of reach. Like a shield, she clutched the book to her still-heaving breasts, and dashed out the door, her hair flowing wildly.

Confusion danced in his head; lust frolicked in his loins. He pressed a hand to his belly to ease the pressure. He flexed his knees to counter the need that almost doubled him over. He searched for some distraction, anything to get that woman out of his thoughts. What kind of game was Juliet White playing? Respect? Why would a woman desire respect?

Baffled, he examined the shelf she had been scouring, hoping her choice of books would offer an answer. He found an empty slot. From the remaining titles on the shelf, he guessed her choice. And frowned. What would Juliet White want with a book on the MacKenzie clan of Scotland?

By God, she *was* trying to impress him.

Chapter 5

Juliet held the breakfast tray to one side to watch her footing on the darkened stairs. Through the soles of her worn boots, she felt the uneven surface of the stone steps. Generations of MacKenzies, their guests, and servants had left their mark. Had Lillian trodden the ancient stairwell? Had she, too, felt the tug of security, the sense of belonging that pervaded this old castle?

Doubts plagued Juliet.

She stopped to lean against the wall. Below, the steps trailed down to the dark pit of the main hall. Above, the pink light of dawn seeped through an arrow slit. How simple her task would be if answers came to questions as easily as darkness fell to light.

A milk cow lowed in the distance. A cock trumpeted in the new day.

During the month she'd been at Kinbairn, Juliet had been diligent in her quest. Cogburn had also sought the answers. But the tavern-goers and tradesmen were as tight-lipped as the castle dwellers and staff. As each day passed, misgivings chipped at her solid theory until what had once been a foregone conclusion now seemed a fitful guess. Did Lillian's child dwell here?

The uncertainty inside Juliet grew, yet knowing the cause only intensified her woe. The orphan in her heart cried out for a home such as Kinbairn. The woman in her longed for the duke of Ross.

Even after weeks, the taste of him lingered on her lips, and her breasts tingled at the memory of his touch. A hundred times she'd relived the rapture of his embrace. A hundred times she'd damned herself for a fool. And beneath every condemnation lay the hope that he wasn't the faithless rogue who had destroyed her sister but the prince who would one day claim Juliet's heart.

The folly of that fantasy brought a sad smile to her face. Any woman would want Lachlan MacKenzie. But unlike sweet Lillian, Juliet would not fall prey to him. He, in fact, would lose to her. She would learn which daughter was her niece and spirit the girl away from the people who called her a bastard. Away from the prejudice of the MacKenzies and secure with the Mabrys, Lillian's daughter would make of her life what she chose.

A ray of sunlight glinted on the pewter tray. Juliet glanced up the stairs to the iron-studded door of the chamber she sought. The path lay clear. She climbed the steps and knocked.

Ancient hinges creaked. The portal opened. Excitement danced along Juliet's spine. "Morning, Gallie."

Her brow furrowed, her brown eyes flitting to the tray, Gallie said, "What do you want?"

Accustomed to reticence and curtness from the chronicler, Juliet said, "Only to deliver your breakfast. Or, as Lottie says, your supper."

Gallie raised an ink-stained hand to her mouth and yawned. With the other hand, she waved Juliet into the room. Eyes twinkling with ribald mischief, the chronicler said, "I take it Cozy's tending to her *other* duties this morn."

Juliet set the tray on a lace-covered table. "What other duties? She hardly lifts a finger."

Gallie poured a mug of honeyed milk and drank deeply. Over the rim she said, "Perhaps she's tending the manly needs of His Grace."

Embarrassment warmed Juliet's cheeks. Her gaze flew to a locked door leading to a vestibule. Beyond that lay the duke's chamber. Were he and Cozy at this moment— She banished the disturbing image and focused on inspecting Gallie's room. If the book was here, she would find it today.

"I'm glad she excels at something," Juliet murmured, perusing the velvet-draped bed, the tapestry-covered walls, and the open wardrobe. "She's hardly a help to Cook."

Gallie chuckled. "Or to the duke himself these days or nights."

The wardrobe contained only dresses on pegs and shoes lined up in a row. With the exception of the privy alcove, Juliet didn't see a hiding place. Out of the corner of her eye, she saw the chronicler shrug and pick up a scone. With her dark hair tied loosely at the nape of her neck and milk foam coating her upper lip, she looked younger than the thirty-five years Cook claimed her to be. Beneath a linen apron, Gallie wore a bright blue frock, the long sleeves rolled above her elbows. Black and red ink stained her fingers, hands, and arms.

She swallowed, rubbed her stomach, and said, "He'll call Cozy back to his bed soon enough. Once he does, she'll flounce around like the queen o' May. 'Tis a puzzle, though, why he's denied himself these past weeks. 'Tisn't like him."

Juliet felt an unwelcome sense of relief. She didn't care a fool's wit about the duke's hiatus from immoral practices. "He has much on his mind, I suspect," she said absently.

The room didn't contain a desk or writing materials. Where did Gallie work?

"A snuggle a day keeps a man's troubles away," said Gallie, plopping into a chair. "He should up her skirts and be done with it."

"He's certainly an expert at that."

"Has he been up yours?"

Aghast, Juliet snapped, "Absolutely not."

Gallie grinned. "Prim, are you? He said as much."

Dignity stiffened Juliet's spine. "I'm different, to be sure. You've milk on your mouth . . . and ink, too."

"Don't try to governess me."

"I wouldn't dare. What do you use to wash off the ink?"

"Soap and hot water."

Juliet pretended not to notice Gallie's sarcasm. "I read in the *Virginia Gazette* that Dr. James Jay is experimenting with disappearing ink."

"What would I be wanting with disappearing ink?"

"I merely thought you might find it interesting."

"It sounds like a silly waste of time. Why write something only to have it disappear?"

Juliet had had enough of Gallie's curtness. "Do you work in here?"

"Work? What work?"

"Keeping the Book of the MacKenzies."

Gallie dropped the scone. It landed with a splat in her mug. "Who told you about that?"

"His Grace. He's very proud of you."

Gallie tried to fish out the scone, which had turned to a soggy mess. "He's as free with his tongue as he is with his tail," she said, walking to the privy. "His rutting is what brought about the secrecy."

Juliet followed. While Gallie pulled back the tapestry and tossed the contents of her cup, Juliet made a quick scan of the alcove. She spied a stack of neatly folded towels and an array of toilet articles. But no books, no ink, not even a blasted quill.

Gallie turned abruptly. "I know what you're about."

Juliet stepped back, fear barreling through her. Had Gallie guessed her purpose? But how? The chronicler absented herself from Kinbairn for days at a time, gathering data for the books. When in residence she sequestered herself in this room. She didn't even emerge for meals. In the last month, Juliet had seen Gallie only twice, in passing.

"What am I about, Gallie?"

The chronicler paused, her hand hovering over the plate of scones, her eyes black as jet, her gaze piercing. "The same as all the governesses who come to Kinbairn Castle. You want him. This coyness is a new trick." She jerked her head toward the locked door. "But I'll tell you what I tell them all. You won't get there through here. Now leave me be."

The insult struck at Juliet's pride. "You're wrong, Gallie. I don't want His Grace. I'm as plain as a post." Never had honesty hurt so much. The duke had kissed her and teased her, but that was merely his way. He meant nothing by it.

Mirth twinkled in Gallie's eyes. "If the men in the Colonies convinced you of that, then you're doiled."

"Doiled?"

"Daft, in English."

Juliet felt she was many things, but stupid was not one of them. Her ignorance of Scottish and the Scots was diminishing every day.

"I wonder," said Gallie, "why you didn't marry one of those Colonials. Surely they can appreciate a comely face and shapely body."

Wishing to steer the conversation away from herself, she asked, "Who teaches the girls between governesses?"

Gallie smiled and gazed at a shuttered window. "I try, but they're wild as barn cats. Except Sarah, of course. They need a real governess who ain't interested in warming a duke's bed."

Juliet smiled. " 'Twould seem, then, that His Grace has found the right person. Lottie said the tinker's arrived. I came to ask if you'd like to accompany me there."

"No governessing today?"

"No. The weather's too nice. I've given the girls a holiday. I thought you and I might become friends, Gallie."

The chronicler studied her stained hands. "I don't befriend governesses."

"Why not?"

Gallie's lips curled in disgust. "Scheming, crafty wenches is what you all are."

"You're wrong about me, Gallie."

"Ha! I'll see a Stuart on the English throne again before I'll believe that blather."

Determination goaded Juliet to say, "Then I'll prove you wrong."

Gallie reached into her pocket and held her hand out to Juliet. "The MacKenzies are here. They're staying in the stables again. Since you're going to the tinker, take this for young Lachey."

Juliet thought of young Grace and the infant with bright red hair. A month ago they'd arrived in the middle of the night. Two days later they'd left for their new home. "The MacKenzies-from-Nigg?"

"Aye."

"Lottie didn't tell me they were at the castle."

"She's angry with you because you caught her spying on Thomas and the butcher's daughter and made her stand in the corner."

"She broke a rule of common courtesy."

Grudgingly, Gallie said. " 'Twas right you punished her. Here."

Juliet accepted the tiny bag. "What is this?"

" 'Tis a piece of coal. Red-haired bairns need it to keep the evil spirits away."

A snicker perched on her lips, but Juliet fought it back. "You are superstitious, aren't you?"

"Aye, and wise to the tricks of your kind."

Biting back a retort, Juliet left the room. As she descended the steps, she began planning a new strategy. Making friends with Gallie wouldn't work. Juliet needed to find out where she kept the books. The devil take Gallie and her rudeness.

Later that day Juliet clutched a jar of honey as she made her way across the crowded inner bailey. A brisk wind whistled down the hay-strewn lane and blew strands of her hair into her face.

All around, the residents of Kinbairn Castle and its neighboring villages mingled, eager to be out-of-doors. Off and on for two weeks, a winter storm had raged, dumping snow on the streets, paths, and roofs. Workers had piled the snow in mud-laced drifts. A layer of ice coated the barren trees and twinkled in the bright winter sun.

Virginia seemed a lifetime away, and much to her surprise, she no longer pined for the mild winter of home, but found herself enjoying the brisk climate of the Highlands.

Frustration tugged at her, but she refused to let it spoil her cheerful mood. It was only a matter of time before she found the bletherin book. She paused, amused at her use of the Scottish adjective. Bless Saint Ninian, she was even beginning to think in the language of Lachlan MacKenzie.

Her heart tripped. But female hearts inevitably tripped

like tin drums for the duke of Ross. Why shouldn't the rogue affect her as well? She was a woman in her prime and as vulnerable to male charm as half the population of Kinbairn and, tragically, her sister Lillian.

A snowball whizzed past and landed smack in the middle of Gibbon MacKenzie's leather apron. The blacksmith roared with anger and dropped a handful of horseshoes. Waving his hamlike arms, he made to chase the young culprit. The lad yelped, darted around the throng, and dashed into the alley beside the alehouse. Now roaring with laughter, Gibbon retrieved the rusty horseshoes and started off again to his forge.

Smiling, Juliet passed the baker's hut and headed for the stables. The aroma of freshly baked scones and grilled bannocks floated on the crisp clean air.

She spied Thomas running toward her, his black greatcoat flapping like the wings of a gawky crow. She tried to remember if she had ever seen Thomas walk anywhere; he always seemed to be in a hurry.

"Glorious weather, eh?" he huffed, his head bobbing with each frosty breath. "His Grace asked me to purchase this. 'Twas the last the tinker had." In his right hand he held a brown bottle with a sealed cork, in his left, a slender wooden box with exotic words carved into the lid.

"The last what?"

"Vanilla."

Confused, Juliet said, "Vanilla in a box?"

His face grew red. He tucked the box under his arm. "Nay, the bottle. His Grace said you'd know what to do with it."

So the duke had remembered the molly-tops. "Take it to the kitchen, Thomas, and give it to Cook. But don't tell the girls."

He nodded and sped off.

As she wended her way to her destination, Juliet pondered the duke of Ross. How could the same man who'd destroyed her sister care so much for her niece? He was a puzzle. With each piece she discovered something new about him.

Of late, political problems in a district called Easter

Ross plagued him. The mere mention of the place ignited his temper. Another duke, the one from Argyll, was involved, too. She'd questioned Sarah. In her precise oratorical fashion, the girl had supplied the geographical and historical data. Easter Ross was located in the middle of the top of Scotland. The district encompassed a peninsula between Moray Firth and Cromarty Firth. Sarah knew nothing about the political problems there. Lottie had said the king would chop off her papa's head if he went to Tain and did what ought to be done to the sheriff of Easter Ross.

The duke had refused to discuss the topic with Juliet. That was fine and dandy with her, for she had no desire to dabble in Scottish politics. She had problems of her own.

She quickened her steps. Perhaps the mother of a babe recently listed in the Book of MacKenzies could lead her to it.

The main room of the stables resembled a campground: the wagon parked to one side, barrels arranged around a trunk, a cauldron bubbling atop the brazier. The smells of stew and people blended with the odor of horses and hay.

Her carrot-colored curls bobbing, Flora MacKenzie emerged from the back of the wagon. She beamed and turned the babe in her arms so he faced Juliet. "Lookit here, Lachey, at the bonnie lady come special to see you."

The grinning child hiccuped and pumped his arms wildly. Guilt riddled Juliet, but she ignored it. What was wrong with her gaining information from Flora if that knowledge did no harm?

She held out a crock of honey. "I'll trade you a sweet for a sweet."

"You needn't have bothered."

"I wanted to."

"Thank you. He'll be teething soon, and a bit of honey always helps." Flora came forward, her breasts bouncing. She wore a perfectly tailored but plain dress of pale blue linen.

Juliet passed over the honey and Gallie's pouch and reached for the child. She tickled him and got an earsplitting screech of joy for her trouble. "He's grown so. The last time I held him, he was no bigger than one of Cook's clootie dumplings."

Flora peered into the pouch. "Is it coal?"

"Yes, from Gallie. But how did you know?"

Flora reached into her pocket and brought out a similar pouch. "It seems that the butcher's wife also thinks my red-haired lad needs protection from evil spirits."

With feigned nonchalance, Juliet said, "Perhaps Gallie will put the warning by his name in the Book of MacKenzies."

Flora gasped. "You know about what's in the books?"

Books? Dear Lord, there was more than one? "I know the duke has secrets to keep," she said. "But tracking one's kin is a wonderful tradition. Just think, little Lachey here is immortalized on those pages."

"Gallie showed you the books?" Flora asked, disbelief in her voice.

"Oh, no. I don't even know where they are. But I'm sure they're guarded well." Juliet held her breath.

Flora smiled. "Aye, they are. You'd have to go through the laird to get to them."

Like an elusive butterfly, the answer floated beyond her fingertips. Casting her net, Juliet said, "I prefer to keep my distance from His Grace, if you ken my meaning. I'd sooner set Mary to fasting than step foot in the ducal bedchamber."

Flora slapped her thigh. " 'Tis a keen one you are, Mistress White. Tankard talk says the laird can turn up a lassie's skirts before you can turn down the covers." Her smile faded. "Mind, though, he only does the willing ones."

Juliet felt the answer fluttering farther out of reach. Rocking the babe in her arms, she primly said, "Well, I hope Gallie never runs out of ink and asks me to fetch it. At least not while the duke's in his chamber." Pasting on a conspiratorial smile, she added, "I like keeping my skirts down, thank you."

Flora's shoulders shook. "Aye, you'd never make it

to the tower steps, let alone the books, before that rogue had yer virtue. Oh''—she put a hand on Juliet's arm—''don't think I was meaning you'd do such a thing. You're much too proper.''

Dizzy relief washed over Juliet. The tower room off the vestibule. That was where the books were kept.

''I should cut out my gossiping tongue.''

''Don't worry, Flora. You weren't gossiping. It's up to me to prove I came here not to seduce a duke but for honest work.'' *Honest.* The lie tasted bitter.

''Don't you worry over that. The townsfolk say you laugh at the laird's romancing talk. They say you truly love the lassies.''

''I do.'' Juliet felt dampness seep through the babe's blanket. ''Uh-oh. He's wet his nappy.''

Flora took the child and changed him. He was cooing when Juliet picked him up again. ''What a sweet baby you are.''

''He's just a smutchy lad.'' Agnes's voice floated from nowhere.

Juliet froze. The babe noisily sucked his tiny fist and blinked his sleepy eyes. Had Agnes heard the conversation? Would she repeat it? No. Agnes was no gossip.

Juliet searched the area but saw no sign of the girl. Flora pointed a finger into the air.

Looking up, Juliet spied her charge sitting on the edge of the hayloft, her leather-clad legs dangling. Since the night Juliet had told the story of Pocahontas, Agnes had pretended to be an Indian chief. She wore a leather headband, only today she'd added pheasant feathers and streaked her face with war paint from Cozy's rouge pot.

Juliet raised her hand and gravely said, ''How, Chief Agnes.''

''How, paleface.'' She scrambled down the ladder.

''What are you still doing here?'' Flora asked. ''I thought you and your sisters left.''

Agnes folded her arms across her chest and glared at Juliet. ''You should wear an apron so he don't piss on your dress.'' She wrinkled her nose. ''It's all he's good for.''

"And I suppose you never soiled anything," Juliet challenged.

"At least I didn't piss a stream in the air and squirt people in the face while they was changing my nappies."

"Now, Agnes," soothed Flora. "He didn't do it on purpose while you were changing him. He's too little to know better."

So that's how Agnes's war paint got smudged.

"I saw Hoots MacBride piss a stream this big on the butcher's stump." She held up a finger.

"Agnes!" Juliet's mouth dropped open. "When did this happen?"

"At Hogmanay. The turning of the new year, in case you didn't know."

Juliet was unfamiliar with most Scottish traditions, and Agnes jumped at the chance to remind her of it.

"Where was your father while you were spying on Hoots MacBride?" Juliet asked.

Agnes breathed on her fingernails and buffed them on her shirtsleeve. "Dancing with our last governess. But she must have stepped on his foot, because he took her off and scolded her."

"You mustn't repeat such things."

"The pissing or the scolding?"

"Either. One is none of your affair and the other is vulgar." Both were vulgar, but Juliet wasn't about to say so.

"Lads are vulgar and stupid. Hoots paid me a penny not to tell his mean old papa or mine." Her chin jutted out. "And if you tell Papa, I'll say it ain't true."

Juliet had no intention of bringing up the subject with the duke of Ross. "Very well. I'll promise not to tell your father if you'll promise not to spy on the boys while they're . . ."

Agnes grinned. "Pissing on the butcher's stump?"

"Or any other place. Do I make myself clear?" Juliet hefted the babe to her shoulder, but immediately regretted it. He grasped her hair in a stranglehold.

"He's the very devil with the ladies' hair." Flora pried loose the little fingers.

"Lads don't do nothin' but piss and spit."

Juliet glared down at her. "Agnes MacKenzie. Apologize to Flora or march yourself straight back to the schoolroom and practice your alphabet for the rest of the day."

Agnes closed her mouth as tight as a Chesapeake clam. Tamping back her own anger, Juliet demanded, "Do I make myself clear?"

"Aye, as clear as Hoots's stream. I beg your humble pardon, Mrs. MacKenzie." She dashed for the door.

"Where are you going?" Juliet called.

"To the tinker's wagon to spend my penny on war paint. He's leaving tomorrow." The door banged shut behind her.

Juliet stifled the urge to punish the girl. After being snowbound for so many days, the children had grown bored and pulled more pranks than usual. The day offered a welcome respite for Juliet. She wasn't about to let Agnes spoil it.

"She's a mite headstrong," lamented Flora.

Futility tugged at Juliet. "Aye. Her father indulges her, and the servants goad her into mischief."

"She'll outgrow her wild streak. The laird's bairns have a hill to climb, being . . . motherless, as they are."

"Who *are* their mothers?"

Flora shook her head. "That's the secret of the books. If the sheriff of Easter Ross found out, he'd tell the king who mothered the duke's children. 'Twould scandalize the court and ruin the lassies' chances of making good marriages."

Juliet thought of Lillian, her life draining away as she brought the duke's child into the world. But which daughter?

"That Smithson hates all the MacKenzies, especially the duke of Ross," Flora grumbled. "Rumor says they were friends once, seven years ago when His Grace went to court to get his title back. They gave him all his lands except Easter Ross, which they gave to Smithson, him being wed to the earl of Tain's daughter. Now there's no one there to speak up for the Scots."

"So you came here."

"Aye, and we like it. I wonder if the tinker has a baby rattle," Flora mused.

Anxious for a few moments alone, Juliet said, "Why don't you go along and see for yourself. I'll stay with this braw lad."

"Oh, I couldn't ask that of you."

"You didn't ask. I offered." She rubbed her nose against the baby's. He giggled and reached for her hair again, but she was too quick for him. Laughing, she said, "It feels good to be out of that castle and in the company of a child who can't sass me or put thistles in my bed."

Flora counted pennies from a purse. "I do need a spool of red thread, and my eldest lad is ready for his own razor and strop."

"You can keep an eye on Chief Agnes, if you don't mind." Juliet clucked the babe's chin. He latched on to her finger. "I'll watch this little papoose."

And think about how I can get into that tower room.

Flora donned her coat. "I'll be back before he wets his nappy again."

The door closed behind Flora. Blessed silence enveloped the stable. Juliet wanted to jump and shout. Sensing her excitement, the infant wiggled. A thump from the back of the building drew her attention. Grooming brush in hand, smug expression on her face, Lottie marched out of the stall where her pony was kept.

Juliet tensed as the girl approached, for Lottie never missed a chance at gossip. Even punishing her didn't help. "What mischief are you about, Lottie?"

Her eyes grew wide. She placed a hand on her chest. "Me? I was just minding my business and grooming my pony."

Juliet didn't for a moment believe the innocent tale, but further questions would only egg Lottie on.

"Cook's making honey cake," Juliet said.

"Mary'll eat it all if I don't hurry." But Lottie strolled out the door as if she had all the time in the world.

Juliet went to watch out the door. The girl walked, not to the castle, but toward MacKenzie's alehouse.

* * *

Eben MacBride droned on about the length of the winter, the shortage of peat, and the high price of MacKenzie's ale. Lachlan had heard it all before. He drained his third tankard of beer and gazed about the crowded tavern. Standing at the counter, Cogburn Pitt entertained a crowd with a story about the Colonials playing a prank on English soldiers. The man from Virginia still complained about the cold, but it didn't keep him indoors. He hadn't argued when Lachlan asked him to help with the repairs to the cottage now belonging to Fergus MacKenzie.

"We'll have sickness aplenty," preached Eben. "Mark my words, folks can't do without fuel."

Lachlan said, "Then open the storehouse, Eben, and fill up the wagons."

Eben spat on the sod floor, then wiped his mouth on the sleeve of his coat. "An' what of the MacKenzies-over-the-burn? Their wagon ain't here. Can't put peat in a wagon that ain't here."

Lachlan gnashed his teeth. Neville Smithson continued to exile MacKenzie families from Easter Ross. Lachlan should be there wiping up the ground with that bastard who called himself sheriff, but here he was, jawing with Eben MacBride about a load of peat.

"All right, Eben. Give the MacKenzies' portion to Fergus. He'll deliver it to them on his way home."

MacBride yanked off his woolen bonnet to scratch his balding pate. "Might work," he allowed. "But supposin' he ain't got the room? Horde o' bairns he's got to ride in the wagon, you know. Got 'im that new laddie, too."

"I'm sure they'll find room."

"Aye, mayhap. But that don't help MacKenzie-on-the-moor. He ain't got fuel for his fire, either."

"I swear by Saint Margaret, Eben, you'd make a tragedy out of May Day. We'll see the peat gets to those who need it."

"I could ask around, I suppose. See who's here and who's going where. Or I might tell that lice bag who calls hisself a tinker to spread the word. Everyone'll be at his wagon today. Ain't a decent pipe to be had from him.'' He spat again. "Nothin' but geegaws and trinkets to make the lassies preen. A man—"

"Had you told the tinker you needed a pipe the last time he was here, he would've brought you one."

Eben's face grew red. "An' that's the rub of it, ain't it? He ought to know when I'm a-needin' my things. He knows right enough when the widder MacKenzie needs her smelling salts and curlin' irons. You'd think he'd have a care about the ones what put the coin in his purse and the ale down his gullet."

"The widow has her own funds."

"An' that's another thing."

He opened his mouth to start in again, but Lachlan cut him short. "Enough, Eben. I'm putting you in charge. Find out who's headed in what direction and distribute the peat. If that won't do it, load up more wagons and deliver the blasted peat. Take Cogburn Pitt with you. He needs something to do."

Eben's pockmarked face creased in a grin. "I ken yer reasons. Wantin' the new governess to yerself, eh?"

Embarrassed that he'd become so obvious, Lachlan said, "I want the peat delivered."

"But that wagon belongin' to MacKenzie-under-the-tanner ain't got a round wheel on it. Scunner wouldn't hire the wheelwright if'n his life depended on it."

Lachlan threw his hands in the air and stomped out of the alehouse, Eben's gripes still ringing in his ears. Lottie almost ran him down.

"Papa, Papa! Wait until you hear . . ."

Ten minutes later, Lachlan dispatched Lottie to the nursery. Itching to give the governess a piece of his mind, he entered the stables.

He heard her voice before he spotted her. Near the far wall, she stood in the aisle between the rows of horse stalls, one arm extended toward a pony, MacKenzie's babe cradled in the other.

"And this one is Sarah's pony. His name is Aristotle." Her laughter had a musical ring and a settling effect on Lachlan. "What do you think of that, Lachlan MacKenzie?"

The bairn awkwardly reached for the horse's mane. "Oh, no, you don't." She stepped back. "You're as quick with those hands as your namesake. Aren't you?" She held him up in the air and jiggled him until he squealed. "You're as handsome, too."

Many women had said those words to Lachlan; others had told him so in much bolder ways. But hearing the lassie admit that she found him attractive marked a moment he intended to savor. Quietly he slipped off his sheepskin coat and eased himself onto a barrel near the brazier. Unnoticed, he watched her.

Her thick blond hair hung in a loose braid that dangled almost to her knees. He pictured her naked and astride him, that fall of hair draped curtainlike about them. He'd grasp her tiny waist and lift her. Those melon-ripe breasts would dangle above him. He'd reach out with his tongue and lave her nipples until she begged him to suckle her properly.

His loins turned to hot stone.

She cradled the babe again and approached a stall housing the most gentle Clydesdale in the stable. The mare stuck her nose into the palm of Juliet's hand. "See this pretty lady?" she said to the babe. "According to Mrs. MacKenzie-the-cook, Penelope here is the only female in the Highlands that Lachlan MacKenzie hasn't seduced."

His first impulse was to challenge the remark, but teasing wouldn't work on Juliet. He'd have to explain the reasons behind his reputation. He'd have to tell her about winning back his dukedom seven years ago, about wanting a duchess who loved him and not his title. He wasn't ready to bare his soul to a woman who wouldn't bare her body. Besides, she would probably return to Virginia in the spring.

Oh, but she had blossomed in the Highland winter. In one month her milk-white skin had acquired a soft and pleasing pink glow. The apprehensive expression in her wide brown eyes had been replaced by an appraising, confident gaze.

She'd said she was good with children. She hadn't lied. But his children were a different, very special brood. She countered Mary's constant questions with queries of her own, so the lass had to think things out for herself. She tempered Sarah's devotion with encouraging statements designed to draw the shy lass from her shell. He'd seen Agnes and Lottie do their best to irritate her. She reacted with patience and humor. The same way she dealt with him.

He took great pleasure in watching her entertain the infant. She didn't disguise the joy she felt at holding MacKenzie's babe.

He blew out his breath and stared at the pot bubbling on the fire. God, he was hot for her, had ached for her since that night in the library. Why had she run away? And what would happen when he finally got her into his bed? Would she grow lazy and demanding, as the other governesses had? Somehow he didn't think so. Still, he couldn't picture Juliet White warming his bed at night and teaching his lassies during the day.

"Why must you always sneak up on me!"

He looked up. She stood stiffly before him, the babe clutched froglike to her breasts. Breasts he ached to fondle and kiss.

"How long have you been eavesdropping?" she demanded.

If lies were raindrops, she was in for a deluge. "I didn't know you were here. I came to see Fergus."

"Oh." Her pretty teeth toyed with her lower lip. She stroked the bairn's back in an up-and-down rhythm that made Lachlan quake inside. Her eyes narrowed. "You didn't hear me?"

"Hear you?" he croaked.

Cocking her head, she asked, "Are you ill? Your voice sounds strange."

He cleared his throat. Thank God his coat lay on his lap or she'd see for herself what was wrong with him.

She stepped close. "Do you have a fever?"

Fever? He was a bletherin furnace from the waist down!

Her lips narrowed disapprovingly. "You smell of ale."

"A man is entitled to his pleasures," he grumbled.

"You're certainly an expert on pleasures."

He bristled. "And you're supposed to be an expert on governing children."

To compensate for her stiffening posture, she lifted the babe higher up on her shoulder. "Have you a complaint?"

She'd given him the perfect opening. So why did he feel reluctant? "Aye. Where were you when Agnes was spying on Hoots MacBride?"

Her confident smile boded ill. "How kind of you to ask," she said sweetly. "I was staving off mal de mer and dreaming of an upstanding and generous Scottish lord who'd appreciate having an honest woman care for his children. Ah, by your expression, I don't suppose Lottie . . . it was Lottie who tattled?"

"Aye, 'twas Lottie."

"I thought as much. Our little reporter didn't happen to tell you the incident occurred on Hogmanay. While, I might add, you were romancing the governess *du jour*."

He felt like a green lad caught with a willing scullery maid. Hell, he didn't have to justify his behavior. " 'Twas past romancing, since she'd been in my bed a dozen times by then."

Her eyes narrowed. "Bully for her."

He ground his teeth. Juliet White was a first-rate governess. Instead of berating her, he should praise her, help her, and he would as soon as he trusted her. He still couldn't accept her reasons for coming to Scotland, even though Cogburn Pitt had verified her story.

"I'm sorry," Lachlan said. "I shouldn't have fallen victim to Lottie's tales. She deserves a spanking."

"I accept your apology. But please don't spank her. You'll only humiliate her, and she doesn't deserve that."

Feeling out of his depth, Lachlan said. "What do you recommend I do?"

"Leave the matter to me. As I've said before, I'm very good with children."

The accuracy of that statement made him laugh. "You're very good with me, too, but you could be better."

"Like your Hogmanay governess?"

The babe stirred. Even when her eyes sparkled with

outrage, she managed to soothe the child. Lachlan longed to see that fire in her eyes burst into flame.

The infant latched on to her hair.

"Drat! That's the second time today."

Lachlan tossed the coat aside and stood. "Stand still. I'll fix it." He gently pried the child's hand free. The babe giggled and drooled, his gray gaze darting from one adult to the other.

"What's this sticky stuff?" Lachlan asked, holding the braid out of reach of the babe.

"Honey."

Their gazes locked. "You'll need a warm bath," he said. "With plenty of soft-scented soap, fluffy cloths, and someone to wash your hair and dry it by the fire."

Tartly she said, "You're willing to play lady's maid?"

"I'd like to play with you all right."

"Only because you're angry with Cozy."

He'd lost his desire for the flouncing, willing maid. He had a raging hunger for a sweet-faced Colonial who possessed a stubborn will he intended to break. "You've been listening to gossip."

"If you think to seduce me, Your Grace, you'll have to do better than that."

Of late, she'd counteracted his suggestive statements with boldness. So far, she'd achieved great success. "Put down the child and I will."

"Your namesake? I wouldn't dream of it. Ah, you're smiling. I wager you're feeling cocky about having this babe carry your name."

"And I'll wager," he murmured, "that if you don't temper that sassy tongue, you'll find out who's the cock and who's the hen. And how a chick is made."

She chuckled and stepped back. "My, my, aren't we the barnyard philosopher today?"

"Very well. I'd rather kiss you than talk to you." Even as he spoke the words, he knew them for a lie. He liked keeping company with Juliet White.

"How delightful," she purred, "that you managed to save a kiss for me."

Was she insulting him? Nay, not Juliet. She was bandying words, a game at which he could equal her.

"I'm trying to give you a kiss, lassie, but it fair breaks the mood when you bring up another woman."

"I'll certainly try to be more circumspect."

She'd be flat on her back if he had his way. He tugged on her braid.

"Let go of my hair."

The command in her voice brought Lachlan up short. Yet there was something very natural about standing here with her, a cooing infant between them.

"And cease your roguish tricks. I don't like them."

She could protest until the Highland clans reunited, but she was affected by the situation, too, for her nostrils were gently flaring and her hands grew still on the child's back. The babe dropped his head to her shoulder and closed his eyes again.

Lachlan leaned close, determined to kiss the stiffness out of her lips. He released her hair and eased his palm around her neck. Slowly he pulled her toward him. She glanced nervously at the child and tried to draw away.

"Don't," Lachlan said. "You'll wake the babe."

He'd anticipated kissing her again. He'd dogged her heels and lusted after her. He'd used every trick of seduction he knew. But the instant his tongue slipped between her lips and her free hand gripped him about the waist, Lachlan knew he'd underestimated the extent of his own yearning. Desire knotted his belly, and with every beat of his heart, stinging shafts of desire darted to his loins.

But his mind raced with questions about Juliet White. He wanted to hear her stories of Virginia. He wanted to know what sort of child she'd been. He wanted to ask if that popinjay in Richmond had ever tried to kiss her a second time. He wanted to know if the Mabry children were similar to his own.

Lachlan nipped at her lips while sucking in breaths of air. The demands of his body overrode his curiosity. He cradled her face in his palm, and with his thumb he coaxed her to open her mouth wide for him.

When she did, he slanted his hungry lips over hers and kissed her with wild abandon. His hand sought her breast. Instead of soft woman's flesh, he encountered the downy head of the sleeping babe. Unexpectedly his heart fell victim to a softer, more tender demand. He needed to coddle this woman, to have her smile at him with tenderness and love, to whisper endearments on a long winter night, to give him a son.

The sentimental thought brought him to his senses. He wanted to bed her. Wanting more meant trouble and heartbreak. He pulled back and said, "Tell me what you feel, lass. Tell me what you want."

Juliet didn't dare answer. She couldn't possibly put into words the blessedly sweet sensations his lips aroused in her.

"Tell me," he coaxed on a breathless whisper, his eyes darkly blue and dangerously attractive.

She dared not define the desire that whistled in her ears, thrummed in her stomach, and sang in her veins. Mere words couldn't begin to describe the mind-stealing, heart-throbbing thrill of being held in his arms.

Her head reeled with shiny new thoughts and bold new visions, but they weren't new to him; he'd seduced scores of women. Including poor Lillian.

Disgusted by her weakness, Juliet moved away from him. She had a purpose here in Scotland. She had pride, too. Too much pride to fall victim to this Highland rogue.

"Having second thoughts about coming to Scotland, Juliet?"

If she told him the truth, he'd send her packing. How could he appear so bletherin earnest? Seeking safe ground, she said, "No, I was merely thinking that Flora will be back soon."

"And you'd be embarrassed if she found you kissing me."

"I did not kiss you. You kissed me."

"You put your tongue in my mouth."

"Your Grace! I did no such thing." She wanted to turn her back on him, but pride wouldn't let her. "You're just a conceited duke who's accustomed to having women fall into his bed."

"Not lately," he murmured and straddled one of the barrels.

"Then perhaps you should declare a new holiday. You seem to be the randiest then. Oh, Lord! I can't believe I said that." Racked with shame, she cursed her wayward tongue.

He stroked his face with his free hand. "I assure you, I can get randier, holiday or not."

Assuming a cool demeanor, she said, "Now that we've had our little exchange, have you anything decent on your mind?"

His great shoulders slumped wearily. "Aye, we always have important guests in the spring. I'd like you to prepare the staff and the lassies."

"Are you expecting that other duke? The one Agnes calls a slimy bootlicker."

He laughed so hard he almost tipped over the barrel. "He's the duke of Argyll. As far as he's concerned, there is no other duke. I'm not sure he'll visit, but we will have titled guests."

"All dukes are the same to me. Here, Your Grace, hold your namesake. My arms are tired."

The sleeping child fitted perfectly in the crook of his arm. He smiled at the tiny boy and said, "Argyll may be more English than Scot, but if he visits, he'll expect you to defer to him."

"And how does one defer to a duke?"

He cupped the child's head in his hand and stroked the bright red cap of curls. "You need practice. You're not very good at deferring to me."

"We don't have nobility in Virginia."

"Will you learn, Juliet? 'Tisn't much to ask."

Blessed Virginia! At last the duke of Ross was asking instead of demanding. "Do you seek favors from this Scottish duke who acts like a heathen Englishman?"

His lips puckered as he strove to keep from laughing. "Aye, you might even have Cook prepare some of your Virginia fare. Perhaps those flopjacks."

"Flapjacks."

He cocked an eyebrow and fairly oozed charm when he said, "Did I fankle it up?"

"Aye, you did."

His expression grew serious again. "Will you show my guests proper respect, Juliet?"

If it meant winning a debt from him, she'd sing a ballad for his important visitors. "It shouldn't prove too difficult. Food, wine, good manners, and clean beds. Except for the duke of Argyll. Agnes says he sleeps under a rock."

Grinning, the duke of Ross rose and placed the child in her arms. His hands lingered a heartbeat too long at her breasts. He kissed the tip of his finger and placed it on her nose. "Don't listen to Agnes. Listen to me."

Baffled by the tender gesture, Juliet watched him don his coat and walk to the door.

He turned. Framed in the bright sunshine of the doorway, he seemed bigger than life. The bulky coat accentuated his broad shoulders and made his hips and flanks appear lean and taut as a mountain cat's. The sun sparkled in his mane of hair and turned the chestnut strands to red.

Her heart drumrolled. "Was there something else?" she asked.

"A wee thing."

He could have asked her to pluck the sun from the sky and she'd have dashed outside to do it. Was she falling in love with the man who had ruined her sister? Juliet shuddered at the thought.

Just before he closed the door, he said, " 'Tis time Agnes started wearing dresses."

Chapter 6

I hate Papa."

The message, chalked on the slate in Agnes's angry scrawl, swam before Juliet's eyes. Conflicting emotions warred within her. The trained governess in her demanded she punish Agnes for her peevish behavior. The lonely orphan wanted to comfort the troubled child whom others called bastard. At times like these, Juliet wished she'd become a shopgirl, a lady's maid—any occupation that didn't tear her heart out.

Perhaps she wasn't capable of coping with these four children; perhaps her own wants blinded her to theirs. Yet Agnes needed her, and whatever the cost, Juliet wasn't about to let that little girl down.

Juliet took stock of the schoolroom. She walked to the windows and drew back the shutters. Winter sunlight flooded the room. In a few moments she'd wake the children. Once they'd washed, dressed, and eaten, this room would come alive. Girlish laughter and arguments would overpower the gentle ticking of the clock.

Behind her, the door opened.

Cogburn strolled inside, stocking cap perched on the crown of his head rather than pulled over his brow. Even indoors, he wore a woolen sweater beneath his waistcoat. The fingers of his gloves peeked from one pocket, and the fringed end of a muffler hung from the other.

"Good morning," he said.

She handed him the slate board. "That's debatable."

He clucked his tongue and shook his head. "Agnes, I take it."

"Yes. She locked herself in the falcon mews last night. When I tried to get her to come out she called me a buggerin' Colonial. I had to resort to threats to get her into the castle and off to bed."

Cogburn put the slate on the table. "I'm not surprised at anything she'd say, not after what the duke did."

"She's just stubborn, Cogburn. She has to start wearing dresses eventually."

"He spanked her over that?"

Juliet went cold inside. "The duke spanked her? When?"

"Yesterday, and in front of Ian and that new MacKenzie lass from Nigg."

Suddenly Agnes's angry declaration became a plea. Juliet started for the door. Why hadn't she checked on the girl again? Why hadn't she suspected Agnes might still be upset?

Cogburn grabbed her arm. "He didn't beat her, Juliet.

He patted her bottom. That was all. She deserved it, too. She had no business bragging about watching that Hoots MacBride relieve himself.''

Juliet jerked free. "The duke humiliated her—and before an audience. Oh, God. I didn't know. I'll fetch her, and then I'll have a few words with His Grace, the scourge of children.''

Cogburn followed her into the hall. "He's not here.''

"Where is he?''

Cogburn shrugged. "He and Jamie rode out before dawn. They took blankets and enough provisions to last a week.''

"How fortunate for him,'' she said under her breath.

The nursery door opened. A maid emerged, lugging a brimming ash bucket.

"Is Agnes awake?'' Juliet asked.

"She ain't here, ma'am. Miss Lottie said the mite snuck out to the falcon coop again. Still sulking, I suppose.''

Juliet grabbed her coat and started down the stairs. Cogburn at her side. The duke of Ross was an insensitive brute. He had the common sense of a half-wit. She'd gladly trade her recommendation from Sir Axel to have the duke before her now. But first she must find Agnes.

Juliet yanked open the castle door. Frigid air slapped her face. Compared to yesterday, the inner bailey seemed deserted, for most of the visitors had left. Through the open gates rumbled the tinker's wagon, kettles and pans dangling from its brightly painted sides. Behind him rocked a cart piled high with hay, a cow tethered to the back.

Juliet stepped over ruts in the muddy thoroughfare and dodged the melting snowdrifts. Beside her Cogburn slowed his stride. Snow crunched beneath their boots. She welcomed the loud noise, for it matched the raw fury roiling inside her.

Cogburn worked his callused hands into his gloves. "Juliet, you haven't forgotten your purpose here, have you? I mean, you're not becoming attached to these children?''

"Of course not." The words sounded false. "I'm merely doing my job."

"What about their father? It's not like you to react so, ah, strongly."

The concern in his voice wore the edge off her anger. "How could I become attached to that scoundrel? He's the man who seduced my sister."

"Has anyone mentioned Lillian?"

"No."

"Then how can you be sure? One out of two people in this land bears the MacKenzie name. And they're all loyal to him."

She wanted to believe the duke of Ross had not seduced Lillian, but she couldn't. Not until she found the Book of MacKenzies. "And how many MacKenzies have a six-year-old bastard daughter?"

"Some have, and they're proud to say who birthed the children."

"He's the one; I'm certain of it."

"Whether he is or not, I wouldn't care to be in his boots the next time he sees you," Cogburn said.

A crow cawed from a nearby rowan tree. Feathers ruffled, the bird paced the naked limb. Juliet smiled unpleasantly. Her demeanor would resemble that of the disgruntled bird when she faced the duke. "He'll wish he'd been born Irish, as Gallie says."

Cogburn pulled the stocking cap over his ears. His nose had taken on a bright red glow. "I remember the time the Mabrys' overseer whipped the stableboy for spilling a pail of oats. You threatened to turn the whip on him."

"He deserved it. The boy was only six."

"You scared the man out of his wits."

"He didn't have any wits."

Cogburn chuckled. "I remember you telling him that, too."

Juliet quickened her steps. "This is different. Agnes worships her father. Poor thing, she must be miserable."

"You'll help her, Juliet. You're very good at that. Now, tell me what luck you've had with Gallie and the books."

Warmed by his confidence, Juliet dragged her mind away from Agnes. "None. Gallie's as friendly as the Mabrys' new footman."

Cogburn whistled. "What will you do?"

"I've already learned where she keeps the books." She pointed to southernmost corner of the castle. "Up there—in the tower room."

"Isn't that the duke's chamber next to it?"

"Yes. The only entrance to the tower is through a vestibule separating the duke's chamber from Gallie's. Since he's not here, I just have to wait till she's asleep. I'll try this afternoon."

But Juliet never got the chance. Agnes wasn't in the falcon mews or the stables. Juliet sent Cogburn to question the shopkeepers and tradesmen while she returned to the castle to question the staff.

With each negative answer, each shrug and shake of the head, Juliet's worry mounted. Logic kept the fear at bay. Kinbairn Castle was home to Agnes. These people had known her all her life. No one would hurt her. She was here somewhere, hiding, mending her torn pride. Once they found her, Juliet would put things to rights.

An hour later she entered the schoolroom. Lottie held the slate board. Her bottom lip began to quiver. Her deep blue eyes, so like her father's, filled with tears. "She's never coming back." She dropped the board, buried her face in her hands, and sobbed.

Juliet drew the girl into her arms. "Don't cry, Lottie," she said, her own voice wavering. "She's probably sleeping in the hayloft."

Mary ran into the room, a hand pressed against her side, a frantic expression in her hazel eyes. "Cozy said Agnes ran away." Mary, too, began to cry. "Something awful'll happen to her. The sheriff of Easter Ross'll get her."

"Oh, no! They say he roasts bairns for supper."

Mary nodded, her mouth pulled down into a frown. "Or he puts 'em in the workhouse. We'll never see her again."

Lottie began to keen.

Juliet's courage plummeted, but she refused to give in

to despair. "Mary, nothing like that will happen to Agnes. Come here." She held out her hand. Mary flew into her embrace. Juliet held them both, swayed, and whispered, "She's here. We just haven't looked in the right spot."

"Did Papa truly spank her?" asked an incredulous Lottie.

"But he never spanks us," wailed Mary.

Sarah appeared in the doorway, her sweet face ravaged with pain. "Oh, Mistress White, Agnes is gone forever," she blurted, running to join the embrace. "Cozy said she's been gone all night."

"Cozy has a tart tongue," Juliet said, aware that she'd voiced the duke's words.

"She didn't even eat her breakfast," said Mary, still clinging to Juliet.

Rays of morning sunlight filtered through the windows of the schoolroom and cast long shadows on the stone walls and floors. Absently Juliet stroked Sarah's hair, but her mind jumped from one awful possibility to another. What if Agnes wasn't sulking? What if she'd fallen and broken a leg? At this moment she could be crumpled in some dark place, praying for rescue.

Juliet shivered and pulled the girls closer. She knew well what it was like to be alone, cold, and hungry. From the day Lillian's ship had sailed, there had been no one to look out for an orphaned child. No one had cared about a little girl named Juliet. Fresh tears for old memories threatened to spill forth.

Quickly Juliet summoned a vision of kind Mr. Strickland, the scholar of Greek. A gentle and considerate man, he'd taught her to trust her own judgment, to take care of herself. But his greatest gift had been knowledge, for he had taught her to read and cipher.

"What will we do?" moaned Sarah.

Juliet knew what she'd do: she would kill the duke of Ross.

Lottie said, "Papa's gone somewhere, and Thomas is in Glenhugget."

"Gallie's asleep," whined Mary.

"We'll get everyone to help," Juliet said. "We'll all work together."

"But how?" asked Mary. "Agnes always tells us what to do."

"We'll each search in a different place. Cogburn is asking around the village." The girls would need more than a search to occupy them. Juliet turned to Sarah. "I don't know the castle well enough to pass out assignments. You do. Will you tell us where to look?"

Sarah's sad eyes seemed to brighten. "I think I could, but I'm not so strong as Agnes."

"Strength comes to different people in different ways. We'll need your strength now, Sarah. Will you tell us?"

The child took a deep breath and wiped her eyes. "Mary and Lottie, you could search the lower floors. Mistress White and I will look upstairs. We'll meet in the hall when we're finished." Uncertainty clouded her heavenly blue eyes. "Is that a good plan?"

Juliet's heart swelled with love. "It's a perfect plan, Sarah dear."

Lottie stepped back and blew her nose. Sarah and Mary did the same.

Sarah stuffed her handkerchief into an apron pocket. "If I were brave, I'd get on my pony and ride everywhere until I found her."

"Agnes rides the best of all," Mary said glumly.

The three seemed again on the verge of tears. Juliet gathered her courage and confidence and set them about the task of locating their wayward sister.

They found no trace of Agnes in the castle proper or on the grounds. By noon, real fear held Juliet in its grip. In a daze of wretched despair, she dashed from the buttery to the battlements, from guardhouse to garderobe. She crawled on her hands and knees to search the darkened corners of the kennels. Frantic, she climbed the hayloft and sifted through the straw. She scoured the scullery. She even searched her own trunk and satchel.

· Hours later, while the girls napped, Juliet found herself in the duke's chamber. Cozy had searched this room; so had Cook. Hoping against hope, Juliet threw open the wardrobes. When she didn't find Agnes huddled among his possessions, Juliet grew angry at him again. She made a shambles of his clothing, yanking everyday shirts and breeches from his trunks and tossing them into a pile with tailored knee breeches and elegant satin coats. The smell of him surrounded her, and even as she cursed him for an uncaring brute, she found comfort among his personal things.

The time had come to call him home.

Instead of exiting to the hall, Juliet stepped into the vestibule. To her left was the door leading up to the tower and the Book of MacKenzies. To her right was the door to Gallie's chamber. Juliet hesitated, then turned right.

She raised her fist and pounded so hard on Gallie's door she thought the wood might splinter. The sleepy-eyed chronicler opened the door.

"Agnes has run off."

Gallie yawned and scratched her head. "She's in the falcon mews."

"No, she's not."

Juliet related the problem and described the search. "You must tell me where His Grace has gone."

Gallie yawned again. "Nay."

Anger and frustration boiled inside Juliet. "Now, you listen to me. I don't care where his latest lovers' tryst has taken him. He must come home."

Gallie stepped back. "Fetch Ian to me. I'll send him for the duke."

Juliet told herself she didn't care where the duke had gone, but she resented the fact that he'd keep his whereabouts a secret.

While the sun still shone brightly, Ian left for parts unknown. Cogburn spent days scouring the countryside, stopping at the farm of every family that had been at Kinbairn prior to Agnes's disappearance. Juliet hoped Agnes might have stowed away in one of the departing wagons. But at each farm the reply was the same: no one had seen Agnes. Cogburn even searched for the tinker, but his destination, like that of the duke of Ross, remained a mystery.

*   *   *

The castle seemed quiet as a tomb. Alone in the library, Juliet stared at the blackened hearth. The fire had burned to white ash long before midnight, but she hadn't the will to rise and light it again. The chill in the room had no effect on her numbed senses.

She tipped her head back. The bowl lamp on the table cast a circle of wavering light on the ceiling. The lantern clock banged the hour of three. After a week without word, the passing of another hour seemed insignificant. She had failed. In her preoccupation with the duke and the Book of MacKenzies, Juliet had committed the worst of all crimes: she had allowed her six-year-old charge to run away.

What if Agnes was Lillian's child? Where was the girl now?

Black despair seeped into Juliet's bones. The vestibule was closed to her; Gallie had locked both her own chamber and the duke's. The books might as well be in Philadelphia. She hadn't even blundered respectably.

Boots tramped in the hall.

"Juliet!"

At the sound of the duke's voice, she leapt from the chair.

He charged into the room. Light from the lamp threw his features into sharp relief. His aristocratic nose flared with anger; worry lines creased his forehead and framed his eyes. One of his braids had begun to unravel.

"Where the hell is Agnes?" he roared.

Her heart jumped into her throat. Wearily she said, "I don't know. I had hoped—"

"Holy Hogmanay, woman!" He jerked out of his sheepskin coat and flung it in a chair. "You don't know?" He stalked toward her, his chest heaving, his hands balled into fists. " 'I'm very good with children.' " He mocked her Virginia accent. " 'You won't regret your decision, Your Grace.' " In his own thundering voice, he said, "No wonder this Mabry fellow drove you from the Colonies. What did you do to his children? Let them wander into the hands of Indians?"

Bitter resentment filled her. She took a step forward.

"How dare you blame me? She ran away from *you* because you beat her."

"That's blather. I hardly touched her."

"Oh, so you admit that you bullied her?"

"Listen to me, *Mistress White*—"

"No!" She closed the distance between them. Staring up into his angry face, she said, "You listen to me." With a stiffened index finger, she poked him in the shoulder. "You drove your daughter away." She jabbed him again. "You lost your temper." He stepped back. She followed him. "You couldn't sit down and talk reasonably with her, could you? Could you?"

He glared down at her, the muscles in his neck bunched tight, the corners of his mouth gone white, his dark blue eyes glittering with rage.

"Answer me!" she demanded.

"If you poke me one more time, I'll—"

"You'll what? Spank me, too? Break my finger? Is violence your answer to raising children and conversing with governesses?" The harshness of her words was her undoing. She withdrew her hand and put it to her throbbing forehead.

"You are not a child."

The absurdity of the comment angered her anew. She clutched her hands to her throat. "Should I be grateful for my age? Will that spare me your wrath, O Great Duke?"

His eyes narrowed and his lips formed a thin line. "You should hold that viper's tongue and keep in mind the perilous state of your livelihood and my daughter."

If he dismissed her, she'd never find the Book of Mac-Kenzies. At the moment Juliet didn't care. "My livelihood?" She choked on the words. "You think I'd worry over a stack of coins when Agnes is out there alone?" A deep, dull pain throbbed in her head. She threaded her hands through her hair and tried to squeeze away the ache. "Good God," she moaned, "she could be hurt. She's lonely and cold. Oh, why can't you find her?"

She turned away. Bitter sobs rose in her throat. She couldn't hold them back. The tension of the last week, the confidence she'd passed on to the other girls, the stiff upper lip she'd maintained, withered like cotton plants in a drought.

Through the misery, she felt his hands touch her shoulders. He turned her around and pulled her into his arms. "You're cold." His hands roamed her back, soothing, comforting. "Don't cry, Juliet," he whispered near her ear. "Trust me to find her. This is my kingdom, remember. No one in the Highlands will harm my daughter."

He hadn't shaved, and she welcomed the rough drag of his whiskers. He smelled of the stables and the crisp winter wind. He emanated security and strength. Juliet's despair dissolved in his embrace. "But what if she's had an accident?"

"She's a sprite of a lassie, my Agnes," he said, a sad smile in his voice. "She could charm her way into Whitehall if she tried."

Juliet grasped his arms. He felt solid, strong, and warm, and his calming words soothed her. Sniffling, she said, "Mary says the sheriff of Easter Ross wants her."

"Nay," he breathed, rocking her from side to side as he often rocked his daughters. "Neville may be my enemy, but he'd not hurt the lassie. All the saints in heaven couldn't help him if he did. He knows that."

Feeling better, she said, "Will you call up your own saints?"

"Aye, and one for Agnes." He pushed the hair back from her forehead and kissed her there. "She'll need a saint of her own when I find her."

Juliet drew back and grasped his necklet. "If you lay one hand on that child, you'll answer to me."

Although he smiled, he couldn't mask the concern that shadowed his features. "I'll talk to her, Juliet."

"Promise?"

"Aye."

She smiled back. "If you don't, I'll box your ears. And there's something else."

"Other than my ears?"

Exasperated, and unsure of his reaction, Juliet chose her words carefully. "You can't go off again without telling me where you'll be. What if Gallie hadn't been here to send for you? What if one of the girls had died?"

A low growl rumbled in his chest. He drew her up and wrapped her in his arms again. Holding her off the floor, he pressed his lips to hers. She clung to his broad shoulders as he ravished her mouth. Anguish and desperation and the sweet taste of his favorite drink flavored the kiss. She felt a burgeoning of trust, the feeling of being cared for.

As if he'd spoken his thoughts out loud, she could read his mind: *I'll find her. I swear by God I'll find her and fetch her back.*

Without thought to the consequences, she thrust her tongue forward and kissed him back. His lips gentled, and his tongue danced and swirled about hers.

When at last he drew away, Juliet almost swooned at the tender expression in his eyes. "What is it?" she asked.

He set her on her feet. She had to work to keep her knees from buckling.

"I didn't think you'd care so much about my children," he said, his voice rife with apology. "Now, lass, keep a lid on that temper." He began to rebraid her hair, which had come loose. "None of the other governesses would have cared. I didn't expect you to be different."

For years the Mabrys had praised her. They valued and trusted her enough to finance her journey to Scotland and offer a home to Lillian's child. But the compliment from the duke of Ross touched Juliet in a much deeper place.

His hands lingered at her waist. "I'll bring her back. But she must be punished."

"You shouldn't have spanked her."

" 'Twas hardly more than a pat or two."

"But you did it in front of Ian and Grace. Would you upbraid Jamie MacKenzie in front of the other soldiers?"

"Nay. 'Twould hurt his pride."

"Agnes has pride, too."

He stared at the lamp. The reflection of the flame glimmered in his eyes. "Too much of it, I'm thinking. She's like her mother in that."

Tender emotions stirred within Juliet, and as she

stood on the castle steps and watched him ride away, she wondered if she hadn't misjudged the duke of Ross.

Two days later Juliet stood in the fletcher's shop and listened to Eben MacBride bemoan the state of everything from the British Empire to his marriage. "Doiled, I was, to string myself up with her," he grumbled.

Juliet pitied his wife. How could any woman tolerate this snaggle-toothed curmudgeon?

Anxious to be away, she said, "Yes, well, that's very interesting, Mr. MacBride. Can you make the bows and arrows or not?"

"Aye, if'n I can find some decent feathers. The sprite's been pluckin' 'em for her Indian garb."

A commotion in the yard drew Juliet's attention. She peered out the window. Joy spread through her.

At the head of a double column of armed horsemen rode the duke of Ross, smiling broadly and waving to the crowd. His mount, a sleek sorrel, pranced and swished its tail. Juliet's heart leapt, for in front of the duke, her head held high, her eyes as big and bright as summer daisies, sat Agnes.

Caught by happiness, Juliet scanned the girl for injury. Her hair was untidy; she appeared thinner than before, but she seemed unharmed in spite of her harrowing experience.

The duke grasped his daughter's waist and set her on the ground. She looked so small, staring up at her giant of a father. Her eyes beseeching, she spoke to him. Juliet bit her lip, for Agnes had at last lost her front teeth.

The duke shook his head and pointed toward the castle. Agnes clung to his leg. He leaned down, and Juliet imagined the loving words he must be speaking. When he straightened again, Agnes bowed her head and trudged off toward the kitchen entrance.

The duke sawed on the reins and headed his mount to the stables. Some of the soldiers followed him, others went their own way.

"He snatched the little bastard back, I see," said Eben.

Juliet spun around. "Mind your tongue, sir! What choice did she have in who her father was and whether or not he married her mother? You've a vile way about you."

His mouth dropped open; his clay pipe tumbled from his lips. With a dull crack the pipe shattered on the plank floor.

Satisfaction loosened her tongue. "Oh, you've broken your pipe, Mr. MacBride. How unfortunate."

Anxious to see Agnes, Juliet exited the shop and crossed the thoroughfare. Jamie MacKenzie waved to her.

"Welcome home," she said. "Where was Agnes?"

He smiled sadly. "With the tinker, poor lassie. I wouldn't want to be in her boots now."

The tinker. Juliet had seen his wagon passing through the castle gates the morning Agnes had disappeared. If only she had stopped him. "Has His Grace punished her?"

Jamie stretched and rubbed his back. "Nay, but Gallie must cut her hair."

Stunned, Juliet said, "Cut her hair? What do you mean?"

" 'Tis the only way. She's got a headful of the tinker's lice."

Juliet gaped at him. Then she dropped the basket and took off like a shot. Looking neither left nor right, she raced for the castle. Dear God, please let me get there in time. Her heart pounding in her chest, arms pumping at her sides, she dodged ice-crusted puddles and leapt over mounds of snow. When she rounded the south corner, she skidded on a patch of ice. Her feet flew out from under her. Arms flailing, she grabbed at a thicket of dead vines. Sharp twigs dug into her palms, but she righted herself and moved on.

She hurried up the steps and flung open the wooden door. The kitchen staff stared at her, their mouths agape.

"Where's Agnes?"

Cook slapped a glob of dough onto the bread board,

but the angry action belied the sorrowful expression in her eyes. "In the butler's pantry, poor wee mite."

Her chest heaving, Juliet dashed past the scullery. She heard the snip-snip of shears and Gallie's voice.

"Yer braids'll grow back, child. Don't fret so."

Too late.

Juliet stopped and braced herself against the cold stone wall. She'd been five years old when they held her down and cut her hair. Even now she could feel the cold metal of the shears against her neck. She could hear the taunts of the other orphans. And she could see Lillian, straining against the hands that held her. Lillian screaming, "Leave my sister alone!"

Like a fist squeezing her heart, the old pain held her. But Agnes needed her.

Juliet stepped into the butler's pantry.

She fixed her gaze on Gallie, whose back shielded Agnes from view. The chronicler wore an orange velvet gown more suited to entertaining royalty than to playing the barber. Cozy stood nearby, holding a stack of towels. Lottie, Mary, and Sarah peeked around her skirts.

"You ought to be ashamed of yourself, Agnes Mac-Kenzie," said Gallie. "And if you splash water on my dress, I'll have His Grace take away your pony."

Gallie moved away. Agnes sat in a huge wooden tub, her naked back stiff, her chin quivering. Without her long hair, the slender column of her bare neck seemed slight. She didn't fight Cozy. The child's eyes, now haunted, were fixed on some distant point across the room.

Juliet swallowed back the sob that rose in her throat. Life shouldn't be so brutal to children.

Gallie's fingers worked the blades of the shears as if testing them. She slipped an apron over her head. "Let down the child's hair, Cozy," she said.

As if she were touching a leper, Cozy grimaced and, with the tips of her fingers, plucked pins from Agnes's hair. The mass tumbled free. Her precious braids were still attached.

Juliet lurched forward. "No!"

Cozy squealed and jumped back. Agnes sat as still as

a statue. Gallie looked at Juliet as if she were a worm on a tobacco plant.

"Put down those shears," Juliet said.

"No," said Gallie, her voice dripping scorn. "You may live with lice in the Colonies, Mistress White, but in Scotland we do not abide the creatures. Be about your business."

Anger blazed through Juliet. "My business is here, *Mistress* MacKenzie. You may rob your children of pride in Scotland, but in the Colonies we treat them with love and respect."

Agnes's stoic expression dissolved. Tears rolled down her cheeks, and her skinny chest heaved. Her small hands gripped the edges of the tub. No longer the proud, defiant daughter of a duke, she looked forlorn, helpless.

"Please, Mistress White," begged Agnes, her voice rough with tears, her words lispy without her front teeth. "May I have my braids?"

On shaky legs, Juliet approached the tub. "Of course, sweetie."

Behind her, Juliet heard footsteps and the whispers of the kitchen staff. They'd come to watch, but she wasn't about to let anyone make a spectacle of Agnes. "You three!" She pointed to Sarah, Lottie, and Mary. "March upstairs and write your spelling words three times each." Whirling, she snapped at the kitchen staff, "You are excused! Immediately!"

The girls scurried off, and so did the staff. Juliet turned back to Gallie. "I know a better way to delouse her."

Gallie's dark eyes narrowed. "What way?"

"Goose grease and sulfur. And plenty of both."

"She'll smell like a barnyard."

"But she'll have her hair." And her dignity.

Agnes came to life. Wide brown eyes, alight with hope, were trained on Juliet. "I like goose grease, Mistress White. I promise I do."

Smiling, Juliet held out her arms. Water sloshed. Her eyes shut tight, Agnes flung herself upward and into Juliet's arms. Warm water seeped through her dress, but Juliet didn't care. Taut arms and legs gripped her in a stranglehold. She snatched up a towel and covered Agnes's nakedness, much as Lillian had cared for her younger sister.

Juliet clung to Agnes and the bittersweet memory of her own past. At length she said, "Cozy, fetch all the goose grease you can find."

Cozy dusted off her hands. "It's in the buttery, and I ain't the milkmaid."

Patience dwindling, Juliet said, "Then have the milkmaid fetch it and another tub of hot water to my room."

"Yes, your highness." Cozy flounced from the room. Gallie put down the shears and took off the apron. Her expression softened as she gazed at Agnes. "I want that hair braided neatly when I get back, and should I find a single nit—"

"You won't," said Agnes. "Mistress White will fix it."

Juliet's senses sharpened. Gallie was leaving. Opportunity was knocking on Juliet's door.

"Where are you going?" Juliet asked.

"On an errand," said Gallie. "If it's any of your concern."

Undaunted by the chronicler's cold stare, Juliet said, "When will you be back?"

"Why do you want to know?"

An outrageous plan began to form. "Agnes must be isolated from her sisters. She can sleep in my bed. I had hoped you might let me sleep in yours."

Gallie's mouth formed an insincere smile, and she looked Juliet up and down. "A clever move, but not an original one, Mistress White. I hope you're as thorough with the lice as you seem to be with strategy. I'll be sure to leave you the proper key."

She meant the key to the duke's chamber. Let her think she was abetting a seduction. "I'll be very thorough, Gallie. I'll pick out every nit."

Gallie breezed out the door. "See that you do."

Emboldened by her plan, Juliet squeezed Agnes, who still held on like a kitten saved from drowning. Hope in her heart, Agnes in her arms, Juliet strolled upstairs.

* * *

Lachlan took the steps three at a time. His legs protested. After days in the saddle, his muscles ached with every step. He wanted a scalding bath and a soft bed. And the Colonial to warm it. She could even rub goose grease all over him and he wouldn't care.

Goose grease. He chuckled at the remedy. Inside, however, he was deeply delighted. According to Gallie, Juliet had charged into the pantry and saved Agnes from the shearing. She'd be happy now, and he couldn't wait to see both her and Juliet.

Not bothering to knock, he stepped inside Juliet's chamber.

"Papa!"

Agnes sat in a hip bath, soapy water up to her pert chin. On her head she wore a towel wrapped turban-style, which teetered as she moved. Juliet knelt beside the tub, a sponge in her hand, a smile on her lips, a bemused expression in her eyes.

Emotion clogged his throat. "Hello, poppet," he managed.

"I'm not a poppet no more." She squared her shoulders and waved an arm about the room. "I'm a sultan and this is my . . . my . . . What is it again, Mistress White?"

Juliet looked up at him. Her brown eyes glowed. "This is your harem, Your Highness."

"And I'm a highness, too!"

Juliet twitched her nose. "You smell like a goose."

"I don't care if I smell like Ian's muck pile. At least I got me . . . my braids."

"Remember," said Juliet, "goose grease doesn't always work, and you must hold very still while I pick out every egg."

"I'll be still as Ian's stuffed badger. It'll work. Won't it, Papa?"

He stepped into the room and carefully lowered himself into a chair. Fatigue seeped into his bones. "I hope it will, lassie—if hope matters."

"Are you ill?" asked Juliet, looking him up and down.

"Nay, just sore from the saddle." It occurred to him that he wouldn't have spoken so frankly to another woman. He shrugged it off; she was simply different. She was openhearted and understanding and kind.

She rose and walked toward him. The damp gown clung to her in all the right places, and he remembered well the way her breasts filled his hands, the way her nipples jutted out.

A mischievous grin played about her lips. She extended her hand. "Goose grease, Your Grace? We've a bit left over."

Lachlan eased himself deeper into the chair and stared at the jar in her hand. So she wanted to play, did she? He lowered his voice. "Only if you apply it to the parts of me that hurt, Mistress White."

She blushed, and quite prettily. "I must put our sultan to bed."

If his daughter weren't here, he'd strip off his breeches, carry the Colonial to his room, and call her bluff.

He took the jar. And noticed her palms. Grasping her wrist, he said, "What have you done to yourself?"

She tried to pull away. "Nothing. It's just a scratch."

Abrasions and bruises covered delicate pads of her palms. One fingernail had broken into the quick. "What happened?"

She darted a glance at Agnes. The girl slumped against the tub, her turban pillowing her head. She was asleep.

"I slipped and caught the dried vines on the castle wall."

His gaze moved from her palms to her breasts, then her mouth. "You'll be sore tomorrow," he whispered, allowing their eyes to meet.

"So will you."

He laughed. Under his breath he said, "I'm sore now, lassie."

She withdrew her hand and walked to the tub. "I'd better put our sultan to bed," she repeated.

Agnes awakened. Lachlan got to his feet and reached for a towel. He held it out and Juliet put Agnes into his arms. "I'll take her to her room," he said.

"Nay, Papa. I get to sleep in my harem."

Juliet fussed with the turban. "I promised her she

could sleep here tonight, Your Grace. Put her in my bed.''

Why was Juliet so nervous? He dried off his daughter, put on her nightgown, and tucked her in bed. Already asleep, she looked like an angel. He touched her down-soft cheek, and his heart filled with love.

"Where will you sleep?" he asked Juliet.

She stood in the candlelight, examining her hands. "Near you."

Certain he'd misunderstood, he said, "Where did you say?"

She folded her hands, but the prim gesture didn't match the glitter in her eyes. "I said I'll sleep near you. In Gallie's bed, Your Grace. I intend to go down in history as the only virgin to sleep within strolling distance of you and awake . . . intact."

Blood raced to his saddle-sore groin. "Tonight?"

"Yes, tonight. Do you object?"

"Nay." He hitched up his breeches and swore to keep his meeting with Thomas brief. "But I'm beginning to feel like a stroll."

Chapter 7

An hour later, keys in hand, Juliet paced the floor of Gallie's chamber. With each pass, the canvas soles of her slippers scuffed the woven rug. For the tenth time since entering the room, she stopped and listened for sounds from the duke's chamber. All was quiet.

The clock struck one.

Excitement quivered through her. In a few moments she would learn which of the duke's children had been born on June 20, 1762, the day Lillian died. She would also learn which MacKenzie man had sired the child.

Would the information exonerate the duke of Ross? Or would the book prove that he'd seduced Lillian? As she paced, Juliet worried over the question. The romantic in her prayed the duke hadn't been the one. The other part simply wanted an end to the uncertainty. Soon she would know the truth.

She harnessed the heady anticipation and looped her index finger through the ring in the candle holder. Holding the light high, she opened the door.

On tiptoe she entered the vestibule. Her breath frosted on the cold air. The candle flame wavered. A thread of light shone beneath the door of the duke's chamber. He was awake. He spoke in muffled tones. She couldn't make out the words. Who was he talking to? Cozy. But the next voice Juliet heard was also male. It was Thomas.

She could turn back now. She could scurry into Gallie's room, lock the door, and wait for a better time, a a time when the castle was empty, save for her.

Urgency pushed her onward.

She closed the door behind her and inserted one of the keys Gallie had given her. By locking herself out, she also kept out the duke. If he decided to take a stroll, as he'd threatened earlier that evening, he would assume she had retired for the night. She grasped the key so tightly the blood rushed from her fingers. Slowly she turned her wrist until, with a dull click no louder than a snap of the fingers, the mechanism slid into place.

Juliet crept to the arched door leading to the tower room. She inserted a different key. Please open, she chanted under her breath. She pushed and jiggled, but the nose of the key didn't fit. She wished and cursed, but the lock didn't tumble. This, then, was the key to the duke's chamber. Like dry wood on a fire, the knowledge ignited her fear.

If he opened his door now, she'd be trapped.

If the key didn't work, she'd be back where she started.

Wishing for an extra hand, she carefully maneuvered the third key into her palm. As smoothly as a hand into a worn glove, the key slid into the lock. Relief seeped through her. Thank you, Gallie, for suspecting I wanted a different key. Thank you for thinking I wanted him.

Juliet stiffened her wrist until the muscles in her arms cramped. Not daring to breathe, she turned her hand.

A deafening click shattered the silence. The candle holder tilted wildly. Hot wax slithered over the rim and pooled in the tender webbing between her thumb and forefinger. Pain raced up her arm. Like a too-tight second skin, the wax began to harden. She sucked in a breath and pulled out the key.

She darted a glance over her shoulder, pulled open the door, and stepped inside. Stairs spiraled up into darkness. The musty odor of stale air and sweating stone permeated the silent space. But above those common smells floated another odor. It was odd and familiar. Ah, well, she'd find out soon enough.

She considered leaving the door unlocked, but how could she search through the books if she constantly worried that he might creep up behind her? She couldn't. With exaggerated care, she wielded the key again and put the ring into her pocket. Cupping her hand around the candle flame, she mounted the narrow stairs.

Juliet had studied this chamber from the castle yard, had envisioned its size and shape. But as she stepped onto a crimson square of the chessboard carpet, she was surprised at the size of the room. She was even more surprised at its contents.

Seated at the table in his private chamber, Lachlan thrummed his fingers on the arm of his favorite chair. The bracket clock on the mantel struck the hour of one. He gazed with longing at his bed.

Across the table, Thomas read the letter to the duke of Argyll. Three times Lachlan had dictated the letter, three times he'd changed his mind.

Thomas looked up, the pen poised over the paper. His narrow face reflected uncertainty. Lachlan knew the expression well. The ever-tactful Thomas was striving for a way to voice an objection to something in the letter. His gaze fell again to the parchment. The candlelight illuminated the white scar that creased his temple and disappeared beneath his black hair. A band of ruffians in a London alley had given him that scar. They'd stripped him of his horse and all his possessions and left him for dead. Neville Smithson had rescued Thomas and brought him to Lachlan. Neville had been a good man seven years ago. What had happened?

That night Lachlan had traded one friend for another, for once Thomas had mended, Lachlan learned three things about the man who would become his steward: Thomas Brodie was fiercely loyal. He possessed a memory for details that surpassed little Sarah's, and he was a master of discretion.

Thomas tapped the parchment with his quill. "Your Grace—" He stopped and jerked his head toward the door to the vestibule. "Did you hear something?"

Lachlan listened, but he heard only the buzz of fatigue. Juliet would be asleep by now. She'd never come through that door. If Juliet White wished to speak with him, she would approach his room from the hall, and she'd have business on her mind.

Until tonight he'd often wished she were more like her predecessors. But none of those flighty and conniving women would have come to Agnes's rescue. He wanted Juliet White just as she was.

"Nay, Thomas. I heard nothing. Let's get on with it."

The steward shrugged. "On the matter of the accusations you bring against Neville Smithson . . ."

Humor bubbled inside Lachlan, but he swallowed it. "Spare me the verbal dancing, Thomas. What's on your mind?"

A smile softened the steward's stern features and revealed a chipped tooth—another memento of the beating he'd taken. "My father would have phrased the letter differently."

"And what would the good ambassador to Spain have done?"

Fondness glowed in Thomas's eyes. "He would have named each of the injured parties."

"So Neville would have to explain himself in every case."

"Precisely. As your social equal, Argyll should, out

of respect, take these charges to the lord chancellor or visit Easter Ross himself. He really can do no less."

"Would you go there were you he?"

Humor twinkled in the steward's dark eyes. "Were I he, I'd buy the finest equipage and acquire the most accommodating and inventive of mistresses. Then I'd lie back and enjoy the long journey to Tain."

Lachlan roared. "Spoken like a true rake, Thomas. I often wonder that a woman in London didn't lay you low in that alley."

"Impossible, Your Grace. At the time, every woman in England wanted you."

Memories, both fond and sad, came to mind. That early autumn seven years ago had been a blur of willing women and flowing wine. Three women he remembered vividly. Sadness and pity still clouded his recollection of the fourth.

He'd had troubles then. He had more troubles now.

"I would say, Your Grace," began Thomas, "that by striking the second paragraph and adding—"

Lachlan got to his feet. "Make it so, Thomas. I'll sign it in the morning."

"You'll be interested in the addition. So will Argyll."

"Very well. Now tell me."

Thomas sorted through a sack of ledgers. "Twelve new families—all MacKenzies, of course—have descended on Squire MacKay in Glenhugget."

"What has that to do with the letter to Argyll?"

"They're from Kelgie."

Kelgie was a MacKenzie stronghold in Easter Ross. "Their occupations?"

Thomas winced. "Groundkeepers at the golf course belonging to Conall MacKenzie."

Rage pumped through Lachlan. He pounded his fist on the desk. "Smithson's a miserable bastard. Who's tending the links? A passel of pastry hawkers from Bartholomew Fair?"

Thomas cleared his throat. "Worse than that, Your Grace." He rose and walked to the liquor cabinet. "Perhaps you'd like another drink."

"Sit down."

Thomas heaved a sigh and plopped down in the chair. "The sheriff, it seems, leased the golf course from Conall and then plowed it up."

The urge to kill raced like a beast through Lachlan. "I swear on the soul of Queen Mary, the idiot has sealed his fate now. Argyll fair lives for golf."

"Smithson's planted tobacco."

"He can plant pansies for all I care. But I'll see him seed those courses again—on his lily-white hands and satin-clad knees."

"You'll be glad to know he didn't touch your personal golf course." Thomas chuckled. "Seems he won't go near Rosshaven Castle."

"At least he's got some sense."

Thomas made a tsking sound. "I had thought Smithson would change once the Lady Bridget took him back."

"Bridget had every reason to toss him out on his ear."

"But they were at court. All men keep mistresses there."

Lachlan thought of his childhood friend. "Not if they're married to Bridget MacLeod."

Thomas shrugged. "Now that that's settled," he said, pulling a bag of coins from his pocket. "I've paid the staff their wages." He held out the bag. "Except the governess."

Lachlan waved him off. "You pay her."

Thomas's head jerked back. "You always pay the governesses."

"This one's different." The statement came so easily.

"Aye," said Thomas. "There's something about her." He squinted and stared at the bag of coins. "Something familiar, and yet not. Do you sense that you know her?"

Lachlan wanted more than to *know* Juliet White. And he would soon, if she didn't keep that sassy tongue still. He chuckled at the thought of a meek and mild Juliet. One thing was certain. He intended to keep her. "You mean you've seen her before?"

"I don't know, Your Grace. I should remember." He dropped the bag. "I don't."

"Nonsense. You never forget anything. What about Cogburn Pitt?"

"A damned likable fellow." Thomas grinned. "Especially after a few pints of MacKenzie's brew. He seems so proud of Mistress White. Why, every time I see them together—"

"When have you seen them together?" Lachlan blurted. Cold jealousy slithered into his gut. He hadn't felt that emotion in years.

The steward's face grew white. "Oh, my goodness," he said, rubbing the scar at his temple. "You're jealous. That means—"

"Nothing," grumbled Lachlan. "It means she's the best governess the lassies have had."

"Hear, hear," Thomas said solemnly. "And have you noticed how she's changed since her arrival? She's blossomed."

Confusion and need caused Lachlan to mumble, "Aye, she's developed a tart tongue and willful ways."

"She's also a bonnie woman, sir."

"Bonnie is as bonnie does."

"She's better than Miss Witherspoon."

Lachlan shook his head. "Cozy's better than Miss Witherspoon."

Thomas winked. "In bed or with the lassies?"

"Enough. Juliet's the best of them all. Give me the bag and I'll pay her."

Thomas handed it over. "Do you distrust her?"

Lachlan wasn't sure. He wanted Juliet White, but for the first time in his life he wanted more than lovemaking from a woman. She hadn't pretended concern for the missing Agnes; she didn't hide her affection for his lassies. What did she think? What made her laugh and cry? Why was she here? The mystery surrounding her presence at Kinbairn brought him to his senses. "Women must never be trusted, Thomas."

"Who knows that better than you, Your Grace?"

"Poor Paris. He learned it well at the hands of Helen of Troy."

"Just so. Still, I worry that some of your former mistresses might change their minds about motherhood."

A familiar ruthlessness filled Lachlan. "That isn't an option open to any of them."

"I know that, sir, but what if Smithson learns their names?"

"He won't. No one ever will." Lachlan sighed. "Have you more business tonight?"

"Aye." Thomas reached for another ledger. "The taxes from Durness and the expected revenue from Lax-ferry's sheep."

Lachlan resigned himself to the work ahead, but his mind stayed focused on Juliet White. Why had she come to his household?

Juliet buried her face in her hands and cursed herself for a stupid, stupid fool. The excitement she'd felt an hour before had sputtered like a dying candle. The wind whistled outside the windows. She splayed her fingers and forced her eyes open.

The leather-bound volume, its cover illuminated with golden letters and a finely detailed stag, lay before her. Six similar books were stacked in a niche in the curved wall behind an unframed canvas.

Anger and frustration twisted her stomach into knots. *The blasted books were written in Scottish.*

Her knowledge of French and Latin didn't help, for the language of the Highlands bore no resemblance to any tongue she knew. Still, she wouldn't give up.

Again, she grasped the binding. Dyed crimson, the leather matched the candle-wax burn on her hand. A series of blisters had formed, but the pain seemed minor compared to the disappointment that ravaged her soul.

She opened the book and tried again to find some common denominator or key to help her translate the words. Like a summer storm rolling over the Appalachians, despair threatened her resolve. She banished it. Of course, her task wouldn't be simple. Not since that black day in an Edinburgh cemetery had she expected simply to scoop up her niece and sally back to Virginia.

She moved her hand down the first column of the yellowed page and stopped on a familiar word: *tues.* Could it be the abbreviation for the day of the week?

The idea put her brain in motion. If the abbreviations were consistent, then she should find similar ones for other days.

She did not. Nor could she make any sense of the other combinations of letters. Only one Scottish name blazed clearly in her mind: MacCoinnich. The bane of her existence, the thorn in her side. The nemesis of her sister. The flesh and blood reason she sat in this rigid room and quaked with the cold.

She glanced at the candle and estimated she'd been in the tower about an hour. Taking a sheet of parchment from her pocket, she picked up the quill and made a list of the words. Once she learned their meaning, she would return to this tower.

She rose and hefted the weighty volume to her breast. The top of the book rested just below her nose, which began to itch. She crossed the circular room. The unframed canvas scratched her sore hand, but she didn't care. She burrowed beneath the canvas and replaced the book, lining up the spines exactly the way she'd found them.

Lifting the candle holder in her uninjured hand, she gave her attention to the painting. She stared again, in awe of Gallie's imaginative creation.

As tall as Juliet and easily twenty feet long, the unfinished canvas illustrated the lives of Sarah, Mary, Agnes, and Lottie MacKenzie. And their governesses. Each section depicted a room or area of the castle. The nursery came alive with four infant faces peeking from swaddling clothes, an elegantly dressed and obviously peeved governess looking on. As toddlers, the girls scrambled across the elegant dining room table and tossed food at one another and at a dark-haired woman with her hands thrown in the air. At about three years old they sat mesmerized at their father's feet while he read them a story. The fireplace in the great hall illuminated his noble features and brought his finely sculpted nose into sharp relief. His hair had been shorter then, his expression endearingly young. A sultry golden-haired governess lounged nearby.

Unable to look away, Juliet studied the other scenes,

drinking in the happy times. The incomplete drawing of Agnes in her Indian garb and Sarah peering at what looked to be a globe of the world lifted Juliet's spirits, for her own image, smiling down at her charges, looked back at her. She was a part of those moments, and even after she left Scotland, something of her would remain. How would Gallie picture Mary and Lottie? The weight lifted, and Juliet felt proud of herself, as proud as she had felt the day young Alton Mabry had begun his studies at the College of William and Mary.

Who would have thought that Juliet White would be pictured on a canvas hung in a tower in a Scottish castle? Who would have thought a woman as cold and secretive as Gallie could have created such a heartwarming chronicle? And signed her name with such flair.

Juliet stood on tiptoe, held the candle high, and scanned the rest of the painting. Her breath caught. At the top, to the left of the MacKenzie stag, were four women, each holding an infant.

Four women with no faces.

Weariness weighted her spirits. Suddenly longing for the safety of Gallie's room, Juliet made a careful inspection of the tower, then descended the stairs.

Before she reached the door, heavy footsteps sounded outside. The duke!

"Juliet," he called out. "Are you asleep?"

Her bones fused. Although she felt cold, her skin grew warm. He would catch her now. Before she could learn the meaning of a few precious Scottish words and climb these stairs again, the duke would dismiss her.

Her heart hammered. She pinched out the candle and crept to the bottom of the steps. Kneeling, she peeked through the keyhole.

He stood in the vestibule, his arms folded across his chest. Feeling absurdly naked behind the ancient door, the key in one hand and the unlit candle in the other, Juliet watched the duke of Ross.

He stared at the floor. She realized he was looking at the bar of light beneath Gallie's door. He thought she was awake. Would he, too, peek through the keyhole?

She hoped not, for if he did, he'd see the bed, perfectly made and completely empty.

He called her name again and turned his head to one side to listen for her reply. When none came, he rocked back on his heels, the movement sending ripples down his muscled legs. Agnes's favorite swearword escaped his mouth. He knocked again.

In one hand he held a leather pouch. He tossed it into the air. Coins chinked as it landed in his palm. Why would he come to her at this hour of the night, a bag of coins in his hand? One possibility sickened her.

He spun around, marched into his own chamber, and slammed the door.

Quick as a frightened hare, Juliet shoved the key into the lock and pushed open the door. Fear buzzed so loudly in her ears that she didn't hear the click of the lock or the whining of the hinges. Once out, she wielded the key again.

The key ring slipped from her hand and clanged to the stone floor. Not daring to look toward the duke's door for fear of finding him standing there, she snatched up the key ring, unlocked Gallie's door and dashed inside. Leaning against the door, she gasped for breath.

In the hall, another door closed.

Footsteps sounded. The duke was coming to the other door to Gallie's room. She'd been so preoccupied with the door to the vestibule, she'd forgotten to lock the door to the hall.

On numbed legs, she walked to the desk, replaced the keys and the candle holder. In her mind she could see him, feel him, standing on the other side. Her eyes stayed fixed on the door, her thoughts on the man beyond it. She heard a shuffling noise.

And watched in complete surprise as a folded square of parchment appeared beneath the door.

Chapter 8

Lottie," whispered Mary. "Where did Papa go this time?"

"Nobody but Gallie knows and she's not here."

"She's never here," grumbled Agnes.

Juliet glanced up from Smollett's *Complete History of England*. The girls sat facing her, their school desks arranged in a half circle. Mary and Lottie flanked the turbaned Agnes. In the back of the sun-drenched schoolroom, Sarah stood on a stool before a pedestal table that held the *Forbes Encyclopedia*. With great care, she turned the oversize pages.

Over breakfast Agnes's sisters had quizzed her about her adventure with the tinker. The expected boasting never came. She had admitted to being cold. She even confessed to being afraid. In retrospect, Juliet thought the experience had been good for the lassie.

In their own way, all of the girls vied for attention. Sarah studied harder, knowing the duke would praise her. Agnes emulated him and ruled the others. Lottie harried the servants to impress her father with her skill at managing his household. Mary questioned him about everything, from why he liked satin bedsheets to why they couldn't have a French chef.

Mary leaned toward Agnes. "You saw Papa last."

Lottie giggled. "She saw the flat of his hand bustin' her bottom."

Agnes stuck out her chin. "He did not bust my bottom."

"Did so."

"Did not."

"Did so."

Agnes clenched her fists, but instead of striking out, she turned a pleading gaze to Juliet.

Startled, yet delighted, Juliet cleared her throat. "His

Grace has gone to Laxferry to visit the earl of Sea-forth."

The girls gaped in surprise. Juliet quelled the urge to giggle. She'd been surprised herself last night when she'd read the duke's note.

Lottie cocked an eyebrow. "He told you where he was going?"

"When's he coming back?" said Mary.

An unexpected sense of satisfaction rippled through Juliet; she felt like a giddy young girl anticipating a special treat. "On Friday."

"A whole week?" squealed Mary. "Why so long?"

Juliet said, "Never you mind. We've plenty to keep us occupied until then. Sarah come back here."

Sarah jumped from the stool and returned to her desk. She fidgeted, obviously anxious to begin her discourse.

Juliet gave a sheet of paper to each of the girls. For the hundredth time, she studied their curious faces, searching for a glimpse of Lillian. Like a bad spirit, guilt invaded her. Deception grew harder as her love for them grew stronger. She felt pride for their father, but envy tainted her admiration. Did he know how fortunate he was?

Mary rattled the paper. "What's this for?"

"I want you to write your birthdays—in Scottish."

"Why?"

Juliet smiled at Mary. "So we can celebrate your birthdays and I can learn Scottish from you. How can I ask Cook to make a cake if I don't know when?"

"A cake?" Mary snatched up her quill and stabbed it into the inkwell.

Lottie sighed. " 'Tis silly. Why must each of us write it?"

Juliet frowned. Lottie could be so obstinate at times. "Because it's only fair. Why should one of you have the task of writing four different dates? Don't you like your birthday?"

Four puzzled faces stared at her. Juliet gazed back at them in confusion. "Did I say something wrong?"

Agnes slipped the feather end of her quill beneath her

turban. "Tell her, Sarah," she said, her mouth twisting to one side as she sought and scratched an itch.

Sarah bolted from the chair. "Midsummer Day," she began, "marks the beginning of summer. In ancient times, the summer solstice was celebrated with pagan rituals. With the coming of kirks and holy men, Midsummer Day was declared a religious holiday. On his travels through the Highlands, Samuel Johnson reflected that the celebrations hadn't changed—only the collector and the amount of taxes differed." As graceful as a nun, she returned to her seat.

The dissertation saddened Juliet; Sarah knew the facts, even recited the irony, but she didn't understand it. Juliet hoped to change the girl from parrot to thinker. "Thank you, Sarah. That was splendid." She glanced at the others. "Lottie, when is your birthday?"

A duchess couldn't have summoned more disdain than Lottie when she said, "Sarah just told you. Didn't you hear?"

"I want a honey cake this Midsummer Day," demanded Mary.

A horrible suspicion invaded Juliet. "Sarah told me Agnes's birthday, but now I'm asking yours, Lottie."

" 'Tis the same," said Sarah. "We were all born on Midsummer Day."

Agnes added, " 'Twas in the first year of the reign of the sixth duke of Ross."

"That's Papa," jeered Lottie. "He won back his titles and his lands the same year we was born."

Juliet wilted into her chair. She should have guessed. Not only did the duke keep their mothers' names a secret, he gave his daughters a collective birthday. How many more setbacks would she encounter in her quest for Lillian's child?

She squared her shoulders. Later today she would ask Sarah to define the words she had copied from the Book of MacKenzies. If none of the words were "birth" and "death," she'd ask Sarah to write those, too. The duke would return before Gallie did, so Juliet had the next few nights to find the information.

She forced a smile and turned to another matter.

"Sarah, tell us about the word I asked you to find in the dictionary."

The girl shot to her feet. Her hands clasped, her posture perfect, Sarah took a deep breath. "Archer. From the Latin *arcarius*. An archer is one who uses a bow and arrow."

Agnes gasped. "Indians use bows and arrows."

"I thought you was a sultan," snapped Lottie.

Weary of the girl's peevishness, Juliet said, "Lottie, why must you be so rude to your sisters?"

"She's rude to everybody," grumbled Agnes. "Not just us."

Lottie stuck out her tongue. "Agnes gets to be everything. She gets to wear breeches and say the Hogmanay poem."

"And have adventures with the tinker," Mary pointed out, smiling vindictively. "She also got lice and a spanking."

Agnes made a great show of ignoring her. "Can a sultan use a bow and arrow?"

Juliet asked, "What do you think, Sarah?"

She jumped from the chair and headed for Dr. Johnson's *Dictionary of the English Language*.

Juliet called, "Sarah, sit down. Tell me what you think."

Sarah blinked, and her winglike brows drew together. She opened her mouth, closed it, then opened it again.

Mary said, "Why can't she look it up?"

"Because I want to know what *she* thinks, not what a book says. You look it up, Mary, while Sarah tells us her thoughts."

"I'll do it." Lottie swung her legs from under the desk.

Juliet stood before Mary. "Stay where you are, Lottie."

Resigned, Mary wiggled out of the chair and trudged to the dictionary. She leaned over the book, her face only a few inches from the page. Juliet had wondered why Mary shied from books and drew letters poorly. Now she knew why; Mary's eyes were weak.

She turned her attention to Sarah. And waited.

"I think . . .," the girl began, hesitantly, "that anyone who has a bow and an arrow could be an archer."

"What if he didn't know how to use it?"

From her perch on the stool, Mary said, "I can't find 'archery.' It must be one of your American words."

"No matter, Mary," said Juliet. "Return to your seat." Spectacles would solve Mary's problem. Would the duke accept his daughter's weakness and correct it?

"He could find a teacher and take lessons to learn to use his bow and arrow," volunteered Sarah.

"Yes, he could, Sarah," said Juliet. "You're very clever."

The girl beamed; her milk-pure complexion glowed with pride.

Mary blew out her breath and returned to her seat. "Who cares about stupid archers, anyway?" she grumbled.

"All of you." Juliet went to the wardrobe and took out the bows and quivers Eben MacBride had made. "You're all going to become archers."

"Hoots!" Mary jumped from her chair. "I'll be the best."

"Ha." Agnes pushed her aside.

They all crowded around Juliet.

"I don't want to," whined Lottie, her nose in the air. "The heathen Indians use those."

"Can you truly shoot a bow and arrow, Mistress White?" asked Sarah, her eyes as big and blue as cornflowers.

"I certainly can. When I was seventeen I won a turkey at the Harvest Fair in Williamsburg."

"We don't have turkeys in Scotland."

Mary giggled. "We have Agnes instead."

"Calm yourself, ladies," she said. "We'll begin practice today, and when His Grace returns, we'll surprise him."

Lottie slid an envious glance toward Agnes. "Does the best archer get a prize?"

"She certainly does. The best archer wins a new dress."

* * *

By night Juliet scoured the Books of the MacKenzies. To her dismay, she found that the information in the books was not listed chronologically. Even Sarah's list of Scottish words didn't help. Each page contained both old and recent listings. Listings she couldn't read. Try as she would, she couldn't discover a method to the entries.

By day Juliet instructed the girls in the sport of archery. With Thomas's reluctant help, Juliet had altered the third-floor ballroom. They replaced elegant chairs and tables with leather targets stuffed with straw. The girls could practice every day in the warm castle rather than shivering outside.

Lottie and Agnes competed against each other; Sarah did admirably well, but Mary was the best archer of the lot. She had trouble reading a book, but she could sight a distant target and hit the center almost every time. She won the new dress and often skipped meals to practice.

Altering the rules, Juliet proclaimed that the winner must fetch all the arrows. Eagerly Mary ran to the targets and retrieved the arrows.

Juliet had hoped to reward Agnes into wearing dresses, but since Mary won the contest Juliet had to insist Agnes wear dresses. The girl had stood quietly for the fittings. She even preened when she donned a yellow dress that had been embroidered, to Juliet's instructions, with tiny feathers.

By Friday the effects of exercise had begun to show on Mary; her face appeared slimmer and her underdrawers often slipped to her knees. Agnes had won her battle against lice. Her sweet face had gleamed with gratitude when Juliet offered to plait yellow ribbons into the girl's braids. Sarah was offering a few opinions without consulting a book. Lottie had curbed her caustic remarks and had even apologized for a few slips.

Late Friday night a sentry announced the duke's imminent arrival. A very proud Juliet summoned the girls to the foyer.

Lachlan wound the traces around his gloved fingers and tapped his foot on the wagon brake. Calling out a guttural command, he pulled back and urged the team of Clydesdales to a walk. Moonlight glistened on their lathered flanks, and the chilly night air turned their breath to puffs of clouds. Wheels creaked and harnesses jingled as he drove the team through the opening in the curtain wall and into the outer bailey. In the road, darkened shapes came to life as cattle lumbered to their feet and trudged away.

Familiar feelings of security and pride tugged at Lachlan. God, he loved his home, his people. Some said he was too protective of Ross and Cromarty; others called him unconventional. He was that, to be sure, but Lachlan felt he ruled with fear and arrogance: fear that the English would take his heritage away again, arrogance that he'd won it back at all.

From the age of seven until his twenty-fifth birthday, he'd been exiled from the Highlands. With MacKenzie-the-cook, he'd lived on a small stipend from his mother's estate. He made a fortune shipping wool to the Colonies and cotton to England. But the money hadn't pleased him. He wanted his heritage. So he'd gone to the English court and made a friend of Neville Smithson. Both wanted boons from the king. They succeeded, but a woman ended their friendship.

Behind Lachlan, Jamie ordered his own team to slow. Like an echo in Smoo Cave, the command rippled down the line of wagons until Cogburn Pitt yelled out the words. Spoken in his soft Virginia drawl, the Scottish words sounded like a lively chorus.

After a week in Pitt's company, Lachlan agreed with Thomas's judgment of the Virginian. Hell, thought Lachlan, any man who loved horses enough to endure elements that made him miserable just for the experience of driving a team of Clydesdales deserved respect. He was a friendly, intelligent fellow, who protected Juliet like a brother.

At the thought of her, Lachlan grew warm. He was becoming accustomed to that reaction, but if the matter were left to Pitt, Lachlan would never do more than dream of her.

"She'll not be used by you, MacKenzie," a red- and

runny-nosed Pitt had declared. "Juliet's a fine, upstand-ing woman. When she served out her indenture to the Mabrys, half the families in Virginia wanted her—for honest work."

Huddled near the campfire, Lachlan had posed the niggling question. "Why, then, did she choose Scotland?"

"Are you complaining?" Pitt had challenged. "If you're unhappy with her, tell her. She'll pack her bags and be off."

The possibility left Lachlan lonely and confused. "Juliet isn't leaving. But she said you were. When?"

Cogburn had gazed into the fire. "In April. I must attend the tobacco auction in Glasgow."

Secretly pleased, Lachlan wondered if Juliet would be different without Cogburn here. Would she turn to Lachlan? He hoped so. She enchanted him. She excited him. She could mock his lusty talk and toss it in his face. Most surprising, he respected Juliet and enjoyed her company. By God, she hadn't given an inch when it came to defending Agnes. Juliet had set her pretty chin, planted her dainty feet, and called him a bully. No governess had dared criticize him so forcefully. No governess had sparred with him so freely. No governess had ever cared for his children more. For that, he could overlook many things, even her motives for coming to Kinbairn Castle.

He'd been wrong to spank Agnes, but the thought of his innocent lass watching Hoots MacBride expose his private parts made Lachlan see red. Juliet had settled him down; then she'd sought comfort in his arms and begged him to bring the lass back. She'd kissed him with desperation. Would she ever kiss him with a woman's need?

As suddenly as a bolt of lightning, desire flared in his loins. He shifted on the hard plank of the wagon seat. He shook his head to banish carnal images from his mind. The chilling March wind cooled his heated senses, but the vision of Juliet remained.

He guided the team through the castle gates and into the torchlit yard. The guards chanted "MacKenzie!" and the residents of Kinbairn poured from their closed shops. Young Rabby MacKenzie waved from his guard post, then hurried down the steps and ran to the main doors of the castle.

Cooking smells drifted to Lachlan's nose and masked the rank odor of his cargo of damp Laxferry wool. The sights and sounds of home filled him with joy and security.

He turned the team toward the stables. The wagon tilted. Out of the night popped Ian. He jumped onto the seat and held out his hands. "I'll take 'em in, Your Grace. Eben and some of the soldiers'll relieve the others."

"Thanks, Ian." Lachlan gladly yielded the traces. He flexed his hands and worked the kinks out of his back and shoulders.

Ian urged the team onward. "I counted eight wagons. 'Tis a fair harvest from Laxferry's sheep. Smelly, too," he snorted.

"Aye," said Lachlan. "Did the lassies cause any trouble while I was gone?"

Ian chuckled. "Nary a prank. The colonial keeps 'em in line like marshal of the troops. She's a bonnie lass. Everyone says so. The smithy's layin' four-to-one odds that you'll keep her. Will you?"

"That depends," Lachlan dissembled. He wanted Juliet, but it bothered him that everyone else knew he wanted her. He should leave her be. But as the wooden doors of the castle came into view, the image his mind formed of Juliet White had nothing to do with his children's needs and everything to do with his own yearning.

He grasped his traveling bag, bade Ian a good night, and leapt from the slow-moving wagon. He bounded up the steps, threw open the doors, and stopped in his tracks.

He felt as if he'd walked into a fairy tale. Like a calming stream, pride flowed through his veins. In the center of the foyer stood Juliet. She'd donned a new dress of leafy green wool. To her left stood Sarah in pink and Mary in blue. To her right stood Lottie in a frilly white dress with red ribbons, and Agnes in sunny yellow, her temple braids threaded with ribbon. She looked the image of her mother. So did Sarah and Mary. Lottie had never favored her mother, except in her regal manner. One thing was certain: they all looked beautiful.

"Welcome home, Your Grace," said Juliet, a smile tilting up the corners of her mouth.

"We thought you'd never arrive," said Mary.

Lottie stepped forward. "Cozy said you fell into a bog."

"Papa never falls off his horse, you jelly-head," said Agnes.

Sarah said, "I'm glad you're home."

He felt a deep sense of comfort, of belonging. "I'm glad to be back," he said gruffly.

He knelt and held out his arms. His daughters rushed into his embrace. He hugged them; they burrowed against him. Nothing, no one, he pledged, would ever hurt these bairns, not ever. Over Lottie's crown of braids, he spied Juliet. Her eyes were moist with tears, but she didn't appear sad, and he wondered what she was thinking.

He wanted to kiss her until she told him. He wanted to pick her up and swing her around. He wanted to ask how she'd managed to get Agnes into a dress. He wanted to thank her for that. He wanted to tell her how much he loved being welcomed home.

Lottie pulled away. Nose twitching, she said, "You smell like a reeky old sheep howker."

"Aye, lassie, but you smell of lilacs," he said.

One by one the girls stepped back.

Mary said, "Mine's lavender because I'm nimble and sweet."

Sarah looked at Juliet and whispered, "Mine's heather because I'm gentle and shy."

Agnes fidgeted with the sash of her dress. "My soap's spice because I'm exotic."

He tapped her nose and said, " 'Tis perfect for you. You look very grown up in your new dress."

For the first time since he could remember, Agnes fluttered her eyelashes. "Thank you, Papa."

Lottie said, "You're only wearing it 'cause Mistress

White told you that heathen Indian princess wore dresses and bathed with soap.''

Mary pushed between them. "Nobody cares about an Indian princess. Will you be leaving again, Papa?''

"Not for a while, lassie.''

"I named all the kings of Scotland,'' crowed Lottie. "And I won Mary's red ribbons.''

Mary stuck her nose in the air. "They were Agnes's ribbons, and I hated them. They're crawling with lice.''

Lottie whirled on her sister. "I hate you, you foosty scunner. I hope fifty lice crawl up your nose.''

"That's quite enough, Lottie and Mary,'' said Juliet. "Unless you'd like to be responsible for an extra spelling test.''

Their mouths snapped shut.

Lachlan stood and approached Juliet. He took her wrist and kissed the back of her satiny smooth hand. "Soap?''

She let out a nervous breath. "Soap,'' she murmured.

Beneath his thumb, her pulse raced in a ratty-tat-tat tempo. Ah, so she wasn't so cold as she appeared. How could he keep his hands off her when she continued to warm his home and heat his blood? Why did she continue to evade him when it was plain she wanted him, too?

"Mistress White taught us to make soap, and we each got to pick our own.''

Mary's voice crashed through his love-struck thoughts. "We drew lots, Papa. 'Tis the . . . the . . . What is it, Mistress White?''

Juliet withdrew her hand. "The democratic way, Mary.''

"Aye,'' piped Sarah. "Just as Mr. Locke and Monsieur Rousseau wrote about it.''

Lachlan stayed close to Juliet. His gaze drifted to the neckline of her gown, to the rise and fall of her breasts. The dress was modest, but the body beneath it brought to mind long, lusty nights filled with breathless sighs and whispers of love.

"Papa,'' said Mary, tugging him away from Juliet, "why are you staring at Mistress White?''

"You never look at governesses that way," said Lottie.

"I bet he scolds her," declared Agnes.

"She's the only governess he hasn't scolded," said Mary.

Lottie crossed her arms over her chest and smugly said, "He didn't scold Miss Witherspoon."

Lachlan came to his senses. In two months, the lassies had learned more from Juliet White than from all the other governesses combined. "Did you thank Mistress White for your soap?"

"Aye," said Mary. "I filled her lamp."

Lottie said, "I hemmed her new dress."

"I polished her shoes," said Agnes.

"I'm teaching her to write Scottish," said Sarah. "But I'm not a good teacher."

"That's not true, Sarah," said Juliet. "I just don't learn as quickly as you. Now." Juliet clapped her hands. "It's past your bedtime. You agreed to go straight to bed if I allowed you to wait up for your father. Now say *guid nicht* to him."

Mary stepped forward. "Papa," she implored, "please don't make us say *guid nicht*. We missed you so."

"We've been waiting all day," whined Agnes.

Lottie said, "We have so much to tell you."

They gazed forlornly at Lachlan. He'd been away so often of late, and each time he returned, his daughters had lost a tooth or grown an inch. But tonight the changes were subtle.

"Sarah even learned to fill your pipe. Don't you want her to show you?" wheedled Mary.

He did. Bless Saint Ninian, he did.

Lottie said, "Agnes smoked it and puked on the rug."

"The pipe didn't make me sick," snapped Agnes. "You did."

"Did not."

"Did so."

He glanced at Juliet. She seemed the picture of motherly patience. Probably because she heard their arguing all day every day. But what was she thinking?

"They're exhausted, Your Grace. They must go to bed."

Mary tugged on his sleeve. "Can Sarah light your pipe?"

He didn't have the heart to disappoint them. "Aye, Mary."

Lottie, Agnes, and Sarah cheered.

Mary clapped her hands. "See, Mistress White, I told you he would let us stay up."

Juliet smiled tightly, "Sir, it's hours past their bedtime."

"Tomorrow's Saturday," said Mary. "We can sleep in. Can't we, Papa?"

"Please, Papa," begged Lottie.

"Very well, poppets."

"I'll say *guid nicht*." Juliet turned, picked up a lamp, and started up the stairs. "I trust you'll put them to bed."

As he watched her ascent, her back rigid, her soft woolen skirt swishing around her ankles, he wondered if he had hurt her feelings by not insisting she stay. He wanted to call her back, to ask her to join them. But he discarded the idea. Too often he thought about Juliet White as family. Including her would only make him want her more. He had no business seducing this governess. He should praise her and treat her well.

An hour later, as he sat with the girls in the library, Lachlan didn't feel so magnanimous. Mary and Lottie squabbled over everything from who could spell the most words to who could run the fastest. Sarah slept fitfully in a chair. Agnes sulked because she hadn't gotten to light his pipe. His head began to pound. His patience dwindled. He should have insisted that Juliet join them. By God, she should have volunteered to stay.

Only when threats of punishment turned to promises of treats did he get his daughters to bed.

A disgruntled and weary Lachlan paused outside Gallie's chamber. He stared blankly at the light beneath the door. According to Lottie, Gallie hadn't returned. Juliet was still occupying this room. Why? She was still awake. Why?

He knocked.

"Who is it?"

She knew the answer perfectly well. Annoyed, Lachlan said, "Your lord and master."

"I've retired, Your Grace," she said in a tone as chilly as a wind off the moors.

She was upset. What had he done? Leaving the matter until tomorrow would make it worse. Women had a way of mulling over problems until a molehill became a mountain. He'd best put to rights whatever was bothering her.

He tested the door and found it locked. "Let me in, Juliet."

She waited so long to open the door that he thought she might ignore him. He stepped inside.

She'd donned her gown and robe and dismantled her hair. Even though a fire blazed in the hearth, she wore a shawl. The long braid lay over her shoulder. His fingers itched to grasp the silky rope, but seduction wouldn't work on Juliet White. At least not tonight.

"I wish to speak with you."

She moved to the writing desk and set the ring of keys next to a candle holder and a stack of papers. "Is that a command?"

Her soft drawl dripped sarcasm. Taken aback, Lachlan said, "Yes, by God. Turn around and face me."

Her back as rigid as a caber, she turned. "I didn't invite you in."

Governesses always invited him in. But none of them acted like Juliet. "You don't look as if you're ready to retire."

Her eyes widened, almost guiltily. "What do you mean?"

"You look as if you're ready to curse me to Aberdeen. Why, Juliet?"

Her whiskey-colored gaze locked with his. "I insist," she said, sounding as businesslike as Thomas on payday, "that you address me as Mistress White."

Mistress White? He wanted to call her sweetheart. He wanted her to call him darling. He wanted to know why she seemed so distraught. Bless Saint Ninian, he even

135

wanted to hold her hand. Softly he said, "You can insist till this castle crumbles, *Juliet*."

She picked up the papers and began rolling them into a tube. "I won't be here when this castle crumbles."

Dread seeped into Lachlan's soul. "Neither will I. Are you leaving?" He didn't like the possibility. He examined her face closely. Had she been crying? Oh, Christ! He *had* hurt her feelings.

"No, Your Grace. I'm not leaving."

She'd probably written to her former employer. Had she told them she wanted to return to Virginia? To be certain, Lachlan took the papers from her hand.

She tried to snatch them back. "Those are mine. You've got no right to barge in here and read my private papers."

One page listed towns in Ross and Cromarty; another listed common verbs. He sagged with relief. "I'm sorry. And thank you for fulfilling your promise to learn Scottish. Here."

She took the papers. With jerky movements, she folded them. Her gaze stayed fixed on him. "I accept your apology. If you'll excuse me . . ."

Casually he said, "You were wearing a new dress tonight. 'Twas lovely."

She heaved a sigh. Lachlan thought he might as well have told her she had dirt on her face, for all she appreciated his compliment.

"Did you hear me?"

She glanced up and looked right through him.

A blow to his groin would have hurt him less. "What's wrong?" he asked.

"Nothing."

He was on familiar ground. He could read her like a book. "A predictable female response isn't like you at all, Juliet. Tell me." He extended a hand. "I'll stay here until you do."

Expecting her to repeat the answer, he was surprised when she knocked his hand away. The papers fluttered to the floor.

"Stay, then." She headed for the door. "I'll leave."

He blocked her escape. When he grasped her shoulders, she grew still. "Please don't leave," he said. "Talk to me."

She stared at his necklet. At that moment, Lachlan wished he possessed the eloquence of the man who'd commissioned the family amulets. Legend said Kenneth MacKenzie could charm the pelt from a badger.

"I want to know what's bothering you. If I hurt your feelings by not including you tonight, I apologize."

"Hurt my . . ." She sucked in her breath and closed her eyes. Light from the wall torch fell on her lashes and cast crescent-shaped shadows on her cheeks. He longed to touch the curling tips of her lashes. He wanted to pull her into his arms and romance the truth from her.

"I didn't mean to."

"You did not hurt my feelings," she said.

"Then what did I do?"

She opened her eyes. Her expression was as stern as a vicar's. "You undermined my authority."

Telling him he had two heads couldn't have surprised him more. "Your authority?"

Hot color stained her cheeks, and her eyes blazed with anger. "I told the children to go to bed. You let Mary cajole you into proving she could control me."

Immediately defensive, he said, "They're my children."

A cool smile appeared on her lips. "They certainly are."

"What is that supposed to mean?"

"It means," she said through pearly white teeth, "Your Obtuseness, that just when I was making headway with *your children,* you blew it to Hades."

"What the devil are you talking about?"

"Excluding Sarah, would you say that your children are well behaved?"

He felt like a lad who'd been caught dulling his father's broadsword. "Nay."

"Would you say that they're polite?"

"On occasion."

"I await that special day. The truth is, with exception of Sarah, your children are rowdy, manipulative, and uneducated. Lottie didn't even know the names of your Scottish kings."

His heart began to hammer. "Scotland has a king. His name is George. He's your king, too."

"Go ahead, try to put the onus on me. I expected as much." She crossed her arms over her breasts, deepening the cleft of her cleavage. "You don't have to respect me. I'm a woman after all, and it's certainly no secret what you think of us. Were I a male tutor, you would have acted differently."

The irony of that statement brought a smile to his face. "I most certainly would have, Juliet."

"Don't try to cajole me with your winsome ways."

"Winsome. I rather like that word."

"Get out."

"Tread lightly, Juliet."

"*Tread* lightly?" she said, fire simmering in her eyes. "Don't you mean *think* lightly? Or better yet, don't think at all." She rose on tiptoe. "Know this, sir. I am not some Boeotian female ready to simper before you and fuel your ducal pride."

Respect put a dent in that pride. "I loathe simpering women. I never said you were dull-witted."

She whirled and began pacing. Unmindful of her steps, she trampled the papers. "Not in so many words, you didn't."

Unease crept up his spine, but his senses stayed fixed on the small of her back. "I think you're very bright."

She stopped and raised her eyes to the ceiling. "Oh, please. Save your pretty compliments for Cozy."

He knew better than to use flattery on Juliet White. What would work? Baffled and certain she'd leave if he didn't get to the bottom of the problem, he said, "What do you want?"

She sighed. "You employed me to rear your children properly. A task, I might add, that would challenge a saint." She knelt and began shuffling the papers into a pile. "I want to do my job without interference." She grabbed another page. "I want you to admit, tomorrow morning in front of the children, that you were wrong to gainsay me." With each demand she slapped a page on the pile. "If you object to anything I do, I expect you to discuss it with me . . . in private." She turned and pointed a quivering finger at him. "And if you say the word 'scullery' in the next five minutes . . . I won't be responsible for my actions." She dropped her hand.

What would she do? Slap him? In a way, he welcomed her anger, but remorse nagged at him. He had been wrong to overrule her. His feelings for Juliet White ran deep, and right now he thought he'd drown in them. "Shall I do it over the flopjocks?"

She pursed her lips until the urge to smile had passed. "I cannot demand your respect. I must earn that, and I shall. But I do strongly request that you keep in mind my position and my purpose here."

Looking for a reply that would satisfy her and return control of the discussion to him, Lachlan sorted through the personalities of all of the women he'd ever known. But Juliet White didn't fit any mold. It was one of the reasons he loved her.

Loved her? Like a storm rolling inland from the Minch, realization thundered through him.

"Well? Will you agree or not?"

Gathering his bearings, he said, "I agree that I was wrong, and I accede to your demands."

She raised her brows.

"Your . . . requests," he amended.

He expected her to gloat. When she merely nodded, Lachlan was again reminded of how different she was and how much he had to learn about her.

"I would also like some time to myself each week." Her direct gaze unnerved him. "How much time?"

"Saturday afternoons and Sundays."

"That was your agreement with Mabry."

Her gaze locked with his, and for the first time since he entered the room, she really looked at him. "You remembered."

Her soft words settled in his heart. "Aye, I remembered. Where will you go?"

"I don't know." She shrugged. "To visit Flora MacKenzie. I like to fish. Perhaps I'll do that when the loch thaws."

Her request was reasonable; no one in the castle worked seven days a week as she did. "Agreed, then. But you must pick your substitute. And if I'm away from the castle during your free time, I'll still expect you to be responsible for the safety of my children."

She smiled. Gallie's plain room brightened. "Of course, Your Grace. Will you be leaving again soon?"

"Probably." And when he did, he would take her along. He'd tell her to pack up the lassies. They'd travel as a family.

"Anything else?" he asked, his mind a jumble of plans.

She frowned. He suspected she had something to say and didn't quite know how to bring it up. "Tell me, Juliet."

"Mistress White," she corrected.

"What's on your mind, Juliet?"

"I'm no expert," she began hesitantly, "but I think Mary needs spectacles. Did her mother, perchance, wear them?"

When he conjured a picture of Mary's mother, he remembered a mane of red-brown hair, a kissable mouth, a husky laugh, and resonant snores. He'd learned little else about the woman—other than her carnal preferences. He hadn't cared to speak with her about anything, either. He thought about Juliet White. She didn't have any carnal preferences. He'd have to teach her every one. That appealed greatly to him.

"Your Grace?"

"Not that I recall."

"Please try to remember. You see, if parents wear spectacles, their children might need them, too."

"How do you know that?"

"Sir Axel needed spectacles, and two of his three sons also wear them."

Nay, he thought. Not Mary. Her refusal to read stemmed from Sarah's proficiency.

"What are you thinking, Your Grace?"

Defensively he said, "Mary's not truly slow."

Juliet gasped. "Of course she's not. She's bright and logical. I just don't think she can see little things such

140

as embroidery stitches or small printing. I've been teaching the girls archery, and Mary is the best by far."

Relief and gratitude poured over him. "We'll get her spectacles from the tinker, and if his won't do, we'll take her to Inverness in the spring."

"Does Mary's mother live in Inverness?"

He knew people who would pay well for that answer, namely Neville Smithson. "Inverness is a sizable city. They'll have spectacles there."

"If you feel uncomfortable contacting Mary's mother, give her address to me. I'll write to her. Many women are vain about such things. Mary might be, too, but if she knew her mother—"

"Mary will never know her mother. Neither will you."

She put the papers beside the keys on the table. "As you wish."

"I wish, as you well know, to avoid the topic of the women who bore my children." He didn't want Juliet to meet those women, for they were mirrors of the shallow, uncaring, and desperate man he'd been seven years ago.

With a tiny shake of her head, she said, "I'd forgotten. Then I'll bid you *guid nicht* again, Your Grace." She picked up the keys and unlocked the vestibule door. Holding it open, she said, "I'm sure you're eager for bed."

"Is that an invitation?" He held out his hand.

She stared at his palm, then leveled a suspicious gaze at him. "Of course not."

"My door's locked. I'll need your key."

"Oh. Here, then."

He took the ring. The ancient metal still held the warmth of her touch. She looked so serious. He wanted to see her smile, to hear her laugh. He knew how. Chuckling at his own ingenious idea, he walked through the vestibule and unlocked his door. With his back to her, he slipped his key off the ring.

"Your Grace," she said softly, "I've one more thing to say."

He turned. She seemed anxious, her eyes gloriously wide.

Her throat quivered as she swallowed. "Please don't try to kiss me again or seduce me. I'm not—" She paused and heaved a sigh that lifted her shoulders. "I'm not your kind of woman."

His chest grew tight. "That's a bletherin lie, Juliet White. But if you insist, I won't kiss you tonight." He had serious plans for Juliet White; he might even change her name. She'd make a fine MacKenzie. She'd give him a passel of sons.

Her fearful gaze rested on his mouth. "Good. May I have the keys?"

He took her hand, put one key in her palm, and folded her fingers over it. " 'Tis the only key you'll need. Feel free to use it at will."

Her stunned gaze followed his hand as he pocketed the keys.

"*Guid nicht*, Juliet, and close your mouth. Someone might mistake you for a Boeotian."

He walked into his room and shut the door, a very feminine moan of frustration echoing in his ears.

Chapter 9

Mary sat back on her heels and blew a strand of hair out of her eyes. "I don't see why I should have to clean and scrub," she grumbled, wringing out a soapy rag. "Lottie's the one who sassed Papa this morning."

Lottie held out the broom and danced a minuet around it. "You're the one who gainsaid Mistress White last night."

"Aye, Lottie's right," snapped Agnes. " 'Tis all your fault, Mary."

Mary stuck out her tongue. "You didn't want to go to bed, either. You're just miffed 'cause you couldn't light Papa's pipe."

"Could so."

"Could not."

"Haud yer wheesht," said Sarah. "We were all wretched to Mistress White. Papa's making us clean her room to atone."

"But I hate servants' work," Lottie said.

Juliet applied beeswax to a rag and resumed polishing the thistle-shaped knobs on the bedposts. "I believe you all offered, after a fashion, to help me disinfect my room so I could return to it."

"I didn't offer," said Mary. "Papa said he'd take away my pony if I didn't. Why can't you stay in Gallie's room until she returns?"

The simple question triggered complex emotions in Juliet. She didn't have the key to the tower room. She didn't read Scottish well enough yet to decipher the books. But she didn't need to know a foreign language to read the message in her employer's eyes. He wanted her. Even more troubling, she wanted him.

"Don't you like Gallie's room?" asked Sarah.

"I like this room more," Juliet lied.

"I'm tired of scrubbing," said Mary. "Besides, today's Saturday. We always play on Saturdays."

"You can. Later."

"The servants should finish this," Lottie declared.

"How will you instruct your servants and evaluate their performance if you don't know the proper techniques?" asked Juliet.

"I want to learn," said Sarah.

Mary glowered. "We wouldn't be working our fingers to the bone if Agnes hadn't run off with the tinker and got lice." She shook the rag at Agnes. " 'Tis all your fault."

"That's a wheen o' blethers, Scary Mary."

"Don't you call me that, you—" She threw the rag into the bucket. Water splashed onto the stone floor. "You lousy scunner."

"Enough," said Juliet. "The sooner you two stop squabbling and start cleaning, the sooner you play."

"Please do stop," said Sarah. "MacKenzie-the-tanner

said we could play with his new puppies this afternoon."

Mary snatched up the rag and slopped it on the stone floor.

Lottie leaned on the broom handle. "MacKenzie didn't have the puppies, Miss Smarty-breeches. His bitch did."

Tears filled Sarah's eyes. Through trembling lips, she said, "You're awful, Lottie MacKenzie."

Juliet sighed in disappointment. Even her best laid plans sometimes failed with these children. If they didn't learn to properly command a household, they'd forever be at the mercy of their servants. If they didn't learn to respect each other, they'd be sorry later. "'No more name-calling, and that goes for all of you. Get back to work."

As soon as they had moved Juliet back into her room, she would enjoy her first free afternoon. She needed some time away from the castle. She needed to sort out her feelings and get control of her emotions. She was becoming attached to these children. She was falling in love with their father. She hadn't a prayer of getting into the tower room.

Sarah put away the last of Juliet's clothes, then stepped forward and reached into her apron pocket. Her face broke into a grin, and her eyes glowed with affection. "I made this for you, Mistress White." She held out her hand. Resting in her palm was a satin pouch bearing neat stitches only she could have sewn. "It's lilac. I'll put it with your clothes, if you like."

Longing choked Juliet. Longing for this sweet child's happiness, longing for a child of her own. But that could never happen; by law, any child she bore would become the property of the Mabrys and would serve them for eighteen years.

She took the tiny sachet and sniffed the delicate fragrance. "Thank you, Sarah. It's exactly what I would have chosen for myself."

"I want one," demanded Mary.

"Perhaps Sarah will show you how to make them."

"Ha!" said Lottie. "Mary squints so much she can't even thread a needle."

"Can so," spat Mary. "I can thread a needle anytime I want."

"And once you have your spectacles, Mary, you'll be able to write the Lord's Prayer on the head of a pin."

"See?" Mary sneered.

"Shall I fetch your satchel from Gallie's room, Mistress White?" Sarah looked around the room. "We've moved everything else."

"Thank you, no—"

"I'll get it." Lottie put down the broom and headed for the door. "I have to go to the privy anyway."

"You don't have to piss," said Agnes. "You just want to see who Papa's visitors are."

Lottie held out her skirt and twisted primly from side to side. "I already know who they are."

Her sisters stopped what they were doing and stared anxiously at her.

"Who?" demanded Mary.

Lottie plucked at a loose thread on her sleeve. "His name is Magnus LaMont, and he's a messenger from the duke of Argyll."

"What about the other man?" asked Agnes.

Mary said, "I'll wager two of your arrows she doesn't know."

Lottie traced the glass buttons on the front of her dress. "I do so."

"Do not."

"Do so." She glided across the threshold. "They're the duke's servants, you salmon-brain."

"You're the salmon-brain," blustered Mary.

Sarah seemed oblivious to their squabbling. "I'm glad you'll be sleeping near us again, Mistress White," she said.

"I'm not," Mary said. "We'll have lousy old Agnes in our room all the time now."

Agnes balled her fists. "I don't have 'em anymore. Ask Mistress White." She turned an imploring gaze to Juliet. "Tell her I don't."

"Agnes is correct. One more outburst from you,

Mary, and I'll take away your bow and arrows for a week."

Shooting Agnes a hateful stare, Mary resumed cleaning the floor.

"Mistress White?" Thomas stood in the hall and peered into the room as if it were a cliff he might tumble over. "His Grace would like to see you in the solar."

A thrill passed through Juliet, but she schooled her features into blandness. The duke had almost caught her sneaking into the tower room last night, but that wouldn't happen again. Not until she managed to get the key back. She feared he might discover her mission, but she feared something else more .Her feelings for him had changed from curiosity to yearning.

"Thank you, Thomas. Tell him I'll be right there."

She turned to the girls. "You've done very well. Now you may go see the puppies."

Mary tossed aside the rag and shot to her feet. "What about Lottie?"

"Don't fash yourself over that. She'll come," said Agnes. "She's always prowling the shops for gossip."

Giggling, they ran for the door.

"Walk, if you please, ladies," said Juliet.

They stopped in their tracks. Agnes bowed from the waist and swept an arm toward the stairs. In a voice that mimicked her father, she said. "After you, my dear Lady Addington. And have a care where you place those dainty feet."

Mary pressed one hand to her throat and in a wilting voice said, "Oh, Your Grace, you are ever the most thoughtful and virile of men. You take my breath away."

Sarah dissolved into gales of laughter.

Juliet felt a stab of envy. Who was Lady Addington? The duke had obviously wooed and won the woman.

Calling herself a jealous fool, she washed her hands and face and tidied her hair. With a spring in her step and a flutter in her breast, she went to see the duke of Ross.

*　　*　　*

Juliet stood in the doorway of the solar. Rays of bright sunlight and an unseasonably pleasant breeze streamed through the open windows. Mugs, pitchers, and dishes littered the sideboard. Where were the visitors?

Alone in the room, the duke stood before one of the family portraits, his arms akimbo, his hands on his narrow waist. From the back, his shoulders appeared as broad as MacKenzie-the-smith's. He wore a gathered shirt of cranberry-colored silk. The rich shade served as a striking contrast to his tight biscuit breeches and black knee boots.

He should wear a cavalier's hat, she thought, perched at a jaunty angle and decorated with a frothy white plume.

A current of wind ruffled his hair and molded the shirt to his muscled torso. Her fingers itched to touch him, to feel again his blazing heat. She shivered and reminded herself that she was not here to gawk at a comely duke who tried to seduce her at every opportunity. Perhaps his preoccupation would aid her in finding the key to the tower room.

"Your Grace?"

He turned and flashed a grin that dimmed the light of day. "Ah, fair Juliet, come hither."

Wariness spread through her. "Has Mr. LaMont brought you good news?" she asked, hoping her voice didn't betray her admiration for this beguiling Highlander.

" 'Tis more than good tidings," he said. A frown wrinkled his high brow. "But how did you know his name?"

"Lottie."

"Ah." Wry humor danced in his eyes. "My undisciplined, snooping daughter."

Juliet found herself smiling, too. "She's changing a little, Your Grace. You handled them well at breakfast."

His chest swelled. "They cleaned your room?"

"Yes. As a reward I told them they could play with MacKenzie-the-tanner's puppies."

He rocked on his heels. "Excellent."

"Tell me. What has happened to please you so? Has it something to do with him?" She indicated the painting.

"It has everything to do with him. With all my forebears. They'd be raising a tankard today, to be sure, were they alive."

She indicated the messy table. "Several tankards have already been raised. Why?"

He folded his arms across his chest. "Because the king has named me overlord of Easter Ross."

"The sheriff has been deposed?"

"Nay, his father-in-law, the earl of Tain, has died."

"I'm sorry for your loss."

"I hardly knew him."

"Will they make you earl?"

"Not when I'm already a duke. He had no sons and I'm his heir."

"What will happen in Easter Ross?"

"It will prosper, as it did before Neville Smithson."

"Congratulations, Your Grace."

He grasped her shoulders and pulled her close. His eyes bored into hers. "Do you truly know what this means, Juliet? Fergus MacKenzie and his family can return to Nigg. Never again will a MacKenzie be forced out of Easter Ross." He closed his eyes and breathed deeply. "The Highlands will prosper again."

Caught up in the excitement. Juliet placed a hand on his chest. Beneath her palm, his heart beat like an Indian tom-tom. She felt safe standing so close to him.

He stared at her hand; then his gaze moved up her arm to her face. Intensity shone in his eyes, and in the next instant, he scooped her up and swung her around. "Bless Saint Ninian, this is a day to remember."

The room spun, and the windows and paintings cartwheeled in and out of view. Juliet clutched at him and grasped the sleek silk of his shirt. His joy seeped into her, filled her, until she found herself laughing and celebrating along with him.

Suddenly the room stilled, but the heady mood still swirled around them. She felt herself sliding down his chest, his arms banded around her.

"I told myself not to do this," he mused.

"Do what?"

He smiled crookedly. "Hold you. Need you. Love you."

Sadness invaded her exuberance. Love? He meant lust. For marriage he would choose a social equal rather than a commoner from Virginia. Did his noblewoman await him in Easter Ross?

"Oh, Juliet," he breathed against her temple. " 'Tis what I've always wanted, but I wonder if I'm able to do what needs to be done in Easter Ross."

Vulnerability underscored his words. "Why should you doubt yourself?" she asked.

He squeezed her. "I have such sad memories of my life there. What if I can't forget those awful times?" His voice broke and his arms trembled, and she sensed desperation in him. "I'm afraid."

Him? Afraid? His confession reached out to her, and she reacted instinctively. She held him tighter, saying, "You're a fair and compassionate man, Lachlan Mac-Kenzie. Who else but you could manage a man like Eben MacBride? Your people respect you, and look to you for guidance and protection."

Softly he said, "Thank you. I don't know what I'd do without you."

His breath smelled of the sweet liqueur he favored, and when his lips touched hers, her senses ignited. He kissed her with desperation, with honest need. She felt engulfed, surrounded by his masculinity. She felt enchanted, spellbound by his nearness. Unable to resist him, she cradled his face in her hands, then wove her fingers into his hair. His tongue slid across her lips, nudging them apart, and just when it slipped into her mouth, her fingers found his braids.

Wildness burst inside her. She felt unfettered by convention, unaffected by the world that existed beyond the boundary of his arms.

"That's it, lassie," he rasped against her mouth. "Hold me. Help me. Show me I'm not alone in what I feel for you. Love me, Juliet."

She did love him. Strange, exotic feelings budded to life within her. She struggled to get closer to him, to burrow inside his strength, to bask in the comfort of his arms. She wanted him to cherish her, to keep her safe, to show her the security she'd never had. She wanted him to hold the image of her inside his heart.

Soon she would leave Scotland. She'd never see this beguiling man again or hear the heavenly sound of her name on his lips. Could it be so very wrong to seek a memory for herself? A memory to savor on cold and lonely nights?

Her hands roamed the tightly corded muscles of his neck, the mantel of his shoulders, the bulging strength of his arms. Even through tightly closed eyes she could envision the amber stones in his necklet and picture the springy hair on his chest curling around her fingers.

Sadness welled inside her, but she beat it back. As sure as the tobacco would flower in Virginia, she would remember every glorious moment she spent in his arms. She would recall every joyous day she spent in his life. Years from now, when the Mabrys' other servants sat on the porch and bragged about their romantic trysts, Juliet would have a sweet and secret memory of her own.

He drew back and his hot gaze seared her. "I shouldn't be kissing you. You're too good a governess."

She struggled for lightness of thought. "You always kiss the governesses."

"You're different."

He would marry someday. He would wed a simpering noblewoman who'd give him sons. But would she care about Mary, Sarah, Agnes, and Lottie? Or would she mistreat them, ignore them?

The possibility tore at Juliet's heart. She clung to the duke of Ross and said, "Promise me you'll always protect the girls. Promise me you'll marry a woman who'll love them."

Fondness darkened his eyes to midnight blue. "Oh, aye," he said. "I intend to do just that."

Then she was kissing him again, touching him, wishing she could be that woman. He enveloped her, and his lips danced with hers and his arms twined about her.

"Ask me to stop, sweet Juliet. 'Tis not the time or the place to kiss you so. But I need you."

Denials and rationalization rose up to protect her. She wouldn't find him listed with Lillian in the Book. He wasn't the father of Lillian's child. She'd see the name of some gin soaker in Glasgow. She would travel to that town and find another Scottish child, a girl who looked just like Lillian, a girl who wanted to go home to Virginia.

"Don't leave me, Juliet." He hugged her fiercely. "I want to take down your hair and wrap it all around me. I want to start kissing you here." His lips touched her brow, then moved to her lips. "But I can't stop kissing your mouth."

Her heart skipped a beat and the blood in her veins sang a gay tune. She gazed up into his passion-dark eyes. She should draw away from him. She should be outraged that she would kiss him and encourage him to seduce her. She should balk at his bold words. But his lips beckoned and his doubts about ruling a block of Scottish soil struck a chord inside her. She knew what it was like to want, to need.

"Papa!"

Lachlan looked up to see Lottie bolting into the room. He stiffened. "Stop right there, young lady," he said. "Go back outside and knock this time."

"But, Papa—"

"Go! Right now."

She slammed the door, then knocked.

"Enter."

He looked down at Juliet, expecting to see desire in her eyes, but passion had turned to shame. Frustration gnawed at him. Out of the corner of his eye, he saw Lottie edging closer.

Hoping to salve Juliet's pride and quell Lottie's tattling tongue, he stepped back and said, "You needn't thank me, Mistress White. I was glad to remove that cinder from your eye."

Her gaze darted to his shoulders, to the ceiling, to the paintings on the wall, to anywhere but his eyes. He knew she couldn't reply; her mind must be a jumble of confusion and torment and need.

"Now off with you," he said to Juliet. "Send a maid

to tidy this room, then help the lassies pack. We're going to Easter Ross."

"Hoots!" cheered Lottie. "Wait till I tell Cook."

He leaned close to Juliet and whispered, "We'll begin with a walk in the moonlight."

"What did you say, Papa?"

"When?" asked Juliet.

"I was speaking to Mistress White."

The color drained from her face. "When are we leaving?"

Awash with the confidence she'd given him, he said, "Tomorrow."

"So soon? I can't possibly be ready—"

"Of course you can. I trust in your efficiency, Juliet."

A peculiar tension shadowed her face. "Where is Gallie?"

"Collecting information for the books."

"Is she coming with us? Shall I pack for her?"

"Nay. Gallie stays here. Thomas is leaving tonight. He'll prepare Rosshaven Castle for our arrival."

"Oh. I should be about packing, then." Juliet hurried past the excited Lottie and left the room

Lachlan plopped into a chair. To his surprise and his extreme discomfort, Lottie bolted onto his lap and pulled a tattered and yellowed envelope from her pocket.

"Lookit, Papa," she said, taking the letter from the envelope and holding it before his nose. "Lookit what I found. It's in English. Will you read it to me?"

Thinking she'd been snooping in the servants' quarters, he opened his mouth to scold her. But the date and the salutation on the letter transfixed him: "20th June, 1762—to my dearest sister, Juliet."

A cold stone fist slammed into his gut. *Nay,* his heart cried.

"What does it say, Papa?"

Ignoring her, he sought the signature: "Lillian." Lillian White. Juliet was Lillian's sister. Lillian had written to her on the day she'd brought a daughter into the world. A wee girl who was now one of his lassies.

Juliet White had come to Scotland to steal the child

away. Nay. It couldn't be. The words were lies. His Juliet was—different. His Juliet was good and kind.

"Papa!" squeaked Lottie. "You're crushing me."

His precious daughter squirmed. The devil himself couldn't steal these bairns from Lachlan MacKenzie. Only God could.

He relaxed his hold on Lottie. "You should be punished for snooping."

"But, Papa—"

"You must never again pry into someone else's things. People won't like you. Do you want that?"

Sprite that she was, she considered it. At length, she said, "Nay, Papa. I do want people to like me. I'm sorry I disappointed you. I won't do it again."

"I know. I love you."

She looked up at him, her beloved face aglow with confidence. "I know. 'Tis why you forgive me when I'm bad."

He kissed her forehead. Handing her the letter, he said, "Put this in the envelope and take it back where you found it. As long as you keep quiet about it, we'll let the matter drop."

"Yes, Papa. It'll be our secret." She wiggled off his lap. Tucking the vile letter into her pocket, she ran out of the room.

In a shadowy corner of his soul, a beast sprang to life. Ignorant of Juliet's purpose, he'd felt soft, warm, and loving. Now that he knew her plan, he felt hard, cold, and vicious. He'd stupidly allowed Lillian's sister to weasel her way into his household and weave herself into his heart. Her verbal sparring, her impassioned kisses, had all been an act. Each of her innocent-sounding queries about the lassies' mothers had been a cleverly devised ploy. She thought to trick him into revealing names because she didn't know which girl was her niece.

The knowledge brought a smile to his face, for he had time to play her game and seek revenge.

The first night in the library she hadn't been looking for a book to help prepare lessons. She'd been ferreting out the Books of the MacKenzies. She hadn't given up her bed to Agnes out of love for the lass. She'd done it to invade Gallie's chamber and the tower room.

In his mind, the beast prowled restlessly. She had stolen into the tower room. He'd almost caught her once. She'd had the keys and notes in her hand. Thank God she didn't read Scottish well enough to decipher the information in the books. The reason behind her promise to learn his language was a lie. So was her desire for him. What other lies had she told?

What of the truths he'd revealed to her? He cringed, thinking of how he'd confessed his fears and doubts to her. At least he hadn't told her the whole story about Easter Ross, about a small boy whose world had been cruelly ripped apart.

Lachlan settled back into the chair and loosened the reins on his emotions. Like a strong tide drawing pebbles from the shore, anger dragged at the love in his heart until only a smooth, desolate beach remained, devoid of care and compassion for a scheming, lying Colonial.

Chapter 10

The duke was returning to Easter Ross to rule.

As she stood on the deck of his yacht, Juliet pitied his enemies.

Since leaving Kinbairn Castle six days ago, the duke of Ross had changed. It had taken the caravan four days to reach the port city of Kincardine, and during that time he had ridden alone. Had it not been for the gossiping Lottie, Juliet wouldn't have learned any of his plans. Had it not been for his daily visits with the children, she might not have seen him at all. He didn't have time for a homely governess who'd foolishly lost her heart to him.

Tears blurred her vision. Her stomach lurched. She turned away from the rising sun and faced the wind.

Salty air caressed her cheeks and dried her tears. She filled her lungs with the tangy breeze, leaned over the ship's rail and gazed into the swirling waters of Dornoch Firth, waters the same alluring blue as the eyes of the duke of Ross.

A school of fish frolicked off the port bow, their sleek silver bodies gliding through the water like sharp needles through fine silk. A family of eager seals broke the surface, their soulful eyes surveying the ship, their whiskered noses twitching. The pups bobbed and chattered; the white-muzzled mother hovered nearby. When one of her babies edged too close to the yacht, she barked and herded her family a safe distance away.

Sadness and loneliness enveloped Juliet. If only Cogburn were here instead of in Glasgow. He'd cheer her. He'd remind her to count her blessings and think of the future. He would be back, though, and then she would have to think about going home, with or without Lillian's child. They couldn't stay in Scotland forever. Especially now that the duke couldn't spare her a moment of his time.

He wasn't ignoring her, Juliet reasoned. He had plans to make and strategies to engineer. He had wrongs to right in Easter Ross. He wasn't excluding her on purpose. He was tending to the business of his dukedom.

He'd sent a herald to each MacKenzie family that had been exiled from Easter Ross. They were to pack their kith and kin and come to the city of Tain. He'd hired a dozen seamstresses and two tailors to fashion wardrobes for the household. He'd even brought along a cobbler.

But he hadn't brought along Gallie.

Frustration chipped away at Juliet's spirits. The Books of the MacKenzies were back at Kinbairn, and her affections were hopelessly tied to a man who couldn't be troubled with matters of the heart.

Behind Juliet, the captain summoned the hands on deck. She lifted her gaze to the docks. The city of Tain loomed ahead. The duke's pot of gold. His Troy.

She had responsibilities of her own. Poor Mary had been seasick since the call to cast off.

Juliet turned to retrace her steps to the cabin. The

hatch flew open. From the darkened companionway emerged the duke of Ross.

He'd unwoven his braids and clubbed his mane of chestnut hair with a blue satin ribbon. The style lent a regal quality to his overtly handsome features. It emphasized the elegant taper of his nose and softened the stern line of his jaw. Freshly shaved and recently tanned, his face glowed golden in the morning light. A frothy white cravat, embroidered with the MacKenzie stag, fluttered beneath his chin. He wore an overcoat and knee breeches of dark blue sheared velvet, a fabric suited to his rugged good looks and tailored to complement his manly form. Brilliant white stockings clung to his shapely calves. Golden buckles adorned his square-toed shoes. In one hand he held a wide-brimmed hat, in the other a spyglass.

Juliet sighed with longing and admiration; from the top of his head to the tips of his toes, Lachlan MacKenzie exuded nobility. Would the residents of Easter Ross look beyond the expertly groomed duke? Would they see and fear the mighty Highland laird who lurked beneath the stylish clothes? For their sake, she hoped so.

He spied her standing at the rail, and his gaze traveled from her windblown hair to her new walking boots. Her heart fluttered like the ducal pennons adorning the masts. In a snap, his expression changed to one of cool regard. She should have anticipated indifference from him; of late she'd seen it often. Her spirits plummeted.

The crew scrambled on deck, reefing sails and singing a colorful ballad about sailing into Tain and downing a tankard in a dockside tavern. The captain yelled out a greeting to the duke, who touched the spyglass to his forehead in salute.

Then he strolled toward her, his lazy gait as perfectly suited to the pitch and roll of the ship as his seat to the back of his prancing stallion.

Hoping to make an impression, she sank into a curtsy deep enough to honor a king. At one time he'd had to order her to show obeisance. Now she did it willingly.

He tried to maintain his stiff composure, but his lips

quirked and his eyes narrowed with mirth. He donned the hat, angling the brim over his forehead. "Up, Mistress White," he said. "You needn't humble yourself here . . . or anywhere. Humility doesn't suit your Colonial pride."

He led her past the upended ship's boat and stopped at the rail. He raised the glass and scanned the horizon.

Juliet grew bold. "Pride had nothing to do with it. 'Twas your fine new clothes."

His gaze whipped to hers. The ocean faded to dull gray when set against the rich blue of his eyes. "Are you flirting with me, Mistress White?"

Had any other man said those words, she would have been insulted. Congeniality was within reach. "Are you fishing for more compliments from me?"

He hooked his thumb in his belt, his fingers pointed negligently at his crotch. "Have I the proper bait to attract you?"

He was the only man who had what she needed. She grew bolder. "You can lure the honey from the bees, and you know it." But he couldn't lure her from her goal.

"Are you offering your honey?" He touched her cheek with the spyglass. "I'll warn you, I have a ravenous sweet tooth."

The brass cooled her heated senses. Laughing, she said, "I know. Everyone knows about your appetite. But remember, I'm different."

Like a curtain falling at the end of a play, insouciance covered his jovial expression. He turned his spyglass landward. "Aye, Juliet White, that you are."

The high collar of her dress grew tight. Yet no matter how uncomfortable she felt, she would not allow him to ignore her any longer. "Lately you seem different, too, Your Grace."

"Different? I don't know what you mean."

If he didn't warm to her soon, she'd scream. "Something seems to be troubling you."

He lowered the spyglass. Squinting, he scanned the land ahead with his naked eye. "Aye, I have certain *problems* weighing on my mind."

Doubt niggled into her confidence. "Are they the affairs in Easter Ross?"

"My problems seem to follow me, no matter where I go. Where are the lassies?"

Disappointment plagued Juliet. The more he shut her out, the more she wanted in. "The seamstresses are dressing them."

"Do you love them?"

"The seamstresses?"

She might as well have spoken the jest in Greek, for he replied, "Are my children happy?"

She wanted to yank that spyglass out of his hand and whack him over the head with it. "Yes, Your Grace. They're happy."

He propped his elbows on the rail. Fine lace peeked out beneath the wide cuffs of his jacket. "They'd be disappointed if you left us, wouldn't they?"

Three of them would, but Juliet couldn't dwell on that. She had to break through the wall of indifference he'd erected. "What about my admirers in Virginia? It wouldn't be fair to deprive them of my company forever. Would it?"

"I thought you'd stay with us for a long time. At least until the lassies are grown."

What was wrong with him? Where was his sense of humor? "But you'll be an old man by then."

Even those strong words failed to rouse him. He shrugged. "I'll have a duchess and a dozen sons to liven up my dotage."

He might as well have driven a knife into her heart, so deep was the pain. "What do you see?"

One side of his mouth tilted in a cocky grin. "My destiny."

Bittersweet laughter bubbled inside her. As easily as he'd conquered her heart, this enigmatic duke would conquer those who awaited him. "Tell me," she said, "where is Easter Ross?"

"In the center of Scotland . . . near the top." He pointed to a distant land mass off the starboard bow. " 'Tis a peninsula surrounded by the firths of Dornoch, Moray, and Cromarty."

"And populated by an evil sheriff and hordes of Englishmen?"

Nothing she said seemed to cheer him, for he emitted a half laugh that held no humor.

"Tell me about Easter Ross."

"Does your knowledge of Scottish history extend to the Battle of Culloden Moor?"

"Yes. The Jacobite Rebellion. When the clans backed Bonnie Prince Charlie."

"Not all the clans."

"The duke of Ross, your father, did."

A muscle in his jaw flexed. "Aye, and he paid the price. He let pride and stubbornness rule him."

Resigned to the serious subject, Juliet said, "So the English took Easter Ross away."

"They took it all away." He tapped the spyglass on the ship's railing. "The titles, the wealth, the estates. At seven years old, I was penniless."

"But when you became a man you got back your property."

" 'Twas mine by right. I always keep what is mine."

Not this time, she thought. "What happened to your mother?"

He pointed the spyglass to the busy docks that loomed closer. "She died in Tain."

"I'm sorry. I wish I could say something to comfort you."

Expecting a bold rejoinder about how much comfort he needed, she was stunned when he said, "You don't know about family loyalty." He pivoted, turning his back on the shore. "Do you?"

She felt naked under his potent gaze. "I would be very loyal to my kin."

" 'Tis a noble sentiment, but a moot point, Mistress White. Since you have no kin."

She had the absurd notion that he knew her secret. But that was impossible. He could never associate her with Lillian. Lightly she said, "You have enough family to make up for my lack of it."

When he didn't reply, she said, "Sarah tells me you have a castle in Tain. Is it grand?"

His gaze followed the flight of a sea gull. " 'Tis smaller than Kinbairn, as I recall, but not so old. I can't picture it now." He offered her the spyglass. "Look for the golden dome."

She raised the glass and tried to sight the ant-sized people roaming the docks and the thumb-sized dome dotting the skyline. Sunlight glinted on the target but the image pitched and rolled with the ship. "Will you show me how?" she asked. Surely he would offer to show her all sorts of things, none of which had to do with the sighting of land.

"Don't hold your arms so stiff," he said, stepping behind her. "Relax."

Relax? She'd slither into a pool if he so much as touched her. The enticing aroma of him, so earthy and masculine, drifted to her nose. The ever-present heat from his body warmed her.

His touch, when it came, would have wooed a butterfly. His face appeared next to hers. The morning sun limned his profile. If she turned, their lips would meet.

The boat tilted. Her head bumped his hat. It soared past her. He reached across her to snatch it. She lost her balance. The spyglass flew from her hand and sailed over the side. Tumbling end over end, the brass sparkled in the sunlight, then plopped beneath the surging blue swells.

Juliet found herself pinned between the rail of the ship and the wall of his chest. The snowy cravat tickled her nose. At the ardent expression in his eyes, her senses teetered. He still wanted her, but a dark emotion lurked in his eyes.

"I'm sorry I lost your spyglass. Is it special to you?"

He pressed closer. "It once was, but not now."

She balled her fists to keep from reaching out to him. "You're cold to me. Why?"

He focused on a point over her head. "A man doesn't stand this close to a woman and remain . . . cold."

Vitality surged through her. "Are you warm?"

"Aye, Juliet. I'm warm all right. Hot, as a matter of fact." He stepped back and pointed to the sailors in the rigging. "But you're a respectable governess. We wouldn't want these man jacks adding your name to their ditty."

She had forgotten the crew, hadn't thought about the pitch and roll of the ship. All she could think about was this man and how much she wanted him. Desperation made her reckless. "They wouldn't, no matter what you did to me. They have too much respect for you."

Muscles bunched in his neck. He spat Agnes's favorite swearword and pulled Juliet to him. Bending her back over his arm he fastened his lips on hers in a punishing kiss. A stranger held her in his arms, a stranger ground his lips on hers. The soft velvet clothing seemed incongruous, for the body beneath it was as rigid as steel. Where was the man who had kissed her with tenderness, bewitched her with his charm, beguiled her with sizzling repartee?

Over the ringing in her ears, she heard the sailors shouting in Scottish. She didn't know the words, but the meaning was embarrassingly clear. They were urging on the man they called MacCoinnich. She'd heard all that before.

A slap from him would have hurt less than such belittling tactics. She felt cheap. She felt degraded. When one of his hands caressed her breast, she felt her pride shrink like sprouts in a drought. She thought her heart might burst with shame.

She twisted away. Their eyes met. "How dare you treat me so callously?"

Had she not known better, she might have sworn he looked hurt, regretful. "I only gave you what you've spent the last half hour asking for."

A hasty exit seemed best. "If you'll excuse me, I'll get back to being a respectable governess."

"Aye, Mistress White. We wouldn't want anyone to think you have any hidden facets."

Now, what had he meant by that? She was more confused than ever.

His lips parted. He seemed to struggle with the words he wanted to say. He blew out his breath. "Mary and Sarah are better?" he asked.

Although certain he'd meant to say something else,

Juliet grasped the neutral topic. "Sarah was never sea-sick. She only pretended so that Mary wouldn't have to stay alone in the cabin."

"I worried about that. I wouldn't expect Sarah to be sick from the sea."

"Why not?"

He watched the nimble crewmen climb the rigging. "Her mother's kin were seafaring people." He clamped his lips together. A muscle ticked in his jaw.

Juliet grew still. Sarah's mother had a family. She wasn't an orphan from Virginia. Sarah couldn't be Lillian's child.

"Or was that Mary's mother?" He shook his head and shrugged. "I can never keep them straight. Come to think of it, I believe it was Agnes's mother. Aye, 'twas. The wee tart has a sailor's tongue."

If Juliet was clever and careful, perhaps she could learn by similar means the names of the other women who had borne his children. Then she wouldn't need the Books of the MacKenzies.

The hired carriage lumbered down Thistle Avenue, Tain's main street. The boardwalks teemed with curious pedestrians, English on the right, Scots on the left. Mouths agape, the English pointed at the ducal pennons mounted on the carriage and gossiped as if they'd never before seen nobility. Their disdainful expressions labeled them adversaries.

On the left side of the thoroughfare, the Scots cheered and saluted. Children with bonnie bright faces rode on their fathers' shoulders, their tiny hands waving wildly.

Pride squeezed Lachlan's throat; nostalgia filled his mind.

Once these streets had been jammed with Highlanders, their plaids distinguishing their clans, their bagpipers playing their songs. He remembered wearing his own tartan kilt and bonnet. Passersby would stop him, compliment him on his grand sporran, and tell him he'd make a fine laird someday.

And now, against odds even Lloyd's wouldn't make, Lachlan intended to rule all of the Highlands. But his success or failure would be measured here in Tain, the hell of his childhood, the purgatory of his dukedom.

The English population here and in all of Easter Ross expected barbarism from the laird of Clan MacKenzie. The Scots expected strength. A seemingly impossible dichotomy.

He didn't want to be in this crowded carriage, but after days in the ship's hold, his own mount and the other horses wouldn't be fit to ride. Ian would bring them along later and supervise the transporting of the household goods.

Lottie, Agnes, and Sarah sat with Juliet on the facing seat. Thomas sat beside Lachlan. Cook and the other servants rode behind in a wagon. Jamie and the soldiers rode in another wagon.

Mary squirmed in Lachlan's lap and raised her head. "Are we there yet?"

"Nay, poppet. Go back to sleep."

She felt so slight in his arms. The poor mite hadn't been able to eat since the ship hoisted sail. Juliet had given the lassie glass after glass of sweetened water, only to see it come up again. Juliet had held Mary and answered the groans of pain with whispers of encouragement. But it was all an act. She didn't truly care about his daughters.

He squelched the softening inside him. Juliet White, sister to flighty and selfish Lillian. Damn that crafty wench for not telling him she'd left a sister in Virginia. Damn them both. And damn him for not connecting the two. How would he, though? Juliet was as different from Lillian as heather from gorse. The surname White was as common to England and the Colonies as MacKenzie was to the Highlands.

"Your Grace." Juliet held out her arms. "I'll take her."

She would never take anything or anyone belonging to him. "Nay." He ignored the flash of pain in her eyes. "We'll be there soon."

"When?" demanded Lottie. "Is it a bonnie castle?"

"Of course it's a bonnie castle, you snaggle-brain," snapped Agnes. "Papa wouldn't have any other kind of castle."

"Lottie, Agnes, look," said Juliet. "There's a tea shop with lace curtains in the window. I saw one like that in Richmond."

They all clamored to see.

"There's a toy shop," said Sarah.

"I want to go exploring," said Lottie.

As they chatted excitedly, Lachlan stared at Juliet. Again she had sensed his need to be alone with his thoughts and had distracted his inquisitive lassies. His. By the bones of his ancestors, these children belonged to him. No one would ever take them away, not even a blood relative.

Juliet White. He glowered at her pretty profile as she looked out the window. Juliet White. The accomplished deceiver disguised as the prim Colonial governess. How could she be so bletherin loyal to his children?

Because she wanted one of them.

How could he have lost his heart to her?

Because he'd been a fool. But no more.

The carriage slowed. On the English side of the lane, a street sweeper paused in his labors. His bright red beard marked him as a MacKenzie. Squaring his shoulders and doffing his bonnet, he shouted. "A MacKenzie! A MacKenzie!"

Passersby paid him no mind. Only the shopkeeper noticed. He snatched the broom, spoke crudely to the sweeper, then marched inside his place of business.

The sweeper waved and yelled, *"Luceo non uro."*

Scots on the other side of the street took up the chant. Lachlan pasted on a smile and waved to the fellow and his counterparts.

"How odd," said Juliet.

"In case you didn't know, Mistress White," declared Lottie, "they're chanting, 'I shine, not burn.' "

"How sweet of you to tell me."

Sarah said, " 'Tis the motto of Clan MacKenzie. Before the Battle of Culloden Moor, the words were carved above the entrance to every MacKenzie household in the Highlands."

Juliet's eyes twinkled with understanding. "It must have been a glorious time for your people, Your Grace."

164

Disappointment stabbed at Lachlan. He used to enjoy that twinkle, had believed in it. But now he knew the real reasons behind her friendly demeanor toward him and his children.

Agnes scowled and shook her dainty reticule. "The bloody Sassenachs scraped our motto off."

"That lady looks like the parson's mother back home," said Juliet, pointing to a sizable woman wearing an acre of black bombazine. The widow glared at the carriage, snapped her parasol shut, and with an air of dismissal, marched into a dress shop.

Lachlan hadn't expected the English citizens to host a parade to welcome him to Tain; neither had he expected to be insulted. Neville Smithson had prejudiced these people. Now Lachlan had to win them over. Seeking encouragement, he waved again to the Scots. They waved back.

Lottie jabbed Agnes in the ribs. "Look there." She pointed out the window on the right side of the street. "That lady's farthingale is as big as Jamie's guard tower."

"They all have silly parasols, too," said Agnes.

Lottie tugged primly at her gloves. "The men don't. They have walking sticks."

Agnes laughed. "They have wigs as tall as Gilderoy's kite. If they didn't use a cane, they'd topple over and smash their foosty noses on the boardwalk."

"But look at the Scottish people," Sarah said. "Papa, why do they stay on different sides of the street?"

"Because they want it that way." He intended to change that, among other things in Easter Ross.

Four voices piped at him.

"Papa. I want my own room."

"Me, too. And my very own wardrobe for my new dresses."

"We all have new dresses."

"Even Mistress White."

Juliet merely smiled. He wanted to shout, "Can't you see what sweet lassies they are? Can you be so cold-hearted as to take one away from her sisters?

He glanced at Lillian's darling daughter and wondered

again how such a schemer could have bred so bonnie a child.

The team slowed, then jerked and turned left onto Clan Row. His street. Looking back, he spied the home of the earl of Tain, now the residence of the sheriff of Easter Ross. Half a mile and a world of difference separated the mansions.

The carriage started the trek up the hill. Lachlan braved a peek at the dainty city castle. His castle. Rosshaven. Memories engulfed him. He remembered every room, every staircase, every stall in the stables. He even remembered the bell heather and the climbing roses in the back garden. As a child he had skipped down this hill and dashed to the other end of the street to play with his friend, Bridget MacLeod.

Those had been peaceful times. Rosshaven had been his home for several months of the year. He'd rolled his hoop in the circular drive. He'd stationed his toy soldiers under the hedgerow and laid waste to a tiny army of light dragoons. The same child had watched the real soldiers come. He'd been ripped from his mother's arms and whisked away under the cover of darkness.

His mother had died that night. His childhood had ended that night.

He'd learned to hold on fiercely to what was his. He'd learned to make his own way. Years later he'd learned to trust again. He'd naively put his faith in Juliet White. Before reading the letter, he'd fantasized about revealing his past to her, about making her his duchess. But he would keep his pain forever locked in his heart.

He felt a tug on his arm. "Why would someone put boards on our windows?" asked Sarah, her cameolike features drawn into a frown.

Probably Smithson's doing. Even though he knew Lachlan was returning today, the bold bastard hadn't lifted a finger to undo his villainy.

Hatred roiled inside Lachlan. His first impulse was to storm to the opposite end of the street and drag the sheriff out by the ears. The English expected such a bold tactic. The sixth duke of Ross intended to disappoint them. He'd beat Neville at his own game.

Thomas cleared his throat. "I wanted you to see the damage for yourself. I've hired every available MacKenzie. The men are repairing the stables. The women are cleaning the sleeping quarters. I'll set them to the outside immediately."

Understanding passed between them. "Good work, Thomas."

"Why, Papa?" repeated Sarah. "Why are the windows boarded?"

"So ruffians won't smash the glass," Lachlan lied.

"Ruffians?" asked Agnes, her spritelike features suddenly alert. "I'll bash them like they was . . . were wiggly bugs."

Lachlan tweaked her precious nose. "I'll do the bashing, poppet. You'll learn your lessons."

"I can clean the windows," declared Sarah. "Mistress White showed me how."

Agnes said, "Where's the sheriff of Easter Ross? I want to see the ugly scunner."

"Agnes," said Juliet, "sit straight and tie your bonnet ribbons."

"I hate bonnets," she grumbled.

"I'll make you a bow," offered Sarah.

Lachlan said, "The sheriff lives at the other end of the street. You're not to go there. Do you understand?"

"Aye, Papa." They said in unison.

The carriage door opened. Lachlan braced himself. He governed more than a dozen estates, all finer than this one and none more sorely in need of work. Still holding Mary, he stepped out and surveyed his domain. He had work to do here, and as soon as he'd disciplined the sheriff of Easter Ross, ensured the safe return of the MacKenzies, and solved the economic problems, he'd hie himself and his lassies back to Kinbairn Castle. What would he do with Juliet White?

The servants' wagon headed for the stables. He wondered if they were still standing.

"It's beautiful, Your Grace," said Juliet, gazing at the marble columns. "You must be very proud."

"I'm proud of the man who built it and the MacKenzies who've lived and died here."

"It's dirty," said Lottie, kicking at a pile of masonry that had fallen from the overhang. "And it's a wee thing."

His gaze raked the face of his boyhood home. "Aye, Lottie. I recall it being bigger myself." He'd last seen Rosshaven Castle from a child's perspective. As a man, he saw a decrepit symbol of dashed hopes and injustice.

Dear Sarah stood on the bottom step, her arms hanging at her sides, her pretty new purse dragging in the grimy marble, her eyes as big as china plates.

Jamie MacKenzie and six subalterns stood at attention on the front steps. Fourteen steps led to the great double doors. Lachlan remembered every crack and vein in the white marble. He studied the ornate capitals that topped each of the dozen columns. Their leafy design still played host to noisy brown wrens. Years ago a baby bird had fallen from one of the nests. He'd tried to save it and failed. But he wouldn't fail now.

"Put me down, Papa," said Mary. "I want to explore."

Yet he held fiercely to his daughter. None of these children would ever know the hardships he'd suffered as a child. War would never touch them. They'd never feel the pain of being torn from their home.

He fixed his gaze on Juliet. She stepped forward and placed her palm on Mary's forehead. "How do you feel, sweetie?"

For the first time since boarding the ship, she smiled. "Not so tapsal-teerie anymore. I'm hungry, too."

Juliet smiled and winked. "I'll wager you are, Mary. Shall we see if she's got her land legs, Your Grace?"

Like salt on a new wound, her false concern stung. He should send her packing. He knew he wouldn't. He should stop thinking about her. He knew he couldn't.

He put Mary down and held her small hand. "Sarah, Agnes, Lottie, come here." He pointed at Juliet. "You listen, too."

"Of course. Come, girls."

When they had gathered around him, he squatted. "None of you are to leave this house, even to visit the stables, without telling me of your whereabouts. Do you understand?"

Lottie stuck out her bottom lip. "But what about the tea shop?"

"Mistress White and Thomas will take you there." Thomas would escort them everywhere; Lachlan had no intention of letting Juliet out of the house with his children. "You're not to go alone. You're not even to walk down these steps without asking permission. Tain is a busy city. There are ruffians and vagabonds here."

"The sheriff could snatch us up," said Mary.

But Lachlan knew he had to worry about an enchanting golden-haired thief who lurked closer to home. "No one will snatch you. And I'm asking you to give me your word."

Sarah put her hand on his arm. With her angelic demeanor, she might as well have been wearing a halo. "I promise, Papa."

Mary said, "Me, too."

Agnes said, "Can we smoke a peace pipe to seal our bargain?"

Lottie said primly, "Of course, I promise. A young lady never goes out unescorted like Agnes always does. Miss Witherspoon taught me that."

"She also taught you to fart without making any noise," said Agnes.

Lottie's face turned bright pink. "I hate you, Agnes MacKenzie."

Juliet stepped between them. "Agnes, a lady never discusses such personal matters. And, Lottie, a lady never uses the word 'hate.' "

"She does if she has Agnes for a sister."

"Enough squabbling," Lachlan said. "We have an agreement." He stared sternly at each of them. "If even one of you breaks her word, I'll sell your ponies and give away your bows and arrows."

Mary gasped. Agnes grumbled her favorite swear-word. Lottie huffed. Sarah said, "We'll behave, Papa."

"Very well. Shall we go inside?"

The small party trooped in, Lachlan bringing up the rear. He found himself holding his breath as he entered the dim interior, then releasing his breath in a whoosh of shock and anger and grief. He was afraid to look up at the chandelier.

He had expected disrepair. He found destruction.

The foyer and parlor were devoid of furniture; the giant Grecian urns were gone, so were the gilt-framed family portraits. A light spot on the wall at the apex of the dual staircases marked the place where the head of a magnificent stag had been mounted. Colin, the first duke of Ross, had felled the MacKenzie hallmark.

The banisters of the twin staircases sagged at odd angles. Sadness choked Lachlan. He remembered his mother gliding down the stairs, her brocade dress glittering with jewels, her slender hand trailing over the banister. Tears clogged his throat.

"Your Grace."

Over the ocean of misery drifted Juliet's soft voice. Compassion glowed in her eyes. He wanted to bury his face in her neck and weep for the home that had lost its soul. Then he caught himself.

"I'll take the girls to the kitchen," she said.

"Very well, but you're not to leave the house. Not any of you."

She ushered his quartet of lassies out of the room. They must have sensed his mood, for even Lottie held her tongue.

Gathering his courage, Lachlan raised his eyes to the fan-vaulted ceiling. He saw the chandelier and thought he might break down. Thousands of droplets of fine Irish crystal had once formed a rose in full bloom. Now the pieces hung like a clump of wilting grapes shrouded by cobwebs.

Twice each year the servants had cleaned the chandelier. Lachlan had looked on for hours as they soaped and rinsed and polished each piece. Then the magic had come. The butler unwound the chain from a cleat on the wall. Amid a tinkling that sounded like fairy bells, the great glass flower had risen into the air again. His mother had glowed with pride.

He thought of the house parties, the visits by other clan chiefs. Sips of whiskey the men had offered him.

Sweet smells of the ladies who'd kissed him. Braw men in their colorful kilts had kicked up their heels and swung their ladies to the tune of the lively foursome reel. He thought of a way of life gone by. He thought of his own task: to meld, without bloodshed, Scottish and English culture.

He saw Juliet coming down the right-hand staircase, her hand braced against the wall. "The sleeping quarters pass inspection, but the back stairs are rotted." She looked at the chandelier. "We'll fix it, Your Grace."

"Nay. It can't be lowered." He pointed to the mass of crystal. "See that chain dangling from the bottom. It must be fed through the other ring in the ceiling. 'Tis impossible."

"Of course it isn't."

Optimism from such a betrayer fired his temper. "What will you do? Stand on tiptoe? You'll have to grow twenty feet to accomplish it."

She pursed her lips, but she didn't retreat. Much too calmly, she said, "We'll get a ladder and another length of chain. Someone hung the chandelier. Surely we can find a way to thread that chain through the ring."

Repairing the chandelier would make only a small dent in the damage to this house and to Easter Ross. "'Tis a dangerous climb. A light is hardly worth the trouble."

"It is so worth it."

What the hell did she know? "'Tis not."

Her voice rose. "It is." Then she laughed. "We're beginning to sound like the children."

She should pout. Her lips should tremble as Lillian's had when she wanted something. She should rail and cry. She should act helpless instead of determined to put his house to rights. He should put her on the first ship back to the Colonies. "'Twould seem, Mistress White, that you've forgotten who's in charge here."

She bristled. "Of course I haven't forgotten. I've been a servant all my life." She pointed her governessing finger at him. "I don't know what's happened to make you give up, but I won't be a party to it."

"Don't you dare jab me with that," he ground out.

She drew back her hand. "Excuse me. Perhaps we should load up the wagons again, return to the ship, and sail home to Kinbairn with our tails between our legs."

Bitterness fueled his words. "You'd like that. Don't pretend you wouldn't." She wanted the Books of the MacKenzies.

She sighed, as if he were trying her patience. "Virginians are not cowards."

"How nice to know. Where are my children?"

"They're with Cook. I'll set them about helping to make *your* castle habitable."

He wanted to throttle her. He wanted her maidenhead. He wanted the conversation over. Since learning the truth about Juliet White, Lachlan teetered between strong emotions. Anger often won out. "Mary's not to help. She's too weak."

A smug smile brightened Juliet's face. "Mary's work won't take long. I propose a wager over the chandelier: if I get the chain through the ring, you must tell me what's bothering you."

'Twas the safest of all wagers. What would be his prize? What did he want? He wanted a loving, compassionate, and honest woman. But there was none to be found. He would settle for the next best thing: lust. "Very well. If you fail to get the chandelier down, you shall come willingly to my bed." She gasped, but he went on. "You'll move your clothes to my chamber. You'll sleep there. You'll perform all the duties of a mistress."

Her glorious eyes narrowed. "You're despicable."

He shifted his weight to one foot and crossed his arms over his chest. "Losing confidence, Mistress White?"

"Why have you stopped calling me Juliet?"

Blessed Saint Ninian, she was a bold one. " 'Twas your request."

A sarcastic chuckle emerged from her lips. "Pardon me, but of late I don't think you have a cooperative bone in your body where I'm concerned."

He had a bone for her. "Have you mistreated my children? Have you lied? Have you come here under

172

false pretenses? What, fair Juliet, could you possibly have done to provoke my ire?"

"I've done nothing. I love your children."

Such pretty lies she could tell. No doubt she'd learned them at Lillian's knee. But how? Juliet couldn't have been more than twelve or thirteen when her sister left.

"Your Grace? I've done nothing wrong."

"Then your imagination is at fault. Will you wager or will you not?"

"You don't want me, so why propose such a forfeit?"

With elaborate nonchalance, he said, "One woman is as good as another. You, however, are convenient."

She struck him. The blow threw him off balance. His head banged against the wall. Good Christ, she packed a dunt any man would envy. Speckles of light danced in his vision, and needles of pain prickled his cheek. He righted himself and rubbed his jaw. "Is the wager on?"

"I shouldn't have struck you." She rubbed her palm. Her brown eyes filled with remorse. "I'm sorry."

He'd pay her back. Tonight. "Then answer me. Is the wager on?"

Smiling in a self-satisfied way, she said. "Yes. I accept the challenge. Meet me here an hour after supper."

Chapter 11

The midday meal was served picnic fashion on the kitchen floor. The duke, Juliet, and the girls sat in a circle near the hearth. Wearing a new frock of rust-colored wool, a white apron, and a starched mobcap, Cook had spread a cloth on the floor and laid out a platter of braised fowls, loaves of brown bread, and bowls of asparagus, parsnips, and fresh peeled oranges.

The duke sat cross-legged. He'd shed his jacket and waistcoat, loosened his cravat, and rolled up his shirt-sleeves. His chestnut hair had come loose from the tie and hung about his shoulders. On one thumb he wore a bandage that sported a bow only Sarah could have tied. Juliet wished his injury were as painful as the suffering he'd dealt her. With honeyed words and a winsome smile, he'd lulled her into believing him innocent of the crime of seducing and deserting Lillian.

On the ship he'd treated Juliet like a tavern wench. In the foyer he'd goaded her into violence. The duke of Ross behaved like the worst of scoundrels toward her. Why? His coldness shouldn't matter, but it did. After they'd eaten and settled the wager over the chandelier, he'd have to tell her the reason behind his callous treatment of her. Then he would have to stop toying with her.

"Cook, you've done a fine turn by this English fare," he said, tilting his head to watch her stir the stew at the hearth.

She smiled, revealing a dimple and those odd teeth. "Always was easy to set a bonnie table at Rosshaven, it being near a port and all." Pushing the mobcap behind her ears, she said, "I remember the time you ate the better part of a dozen green apples fresh off a ship."

He smiled and shook his head. "Aye, and for two days I didn't dare venture far from the privy."

Lottie unfurled her napkin and made a great show of placing it on her lap. "In case you didn't know, Mistress White, Papa and our grandparents used to visit here. He was six years old, just like us. Cook helped him escape when the soldiers came."

"What soldiers?" Juliet asked.

Sarah said, "After winning the Battle of Culloden Moor in April of 1746, the duke of Cumberland and his army scoured the Highlands to find our Bonnie Prince and his supporters."

"We know that part, Sarah," said Agnes, waving a leg of fowl. "Cook bundled our papa in a blanket. She and Papa crept ever so cautiously into the night. They crawled under the bracken and waded through icy burns. Those wicked English soldiers wanted to chop off his head, but Papa was too brave and crafty for them."

All four girls gazed raptly at him.

He laughed. "You lassies have the tale twisted. 'Twas Cook who saved me, not the other way 'round."

No wonder he enjoyed such a special relationship with the woman. Juliet pictured a reed-thin Cook bravely leading a frightened lad out of danger. It sounded like a fireside tale, but then all of Scotland seemed romantic to Juliet. "My compliments, Cook," she said, "on your bravery and your cuisine. I love asparagus."

"We all need a hearty meal," the cook replied. "Who would've imagined we could make Rosshaven livable again . . . in the space of one morning?"

They had worked hard, every one of them. Lottie and Mary had helped the hired maids scrub the pantry and the kitchen; Sarah and Agnes had helped Juliet unpack the trunks. The duke had supervised repairs to the castle. Thomas had acquired mattresses and beds, wardrobes, and tables. Even though all of the rooms weren't furnished, the family would sleep in clean beds. They'd also bathe in an upstairs chamber that Thomas called the bathroom. Juliet called it decadent beyond belief.

Sarah spooned parsnips onto her plate. Mary began piling her own with too much of everything. The duke reached out and exchanged his empty plate for Mary's full one. "Thank you, poppet, for serving me."

Mary stared dreamy-eyed at the overflowing plate, but served herself moderate helpings.

"Papa," said Lottie, "did you hurt your thumb on the banister?"

"Nay. 'Twas the hammer and my poor aim."

"But you fixed the banister," Sarah said proudly. "And I fixed your thumb."

"I'll test it by sliding down," bragged Agnes, "after I have my bath in that tiled pool upstairs."

Juliet put down her fork. "Young ladies do not slide down banisters. Do they, Your Grace?"

"Nay, Juliet." His mocking grin made sarcasm of the informal address. "Nor do they make foolhardy wagers."

Juliet stared straight back. Let him enjoy himself while he could; she would win the wager. But secretly her love for him made her want to lose.

"If you don't be needing anything else," said Cook, "I'll be taking Jamie and the others their supper."

"Thank you," said the duke. "That will be all."

She stacked several loaves of bread into her apron and tucked the hem into the waistband, making a pouch. Using a smithy's leather glove, she lifted a kettle of steaming stew from the fire and left through the door leading to the stables.

Throughout the meal the girls questioned the duke on everything from who lived in Easter Ross to how many fairs the district hosted. Juliet was reminded of the picnics the Mabry family had enjoyed. Those had been happy outings. The children swam and fished in Sandy Creek until they dropped from exhaustion.

She braced herself for an onslaught of homesickness, but it never came. She knew, though, that the next time she sat on the bank of Sandy Creek her mind would travel to Scotland and another picnic. But she would have her niece to cherish.

Her stomach grew queasy. She couldn't allow herself to become so attached to this troubled Scottish duke and his adorable children. She reached for an orange and tore it into sections. The pungently sweet aroma masked the musty odor of neglect that still permeated the castle.

The kitchen door opened. Looking over her shoulder, she saw a stranger walk in.

He wore a jacket and breeches of sunny yellow satin, a white cocked hat, and bucket-top boots. A gleaming dress sword dangled at his hip. He possessed the sort of timelessly attractive face that often appeared atop marble statues. He wore his fair, stick-straight blond hair fashionably clubbed at the nape of his neck.

Who was he? She glanced at the duke. Sarah was reciting the names of every titled family living in Easter Ross. But the duke wasn't listening. His attention was focused on the visitor. While his expression remained impassive, his clenched fists and taut jaw bespoke a mountain lion ready to attack.

The visitor swept off the hat and made an elaborate

bow. "Your Grace," he drawled in a voice as bland as unsalted potatoes.

"Who are you?" said Lottie.

"I'm Neville Smithson. Who are you?"

"Oh, no!" squealed Lottie.

"The sheriff of Easter Ross!" exclaimed Agnes. She scrambled to her feet, dashed to her father's side, and shook a tiny, threatening fist.

Mary scooted into the duke's lap. Sarah's fork clattered to her plate. She crawled on hands and knees to her father and burrowed under his arm.

Lottie beckoned agitatedly to Juliet. "*Pst!* Come here, before he gets you."

Juliet swiveled to face Neville Smithson, the man who struck fear into the hearts of little girls, the man who exiled kind people like the MacKenzies-from-Nigg, the man who was the nemesis of the duke of Ross.

Smithson appeared stupefied. His clear blue eyes stared in shock and disbelief at the duke's daughters. "By Saint George's bones, MacKenzie," he said, pointing to either Mary or Sarah, "that one looks exactly like—"

"Smithson!" yelled the duke.

Three of the girls gasped; Mary began to cry.

"And that one," said Smithson. "She's the image of—"

"No one you know," said the duke.

Juliet's breathing grew shallow. She followed Smithson's gaze, but could not determine which of the girls he'd spoken of, for he scrutinized each one in turn.

He knew their mothers.

Exuberance dashed through Juliet. The duke's enemy could tell her what she ached to know. She wouldn't need the Books of the MacKenzies.

"Juliet," said the duke, "take the lassies upstairs. I'll meet you in the foyer as we arranged."

She hesitated. The girls could find their own way. They would be safe upstairs. The chandelier could wait until tomorrow. What if the sheriff had known Lillian? "Surely, Your Grace, it would be rude for me to desert you and our guest."

"Ah, Juliet," said the sheriff in the clipped speech of an upper-class Englishman. "Thou art a maiden passing fair. But then again, our Highland rogue has a propensity for beautiful women." He cocked a golden brow and stared inquiringly at her abdomen. "Doesn't he?"

Did he think she, too, would bear the duke a child? Her skin tightened and her blood heated. Blessed Virginia, she'd been insulted enough today. "If knowing four beautiful women resulted in these lovely children, I would say his propensity was worth the while. But I am, for your information, merely their governess."

He smiled a choirboy smile and extended a hand to help her up. "You're a welcome addition to our dull society here in Tain. And your accent is—"

"Don't you touch our governess," said Agnes, holding tight to her father's sleeve. "If you hurt her or try to roast any of us, our papa will bash your head and cut off your balls."

Laughing, Smithson said, "I'd like to see him try."

"Agnes MacKenzie," admonished the duke, "*haud yer wheesht!*"

Although his eyes darted from Juliet to the sheriff, the duke addressed his daughters in Scottish. His speech sounded like a Highland rill flowing smoothly to the sea. She couldn't decipher the meaning, but suspected he was reassuring them.

The sheriff sucked in his breath. "I expected trickery from you, MacKenzie," he said, "but I never thought you'd stoop to terrorizing children. I thought you only sired them."

He'd understood every word the duke said. Neville Smithson spoke fluent Scottish. The seed of an idea germinated in Juliet's mind. Neville Smithson could be the key to unlocking the secret identity of Lillian's child.

The duke set Mary off his lap and got to his feet. The girls huddled together, their eyes still wide with fright, their hands clasped.

Although shorter than the duke by several inches and lighter by at least a stone, Neville Smithson stood his ground. Seeing them face to face, Juliet noted other differences between them. Neville, with his intelligent eyes that saw too much and his dashing good looks, personified English arrogance. The duke of Ross, elegantly handsome and dangerously powerful, epitomized the charm and unconquerable spirit of the Scots.

As opponents they were well matched indeed.

"Juliet, you and the lassies are dismissed." Lachlan kept his voice even, but if she didn't take his children upstairs in the next thirty seconds, he'd make her very sorry. Their eyes clashed in a battle of wills. He knew what she was thinking, that she meant to nurture a friendship with Neville. The knowledge made Lachlan angry. There'd be hell to pay if Neville found out who Juliet was.

To his relief, she lowered her eyes and led the lassies out.

"This way, Smithson." Lachlan left the kitchen and went to his study. Behind him, Smithson's sword rattled. Lachlan felt a prickling between his shoulder blades, and cursed himself for turning his back on his enemy. Beneath the fancy clothes lurked an ambitious scoundrel who'd forsake his own blood kin to better himself. Not this time, though, for Lachlan had a mandate from the king. Retaining Neville as sheriff had been a goodwill gesture to save face for Bridget, Neville's wife, Lachlan's childhood friend and the daughter of the recently deceased earl of Tain. But if Smithson said one more thing about the lassies, Lachlan would slice out his heart.

As he made his way through a maze of pails and mops, boxes and baggage that lined the narrow hall, Lachlan considered his options. He knew he should send the lassies back to Kinbairn Castle, but that was out of the question, for Juliet would have to travel with them. His stomach grew tense at the thought of her leaving, but only because he had to keep her away from the Books of the MacKenzies, he assured himself. Besides, he had Neville and the MacKenzie-hating English citizens of Easter Ross to deal with.

Once in the study, Lachlan threw open the shutters. The outside boards had been removed. Sunlight blanketed the sparsely furnished room. He seated himself and motioned to the other chair. Smithson took out a silk handkerchief and dusted off the cushion before sitting.

Lachlan laughed. "Better wipe the arms, too. We wouldn't want you to soil those fancy sleeves."

Smithson curled his lip and surveyed the room, which contained only the chairs. "Still the Highland barbarian, eh, MacKenzie?"

"As I remember, the ladies at court called me the Highland rogue and you the archangel. But if you're an angel, bagpipes can fly."

"Bagpipes are banned, along with your Scottish tartans. How many years has it been, MacKenzie? Six? Seven?"

"Too few to suit me," Lachlan said. "Why have you graced me with your charming presence?"

Smithson slipped the handkerchief under his cuff. "To pay my respects to the new overlord. And to tell you to get out of Easter Ross."

As smooth and as dangerous as a well-honed blade, that was Neville Smithson. His narrow mind and strict adherence to English law had brought ruin to the Scots in Easter Ross. Lachlan tamped down the rage boiling inside him. "Indeed. In that case, prepare yourself for disappointment. At the request of the king, I anticipate a lengthy sojourn in Easter Ross, marked by the home-coming of all of the MacKenzies."

Strong manicured fingers gripped the chair arms. "The king is an idiot. He doesn't know how to rule Easter Ross."

So, thought Lachlan, Neville's hatred wasn't reserved for MacKenzies after all. Odd, since Neville had bowed and scraped to the king seven years before to win the office of sheriff. "Neither, it would seem, do you."

Through clenched teeth, Neville said, "The MacKenzies are a blight. They blacken the bonnie face of Easter Ross. They're where they belong—with their own kind."

"Your bigoted thinking and your English code of justice started the problems here. Whether you like it or nay, the Scots are coming back."

"According to the king's writ, you cannot interfere

with my rule. You may have persuaded him to give you back Easter Ross, but it will not fall into your ducal lap. You have the title, and you'll receive the rents, but I have the power."

His own benevolence gnawed at Lachlan. "Oh, but I've been encouraged to advise you." He leapt to his feet. He placed his hands over Smithson's, then leaned so close their noses almost touched. "And I advise you of this: you have almost bankrupted Easter Ross with your tight-fisted laws, your uncompromising ways, and your ridiculous tobacco fields. The MacKenzies will return."

His face mottled, Smithson blustered, "But they have no place to live."

Lachlan smiled and stepped back. "Then have your English carpenters build them houses and boats to replace what you've stolen. Do I make myself clear?"

"They cannot make a living here."

"Not when you bring in Englishmen to undercut their prices."

"That's a lie."

"Oh? I suppose you weren't responsible for the arrival in Nigg of a certain English cooper."

"You've spoken with Fergus MacKenzie."

"Aye, he came to me for help, as your victims often do."

"I don't suppose your MacKenzie-from-Nigg happened to mention that his business failed because he formed a union whose members refused to give credit to English customers. Or that said union members refused to speak English, which they know as well as you and I."

"This is Scotland, damn you. We speak Scottish here if we choose."

"Not if you're a cooper who wants to sell barrels to the English residents. Damning me won't change that."

Lachlan hadn't anticipated another side to the story. "The English can learn Scottish."

Smithson toyed with the plume on his hat. Stubbornness shone in his eyes, the rigid set of his jaw. "They won't have it shoved down their throats."

"Send them back whence they came."

"To the slums of Whitechapel? The rabbit warrens of Shoreditch? I thought you were a man of compassion, MacKenzie. They were starving, dying, in London. Would you deny them a second chance in Easter Ross?"

Lachlan stepped back. "Nay," he said honestly. "But I won't have them causing trouble. Remember, the Mac-Kenzies are back to stay."

Smithson shook his head. "They'll adhere to the law. I govern here."

"Then we've a battle to come, for *I* govern Easter Ross."

"We'll see about that." Smithson stood and walked to the door. "A warning, MacKenzie. Keep your soldiers on a short leash or I'll lock them up." As if he hadn't a care in the world, he strolled out the door.

Lachlan's hands balled into fists. He'd love to let loose his anger. He'd love to kick that worthless bastard back to London where he was born. But even as the thought formed, he checked it. He and Neville had been friends once. Lachlan had even consoled Neville when Bridget packed her bags and her young son and left the English court for Tain.

But once Neville was named sheriff, he'd come to Bridget and healed the rift. In the process, the economy of Easter Ross had suffered. The king expected violence from a Highlander; so did the English in Easter Ross. They were in for a surprise.

But how could he win the English over? True, he'd gained the king's favor seven years ago. A mere passel of English citizens shouldn't be too difficult. And he knew Neville well.

Keeping Juliet out of the sheriff's clutches posed a trickier problem. But once Lachlan made her his mistress, and word got around, Smithson wouldn't receive her. If he did, even the king would support Lachlan for defending what was his. *His.* Bitter regret filled him. He had dreamed of sharing his life with Juliet, of sharing his problems and his children. An impossibility now. Before she learned the damaging truth about his lassies, Lachlan would find another governess and pack Juliet

White off to Virginia. Alone. But in the meantime, he'd damned well enjoy her.

Starting tonight.

Juliet felt as confident as a gamester with a stacked deck of cards. Whistling the song "To Anacreon In Heaven," she and the girls descended the stairs. In honor-guard fashion, Sarah and Agnes led the way. Mary followed, her child-sized bow hooked over her shoulder, her arms swinging. How wonderful, Juliet thought, that this once chubby and sedentary child now marched through her days with the vivacity and confidence of a warrior queen. Lottie, still miffed over the sleeping arrangements, brought up the rear.

For the hundredth time, Juliet wondered which of them was her niece. Soon she would seek out Neville Smithson and learn the answer. Then, when Cogburn returned, she could sail home, saving Lillian's daughter from the stigma of bastardy and sheltering her in the home of the Mabrys. The duke would find a duchess, a woman befitting his station. Life would go on. Why, then, did this proximity to success make her feel sad?

In the foyer below, the duke lounged on a settee, his head resting at one end, his long legs draped carelessly over the other. He looked like a sleek, pampered cat awaiting a fat, juicy mouse.

But he wouldn't get a taste of Juliet White. He'd have to look elsewhere for his prey. The thought of his seducing another woman brought a queer lightness to her stomach. She decided it was frustration over the breach between them. But that would soon come to an end. He'd tell her what had made him so moody. They'd discuss it. Things would return to normal. His daughters wouldn't be affected. He would once again become the teasing, happy man rather than a relentless, lusting stranger.

He didn't want Juliet for anything more than a mistress. He had what Mrs. Mabry termed "a man's needs," an odd condition that didn't seem to require any woman in particular, but a female in general. A familiar yearning stirred in her breast. She wished he wanted her and her alone, even with all her foibles and imperfections.

As the troupe descended the curved stairway, the amber and purple shades of sunset streamed through the fan windows and glass panels surrounding the double front doors. The marble floors and whitewashed walls glistened like beaten gold. Overhead, through a coating of dirt and cobwebs, glorious reflected light twinkled on the sagging, broken clump of the chandelier.

Agnes leapt' the last two steps and dashed to her father. "Papa! We're here."

With the grace of a dancing master, the duke got to his feet. "So you are, poppet."

Sarah said, "Mary's going to repair the festoon, so we can see our grandmama's chandelier."

He patted her head, but turned to Juliet. "I thought you were going to fix it, Juliet. That was our bargain. Or have you forgotten?"

Confidence brought a smile to her lips. "How could I forget the wager I intend to win?"

"I meant," he said patiently, "that you would do it yourself."

"Oh, nay, Papa," said Sarah, seating herself primly on the settee and patting the space beside her so Agnes could sit. "Mistress White didn't pack her bow and arrows."

Agnes plopped down, saying, "Besides, Mary's the best archer."

Lottie kicked the leg of the settee, grumbling, "I don't care about that foosty chandelier, Papa. You promised we could have our own rooms. I want to go home."

"No more whining, Lottie," he said, "or you'll be confined to your room for the remainder of our stay here."

She stood as rigid as a soldier awaiting a firing squad. Her sisters craned their necks and pointed to the broken chandelier. The duke approached Juliet, his boots clicking on the marble. He took her arm and led her out of earshot of his daughters.

His eyes glowed a steely blue, and the set of his mouth bespoke displeasure. Unease crept over her.

He stood so close she could smell the earthy fragrance

of his shaving soap. He'd taken off his cravat, and his shirt lay open at the neck, revealing tufts of curling hair. He'd shed the stag necklet. The absence of the primitive jewels lent him a courtly air.

Seeking a reason for his remote expression, she studied his face. "What's wrong?" she asked. "Did the sheriff bring upsetting news?"

"Forget Smithson." He stepped back and focused on his hand. Rubbing a thumb over his fingernails, he quietly said, "I distinctly remember you saying that *you* would fix the chandelier." His voice grew hard and cold as stone. "I forbid you to use my children as pawns."

Baffled, she said, "Pawns? I don't know what you mean."

His gaze locked with hers. "What if Mary fails? How could you put your own ambition above her feelings?"

His concern for Mary softened Juliet's heart. She grasped his hand. "She won't fail, Your Grace. She's a marvelous archer. You'll see."

"Papa!" yelled Mary. "Can't you and Mistress White talk later? The light's fading."

Indecision creased his brow. He looked like a man torn between indulging his precious daughter and risking the ruin of her dreams. "Go ahead, then," he said softly. "Let her do it. But I have my price, Mistress White."

With great ceremony, Agnes presented Mary with an arrow. Tied above the fletching was a long, sturdy string with a wooden ball attached to the end.

"I whittled the point myself," Agnes said solemnly, touching the arrow tip with her thumb. "It's as sharp as Miss Witherspoon's tongue."

The duke's stern expression melted into one of paternal love. He crouched beside Mary. "Do you know what to do, poppet?"

"Aye. I'm to put the arrow through that chain." She pointed to the chain that dangled from the bottom of the chandelier. "Then I'm to retrieve the arrow and shoot it through that ring on the ceiling."

"Neither will be easy shots, love."

Sarah tugged on his sleeve. " 'Tis for Mary, Papa."

He smiled and said, "Of course. But remember, Mary, we can always call in some workman with a tall ladder."

"You won't need to, Papa. I'll fix it now." Her lips pursed in concentration, Mary walked in a circle. Judging the distance, she stared up at the chain, then considered and discarded vantage points throughout the room. Her decision made, she climbed partway up the stairs. She planted her feet and nocked the arrow. One eye closed, her fist drawn back to align with her cheek, she took aim.

Tense silence pulsed through the room. A twang sounded. Mary's hand flew from the bow. "Damn!" she exclaimed.

The arrow sailed past the chain and plummeted to the floor, the twine and wooden ball trailing.

Juliet felt the duke's gaze drill her. She looked at him and immediately regretted it, for his expression boded ill. As clearly as if he'd spoken, the look said, "You'll be on your back before moonrise."

Her heart pounded. Her palms went damp. He'd never forgive her if she caused his daughter's humiliation. She'd never forgive herself, either, for no wager was worth undermining a little girl's self-confidence. But it was too late to turn back now.

"I'll get it, Mary." Agnes raced to the arrow, picked it up, and examined the point. Then she checked the fletching to make sure it would fly true. She walked to the stairs with Sarah a pace behind, carrying the twine like a lady-in-waiting holding the bridal train.

As serious as generals discussing an important military maneuver, the girls conferred. Agnes and Sarah returned to their place beside Lottie. Mary nocked the arrow again.

The shot whistled through the air. Like thread through the eye of a needle, the arrow slid through a link in the chain. The twine followed until the ball smacked against the chain and lodged there. The arrow, its purpose temporarily served, dangled to the floor.

"Hurray!" Agnes, Lottie, and Sarah hugged one another and danced in a circle, their braids flopping.

Juliet let out an agonized breath of relief. The duke bounded up the stairs and swung Mary into his arms.

Grinning a gap-toothed smile and waving her bow, Mary said, "Hoots, Papa. I did it!"

He held her in the air. "Aye, you did, lassie. 'Tis proud of you I am."

"Did you see, Mistress White?" shouted Mary. "I did it!"

Juliet clapped. "Wonderful, Mary!"

Emotion choked Juliet. She wished Gallie were here, but not because of the books. This moment should be pictured on the canvas in the tower room. Mary in her father's arms. Mary, triumphant, her father showering her with love and praise. What if Mary was Lillian's child? Would she willingly leave her sisters and the father who loved her? Juliet couldn't think about that now.

Agnes fetched the arrow and, taking care not to break the twine, brought the arrow to Mary again. Equally spectacular, the second shot sailed through the center of the ring on the ceiling.

The audience cheered again.

Agnes retrieved the arrow and took it to her father. Hand over hand, he pulled steadily on the twine. Glass tinkled. The clump of crystals moved as the chain snaked upward, drawn by the leading twine. The ball slipped easily through the ring on the ceiling, the chain following.

Amid a symphony of rattling crystals, dust drifted to the floor. Like a crumpled marionette brought to life by the hands of its master, the clump of glass began to spread, stretching the cobwebs and taking the shape of a flower.

Oohs and aahs sounded as a magnificent crystal rose unfolded, the petals nearly spanning the rounded ceiling.

Thomas and Cook entered. "Bravo!" said the steward, climbing the stairs. "With soap and water, it'll be as beautiful as ever." He held out his hands. "I'll take it from here, Your Grace." He smiled down at Mary. "You're a clever lassie."

Mary beamed. Agnes yelled, "I told you she could do it!"

The duke handed over the chain. Side by side, he and Mary descended to the foyer. Sarah, Lottie, and Agnes surrounded their sister, tugging on her arms and all chattering at once.

Cook said, "This calls for a celebration. Come along, lassies. I've made a batch of lemon tarts."

The others trooped out, laughing and talking. Juliet started to follow, but the duke caught her arm, his expression shifting from jubilation to malicious glee. "You lose the wager. I'll expect you in my room as soon as the lassies are asleep."

A shiver of shock coursed through her. "What?"

His brows shot up and a knowing grin widened his mouth. His hand caressed her arm, the gentle touch soothing her jangled nerves. "You're not so indifferent to me after all, are you?"

Juliet gritted her teeth. "Indifferent? I'm appalled that you think *you* won."

He chuckled and tapped her on the nose. "I assure you I did, *Mistress* White. The wager was that you'd get the chain through the ring. Not Mary."

Like a thick fog, rage descended on Juliet. "A trick of wording. I made sure the task was done. You can't expect me to become your mistress over a chandelier."

He grew pensive. "Perhaps we should call it a draw, then. We both won. Now we can both collect the fruits of winning."

"What do you mean?"

"I'll answer any questions you like. So long as you ask them in my bed."

Juliet stared. Any questions she liked! Here was the golden opportunity to learn the identity of the girls' mothers. But to gain the information she'd have to trade her virginity. She was treading dangerous ground, but she was desperate.

He stood waiting, gazing at the chandelier. His eyes seemed cold and distant, as if an old memory clouded his thoughts. "Juliet? Shall I expect you tonight? Or will you renege on our bargain?"

Excitement and desperation overwhelmed her scruples. He dared question *her* honor! When *he* was the one asking *her* to lie naked with him. He would take her virginity. She would trick him into telling her which girl was her niece.

She looked him in the eye and recklessly said, "I'll be there, Your Grace."

Chapter 12

Later that night Juliet stood outside the door to the duke's chamber, her heart beating a wild rhythm, her feet anchored to the stone floor. Once she walked through that door, her life would change.

But hadn't her life changed irrevocably since she stepped foot on Scottish soil? At uncomfortable moments like this she wondered if she knew herself anymore. What had happened to that principled, morally upright governess from Virginia?

She'd fallen in love with a rakehell duke. She wanted him in every wanton way—he'd seen to that. But what did he offer in return? Certainly not the love she craved, and absolutely not the devotion she might have expected from a husband. She mustn't forget Lillian, who surely had stood in a similar spot. She must remember what he'd done before.

Downstairs a door slammed. Juliet jumped. What if someone saw her standing outside his door? She laughed softly. If the duke had his way, she'd be spending all her nights in his chamber. But she needed only one night to discern the truth. So why was she quaking like a frightened virgin? She'd devised a plan for this meeting, hadn't she? The only unknown stemmed from her virginity. Which she intended to keep.

She took a deep breath and pinched color into her cheeks, then knocked on the door. It swung open so quickly she wondered if he'd been standing just behind it.

"I've been waiting for you, Juliet." He waved her inside, a glass in his hand, an indecent smile on his face. He'd reverted to his Highland braids and primitive jewelry. He wore a robe of sapphire-hued velvet. His legs and feet were bare. Was he naked beneath the robe? Apprehension skidded down her back.

"The children were too excited to sleep."

Amusement softened his mouth. "So am I."

"Shall I tell you a bedtime story, too?"

"Aye, and tuck me in before you do."

Maidenly modesty caused her to stare at the hem of his robe.

The telltale wrinkles on his toes gave evidence of a recent soak in the tiled bath. Her senses caught the pleasant smell of his shaving soap, and her gaze veered to his freshly shaven cheeks. Curling strands of chestnut hair clung to his neck. A drop of water dangled from the end of one of his braids. He hadn't been waiting, he'd been bathing.

The liar. He'd been preening for her, too.

"Your hair's still damp." He lifted the braid that lay over her shoulder. "Come by the fire and dry it. Although you'll probably be warm with all those clothes on."

"I'll be fine."

"Oh, I expect so."

A thick floral-patterned rug stretched almost to the walls of the rectangular room. One door led to his sleeping chamber; the other to the bath, where she and the girls had bathed earlier.

A pair of standing candelabra, each hosting a dozen lighted tapers, illuminated the room. A leather chair, a tapestry chaise, and a claw-footed table from Kinbairn Castle had been arranged near the fireplace. The walls were bare, as was the bank of windows that framed the fireplace and overlooked the moonlit garden. Logs blazed on the hearth, but no matter how warm she became she would never let him know. She seated herself on the chaise. "Do you miss the odor of peat?" she asked.

"Aye, and I miss Kinbairn Castle. I always do."

"In comparison, Rosshaven seems an elegant doll-house." And the duke of Ross seemed a scary twin compared to Lachlan MacKenzie.

"Would you like a drink?" he asked.

Knowing he'd asked the same question of dozens of women, Juliet grew tense. Compared to the sophisticated court ladies he'd known, she probably seemed a country bumpkin. That sparked her ire. Why should she care if this rake found her provincial? She'd have her answers before he got her into his bed. "Yes, I'd like whatever you're having."

"You can be sure we'll enjoy the same pleasures tonight, Juliet."

"That sounds ominous. I came here to settle things between us."

"Then we're of a like mind. Take this, lassie," he said around a chuckle and handed her his glass. "Make yourself comfortable."

"I'd have to go to Virginia to do that," she murmured.

He tossed back his head and laughed. Oddly the sound put her at ease. How long had it been since she'd heard him laugh? Shoulders shaking, he poured himself another drink. "You're nervous?"

She stared into the drink. "What a silly thing to say. Of course I'm nervous. I've never been ravished before."

"Do you like it?" he asked.

"The idea of being ravished?"

He folded his lean frame into the chair. Firelight twinkled in his eyes. "Nay, the Dram Buidheach. And I promise to ravish you quite thoroughly. You'll like that, too."

He could promise until the moon burst into flames and she wouldn't believe him. She knew his methods, and tonight she was prepared to combat them. "Maybe a Colonial won't like the idea of being ravished."

"Women are women, no matter their homeland."

Smiling, she sniffed the drink. "It smells like the licorice candy I often buy from the mercantile in Williamsburg."

He tipped his glass toward her. "Taste it."

The thick liquor spread over her tongue and dissolved like marzipan. "It's very good."

"Take small sips, Juliet. It's very potent."

Feeling brazen, she said, "Like you?"

"Oh, I'm much more potent. The liquor will warm your belly, but I'll set you on fire."

"Do tell."

"Don't doubt me, Juliet, for I'm a man of my word."

His voice seemed to come from deep in his chest. Her eyes were drawn to the mat of curling hair that emphasized his masculinity, and to the necklet that marked him a king among his clan. Her gaze moved to his waist and lower. His robe had parted, revealing tight white knee breeches.

Relieved that he'd covered that part of himself, Juliet knew the time had come to set her plan in motion. Still, she would have to work up to asking him what she really wanted to know. "How long will we stay in Easter Ross?"

He slipped lower into the chair. "I expect we'll stay here through the summer. Certainly no longer. Now come here."

"No." The denial flew from her lips. "You haven't spared me the time of day since we left Kinbairn Castle. Why the sudden interest in me now?"

He wagged a finger at her. "I've answered you. Now I want my due. Come here and kiss me."

Her heart leapt into her throat. She jostled the glass, nearly dropping it. At this rate she'd be flat on her back and compromised before she could ask him the important things. Her stomach quaked at the thought. She knew she must not succumb to her own weakness.

She stared at the thin line of hair that trailed down his chest and disappeared below the waistband of his breeches. She even allowed her eyes to focus on the manly bulge at the juncture of his legs. Weakness spread through her.

"Do it, Juliet, or the bargain's off."

The ultimatum stung her pride. He wasn't concerned about her feelings because he didn't care about her. She

did want to kiss him, though. She longed for the close-
ness they'd once shared. She wanted to embrace the
happy, loving man he'd been before coming here. She
needed him to hold her, to woo her, to take her to the
place where all she could think of was him. But tonight
she would distract him and when passion held him in its
thrall, she'd find out what she needed to know.

"You needn't rush, Your Grace. I know why you
wanted me to come here tonight."

"And I know why you wanted to come."

The cocky statement made her see the futility of her
own yearnings. She was a convenient bedmate, no
more. She looked on the bright side of his preoccupation
with lust; he couldn't have an inkling as to why she
questioned him.

Now certain of her purpose, she gulped down the contents of the glass, rose, and took the two steps that
brought her before him. His dark blue eyes glittered with
confidence. She bent over and gave him a maidenly peck
on the cheek.

"On the lips, and with your mouth open."

His bold command should have shocked her. Instead,
she admitted to herself that she'd missed his lusty talk.
Bending again, she took his bottom lip between her teeth
and moved slowly back and forth, her eyes riveted to
his. He tasted of the sweet liqueur and smelled of the
loamy woods in spring, but she blocked out the sensual
images and concentrated on his eyes. When his expression softened and his lids slowly closed, she drew back
and returned to her seat.

"Very nice, Juliet." He sank lower into the chair, his
legs splayed. " 'Twould seem I taught you well."

"Don't flatter yourself, maestro. You've changed
toward me. Why?"

He blinked again, seductively, the expression a perfect complement to his lazy pose. "A kiss like that
would change a monk."

"You're evading the question. The bargain's off
unless you tell me why."

"You'll have to be specific."

"Why did you kiss me so brazenly aboard the ship?"

His brows shot up. "Brazenly? That was a mere peck on the cheek compared to what I'm about to do to you."

Let him think whatever he would about the night to come. "You were angry. You hurt and embarrassed me on purpose. Before we left Kinbairn you were loving and friendly toward me."

He stared into the fire. Flames danced in his eyes. "Things have changed since we left Kinbairn. I know you better. You know me better. 'Twas not my intention to hurt you. Take off all your clothes and I'll show you how sorry I am."

Breathless with rage, she blurted, "You're talking around the question. I want a direct answer."

"Very well, Miss Persistence. I must solve the problems in Easter Ross. I couldn't let my desire for you distract me."

"But your aloofness began *before* we left Kinbairn."

"Aye, and my problems began seven years before that."

"What problems?"

"The answer to that will cost you your shawl."

The wrap wasn't much, considering she had donned at least a dozen pieces of clothing.

He held out his hand. "The shawl, Juliet."

She jerked it off and threw it at him.

Fingering the soft wool, he chuckled. "I received information that distracted me from wanting you in my bed."

"Such as?"

Distress flickered in his eyes. "The earl of Tain died. Easter Ross was suddenly mine to govern—alongside the sheriff."

"But you said the problems began years ago at court."

"They did. The day Neville Smithson became sheriff. He's English. The Scots here won't accept him or his rigid laws. He doesn't respect them."

"Why do you tolerate him?"

He grinned. "I'll tell you after you take off your dress."

She had an answer for that scandalous request. "Your

daughters respect me. I must set an example for them. If they knew—"

"They would better obey you. I'm an expert on my children. Now the dress."

She could afford to forfeit the dress, because she was wearing enough garments to last for almost a dozen questions. By then she'd have gotten the best of him.

Standing, she unbuttoned the dress and took it off. Carefully folding it, she started what she expected to be a small pile of clothing on the floor beside her.

He frowned. "How many petticoats do you have on?"

"Does that mean you want to play the examiner?"

His eyes grew large, his smile inviting. "I'm very good at examinations."

"You're not very good at answering questions. Why didn't you dismiss the sheriff when the king named you overlord?"

"I retained Neville because eleven years ago he married an old friend of mine." Waving a hand, he said, "Now ask away. But remember the price."

"Why were the girls born so close together?"

"I had an entertaining year at court."

"Winning back your dukedom?"

"Aye. That's two questions. Dispense with your stays and one of those petticoats."

Still feeling confident, she removed her stays and one petticoat. "What was Neville Smithson doing at court?"

"Winning the post of sheriff and seducing women."

"But he was married."

He chuckled. "That hardly matters to most men. You'll perhaps be encouraged to know that Neville was estranged from his wife at the time. The chemise, please."

That would leave her breasts bare! Why hadn't she expected such a trick? Oh, but she had a trick or two. "You'll be encouraged to know that I'll have to remove my petticoats first."

"Not quite. Just slide the straps down over your shoulders and lower the chemise to your waist. I want to see your breasts."

Misgivings plagued her, but she'd come too far to retreat. He probably thought she ached to be seduced. He was probably correct, but, dear God, the feelings he aroused were tender and loving, not cold concessions to a business arrangement. She found strength in the assessment of their situation, for if she insulated herself, he wouldn't break her heart.

"The chemise, Juliet. Now."

The straps fell free, but she had to work to get the garment, designed to be pulled over her head, over her breasts. At last the fabric lay bunched at her waist. With shaking hands, she shielded herself.

"That will not do. Reveal yourself to me, Juliet."

Humiliation flooded her, but his cool appraisal made her brave. She dropped her hands.

He licked his lips. "Lovely."

That was when she noticed his toes. They were curled into the carpet, the skin white with strain. Higher, the tendons of his ankles were stretched as tight as bowstrings, the muscles in his calves knotted like clenched fists. Hope spread through her, for he wasn't so indifferent as he would have her believe.

"I'm at your disposal, Juliet. Ask what you will." From his tone they might as well have been discussing fabrics for drapes, but his body told a different tale.

"Why haven't you married?"

"I was too busy ruling my dukedom. Come here. I want to suckle your breasts."

Mortified, she crossed her arms.

He heaved a sigh. "I'll count to ten. One . . . two . . ."

She felt pushed and pulled; shame held her motionless, yet the prospect of having his mouth on her breasts titillated her. She walked to him.

He patted the arms of the chair. "Put your hands here and lean over me."

Her breasts seemed heavy, swollen, the nipples contracting. She glared at him.

"I assure you that in five minutes you won't loathe me. You'll like me very much."

To her delight, Juliet saw his nostrils flare and his jaw

clench. She gripped the leather chair arms, still warm from his skin, and leaned over him.

His mouth opened wide, and he pulled one jutting, itching nipple into his mouth. Her nails gripped the leather, and her arms grew stiff. He blew softly, setting off a chain of sensual eruptions that headed straight for her belly and knotted there, pulling and straining.

"Give me the other."

Frail with yearning, she twisted enough to give him the access he wanted. When his teeth grazed the waiting nipple, she groaned in ecstasy and leaned into him until he suckled her fully, his tongue dragging, then circling. Her fingernails bowed and her arms began to quiver.

Abruptly he drew back. With a loud smack, her nipple popped free of his mouth. "You may take your seat."

She blinked in dazed confusion and almost begged him to continue, but his bland expression set her feet in motion.

She didn't bother to cover her breasts as she sank onto the chaise. Sweat glistened on his chest, which heaved with every breath. So he wasn't the master of his own desire. Gratified, she said, "Why don't the mothers of your children ever come to see them?"

His head jerked back and his gaze darted from the fireplace to her stack of clothes. Blessed Virginia! He was nervous. Her confidence soared. Then a smile curled his still-wet lips.

She didn't relish hearing what he had to say.

He held up his index finger. "Lottie's mother . . . impossible." He held up his middle finger. "Mary's mother . . . very improbable."

Juliet's stomach plummeted.

He held up his ring finger. "Sarah's mother . . . unlikely." He added his little finger to the others. "Agnes's mother . . . out of the question. And that, my dear Juliet White, will cost you four petticoats."

Feeling like a simpleton she said, "Take your despotic demands and go to the devil."

He started to rise. "I'd rather go to bed with you."

"Stay where you are."

He relaxed in the chair. "Stand up and take off those skirts."

Hadn't she expected as much? And what did this one night matter? She stood and stepped out of the petticoats. Folding them as one, she added them to the pile. She seated herself on the edge of the chaise and tugged at the short chemise, but couldn't pull it past her knees.

"Why don't you rest back on your arms so the light falls on your breasts?"

"I'm asking the questions here."

He grinned and slung his legs over the arm of the chair. "I await your next query."

"Have you sired other bastards?"

"Nay."

"Why not?"

"Your right stocking for the answer to the first question, your left for the second."

Defiance plowed through the muddle her mind had become. "I can't take off my stockings until I've removed my shoes." Silently she gave herself high marks for cleverness.

His teeth gleamed white through a boyish grin. "Call the shoes a boon for me?"

"Don't even think it."

He frowned. "Shoes shouldn't count."

"Why not?"

"Pardon?"

"Why are you going on about shoes?"

He slapped the arm of the chair. "Aha! That's two questions. You forfeit two shoes."

"You tricked me!"

With exaggerated patience, he said, "Juliet, I'm trying to seduce you. You liked the feel of my mouth on your breasts. Admit it."

Her traitorous nipples contracted. He jiggled his eyebrows.

"I'll admit no such thing," she said primly, an odd sound since her body sang with yearning.

"Very well," he conceded. "Take off the shoes and I'll enlighten you as to the modern man's method of controlling the number of his bairns."

She kicked off her shoes and waited.

His feet hit the floor. From the table he retrieved a box exactly like the one she'd seen Thomas fetch from the tinker in Kinbairn.

"What's in it?"

"Come and see."

The rug felt soft beneath her stockinged feet. The chemise slipped down on her hips. She hitched it up.

He flipped back the lid of the box and revealed a row of at least a dozen little envelopes. She raised her curious gaze to him.

"Condoms. A woman puts this on her lover's ready manhood. The condom catches his seed so it doesn't penetrate her womb."

Frowning, she said, "They're very small."

He roared with laughter, his shoulders shaking, his eyes watering.

Miffed, she said, "I won't put that on you."

Dabbing a tear from his eye, he said, "Very well, I'll do it if I must."

He was laughing at her. Enraged, she planted her hands on her hips, causing her breasts to bounce. His expression sobered, and he stared at her nipples.

"Don't," she breathed, unable to move.

His eyes locked with hers. "Kneel between my legs, Juliet."

Stubbornly her own legs stiffened. But deep inside, warm sensations fluttered from her breasts to her belly and spread like rippling waves over her skin. His foot grazed her ankle and started upward on a slow journey to her knee. The feel of his naked flesh against her stocking-clad legs robbed her of breath. He reached out and, with excruciating slowness, rolled the stockings off her legs. Thoughts of Lillian offered no protection from the commotion of exotic thoughts his touch aroused.

"Kneel."

Her legs buckled, and as she dropped to the floor, he came forward, grasping the hem of her shift. In one smooth motion, he slipped the garment over her head.

Her hands flew to cover her woman's mound, but just

as quickly he captured her wrists and drew her hands away.

"Sweet Saint Ninian," he hissed, his hands shaking.

Trapped at his feet she was embarrassed to tears. It reminded her of that first night in his castle. He'd ordered her to curtsy. He was now ordering her to yield herself to him. "I'm just another conquest to you."

His gaze flicked to hers. Kindness lurked beneath the passion. He blinked. The tender emotion vanished. "Crawl on my lap and I'll let you know if you're just another woman, Juliet White."

Like a slap in the face, the retort brought her out of the passion-drugged stupor and reminded her of her station in life and her purpose in Scotland. She'd asked a question. He'd taken his turn. She'd been seeking reassurance. He'd been keeping to their bargain. She was playing for keeps. He was playing for fun. She dropped her lashes quickly to hide the pain his words inflicted.

"Look at me, Juliet."

He'd spoken softly, yet she felt his breath on her cheek. She glanced up. His beloved face filled her vision, his eyes a deep, luminous blue, his expression a skillful parody of longing. Then she saw something, just a flicker that was no pretense at all.

Oh, what tricks this Highland rogue could play. The painful truth lashed at her tender feelings until she thought she might cry out in agony. But like a cloak of warm wool worn on a bitter night, reality wrapped Juliet's heart. As her eyes drifted shut, she remembered Lillian and braced herself to accept his kiss and his lust.

The touch of his mouth on hers was feather-light, seductively sweet. The feel of his warm hands on her sensitive breasts brought a gasp to her lips. His tongue swept into her mouth and foraged deeply, wildly, seeking the passion she withheld, then teasing, enticing, until she acquiesced and kissed him back. Her tongue cavorted with his, twirling and sliding, while her head spun and her body flamed. She teetered and grasped him to keep from slithering into a pool of wanton need.

Then his hands clutched her waist, and never taking his mouth from hers, he moved her back just enough so he could slide from the chair and join her on the floor. He jerked off the robe, tossing the garment aside. His braids brushed her cheeks, and without thinking, she clutched the slender plaits to keep his mouth on hers. He groaned softly and easing his hands below her breasts, brought her against his chest. Then he moved her from side to side. The drag of crisp, curling hair on her tightly budded nipples sent a storm of shudders to the top of her head and the soles of her feet. Frantic need and confusing desires pulled at her; she felt light as a feather, heavy as a rock.

She swayed, increasing the friction against the touch of his body. His hands roamed her waist, her hips, her thighs, then cupped her bottom and drew her against the solid, insistent heat of him.

"Touch me," he entreated, tugging at her hand. The braids slipped through her fingers. The springy hair on his chest tickled her palms. Muscles rippled beneath her touch—the tapering slope of chest to waist, the pulsing strength that strained against his breeches. Feeling him fully aroused, knowing she'd brought him to this state, sent her own need spiraling out of control and gave her a sense of power and deep, heartfelt satisfaction.

"The buttons," he rasped. "Free the bletherin buttons."

As if from a distance, she watched while her hands worked at the fastenings. His flat belly heaved. His hands stroked her arms, urging her on, and when she didn't move quickly enough, he reached for the placket himself. That was when Juliet saw his thumb, blackened and swollen. Instinctively she drew it to her mouth and placed a healing kiss upon the injured nail.

A pained sound escaped his lips. She looked up at him and found his dreamy gaze fixed on the thumb between her lips. She withdrew it.

"Put it back."

She did, and as if enthralled, he continued to stare at her mouth. Then his hand was on her wrist, gently pulling until his thumb almost escaped her lips, then pushing it back, guiding the movement of his thumb, tracing the shape of her mouth.

Wanton feelings burst into flame, and a wave of heat lapped and rolled upward, singeing her breasts, scorching her skin. She swayed as if in a trance, unable to tear her gaze from his face. Heavy-lidded and midnight blue, his eyes drew her in, his expression fanned the flames that licked her from the inside out.

He pulled his hand from her mouth and replaced it with her own. "Touch your fingers on your tongue."

Like a puppet dancing on strings at his command, she laved her fingers, but rather than shock her, the motion brought a flood of wetness between her legs.

His breath came out in a rush. Cloth was rent. A button flew into the space between them, tumbling, the light of the fire catching the smooth lozenge of polished bone.

His manhood popped free.

She gasped.

He sighed. "Sweet, sweet Juliet. Your mouth makes me wild. See how much I want you?"

The naive and lurid picture her mind had formed fled like a sparrow before a hawk. A man's lust was a thing of beauty, boldly shaped and vigorously alive. The urge to touch him pulled at her until her hand would not be still.

"Lick your fingers again first," he said, his eyes boring into hers.

His gaze never strayed. All rapt attention, he urged her with his intense expression. Anxious to please him, she rubbed her fingers across her tongue. Shock barreled through her, and the pads of her fingers seemed suddenly magic, the nubby texture of her tongue oddly alive. He tugged on her wrist and drew it downward. Her fingers touched the satiny crown of him, and the slick spittle glistened gloriously in the firelight. Lethargy set in. Like an illness that sapped the body's strength and sucked the soul's will, need and love for this man consumed her.

"Kiss me," she begged, craving his lips, yearning for his touch.

"Aye, everywhere," he breathed just before his lips crushed hers and his tongue stabbed deep into her mouth.

She wanted to crawl inside him and languish for a lifetime in his solid strength, his sheer power.

"Squeeze me, love. Hold me fast."

Somehow she knew what he meant, and her hand circled him, fingers straining to meet thumb. He pulsed with life and vigor, a thick lance of hot steel beneath a velvety sleeve of warm flesh. His hand slid over hers and showed her the stroking motion he liked. Once the rhythm was set, his tongue began to imitate the movement. When she thought her head might explode, he sent his hands in different tormenting directions: one teasing her nipples to pointed perfection; the other sliding between her legs and the moistness that awaited him. Awareness seeped from her pores. Need became desperation.

Against her mouth, he urgently whispered, "Spread your legs."

Twisting his wrist, he spread her wide. Her legs ached from kneeling for so long, but when the cool air touched her drenched and heated skin, all sensations vanished save those he controlled.

He touched her in a place that suddenly became a trigger. A shaky groan escaped her lips and passed through his. He sucked in the sound and breathed back, "Blessed Scotland, Juliet, you're a woman to savor."

A long finger slipped deeper and deeper inside her. She jerked and tried to draw back. He soothed her with Scottish words and soft lips, but his finger pressed relentlessly upward.

At last his hand stilled. "Ah," he sighed. "There it is. I love the feel of this."

"What?" she whispered against his mouth.

He smiled against her lips. "A maiden's gift, a man's treasure."

She felt a stinging pressure, a tightness. Before she could tell him her gift was his to take, he withdrew and swept her into his arms. The room spun. She felt empty, lost, as if she were teetering on the lip of a bottomless well.

"Get the box."

Through a whirlpool of desire she did as he asked.

He strolled into the darkness of his sleeping chamber and laid her on the mountainous feather bed. Air whooshed from the mattress, and she seemed to float, suspended between the heaven of his arms and the glory of what lay ahead. His breeches gleamed white in the blackness, and she watched, engrossed, as he pushed them to the floor. Then he was over her, his legs sliding between hers, his fingers entwining with hers, his warm belly flush against hers.

Hot, hungry lips devoured her. His scent surrounded her, and his maleness caressed her, nudged her, and instinctively her legs parted.

"Aye, Juliet, open yourself to me. I won't hurt you, love, for you were made for me. Do you understand?"

Unable to speak, she nodded.

"Guid, for this will be a night to remember."

Remember.

Like a rock through a window, the word shattered her lustful stupor. She'd forgotten her purpose. Here she was, flat on her back, about to be ravished by the duke of Ross.

"Don't shy away, my virgin Juliet. Don't be afraid."

He sounded so confident, and why not? He was a master seducer. He had performed a similar seduction on Lillian. Had that poor soul endured the labor of childbirth with a heart broken by this man? Had she gone to her grave with his name on her lips?

Heart aching, Juliet tried to draw away, but her body, honed and primed for his loving, refused to obey. She hated herself for writhing against him, opening herself more at his urging. Unerringly, his manhood found her, and with gentle but commanding force, he pushed forward.

"Wait."

He stopped and shifted his weight to his elbows. Limned by the candlelight spilling from the outer chamber, he loomed above her. The Highland rogue. His watchful eyes studied her.

A voice in her mind told her to be silent, but she couldn't. "Tell me something."

On powerful arms, he lowered himself enough to kiss

her sweetly on the nose. "Anything, dear. Shall I begin with 'I love you'?"

He could see her face, but could he read the pleasure his declaration wrought? She hoped not. "Are the mothers of your children alive?"

He stiffened, his sensual mouth snapped into a tight line. What would he do?

Lachlan considered bolting from the bed, but he couldn't fight the passion that hammered in his loins and gnawed in his gut. But beneath the lust and the need, the lonely man cried out for love. He wouldn't find it here.

In a matter of seconds he'd know the sheer pleasure of breaking through her maidenhead. In a matter of moments, he'd have her panting, clawing at his back, riding the bliss of her first climax. After enjoying her for an hour or so, he would find his own release.

Through a torturous mist of physical need and soul-deep disappointment, he heard Lillian's younger sister repeat the question. His heart grew as hard as his manhood. "Nay," he lied. "They're all dead."

Her breath came out in a soft gasp, as if she felt relieved. Her hands snaked up his arms, his neck, and to his braids. Grasping them, she performed the woefully unoriginal act of tugging him toward her. "Make me yours, then," she breathed against his mouth. "Love me."

Faking a chuckle, he said, "My pleasure," and in one swift stroke, breached her maidenhead.

Tremors of ecstasy ripped down his spine and curled his toes. Good Christ, being inside this deceiving witch was like coming home after a long, weary journey. His body strained to get deeper inside her, but conscience held him back. Damning himself for the noblest of fools, he stayed still, giving her woman's muscles time to stretch, giving her devious mind a moment to gloat.

He felt like a slave to his body's needs and cursed himself for not keeping Cozy in his bed. But he hadn't wanted another woman since the day he'd laid eyes on Juliet White. Hereafter he would enjoy her every night, every time the urge struck him for as long as she stayed in Scotland. He'd be careful, though, for he didn't intend to sire another child.

Thinking of that, he pulled out of her and donned a condom. She watched, her eyes dreamy with passion, yet alert with curiosity.

He sank into her again, and she clung to him, her arms and legs clutching his, her hidden muscles clutching him in a more intimate, rewarding way. Warm tears rolled down her cheeks.

"I love you," she cried, covering his face with kisses. "God help me, but I'll always love you—until the day I die. Oh, please, Lachlan, don't ever close me out again."

Lachlan bit his lip to keep from pouring out the words that would let her know she'd hurt him again, that she'd slipped into his heart and cut out a hole no other woman could fill. He clenched his fists to keep from shaking her, from swearing that Scotland would conquer the world before she'd take away Lillian's precious child.

Delicate fingers tripped over his ribs. In a musical voice, replete with feminine satisfaction, she said, "Have you fallen asleep?"

He chuckled, buried his face in her neck, and let the needs of his body consume him.

Enjoy her, his mind said.

All in good time, his body replied.

Chapter 13

Vibrations rumbled in Juliet's ear and dragged her from sleep. Furnacelike heat bathed one side of her body; cool cloth the other. Her eyes drifted open and focused on the amber stag in his necklet.

The duke of Ross. Naked, beside her.

Although his eyes were closed, she knew he was awake. He held her tenderly, as if she mattered to him. Cradled in the curve of his arm, her head resting on his shoulder, her leg draped over his thigh, Juliet felt safe, cherished.

Shivers of excitement blanketed her skin and rekindled a tingling awareness in her breasts, her palms, her woman's core. Places he'd touched. Places he'd sworn to touch again.

Bars of light, tinted the pink-gold of dawn, seeped through the shuttered windows and fell across the embroidered counterpane. The linens smelled of honey and almond and love-sated bodies. He'd massaged her back, breasts, and thighs with an exotic oil, and then he'd—

"What about Mistress White?" Lottie's voice, muffled by the closed door, crashed through Juliet's mind. She tensed.

The duke's eyes drifted open. He caressed her arm and whispered, "The door's bolted, love. She can't come in." Louder, he said, "Mistress White had a nightmare, Lottie. She's fine. I've allowed her to sleep in. You needn't fash yourself."

Now Juliet knew the source of the vibrations that had awakened her: his voice. She started to move away. "I'll go to her."

"Nay." He drew her back. "You'll stay here where you belong." Her breasts touched his ribs.

"Was a ghouly-ghost chasing her?" queried Lottie, her voice squeaky with concern.

"Nay." His lips touched Juliet's forehead. Softly he said, " 'Twas a much more fearsome and hungry beast."

Regret choked Juliet. She'd come to him last night certain she could resist his seduction and glean the information she needed. The only thing she'd resisted was the urge to blurt out the truth about her mission in Scotland. The only helpful information she'd gleaned was that all of the girls' mothers were dead.

"Did she scream and hide under the covers, Papa? I didn't hear her."

Juliet remembered the intimacies they'd shared, the labored breathing, the moans of pleasure, the urgent need to touch and to be one, the reluctance to part, the craving to make love again and again. Traitorous desire curled in her belly. She stretched. Her leg touched him intimately. He was hard and ready. She snatched her leg back. "I must go."

"Did she, Papa?"

He sighed and pulled Juliet over him, burying his head in her neck, drawing up her legs, lifting his hips to hers. Fresh need thrummed inside her.

"Lottie, you're making a nuisance of yourself. Remember what I said about confining you to your room?"

"But, Papa . . ."

His gaze met Juliet's. "Tell me something that will make her leave."

She wanted desperately to be alone with him, to explore the wondrous feelings he aroused, to bask in the security of his arms. To find out which girl was her niece. "Only if you tell me something."

Had she not known better, she might have thought he was disappointed. "All business, aren't you?" he said. "Kiss me first. Then tell me."

Juliet clutched his braids and, putting her lips close to his, whispered, "Remind her that Thomas hired two new maids yesterday. Say that Cook will need her help to supervise them." Her lips floated to his. His tongue slithered into her mouth, then retreated, reminding her of another, more intimate joining.

"That's my clever lass," he breathed softly, cupping her hips and holding her still while he moved against her. "You're beautiful in the early light of morn. Your hair glistens like sunshine on gold cloth. Your skin glows with the flush of our loving."

Pure pleasure rippled over Juliet. She had never expected to hear such sweet things, and like a lonely child aching to belong, she clutched the words to her heart.

He related the information to Lottie, adding, "And have Thomas heat the bath straightaway. And, Lottie . . . Mistress White's nightmare will be our secret."

"We have two secrets now, Papa." The girl retreated, slamming the outer door of the duke's sitting room.

He pulled Juliet down. Then his lips were on hers, his

tongue delving deep, twining with hers, calling up her passion, urging her to that wanton wildness of the night before. Snaking a hand between them, he touched the center of her. A storm cloud of desire roiled inside her, thundering across her breasts, her arms, her legs. Her head grew light with longing, her body weak with need. Her heart grew soft with the love she felt.

He drew back, his head sinking into the down-filled pillow. In a heartbreakingly tender gesture, he touched her cheek. "Are you sore, lassie? Did I love you too long and too often last night?" he asked, hope to the contrary shining in his heavy-lidded eyes. "I did promise not to hurt you."

He'd have her confessing her love again if she wasn't careful. "You didn't hurt me. But I can't stay here. Lying abed all day wasn't part of our bargain."

He sighed. "I want something. You want something. Let the bargain resume."

He didn't care about her. He liked playing games. He only cared about satisfying his manly needs. Hardening her heart, she said, "Did you love Lottie's mother?"

A roguish grin illuminated his face. "I love all women. Lift your knees. Ah, yes." His palms caressed her cheeks. The crown of him slipped inside her. "I remember this place well, warm and snug and perfect for me." Sinking deeper, his eyes drifting shut, he said, "Tell me if I hurt you. I'll stop and go very slow. I'll soothe you. I'll make you ready for me."

Like a ripe persimmon, she'd fallen into his arms and his bed last night. Now she had to play her own game. "Your Grace—"

"Lachlan," he insisted, kissing her neck, her shoulder. "I thought we settled that last night."

They had. She tried to deny her longing for this Highland rogue, but the feel of him moving deep inside her, the touch of his wet lips on her breast, the drag of his tongue, banished all questions, all thoughts save those of him.

"Lachlan." He blew the word against her budded nipple. "Say my name, Juliet."

Knowing she shouldn't, knowing she had no choice, she said, "Lachlan."

"Sit down, Juliet."

Her breath caught. The lusty rake expected her to make love to him. Love. Ha! He wouldn't know love if it were mounted in gold and attached to his necklet. She dragged her mind back to her task. "First answer a question. Where was Mary born?"

"Sit down . . . slowly . . . and I'll tell you."

Hating him, hating the wanton she'd become, Juliet flushed and snuggled downward. The movement drew him deeper inside her.

"Mary was born in Rouen. Lift up."

Casting off her pride, she obeyed. His hands gripped her waist, but the gesture paled against his deeper possession of her. He filled her, and started an itch that craved to be scratched. She wanted more. She knew the way to get it. But could she ever get an answer to the only question that truly mattered: Lachlan, do you love me? "Sarah's mother," she said. "Why didn't you marry her?"

"Because she didn't love me. Sit down . . . and quickly."

Like a rock tossed into a pond, Juliet complied. Breath hissed through his teeth. A shiver passed through her, wiping out coherent thought, leaving only need and a wild craving for a man and a future she couldn't have.

"Ask away, Juliet."

Do you love me? "Lottie." The name came out in a rush of breath. "Where was Lottie born?"

He chuckled. "Kent. Move up again, Juliet."

"So she's actually English."

"Half."

Through a fog of painful yearning, she said, "The sheriff recognized her, didn't he?"

Groaning, shaking his head, he ruefully said, "Bringing up my enemy is an excellent way to stir my passions, lassie. Very well. Your rewards are at hand."

With unrelenting strength, he maintained the rhythm that pried her out of her shell of modesty and tossed her into an ocean of delight. With unerring accuracy he touched the places that brought her the most joy. He knew those well, for during the long night he'd coaxed and questioned, persisted and hammered at her until she had told him that she wanted to swoon when he sank deep inside her and held himself still. She'd confessed that her skin tingled when he suckled her breasts and that the feel of his lips on her stomach, on the tender underside of her arms, on the inside of her legs, made her want to scream.

Past games and tricks forgotten, she allowed her hands to roam his chest, her nails to brush his ribs, while her body rocked against his.

"That's the way, lassie. Open your mind to the passion. Feel me within you. Take me fully."

Her eyes drifted out of focus while her senses spiraled out of control. Glorious colors from Sunday pink to holiday red sparkled in her mind, and her heart soared until she thought it might fly from her breast. Loving this lusty and generous man made her feel complete, cherished, like a precious gem in the treasure chest of his affection.

"Not so fast, my sweet," he rasped against her neck, slowing his pace.

Beyond heeding him, she uttered the question that she knew would drive his passions to the limit. "Oh, wilt thou leave me so unsatisfied?"

Grasping her, he sat up, pushed her back, and braced himself above her. Suddenly their positions were reversed. "Lift your hips." She did, and he tucked a pillow beneath her, then looked down at his handiwork. She looked there, too. And the picture of him joined with her, moving into her and easing out, brought a new jolt of excitement. She felt him quicken. Looking up, he grinned. " 'Tis a bonnie sight—you beneath me, your glorious hair flowing around you, your sweet body sheathing me in silk, me filling you, pleasing you."

His eyes glowed with blue fire and his nostrils flared. Bars of light fell over his nose and cheeks. She traced the sunny stripes.

He stilled his hips. His eyes bored into hers. "Why are you looking at me like that?"

"You look like a Shawnee Indian brave wearing his war paint."

He drew his brows together and bared his teeth. "I am. And I'm on the war trail."

She chuckled. He could be so charming when the mood suited him. "Not war *trail*. War*path*."

"I favor this path."

"So do I."

He spat Agnes's favorite swearword and began the quick, deep strokes that signaled the coming of his own climax.

Juliet grasped his narrow waist. Tightly corded muscles, damp with sweat, flexed beneath the pads of her fingers. He stiffened and withdrew so quickly she gasped in shock. Emptiness tugged at her, and her intuition screamed he'd left her on purpose. He fell forward, his head dropping to her shoulder, his breathing raspy. The muscles of his belly rippled against hers.

In an odd way, she felt rejected. "Is something wrong?" she asked.

He held her tightly and rolled so they faced each other. The mattress felt unduly wet.

Grinning, he said, "Many things are wrong, but none in this bed. Because, my sweet innocent, making love to you feels bletherin wonderful." Through the sentiment, his voice sounded strained.

"You're evading the question. Your loving was different this time." Hearing such bold words on her own lips shocked Juliet, but she had to know.

"One night in my bed and already you've become an expert."

"Why?"

He opened his mouth, closed it. She persisted.

" 'Tis your woman's imagination," he said much too lightly.

" 'Tis not."

"Love me again, then," he said. "And we'll put it to the test."

An hour later, as they languished in the tiled pool, the heated water swirling about them, Juliet still wondered at the odd ending to his lovemaking. He lay beside her, his head resting on the top step, his arms draped over the tiled rim of the pool.

Built into a corner of the castle, the bath was lighted on two sides by high windows, the panes set with tiny pieces of yellow glass that formed a thistle. The symbol was repeated in alternating white tiles on the ceiling, walls, and floor, and in the tub itself. In each corner of the room stood a brass brazier. Towels hung from pegs above a shelf stocked with soaps, perfumes, and sponges. A wooden boat with a tattered sail lay atop a pile of carved animals.

"Do you like the bath?" he asked.

"It's very decadent."

"That wasn't an answer."

Miffed by his secretiveness, she moved to the other side of the pool. "When you give me an answer, I'll give you one. That was our bargain, as I recall."

His eyes narrowed, lending determination to his handsome features. "I merely wanted to know what you thought. That sort of question shouldn't be a part of our agreement."

They shouldn't have an agreement at all, because with every encounter she loved him more. Angry that she couldn't control her emotions, she said, "Oh, I see. *You,* in your infinite wisdom, get to establish the boundaries of the bargain while I, in my naïveté, have no say."

"Juliet," he said on a weary sigh, "we needn't belabor the agreement. You're my mistress. You make me very happy. But that doesn't mean I have to explain myself to you."

Hiding the hurt his words dealt her, she said, "I'm sorry I became your mistress."

"You weren't sorry half an hour ago. 'Blissfully alive' is what you said, just before you bit my shoulder."

She spied the mark her teeth had left. Shamed to her naked toes, she slid deeper into the water.

"I left you quickly so I would not give you a child."

She should be grateful, but in her heart she felt used. Suddenly she hated the topic of making love. "What happened to your parents?"

He plunged under the water, then surfaced, shaking his head. Gliding to the pool's edge, he crossed his arms on the tile and rested his cheek on his hands. His eyes found hers. "After the defeat at Culloden Moor, my father fled to Italy. He died there."

"Was your mother with him?"

His eyes drifted out of focus. "Nay. English soldiers hanged her from the chandelier."

Juliet's stomach pitched. "Oh, God." He had gazed so wistfully at the chandelier; now she understood why. "I hate this cruel country."

He blew out his breath. "You once told me not to pity you. Please return the favor. My mother died doing what any parent would do. She distracted the soldiers so Cook could take me to safety."

Love pushed her forward. "I'm so sorry."

He lunged away and ducked under the water again. He surfaced at the other end of the pool. Arms spread, he rested there. "Let's talk about something else."

Aching to comfort him, but knowing that he would refuse, she said, "What will you do about the sheriff?"

Over the gentle lapping of the water, he said, "I'll try to undo the mess he's made of Easter Ross. Somehow the Scots must accept the English and vice versa."

Latching on to the safe topic, she said, "Mr. Mabry has the same problem when he acquires a new slave or bond servant."

He tilted back his head and stared at the tiled ceiling. "I've heard about the cruel methods used on slaves. I'll not take a whip to anyone in Easter Ross. Except that bastard Neville."

Immediately defensive of the kind man who'd welcomed an orphan into his family, she said, "Mr. Mabry doesn't use a whip, never has. I'll tell you his method if you'll tell me where Sarah was born."

His gaze still fixed on the ceiling, he said, "Why do you care?"

"I always care about my charges."

"How nice." Sarcasm dripped from his words.

He'd never know how dear his children were to her. Years from now, she would worry about them. She'd wonder if life had been kind to them. Had they married well? Had they borne their children safely? She wouldn't be here then, but she could protect them now. From beneath the lies and the deceptions, the truth emerged. Juliet couldn't hold it back. "I believe the sheriff knew their mothers."

"Why do you think that?"

"Because of what he said and the way he looked at them. Don't lie to me. I want to be prepared if anyone else notices the resemblance."

"I won't allow Neville near them."

"And I won't have them hurt by a careless stranger."

The duke rolled his head toward her. Water dripped from his braids. "The person who dares hurt my daughters will suffer the force of my wrath. And to answer your question, Sarah was born in Aberdeen."

Guilt snaked through Juliet, but she had to know about the woman who had borne Sarah. "And her mother is dead?"

"And buried," he roared, the echo of his voice bouncing off the tiled walls. "Explain Mabry's way."

If the duke told the truth, which she doubted, none of the girls had been born in Edinburgh. And none was Lillian's daughter. Her woman's heart prayed it was so.

"Well? I'm waiting."

Her thirst to find him innocent had been momentarily slaked. "If a bond servant balks at working with a slave, Mr. Mabry assigns the two of them a cooperative task and offers a morning without work as reward. During planting time, one man must drive the plow while the other man sows the seeds. The men compete with other teams."

"Aha." His brows arched. "If they want the reward, they must put aside their differences and work together to achieve a common goal."

"Precisely. And since all men are greedy at heart—oh!" A torrent of water cascaded into her face.

"Greedy?" He leered, holding out his arms and growling like Lottie's ghouly-ghost. "I've a greed and a lust for you."

Juliet dashed from the bath, snatched up a towel, and

scurried to her own room, the sound of his laughter echoing from the bath.

Later that day, her spirits high, her charges chattering excitedly, Juliet watched impatiently as Thomas handed down their packages. The carriage rocked to and fro on its wheels. The horses blew and pranced in place, their iron-shod hooves clacking on the brick drive. The steward had acted as escort during the shopping excursion. While she had been grateful for his help, she suspected he hadn't come along of his own volition.

"Thank you again, Thomas," she said.

A sack of Indian corn under one arm, swatches of drapery cloth under the other, he looked nothing like a capable steward and everything like a harried footman. "My pleasure, Mistress White," he replied, bowing from the waist. The corn shifted in the sack, almost throwing him off balance. He righted himself, saying, "After you."

Juliet sailed through the door but stopped in her tracks. Beside her, Lottie and the other girls stopped, too.

Holland cloth covered the marble floor of the foyer. The chandelier had been lowered. Half of it sparkled like diamonds. Around it worked two maids with buckets of soapy water and soiled rags. Juliet felt a sinking sensation just looking at the chandelier and remembering the duke's mother.

"*Guid* day, 'Ello. ma'am." The maids said in unison, bobbing curtsies.

The taller servant possessed the milky skin of English porcelain. The shorter had the ruddy complexion of a Highland rose.

Lottie marched up to the taller of the maids. "Who are you?"

She stuffed a towel into her apron pocket. "I'm Polly, miss. 'Ow do." She spoke with the same accent as the Mabry's parlor maid, a bond servant from London.

"Where's Anna?" demanded Lottie.

Polly eyed the other maid, who'd turned her attention

to soaping a strand of crystals. "She's upstairs in the bath."

"Doing what?"

"Cleaning, miss. She and my sister, that'd be Daisy. Excuse me, miss." She pulled out the towel and took the strand of dripping crystals from her counterpart.

"You're very industrious, Polly," Juliet said.

"I ain't one for slovenly work, ma'am. Besides, His Grace said if we finished before the upstairs maids, we could begin our duties an hour later tomorrow. Didn't he say so, Elaine?"

The Scottish maid eyed the yet-to-be-cleaned half of the chandelier. "Aye, but—"

"No buts," said Polly. "Them upstairs'll be doin' our chores come the morrow, and we'll be abed."

The maids, one Scot, the other English, worked as a team. Respect for the duke of Ross warmed Juliet. He'd wasted no time implementing Mr. Mabry's method. She felt pride, too, for her part in helping the duke right the wrongs in Easter Ross.

She led the girls to the parlor, where they conferred over fabrics for drapes and discussed their visit to the tea shop. Once the chandelier was clean and hoisted with great ceremony to its sparkling perch, the girls dashed off to groom their ponies.

The rap-rapping of the door knocker drew Juliet's attention. When the footman failed to appear, she went to the front door. Peering through the glass panels, she saw the sheriff of Easter Ross standing on the stoop, a strikingly beautiful woman on his arm. Her dress and hat of moss green watered silk complemented her hazel eyes and reddish-brown hair. The sheriff was resplendent in oak brown velvet. He even carried a walking stick. Their fancy clothes were more suited to a royal ball than to a late afternoon visit.

Excitement clutched Juliet's stomach. This was her chance to question Neville Smithson without the duke interfering. Tidying her hair, she opened the door.

"Ah, Juliet, how fair thou art," the sheriff said, bowing from the waist.

"Please, Sheriff, no more theatrics," she said.

He looked her up and down, and nodded, as if to say he approved. "May I present Lady Catherine Munro, countess of Beauly. Catherine, meet Juliet, governess to the MacKenzie brood."

The woman, who seemed oddly familiar, didn't bother to respond. Turning sideways, she wedged her panniered skirts through the door and glided to the entry table. Tossing off her muff, she fingered the calling cards on the silver tray. Choosing one, she raised it almost to her nose and squinted to read the name.

The gesture struck Juliet as both rude and curious. She glanced at the sheriff. He watched her closely, his pale blue gaze intense. He seemed to be waiting. But for what?

A knowing grin softened his features. Pointing with the walking stick, he said, "Catherine and the duke are old friends. When she learned he'd returned to Easter Ross, a plague couldn't have kept her away."

The derision in his voice sounded like a warning. Juliet's gaze whipped to the woman. Where had she seen such hazel eyes? And the woman needed spectacles. Just like Mary. Her chestnut hair matched the shade of Mary's. An old friend of the duke.

Juliet's stomach tightened. A chill seeped into her bones. With eerie certainty she knew that the woman before her was Mary's mother.

She wasn't dead. The duke had lied.

"Stop gawking," the woman said to Juliet, "and inform His Grace that we have arrived." She removed her seal-lined coat and held it out to Juliet. "Take care of this."

Gathering her composure, Juliet took the garment and laid it on the settee. "His Grace is out," she said.

Like icy fingers, cold hazel eyes raked Juliet. "We'll wait."

Chuckling cruelly, Neville said, "A pity you didn't bring your son, Catherine. The duke's daughters could have entertained the babe."

"I think not." Finality flavored her words.

"Ah, yes. He is a bit young yet, and legitimate."

A disdainful smile accentuated the wrinkles around

the countess's mouth. "Sensitive about that, are you, Neville?"

He laughed. "Of course not." To Juliet he said, "Where are the girls?"

Fierce protectiveness seized her. "They're busy. If you'll wait in the parlor, I'll order tea."

"That would be splendid." Catherine took his arm. He ushered her into the parlor.

A stupefied Juliet made her way to the kitchen. The woman named Catherine had another child. A son, but he was only a babe. Yet she had abandoned Mary. Unless she'd come for her.

Juliet wanted to race to the stables and stand guard over Mary. She never got the chance, because just as she was relaying the tea request to Cook, the girls strolled into the kitchen.

"The sheriff's here?" said an awed Sarah, straw spiking her braids.

"I want to see the slimy bugger," declared Agnes, swiping the air with a quirt. "I'm not afraid."

Juliet stiffened her back. Desperate to get them upstairs and out of sight, she said, "You'll do no such thing, Agnes MacKenzie. All of you, go to the schoolroom and wait for me."

Sarah and Mary slumped in relief. Curiosity shone on Lottie's face. Agnes brought the quirt to her forehead, and like a field general signaling a charge, she extended her arm and marched to the stairs. Her sisters followed. So did Juliet.

Neville stepped into the foyer. The woman named Catherine stood in the doorway to the parlor. Spying him, Agnes dug in her heels. Like ninepins, her sisters bumped into one another. The quirt began to quiver. But the sheriff wasn't looking at Agnes. He was staring at Mary.

Juliet rushed to the girl and draped a protective arm around her shoulders. "If you'll excuse us, sir."

"Such charming children. Wouldn't you say so, Catherine?"

"Of course we're charming," said Lottie. "Our father is a very important duke."

Juliet watched the countess. Her haughty mask of insouciance fell, and for a moment she devoured Mary with her eyes. In that instant Juliet wished she were a man, strong enough to pound the sheriff to pulp. What was his purpose in bringing Mary's mother here?

"You might be interested to know, Catherine," he continued, "that all of His Grace's daughters were born to different women. The gossips say one of them is a royal princess. Which one do you think?"

Hatred smoothed out the countess's features. "I think you're unwise to pursue the subject. His Grace protects their identity."

Mary looked up at Juliet. "Why are they discussing us like we aren't here?"

"Because they're rude," said Lottie, her expression older than her years.

Juliet could take no more. "Off with you, girls," she said, pushing Mary toward the stairs.

A bewildered-looking Sarah curtsied to Mary's mother and the sheriff. All dignity, Agnes led the troupe upstairs. "We haven't time for the likes of them."

When they were out of sight, Juliet opened her mouth to excuse herself. The front door flew open. In walked the duke of Ross.

He wore an azure waistcoat embroidered with the MacKenzie stag, and a wide-brimmed beaver hat with a white ostrich plume. Dust coated his riding boots. A cocky grin wreathed his face.

Weak with relief, Juliet wanted to rush into his arms. Then his gaze moved to the countess of Beauly and his features darkened, with what emotion Juliet couldn't tell.

A slow smile transformed Catherine's face. She approached him and sank into a low curtsy. "Welcome to Easter Ross, Your Grace, and my belated congratulations on winning back your title. I always knew you would. You're very good at getting what you want." The liquid quality of her voice and her sultry expression left little doubt that she'd like to express her admiration in his bed.

Jealousy bit at Juliet. The duke had given this woman

a child, a child she'd abandoned, a child he cherished. They shared a past that Juliet had no part of. Unprepared for the soul-deep pain that ravaged her, she said, "I've asked Cook to bring tea. I'll take my leave now, Your Grace."

Lachlan watched her mount the stairs. He knew that posture well; her back was stiff as a poker, her knuckles white as snow on the handrail. Had she noticed how much Mary favored Catherine? Had Neville blurted out the truth?

Disgust swept over Lachlan, and he had to strain to keep from tossing Catherine out the door and bashing Neville's perfect face. The whole episode was surely a result of his conniving.

Lachlan said, "What brings you here, Neville?"

All innocence, the sheriff said, "Merely paying my respects, Your Grace, and accommodating dear Catherine. She was eager to renew your acquaintance. But now I must bid you both adieu." Twirling that silly cane, he strolled to the door.

Catherine toyed with Lachlan's cravat. "But I have all day." His stomach pitched in revulsion. "Your daughters are looking well," she purred.

An ugly, terrifying thought occurred to Lachlan. Did Catherine want her daughter back?

Over her shoulder, the countess said, "Do enjoy yourself in Kelgie, Neville."

Immediately alert, Lachlan said, "Kelgie?" Kelgie was the last MacKenzie stronghold in Easter Ross. "What business have you there?"

Waving his hand, Neville said, "Trivial matters. A ship to christen. A babe to kiss." He bowed to Catherine. "Good-bye, my dear. Since your husband remained in Beauly, I trust His Grace will see you to your lodgings . . . safely."

Coy laughter erupted. "Of course he will . . . later. Won't you, Lachlan?"

How had he ever desired this shallow woman? Youth, he thought, had come with blinders and an insatiable appetite. He wasn't blind now, and he could manage Catherine and the sheriff.

"I'll walk out with you, Neville," he said, peeling Catherine's hands from his chest and opening the door.

Once outside, he turned on Neville and dealt him a roundhouse dunt. The sheriff flew back and crashed against a column, then slid down, his arms and legs splayed. Blood gushed from his nose. "That's just a taste of what you'll get if you ever dare threaten my lassies."

"You bloody bastard." Neville slammed down the cane so hard that it cracked.

Lachlan laughed. "Unlike your mother, Neville, mine was lawfully wed at the time of my birth."

Shaking his head, the sheriff levered himself to his feet. "You take great pleasure in reminding me of that, don't you? At least my father wasn't a traitor."

Backing the Bonnie Prince had been grounds for treason—if you viewed the Jacobite Rebellion from the English point of view. "And I'm not subject to the sins of my father. You, however, still are. Put the past behind you, Neville, and don't ever darken my door again."

"You'll rue the day you dared set foot on my turf."

Family pride fueled Lachlan's rage. For hundreds of years, the MacKenzies had ruled all of the western Highlands. "Your turf? You've made a wasteland of Easter Ross. But I intend to correct that." Wiping his hands, Lachlan strolled inside, ready to deal with Catherine Munro.

Juliet, he realized later that night, presented a much bigger problem. Lounging in a chair by the fire and sipping his favorite drink, he waited for her. He'd expected her to be upset over Catherine's visit, but hadn't counted on her defiance.

An hour passed, then another. If she didn't march herself into his chamber in five minutes, he'd go after her. She was his mistress, dammit!

Where the devil was she? Springing to his feet, he went to her room. Empty.

Childish laughter spilled from his daughters' chamber.

He paused, unnoticed, in the doorway. Across the room, Juliet sat on the floor before the fireplace, a long-handled skillet in her hands. Mary and Sarah sat to her right; Agnes and Lottie to her left. All wore bedclothes. Four pairs of curious eyes were trained on the flames that licked at the skillet. Mary, her head bowed over a book, read aloud.

Tenderness touched him. Although she'd come here for devious reasons, Juliet White had enriched the lives of his lassies. She'd taught them to enjoy themselves. She sensed the greatest need in each of them. She'd tempered Agnes's willful ways. She'd imbued Sarah with confidence. She'd given Mary the ability to read. She'd tamed Lottie's sharp tongue. She'd taught them to love and respect one another. Deep in his heart, he knew she loved them. He even condoned her reasons for coming to Scotland, for he sympathized with an orphan who longed to shelter her only kin.

She'd helped him, too. This very day he'd used her suggestion a dozen times. A wheelwright named Mac-Kenzie worked in tandem with an English carriage maker. The *Tain Crier* would henceforth be printed in both Scottish and English. Two ferries now operated between Cromarty and Easter Ross proper: one the *Goodly Anne,* the other the *Highland Gull*.

His eyes kept straying to Juliet, to the delicate line of her jaw and the perfect bow of her lips. Curling strands of baby-fine hair framed her face and gave her a childlike air. But such an observation was pure deception, for Juliet was a woman from the crown of her lovely head to the tips of her dainty toes. He pictured her in a gown of lush red velvet, the bodice cut low enough to hint at the bounty beneath, the waist nipped tight enough to follow the natural curves of her womanly form. He saw rubies draping her neck and dangling from her ears. He saw love in her eyes and a smile of pure happiness on her lips. He saw a portrait hanging in the great hall of Kinbairn Castle. A portrait of his duchess of Ross.

The contents of the skillet came to life. Lachlan put his imagination to rest. Popping sounds filled the room. The girls squealed and clapped their hands.

"Listen!" said Sarah.

Mary looked up. Firelight turned the lenses of her

new spectacles to disks of light. "It pops and sizzles just like you said it would, Mistress White."

"Hoots!" shouted Agnes and Lottie.

Juliet's face broke into a smile so full of joy, so endearingly lovely, Lachlan thought his heart might burst. He wanted to bind her to him. He wanted to give her children of her own. He wanted to see the first strand of gray appear in her hair. But could he ever trust her? Would he ever hear the truth from her lips? Suppressing his sentimental thoughts, he said, "Am I invited to this party?"

Gaiety slipped from Juliet's face. His daughters, however, cheered.

"Sit here, Papa," said Sarah, scooting close to Mary to make a place for him beside Juliet.

"We're popping Indian corn," said Agnes, as excited as a bride at Hogmanay.

Amused, he said, "What's that?"

Agnes lowered her brow. "We don't know exactly. It's a surprise. But Mistress White says all little girls like popping corn."

Would that Mistress White liked a Scottish duke so well, thought Lachlan. "Another Colonial treat?"

"Dukes can like it, too," said Lottie. "Can't they, Mistress White? Papa liked the molly-tops."

Juliet shot him a look that said he could take his likes to China. Undeterred, he sat cross-legged beside her, making sure his knee touched hers. His children would be devastated if she left. His own life would be empty without her. He must think of a way to keep her.

When the skillet was empty and the children were full, he watched in tender awe as Juliet removed the spectacles from a snoozing Mary.

Marry. That was it. He'd marry Juliet. That would keep her here, bind her to him legally. He'd make her love him. In return she would give him sons.

Pleased with himself, he carried the lassies to bed and tucked them in. A sleepy Lottie refused to let go of him; he had to pry her fingers from his robe.

"I'll say good night, Your . . . Lachlan," said Juliet from the doorway of her chamber.

Admiring the way the firelight glistened in her hair and anticipating the seduction to come, he walked toward her. She stepped back and started to close the door.

"Juliet . . ."

Soft brown eyes, rife with challenge, met his. Confident, his mood suddenly buoyant, Lachlan held out his hand.

"No."

He'd crawled into this woman's heart and found a haven of compassion and love. He wasn't about to let her go. He walked through the doorway and bolted the lock behind him. "You're angry with me."

Looking him straight in the eye, she said, "You lied."

So she *did* guess. "Will you cross your heart and swear you've never lied to me?"

She whirled, giving him her back. Like a pendulum, the thick braid swished over her hips. "Don't change the subject. You lied about Mary's mother."

"Aye."

"Did you see her home safely?"

"Nay, Jamie did."

"I hate her for abandoning Mary."

"So do I. But I'm grateful, for I got to keep the child."

"Why didn't you marry her?"

"Because I didn't love her. Because she wanted a wealthy and titled husband."

"You're wealthy and titled."

"I wasn't seven years ago."

She bowed her head and twisted her hands. "Will she try to take Mary away?"

"No one will ever take any of my children away."

"Catherine might use Mary if she thought it would please you."

"She couldn't, in a thousand years, please me. But you do."

"Huh."

"Turn around, Juliet."

"No. I won't be seduced by a liar."

Regret swept over Lachlan. So he reached into the

past and sought a truth that Juliet would accept. "The women who bore my children were selfish creatures. They were more concerned with the pleasures at court than with the joys of motherhood. Had I not taken my lassies, they would have been sent to orphanages." An old pain ripped at him. Suddenly he was back in Rouen, stalking the halls of the great public orphanage, his tortured mind fleeing from one desperate thought to the next. He'd found the squalling Mary wrapped in a dirty satin sheet that still reeked of her mother's perfume.

Love had overwhelmed him that day.

He thought of the child Juliet had been—an orphan.

Love overwhelmed him now.

Softly he said. "I won't lie to you again, Juliet."

When she didn't move, he stepped behind her and rested his hands on her waist. As he felt the flaring curve of her hips and smelled the lilac fragrance she favored, an odd thought occurred to him. Were she any other woman, he'd be caressing her breasts, doing his utmost to get her beneath him. But he wanted more from Juliet White. He wanted her confession, her heart. He wanted her pledge, her love. He wanted her forever. The unexpected occurred to him. What if she was pledged to another? What if she wasn't free to marry? He'd fix that, even if he had to go to Parliament. Sadly he realized he knew little about the woman he loved; he'd taken her explanations for gospel.

Leaning close, his lips touching her temple, he said, "Forgive me. I didn't mean to hurt you."

"You didn't hurt me. You can't seduce me again, either. I'd like for you to leave."

"And I'd like for you to marry me."

She turned so quickly, her braid slapped his arm. Watchful brown eyes peered into his soul. "Don't toy with me. I can't be a duchess."

He knew a lie when he heard it. He caressed her braid and pictured her hair flowing down her back, the Ross coronet wreathing her head. "I think you'll make an exceptional duchess. You'll bear me fine sons and more lovely daughters."

"No. I can't marry you."

"Why not?" He braced himself. "Are you promised to another?"

"I truly don't wish to discuss it."

He had time to win her. And who better than the Highland rogue to woo this alluring golden-haired beauty? "We don't have to talk now, Juliet."

"I won't come to your bed either."

"Very well." He swept her into his arms. "Then I'll come to yours."

Within minutes her heated protests turned to soft sighs of passion. Keeping a tight rein on his own desires, Lachlan explored the delicate arches of her feet, the enticing curves of her calves, and the velvety-soft skin of her inner thighs. He moved higher, eager to taste her fully. When she protested, he told her he was hungry for her. He accused her of leaving him to starve. He called her a coward. The flower of her femininity unfolded, revealing dew-kissed petals and a center so luscious and lively he almost lost his seed.

She writhed beneath him, her fingers threading through his hair, her breasts heaving with excitement. When she moaned, pleading for release, her hands drawing him upward, he stopped.

Love overrode his conscience. "Say you'll marry me, Juliet," he whispered against the lips of her femininity.

She shook her head, sending her glorious hair cascading over the edge of the bed. "You don't understand. Please don't make me beg."

"I want you."

"And I want you," she said, her eyes dreamy with passion.

Noble intentions fled. Rising above her, he opened her legs wide and, in one smooth, deep stroke, buried himself in her softness. She gasped and, with fingers, teeth, and hidden muscles, held him fast.

"Show me you love me," he said. "Lift your hips. Hold me. Touch me with your hands."

She started to cry out. Remembering his sleeping lassies in the next room, Lachlan covered her mouth with his own. He felt her tense, then go limp with satisfaction. Sweet joy poured through him.

His own need raged, and as smoldering desire became blazing passion, he grasped her hips and held her still. Panting, his heart pounding, he almost freed his loins.

Cramps clutched his belly. His conscience screamed that he would regret giving her a child. He thought of his children in the next room and knew that he couldn't give his seed to another woman—not until he was lawfully wed.

He awakened later to an empty bed. Where had Juliet gone? Thinking she might be in the privy, he waited for half an hour. Then he donned his robe and peeked into the darkened nursery. One of the beds was empty. Suspicion sharpened his senses. What if Juliet had taken the missing lass?

He raced into the hall and headed for the stairs. At the sound of Juliet's voice, he skidded to a halt, the marble floor icy beneath his bare feet. Quietly he approached the door to the upstairs privy, but stopped short of the threshold.

". . . houses are made of wood and bricks, because Virginia has many forests."

"Mistress White?" Lottie's voice sounded muffled.

"Yes?"

In a weak voice the girl said, "Why didn't my sisters get sick?"

Juliet had a smile in her voice. "I think you have a delicate constitution where popping corn is concerned."

"Oh." At length Lottie said, "Mistress White?"

"Yes?"

"You won't tell anyone, will you?"

"Not if you don't want me to."

" 'Twill be our secret, won't it?"

"Yes."

"Papa and I have a secret. I was very bad, but he promised not to tell if I never snooped again."

Lachlan tensed. Would Lottie confess to taking Lillian's letter from Juliet's satchel?

Juliet said, "You're a very obedient girl, Lottie. I'm proud of you. And you mustn't tell that secret, either.

You gave your word. It's very important to keep your promise."

Another silence ensued. "Mistress White?"

"I'm here, Lottie."

"Papa beat up the sheriff today. We saw it from our window. Agnes wanted to run downstairs and kick him in a place a lady doesn't say."

"Agnes is a willful lass."

"Aye. Did you ever want a sister?"

Lachlan peeked around the corner. Juliet sat on a bench outside the draped door to the privy, her face a picture of abject misery. She'd thrown back her head, exposing the lovely column of her neck. Twin trails of tears rolled down her cheeks.

Pain squeezed his chest. She was thinking about Lillian, the sister she'd hardly known, the sister she thought he'd seduced.

"Did you?"

"Sometimes." She clamped a hand over her mouth to stifle the sobs.

Lottie said, "You sound funny. Are you sick, too?"

"No."

Her pain reached out to him, and for the first time he understood her dilemma. Her indenture and youth had prevented her from coming to Scotland when she'd received Lillian's letter. For years she'd worried and wondered about her sister. He wanted to go to her, to wrap her in his arms, kiss away her tears, and tell her the truth. But he couldn't, not until he knew he could trust her.

"Mistress White?"

Her teeth closed over her bottom lip. The tears flowed faster. Swallowing back the anguish, she said, "Yes, Lottie?"

"You won't ever leave me, will you?"

Juliet fell forward, burying her face in her hands. Her shoulders jerked. Her braid swept the floor. In a small voice she said, "No, Lottie."

"Good. We need you very much."

Lachlan made his way back to her room, but his mind stayed fixed on the sad image of Juliet. She didn't know which of the girls was Lillian's child. He couldn't blame her for wanting to find and care for her own niece.

He smiled, thinking of the pleasurable task ahead. Juliet had never been courted. He would woo her, win her, then someday he'd tell her the story of Lillian and her child.

Chapter 14

A fortnight later Juliet sat in the parlor in awe of the duke of Ross.

From his spot on the settee beside her, he held court. His subjects today, Edward and Henrietta Worthingham and Fergus and Flora MacKenzie, appeared just as enthralled as yesterday's group, and the group before. Last night, however, the duke and Fergus had had a lengthy meeting. Fergus had organized a coopers' union last year and neglected to tell the duke. The duke had unleashed his anger and given Fergus a choice between emasculation and prosperity. Fergus had made the right decision.

Wearing an oatmeal-colored waistcoat and knee breeches, the duke chatted like an amiable gentleman, but Juliet knew another side of him. After last night, Fergus did, too.

Seated on matching sofas and facing each other, the MacKenzies-from-Nigg and the Worthinghams-from-Tain enjoyed tea, which Sarah served today, while her sisters had their own tea party across the room.

The daily ritual took a familiar, friendly turn when the duke leaned back and casually crossed his legs at the ankles. Silk stockings clung alluringly to his muscled calves. Unseen by the guests, he slipped his hand beneath the folds of Juliet's new gown and strummed his fingers. Beneath the table, the toes of his shoes twitched as if to a lively tune. "I think MacKenzie knows you're a frank fellow, Worthingham, so you needn't powder your words for us." Amazingly, he didn't sound impatient.

The Englishman set his teacup near the plate of short-bread on the table. An oily strand of graying brown hair slipped from beneath his jet black periwig. "I can understand the coopers wanting a union. It worked for the stonemasons in Brighton. But I can't negotiate the purchase of their barrels"—he shrugged—"if we don't speak the same language."

Juliet said, "But Mr. MacKenzie speaks English perfectly."

The duke turned his deceptively mild gaze on Fergus.

He wore a camel brown waistcoat with black-and-tan checked knee breeches. Flora, in a green-and-white striped day dress, her fiery curls tamed with ribbons and faux butterflies, brightened his conservative attire. They hardly resembled the bedraggled couple that had fled to Kinbairn Castle last winter.

The cooper folded his callused hands in his lap. Juliet gave him credit for not squirming. "We might've been a bit stubborn in our dealings with Worthingham." Fergus's gaze met the duke's. "But the sheriff set it off. We Scots had no one to stand up for us."

Grinning, the duke said, "You do now. I'll deal with Neville Smithson."

Fergus settled his thick body into the cushion. Flora beamed. "We always could count on your help, Your Grace."

Juliet said, "A union seems reasonable. Mr. Worthingham, what do you have against unions?"

"Nothing. The language and my bank balance are the problems."

"All of our foremen will speak English," said Fergus. "And your company can have the barrels on consignment."

Worthingham said, "I'll gladly pay you within thirty days, barring the unforeseen, such as a storm closing the port."

"Fergus?" The duke's hand went to his temple. He reached for a braid, which wasn't there. He ran a hand over his hair.

"I'm for it, Your Grace. So long as the sheriff isn't involved."

Henrietta Worthingham's hand stilled, the teacup halfway to her puckered lips. "Has he returned from Kelgie?"

"Nay," said the duke, hiding his displeasure at the continued absence of his enemy.

Henrietta smiled at the MacKenzies. "Lady Bridget, the sheriff's wife, is a generous soul, although she doesn't often leave home these days. She's in the family way again."

"She is, poor thing," said Flora, shaking her head. "And she's still mourning the death of her father."

Fergus said, "And the sheriff's mourning the end of the title. He'd set his sights on being named earl of Tain after the old man's death."

Henrietta declared, "I say the title should go to a Scotsman. An agreeable one. Not a smarmy opportunist like Smithson."

The duke leaned forward and started to push to his feet, but thought better of it. "Well put, Mrs. Worthingham. And I want to thank you, and you, Flora, and my dear, Juliet, for enduring this business discussion. Gentlemen, shall we send word of the agreement to the *Crier?*"

"Perhaps our guests could pen the stories," Juliet said.

To date, getting the local paper to print the news in both English and Scottish had been the duke's greatest coup.

Worthingham patted his wife's hand. "My Henrietta will pen the English piece herself. She has a flair for words."

A charming flush wound its way up her wrinkled cheeks and disappeared beneath her powdered wig. "You always do flatter me, Mr. Worthingham."

Not to be outdone, Fergus said, "My Flora will write the Scottish version."

"I might need Mrs. Worthingham's assistance," said Flora.

Henrietta smiled. "I doubt you will, Mrs. MacKenzie, but I'm at your disposal."

A pleased Fergus reached for a crumpet. The plate of English fare had intentionally been placed before him.

Sarah left her place on the window seat and approached the English guests. Wearing her best pink velvet gown and her best manners, she said, "Would you care for more tea?"

"Of course," said Worthingham. "You pour so prettily."

As graceful as a swan, Sarah filled his cup, then turned to the cooper. "Will you try the gooseberry conserve on your crumpet? Mrs. Worthingham made it herself."

"Thank you, nay. I've eaten my fill and 'twas delicious."

With a bejeweled hand, Henrietta indicated Lottie, Mary, and Agnes, who sat at a smaller table across the room. "Marvelous children, Your Grace. You must be immensely proud."

The duke turned the full force of his charming smile on Juliet. "Aye, that I am. But thank Mistress White. The credit belongs to her."

She almost returned his smile. No one in Tain had called the girls bastards. Fighting the thrill she felt beneath his open admiration, she managed to say, "The credit belongs to the children themselves. They are a governess's joy lately."

Henrietta cleared her throat. "How wonderful to see such devotion. Our governess abandoned us for a family in Burgundy."

The duke rested his hand on Juliet's knee. "Before I'd let Juliet abandon us, I'd marry her."

The declaration hung in the air. He hadn't been joking, he'd been trying to get a reaction.

Four small voices yelled, "Hooray for Papa!"

Opposing emotions warred within Juliet. She should slap her lover. She should show respect for her employer. She should challenge his veracity. He didn't truly care about her. He was more interested in the welfare of his children and the politics of Easter Ross.

Knowing how important this meeting was to him, she said, "He calls me Juliet only when he wants me to forfeit my day off."

The ladies tittered. The men hummed in agreement.

By day, the duke entertained the citizens of Easter Ross, English and Scottish alike. He fawned over the babies, complimented the women, boasted to the men, always with Juliet at his side and the girls close by. By night, he wrapped Juliet in his arms, loved her tenderly, and in the aftermath of passion inquired about her life in Virginia, at the orphanage and with the Mabrys. He asked her opinion on the political problems he faced. He discussed his strategies. He made her forget why she'd come to Scotland. He made her feel safe about Lillian's child.

He took her hand.

"Are you handfasted?" asked Fergus.

"Aye," said the duke, grinning like a smitten youth.

Sarah whispered, "Hoots." Her sisters gasped in shock.

Mrs. Worthingham's cup clattered against the saucer.

Confused, Juliet tried to pull her hand away. He held it fast. Handfasted. What on earth did it mean?

"Your Grace?" Jamie's voice interrupted the buzz of comments.

He stood in the doorway, bonnet in hand. His forehead gleamed white while the rest of him bore a coating of dust. His stern expression boded ill.

The duke got to his feet. "Pardon me, please."

"Thank you for having us, Your Grace," said Worthingham, extending his hand. "And welcome home. When next we three meet, I hope it will be on the links of your golf course."

Feigning a serious expression, the duke said, "Only if both of you allow me a few strokes. I'm out of practice."

He bade the ladies good day and went to Jamie. Heads bent in conversation, they walked toward the stairs.

When the guests had departed, Juliet took the girls to the schoolroom. There she learned to her great consternation that a handfast was a predecessor to marriage. No wonder the duke treated her with such familiarity in the presence of guests; he'd all but told them she was his lover and would become his wife. She'd fantasized about being his duchess, but those were only games she played when her spirits were low.

Her spirits weren't low now. Boiling mad, she sent the girls to the kitchen and made her way to the duke's chamber.

Gold brocade now draped the shuttered windows. Small tables covered with papers and lamps filled with scented oil gave the impression that a decent man rather than a scoundrel lived here.

Not spying her quarry in the outer chamber, she entered the bedroom. Not seeing him there either, she peeked into his dressing chamber. A bench ran almost the length of the narrow room. Trunks and racks of clothing lined the walls.

Wearing only a shirt and stockings, the despicable duke of Ross cut a most appealing figure. His back toward her, he surveyed the wall of shelves that contained his shoes and boots. Stretching, he reached for his riding boots. The movement drew up his shirttail, exposing rigid and powerful thighs covered with honey-colored hair. The boots came tumbling down. He bent over, revealing taut buttocks and interesting parts no lady should see. Parts she was tempted to kick.

She must have made a sound because his head jerked around. He'd plaited his hair again. The smile he gave her sent shivers down her spine.

"Watching me, were you?" He wiggled his eyebrows. "I was watching you, too, today. You look lovely in that dress. Remind me to order something else for you in yellow, perhaps a brocade or a watered silk. And a chocolate brown riding habit with one of those charming hats."

She turned her back on him.

"Don't be modest, Juliet," he said, coming toward her. "You see me naked every night."

"*Haud yer wheesht!*" She pulled the door closed.

He tried to pull her into his arms.

She pushed away and moved around the bench to the far end of the chamber. "How dare you tell those people we were intimate?"

He looked so innocent she wanted to throw something at him. "In God's eyes we're married."

"Don't bring God into this. If you'd married every woman you seduced, you'd be a bigamist fifty times over."

"I never handfasted with any of them."

At the inadequate answer, fresh anger ripped through her. "Bully for me."

"Juliet," he said as if dredging up patience he didn't have. "A handfast marriage becomes permanent only if the woman conceives." He flecked dirt off the heel of one of the boots he held. "I take great pains to see that you do not."

Like a blow, the admission stung. He didn't want to marry her. He wanted a governess for his children and a mistress to ease his manly needs. "I see. You wish only to satisfy your lust. If you have no intention of giving me a child, then what's the point of this handfast marriage?"

He continued to stare at the boots in his hands. "Could we discuss this when I return?"

The weariness in his voice took the edge off her anger. "You're leaving?"

"Aye." He sighed. "For Kelgie."

"What's wrong? What did Jamie say?"

His jaw tightened, his eyes narrowed. He dropped to the bench. "Neville brought in a fleet of Cornish fishermen and docked the MacKenzie boats."

Suddenly her own problems seemed insignificant compared to his. She went to him. "What will you do?"

On a half laugh, he looked up at her and said, "What would I like to do? Or what will I really do?"

Her heart softened. "Both."

He rested his head against her leg. "I'd like to ship those fishermen back to England where they belong. Then I'd like to kill Neville."

Concern for her troubled Scottish duke welled within Juliet. The problems between them could wait. She cupped his head in her hands and held him close. "But you won't."

"Nay. I'll show him the error of his ways and send the fishermen back to Cornwall."

She sank her fingers into his hair and massaged his scalp. "He's still angry because you knocked him down."

Chuckling, he grasped her waist and said, "I blackened his rotten eye, I'll wager." Craning his neck, he looked at her. "I need you, Juliet. I need your sensible, objective mind. I need your loving patience."

She felt his power, his allure. The air filled with the smell of his soap and the excitement of his affection. "What will you do to him?" she asked.

He turned his head to one side. "You didn't bolt the door."

"You didn't answer me."

"One day we won't need to sneak around." He rose, fastened the bolt, then returned to her. His eyes had turned a deep blue. "Will you put your arms around my neck, Juliet? Will you kiss me good-bye and wish me fair luck?"

Lulled by his seductive tone, she draped her arms around his neck and stood on tiptoe. "Will you answer me?"

"And much more," he said, his arms surrounding her, his lips devouring her.

What if he was injured? What if he never returned? She'd been so concerned with her own troubles, she hadn't stopped to consider his. She tasted desperation on his lips and felt the struggle within him. He was a Highland chieftain born to lead men and rule a kingdom; he was a titled nobleman bound to bring peace to his hard-won dukedom. She had few tools to help him in this new battle, but he would win, and long after a Colonial governess named Juliet White had gone to dust, history would immortalize the sixth duke of Ross. She prayed it would remember him kindly.

"You'll win with Neville," she whispered between kisses.

"I don't see how," he said against her cheek. "I'm a

stranger, an enemy to the English people here. Neville is their champion."

"He's no match for you. You're too clever, too determined."

"Truly? I don't think so."

"I'll wager I can change your mind."

Framing her face in his hands, he stared deep into her eyes. "Ah, lassie, what would I do without you?"

Her heart took flight and her body dissolved into a pit of aching emptiness. His tongue filled her mouth; his anguish reached out to her, calling her, needing her. Skilled hands peeled away her bodice and skirts while her fingers gathered up his shirt and slipped beneath it. She molded his trim waist and eased her hands over his naked buttocks. Cool, sleek skin grew warm beneath her palms, and she kneaded and caressed him, drawing out the tension, building up the heat.

He broke the kiss, and warm, seeking lips traced her jaw, the sensitive spot below her ear. The edges of his teeth toyed with her earlobe, kindling a fire and making her shiver.

"Sweet, sweet Juliet," he whispered, just before his mouth closed over her ear and his tongue peeked inside.

Her knees buckled, but he was there to hold her up, then gently laid her down. The worn wooden bench touched her spine, but her senses were trained on the man standing above her. A hungry need gleamed in his eyes, and he reached down, grasped her thighs and pulled them apart, exposing her.

"Take off your chemise," he said, his gaze fixed on the part of her that ached for him.

Her feet touched the cool floor. Her hands found the hem of the garment and pulled it over her head. In a daze of anticipation, she waited.

He traced the garter above her knee, then moved higher, leaving behind a trail of quivering flesh. Deft fingers found her, opened her gently, then eased inside. His eyes drifted shut, and his mouth curled into a smile of pure delight.

"Take off your shirt, Lachlan."

"By and by."

His free hand circled a breast, then he dropped to his knees and took a nipple into his mouth, laving, suckling, provoking a wanton urge that shot straight to her belly and lower. Her hips rose to meet his hand. He groaned, working his finger deeper, and with an unerring thumb, he found the key to her passion. She cried out. His mouth covered hers in a kiss that took her breath and her will away.

"Take off my shirt," he rasped against her lips.

Like a child tearing at Christmas wrappings, she yanked off the garment.

He tunneled his hands beneath her shoulders, and the blazing heat of his body settled over hers. Laughing, thinking of such a big man lying on a wooden bench, she said, "I didn't think we'd fit."

He gazed down at her, his expression soft, sincere. "Prop your feet on those trunks, and I'll show you how well we fit."

"I don't think I can move my legs."

Grinning and rotating his hips until she felt him nudging at her, he said, "Try. And I'll give you a delightful reward."

She did, and when her legs were spread wide, her feet braced, he pushed forward, sinking deep, filling her, then thrusting with a rhythm as natural as breathing. He anticipated her passions, and like a miser doling out precious coin, he brought her to the point of ecstasy, only to stop and wait until she begged for more.

Levering himself up, he said, "Look at me, Juliet."

Through the maze her mind had become, awareness slowly emerged. Her eyes drifted open. He loomed above her, his braids dangling, his nostrils flaring, and in the deep blue of his eyes, she discovered a passion that surpassed her own.

He began moving again, and a moment later, her toes curled, her hands clutched, and a release as sweet as a glimpse of heaven burst inside her. He moved quicker, grinding his hips on her, intensifying her pleasure, prolonging her release. He gasped and his belly jerked. A moment later she felt him pulsing within her, warming her, soothing her.

When her heartbeat slowed and her breathing eased, she said, "Lachlan, *Lang mae yer lum reek.*"

"Thank you, lass. I'll need a bit of luck."

"You'll be careful, won't you? You'll come back safely?"

"Aye, and I expect a friendly greeting."

She tried to dredge up anger and failed. "Not one so friendly as this. You must say you were joking about the handfast marriage."

He bolted to his feet and yanked on his riding breeches. "That would be foolish."

Suddenly wary of him and conscious of her own nakedness, she put on her chemise. "Why?"

"Because." He planted his hands on his hips. "Given my fertility, and your enthusiasm on that bench a moment ago, 'tis safe to say you may *now* consider yourself truly wed to me."

Panic seized her. He'd given her his seed this time. She must return to Virginia. By law, any child she bore would serve the Mabrys for eighteen years. "But you said you wouldn't give me a child." She sprang to her feet. "You promised."

"Juliet." He took her hands in his. Smiling down at her, he said, "You can tell me anything, you know. I care for you. My children care for you. We should speak truthfully to each other."

Her life loomed before her. Once she'd thought herself fortunate. Now her future looked dim and lusterless. But she'd given her word to return to Virginia. Unable to hold his gaze, she bowed her head and told him a piece of the truth. "I can't have your child."

"Look at me." He dropped her hands and stepped back. Sorrow ringed his eyes and sadness tinged his smile. "Juliet . . ." He hesitated, his great shoulders slumped, his mighty arms dangling at his sides. He looked like a small boy suffering life's greatest disappointment. He did need her now, to watch his children, to take his mind off the problems he faced. His troubles would pass, his daughters would prosper. He wouldn't need her then. He'd need a blue-blooded duchess.

Hoping to remind him of such realities, she lightly

said, "You're the laird of Clan MacKenzie. No upshot English sheriff stands a chance against you. I'll be here when you return. But I cannot be your wife."

As if she'd thrown a bucket of water on him, he grew stiff and stepped back. In a tone reserved for underlings, he said, "You may not have a choice in the matter. But don't worry, I'm accustomed to women who don't want my children."

Her hands turned to ice. "What do you mean?"

He picked up his shirt and boots and walked to the door. Although he stood only a few steps away, he might have been on another continent, so distant was his expression. "I meant exactly what I said. None of the women who bore my children wanted them. Don't leave the house without Thomas."

He stalked out the door. She dropped to the bench and sat as still as a stone, but her emotions teeter-tottered from soul-deep despair to painful regret. She couldn't stay in Scotland. And in her heart she knew she couldn't take Lillian's child away from the father who loved her.

Chapter 15

Lachlan leapt from the boat and onto the dock at Kelgie. Tiny crabs and silver bugs scurried for cover. Lanterns dotted the pier and winked in the distance, marking the perimeter of the village. Off to the west and hidden by darkness lay the infamous tobacco field that had started the problems in Kelgie. In the harbor, fishing boats rested at anchor, their naked masts spiking the moonlit sky, their English crews bedded down for the night. Now that he knew why Neville had brought the Cornish fishermen here, Lachlan had second thoughts about sending them home.

The pier rocked. Jamie tramped behind Lachlan. The hollow sound of their boots on the wooden planks drowned out the quiet lapping of Cromarty Firth. The night mirrored Lachlan's black mood.

Unbidden, a vision of Juliet rose in his mind. Self-disgust swamped him. He should've known better than to let down his guard. He'd spent a fortnight courting and befriending her. For naught. All he had to show for his efforts was a bruised pride and an aching heart. No more, though. He'd come to know the real Juliet; in the matter of loving a man and wanting his children, she and Lillian had been cut from the same cloth.

"Your Grace." Jamie's hand touched Lachlan's shoulder. "Shall we go straight to the squire's?"

Problems with Juliet White would have to wait. The trouble with Neville Smithson and Squire Conall MacKenzie would not. "Aye."

Lachlan followed Jamie through the narrow streets, past the noisy taverns, and up the steep hill to the squire's cottage. Logic told Lachlan he'd been here as a child, for these MacKenzies were second cousins to his own father. But he couldn't conjure up a memory of the once-prosperous fishing village that was ruled, according to Jamie, by a stubborn, petty-minded Scotsman.

When they reached the cottage Lachlan pulled the bell cord. In the yellow light of twin lamps, he could make out the faded shape of a stag on the iron-studded doors.

"Who goes there?" a woman called out in Scottish.

Jamie yelled, "The duke of Ross and Jamie MacKenzie."

One of the doors swung open. The woman standing on the threshold needed no introduction to announce her heritage, for the flaming red hair, the milk-fair complexion, and the distinctive nose marked her as a MacKenzie. Her stylish gown of emerald brocade seemed out of place beneath a soiled cotton apron.

She curtsied and waved them inside. "Welcome, Your Grace." She smiled a bit too sweetly. "To pandemonium." Pivoting, she glided toward the main room.

Lachlan glanced at Jamie, but the soldier's gaze was fixed on the woman. None of Jamie's tales of the problems in Kelgie had included a female—a female he obviously favored.

"Who's the lass?"

Jamie smoothed back his hair. "Muirella MacKenzie," he said without inflection.

"The squire's wife?"

"Daughter."

Amused by Jamie's feigned nonchalance, Lachlan said, "She's a bonnie one."

"Aye," the soldier grumbled. "If ye've a whip and a shield in hand."

The remark lightened Lachlan's dark mood; he felt better than he had since leaving Rosshaven two hours ago. He slapped Jamie on the back and strolled into the hall.

The smell of mutton, onions, and fresh-baked bread permeated the spacious room. His mouth watered. He realized he was hungry—hungry for peace, starving for tranquillity in his life.

From his spot at the head of the long trestle table, Squire Conall MacKenzie rose. Yanking his napkin from his shirt collar, the red-bearded Scotsman pushed back his chair, hitched up his leather breeches, and came forward. A head shorter than Lachlan and twice his age, the squire didn't seem capable of causing the trouble Jamie had spoken of.

" 'Tis a bonnie day in Easter Ross," said the squire in Scottish. He eyed Lachlan from head to toe. "Yer the image of yer grandsire, even if ye are thrice his size, Lachlan MacCoinnich. Hae ye eaten?"

"No, we haven't." Intentionally, he spoke English.

The squire shrugged. "Take a seat. Ye, too, Jamie. Muirella will bring yer meal and a tankard o' my best."

Lachlan maneuvered his legs between the bench and the table. The kitchen door flew open. The lassie brought two tankards and a pitcher. She poured the beer, handed Lachlan a frothy mug, but didn't serve Jamie.

"Is that mutton I smell?" Lachlan asked.

Wiping her hands on the apron, Muirella said, "Aye, Your Grace. There's carrots and neeps 'n tatties, and broonie, too, if you've a sweet tooth."

"Mind yer waggin' tongue, lassie," said Conall. "They'd rather eat the food than listen to you."

Fire snapped in her eyes. Her hands flew to her hips. "Aye, yer lordship."

Lachlan put the tankard to his mouth to hide a smile. From the corner of his eye, he caught a glimpse of Jamie. Staring at Muirella, the soldier looked like a golden eagle patiently waiting for a fat moorhen to take flight. So, thought Lachlan, Jamie the bachelor wanted the fiery lass.

"What are you looking at?" she demanded of Jamie.

"Your hips." He reached for the other tankard. "I favor the way they sway."

Her palms slapped the table. Leaning forward, she glared at him. "You listen to me, Jamie MacCoinnich. I'll tell you one more time. Bonnie Prince Charlie'll sit on the English throne before I give you the time o' day. You be rememberin' that." She flounced off.

Jamie's jaw worked, and his determined gaze locked on the departing figure.

Lachlan chugged down the beer, then refilled his tankard. "More?" he asked Jamie.

The soldier winked. "I ain't had the first dram yet, but my thirst is a-building."

Beer almost spewed from Lachlan's mouth. He swallowed and said, "Did you bring a whip and shield?"

Jamie clanged his mug against Lachlan's. "I got all I need, Your Grace. The lass is a kitten when we're alone."

"Salutations on gettin' back yer dukedom," said Conall. "The way I see it, we'll hustle off those Cornishmen first thing tomorrow."

Immediately attentive, Lachlan put down his mug and said, "I'll deal with the Cornishmen, Conall. Let's talk about you and the sheriff of Easter Ross."

He spat on the floor. "A blight on the bonnie face of the Highlands."

The more Lachlan learned about Neville and his asinine dealings with the MacKenzies, the more he regretted having won back the district. Part of the trouble was his own fault, though, simply because he was laird of Clan MacKenzie. "You docked the fishing fleet."

Conall held up his arms and raised his eyes to heaven. "Smithson exiled the coopers from Nigg. There ain't a decent Scottish-made barrel to be found in Easter Ross. What was I supposed to do?"

Lachlan prayed for patience. "You weren't supposed to dump a load of fish on Neville's lawn, Conall."

Conall assumed a belligerent expression reminiscent of Agnes the day Lachlan had caught her putting fleas in Lottie's fancy underdrawers. "The buggerin' Sassenach plowed up my links."

Jamie had done his work well; Lachlan was prepared. "You leased him the land, Conall."

Sputtering, the squire said, "But not to grow tobacco! The weed don't flourish in Scottish soil."

Every MacKenzie in Easter Ross had suddenly become an expert on the growing of tobacco. And at Neville's expense. Unwanted sympathy reared its head. Lachlan's first thought was to ignore it. But he must be objective. He must rule these people fairly. Conall must give his side. "Did you specify what Smithson could and could not do with the land?"

Bushy brows met in the center of Conall's forehead. "Nay, I didn't specify. Didn't think I had to."

"Until the lease expires, you're welcome to play my golf course whenever you like."

Sulking, Conall speared a hunk of meat. "What about the MacKenzie coopers? I ain't puttin' tuppence in the pockets of that Sassenach who calls himself a barrel maker."

"Fergus MacKenzie has returned to Nigg. His union will be making barrels again. Where are the fishermen of Kelgie?"

"In the taverns, Your Grace, drowning their sorrows." Muirella sashayed to the table, a platter in her hands. She'd removed the apron. A generous bosom poured from the lace-trimmed neckline of her bodice. "Da, will ye stop yer blather long enough for His Grace to eat?"

Conall pointed his finger at her. "You watch yer dicey tongue, lass, or I'll take a strap to yer bottom."

Ignoring him, she placed the platter before Lachlan. Bending over, she said, "Take your fill, Your Grace."

Jamie sucked in his breath.

Lachlan coughed.

Throughout the excellent meal, Conall griped about the sheriff and praised the Clan MacKenzie. Muirella sassed her father and taunted Jamie. After the whiskey, Lachlan took his tried patience and exhausted body outside.

He lit his pipe and leaned against the building. The cool night air smelled of fish and people and problems. He longed for the tranquillity of Kinbairn Castle and the peaceful existence he'd known months before. Before Easter Ross. Before Juliet.

Weary, he couldn't summon the strength to quell the hurt that pierced him. Trust was a fragile, precious thing, and he didn't often bestow it. He'd been so certain of her love for him, for his children, that he hadn't bothered to question her motives. Even with proof staring him in the face, he'd looked for the best in her. He'd found it, too. But she wouldn't have him.

The door opened. Jamie stepped into the pool of light. Spying Lachlan, he said, "Care to take a walk, Your Grace?"

Lachlan pushed away from the wall and started down the road. "I thought you'd be helping Muirella clear the table."

Jamie laughed. "The lass'll be clearing my table soon enough."

"If anyone can soften her heart, it'll be you, Jamie. But, blessed Saint Ninian, she's a handful."

Jamie grew thoughtful. "I think I'm in love."

Lachlan drew on the pipe. With a sensible and fair man like Jamie in Easter Ross, petty squabbles could be avoided. "Would you stay here, Jamie?"

"Truth to tell, I favor Kelgie." He waved a hand over the village below. "The salty air, the people."

"The women?"

Laughter rumbled in Jamie's chest. "Aye, I like one well enough."

Footfalls sounded behind them. Jamie turned. "What in Saint Ninian's—" He made a grunting noise, and like a fallen oak, then crashed to the ground.

Lachlan turned. A fist slammed into his face. Pain exploded in his jaw. He staggered but managed to stay on his feet. Shaking his head to clear it, he looked for his attackers. He found himself in the center of a ring of at least a dozen shadowed figures.

Flint struck steel. A lantern sprang to life, illuminating the slightly altered face of Neville Smithson. Lachlan hadn't blacked the bastard's eye; he'd broken his nose and the bastard wasn't too grateful.

Lachlan lunged. Neville stepped out of reach. Four pairs of hands locked on Lachlan's arms. He yanked in vain against the combined strength of the sheriff's cronies.

"What are you doing here?" demanded Smithson, his features distorted by the lantern light. "Cozying up to Conall?"

Anger and common sense fought a battle inside Lachlan. He was woefully outnumbered. Jamie could be injured or worse. Still, Lachlan couldn't back down. "I'm doing the same thing I always seem to do: I'm cleaning up your mess."

"Go back to Kinbairn. I'll deal with Squire Mac-Kenzie."

Patience fled. "The way you have dealt with the others? Blessed Saint Ninian, Neville, you've made a shambles of Easter Ross. The English hate the Scots. The Scots hate the English. I see a war coming. You haven't governed here. You've caused dissension. What's happened to you?"

Neville sneered; the crooked nose lent an evil quality to his archangelic face. "I've learned my lesson. I know how to deal with MacKenzies."

The lantern jerked. The pool of light fell on Jamie. His chest rose and fell. Lachlan relaxed. He knew how to deal with his enemy. "If you want violence, Neville, you'll get it."

Smithson chuckled wickedly and pointed to his bent nose. "You should know about that."

"You had no right to bring Catherine to my home."

"She insisted, and as sheriff I thought it my duty to oblige her."

Fierce protectiveness toward the lassies rose in Lachlan. "Don't ever do it again. And don't start a war you can't win."

Neville cocked his arm. "First battle to me."

Lachlan tried to duck, but the hands held him fast. The blow hit him square in the nose. He heard a crunch. Pain knifed through his head. The next blow slammed into his gut. His breath whooshed out. Another blow doubled him over. His knees turned to jelly. His stomach roiled.

The arms released him. He crumpled to the ground. His assailants disappeared into the warrenlike alleys.

His head throbbed as if a spike had been driven into his face. Warm blood trickled from his nose and seeped into his mouth. He spat out the viscous metallic taste. Taking a deep breath, he clutched his nose and jerked it back into place. And almost left his supper in the lane.

Neville would rue this night, and Lachlan knew the way to get the slimy bastard to see reason. First, he'd put Jamie safe in the arms of Muirella. Then he'd head for Tain and do what should have been done long ago.

"Tell us the story of the starving Pilgrims and the Indians who gave them food," said Mary.

Agnes plumped her pillow. "Nay. Tell us the story about the slave boy who saved the tobacco field from burning."

Wearing mobcaps and flannel sleeping gowns, the four girls perched on their beds. Juliet sat on a chair by the lamp table.

Lottie said, "I want to hear about the beautiful princess who had lots of servants."

"We've heard those." Sarah lay on her stomach, her chin propped on her hands. "Tell us a new story about a poor orphan girl who finds out that her mother is a fairy princess."

"Very well," said Juliet, "but I'll have to think about that one."

A sad story came to mind—the tale of a Virginia governess who came to Scotland with grand visions of finding her sister's child. Instead of celebrating a reunion, the lonely bond servant had fallen in love with a nobleman and his four motherless daughters.

As soon as Cogburn returned she'd leave Glasgow, empty-handed, empty-hearted. Never again would she see these adorable children. Or their incredible father. At the thought of Lachlan, pain constricted her chest.

He hated her now, misunderstood her. Perhaps that was best. Life would go on for him, she thought morosely. He'd have Lillian's child and the other girls. Juliet would have only memories.

Mary was not her niece; unexpectedly, the information saddened her. Dear Mary. Anyone would be proud to call her their own.

A knock sounded at the door. Thinking it might be the duke, Juliet jumped. Oh, dear, she knew she must look a mess. Quickly she smoothed back her hair.

The door opened. Cook stood on the threshold. A worried frown wrinkled her brow and her hands plucked at her apron.

"Please come, Mistress White."

At the urgency in her voice, Juliet pushed from the chair. "I'll be back in a moment. Don't touch the lamp."

She walked to the door and tried to pull it closed. The oak panel stuck in place. Turning, she saw four worried faces staring up at her. "Get back into bed and stay put."

Grumbling, the girls obeyed. Juliet closed the door.

Once in the hall, Cook broke into tears. "He's done it now, and Saint Ninian help us." She dabbed at her tears with the skirt of her apron. "I tried to doctor him, but he'd have none of it. And the boy, bless him. Kidnapped. 'Tis a shame is what it is." She grasped Juliet's shoulders. "You must help His Grace."

Hardly able to breathe, Juliet said, "Is Lachlan hurt?"

Cook nodded. "Aye, indeed. And he bloodied my best set of towels already."

Juliet grew cold inside. "Where is he?"

Her voice muffled by the apron, Cook said, "His study."

"Have you sent for a doctor?"

"Nay." She sniffed. "Wouldn't let me."

Juliet raced down the stairs. The door to the duke's study stood open. Seated behind his desk, his head down, he held a towel over his face. Framed by the two wing chairs, he was the image of a defeated warrior.

He lifted his head. The breath stalled in her throat.

A massive swelling hid his elegant nose. Black-and-blue rimmed both eyes, the right one a puffy slit. Blood caked his upper lip and stained his shirt.

"Sweet Virginia," she whispered and started toward him. "What's happened to you?"

He waved a blood-soaked towel. "Go back to bed, Juliet," he said, his voice hollow and nasal, like that of a child with a cold. "This is none of your affair."

The heated words spoken that afternoon hung between them and held her motionless. "Don't shut me out," she said softly.

He dropped his head. "I can't. You've already done that."

She skirted the wing chairs that faced his desk. "Let me see. What happened to you?"

"I ran into the sheriff's fists." He motioned her away again. " 'Tis nothing, Juliet."

"Oh, Lachlan, fighting is no way to settle your differences." She pried his hand from his face, took his chin in her palm, and studied the bruises, the once-elegant nose. Her stomach floated to her throat.

"Am I still a handsome devil?"

His flippancy took the edge off her shock. "Ice will reduce the swelling. Give me that." She took the towel from him and wiped the blood from his upper lip.

He winced and tried to jerk away. "Are you trying to finish what Neville started?"

She held him fast. "Be still."

A rustling noise sounded behind her. Turning, she

spied a boy of about ten seated in one of the chairs. He shot to his feet. Lanky and fair-haired with clear blue eyes and the beauty of an angel, he reminded her of someone. He wore only a sleeping gown, which dangled above his skinny ankles and slippered feet.

The boy Cook had spoken of. Kidnapped. By the duke?

"How do you do?" He bowed from waist.

Her gaze whipped back to the duke.

The hollow sound of his voice came through his nose. "Meet David Smithson. David, this is Mistress White, governess to my children. David is our guest."

Cook marched into the room. "Guest!" she spat. "Ye kidnapped him. As if there ain't enough trouble in Easter Ross already. You had to go and—"

"*Haud yer weehsht,*" he hissed, then grunted in pain.

Stunned, Juliet looked from the boy, who busied himself with a brass paperweight, to the duke, who appeared ready to faint.

"Cook," she said, "fetch ice from the snow box in the cellar and clean towels. And laudanum."

Cursing under her breath, the woman left the room.

The duke grasped Juliet's wrist. "I don't need your help. I don't want laudanum."

"That's unfortunate, because you're going to get both." To the boy she said, "Don't be afraid, David. No one will hurt you."

Cocking his head to one side, the boy stared at her as if she'd spoken in Greek. "I'm not in the least afraid, Mistress White. His Grace of Ross has merely chosen the Highland way to settle his differences with my father. I'm perfectly safe."

Aghast, Juliet said, "But he kidnapped you."

David returned the paperweight to the duke's cluttered desk. "You mustn't be alarmed. Kidnapping is a time-honored tradition among the clans of Scotland. It offers my father and His Grace the opportunity to come to agreement on whatever it is that stands between them. Why, in the fifteenth century, the Gordons and the MacDonalds effectively ended a twenty-year feud by the kidnapping of—"

"Enough, David," growled the duke. "Sit down."

Neville's son smiled apologetically and sat down. He gazed unaffectedly around the room. He was enjoying the adventure.

Furious at the duke, Juliet said, "How could you snatch that child from his bed? It's barbaric."

"I had no choice," he grumbled. "And stop shouting like a fishwife."

Her heart ached at the pain he couldn't hide. Still, he'd done a dreadful thing. "You look terrible."

"Then don't look at me."

"Actually, he looks a good deal better than my father did a fortnight ago. The duke broke my father's nose, you see. It still sports a rather ugly kink on the bridge. But I'd say it was tit for tat. Wouldn't you, Mistress White?"

The duke opened his mouth. Juliet slapped the towel over it. He sucked in his breath.

She smiled. "I'm not sure what to say, David. Except that I think we should be quiet about the idiocy of overgrown boys."

"Of course. I do apologize for rambling on, as Mother says."

The duke's fist hit the desk.

David resumed his inspection of the room.

Cook returned, carrying a bowl of hard-packed snow and a stack of towels. Juliet broke the snow into small pieces and wrapped them in a towel.

"Lean back. Or better yet, let me help you to bed."

"I'm fine."

At the absurdity of the statement, Juliet's patience snapped. "You're going to bed." She grasped his arm and tried to pull him to his feet.

"Ouch!" He drew back.

"Let me see." She lifted his shirt. Rippling muscles blossomed with bruises. "Get up this instant."

With great effort, he lumbered to his feet. She ducked under his arm and wrapped her own around his waist. "Upstairs."

He sighed, but allowed her to guide him around the

desk. "David," he said, his voice as hard as stone, "you're not to leave this house. Do you understand?"

The boy's eyes grew large. "I wouldn't dream of it, Your Grace. I'm well aware of the rules of kidnapping. My mother's a MacLeod, you know. They and the Munros—"

The duke groaned.

"Yes, well," stammered David, "I don't suppose you'd be interested at this time."

Baffled, Juliet said, "Wait here, David. I'll be back. I'll put you in a guest room. Tomorrow I'll see you home."

"Nay," said the duke. "He stays here, and you stay out of Scottish affairs."

"The duke is absolutely correct, Mistress White. Nothing would be solved by returning me. This way, my father and His Grace will—"

"David . . ."

The boy stopped and nodded vigorously.

"Sit down at that desk, David, and pen your mother a letter," Juliet said. "Tell her you're unharmed and in no danger."

"May I, Your Grace?"

"Aye, David," he said.

He attempted another step. His knees buckled and his weight landed on her shoulders. Juliet staggered, but managed to brace her legs and stay upright. His arms dangled and his head lolled to one side. Veering left and right, she guided him to the stairs. "Hold the rail."

"I don't need your help."

"Humor me."

He continued to grumble that he was all right. But when they reached his bed, he collapsed. Juliet placed the snow-filled cloth on his face.

She removed his shirt and boots. Purple and red splotches painted his arms and chest. She gently touched his swollen ribs.

"It looks worse than it is," he said tightly. "Don't trouble yourself."

"I'm just trying to help. Stop being so stubborn and prideful."

"My pride is not the problem, Juliet."

"Look on the bright side. If the sheriff managed to do this to you, I'm sure you left him in a worse state."

On a bitter half-laugh he said, "I never landed a punch. A dozen of his thugs saw to that."

"You fought a dozen men?"

" 'Twasn't much of a fight, Juliet."

"That's unfair. Neville Smithson should be more like his son."

"The lassies together don't ramble on as he does."

"Sarah sometimes does. David's afraid. He has pride, too, you know."

"Aye. From his mother's side."

Juliet bathed his wounds, then poured the laudanum into a glass of water. "Here, drink this."

With one good eye, he glared at her. "I don't want it."

"Drink it."

He clamped his lips shut.

"I could fetch David. I'm sure he can find the words to convince you."

"Will you leave me be if I drink that vile concoction?"

"Yes." She held the glass to his lips.

He gulped it down.

"I'll just say good night to the girls, then I'll be back."

"Nay."

She took his hand. "I know you're angry with me, and I'm sorry for that. I didn't mean I don't *want* a child from you."

He turned his head away. "I understood perfectly what you meant."

"It's just that I can't have a child."

"You needn't belabor the point."

Pain tore at her. "Please try to understand. There are things in my life—" She stopped, unwilling to bare her soul to the man she couldn't have, to the man who'd been responsible for Lillian's death.

"I understand more than you know, Juliet White."

"What is that supposed to mean?"

He yawned. "Whatever you choose."

She got to her feet. Now was not the time for such a discussion. "Rest. I'll be back."

On leaden feet, she walked to the girls' room. The rumpled beds were empty. She blew out the lamp and went downstairs. When she reached the duke's study, she heard Agnes's voice.

"Who are you?"

"I'm David MacLeod Smithson. Who are you?"

"I'm Agnes Elizabeth MacKenzie."

"I'm Mary Margaret MacKenzie."

"I'm Charlotte Antoinette MacKenzie."

"I'm Sarah Suisan MacKenzie."

"Forgive my appearance," he said. "I usually don't appear in public in my nightclothes."

"What are you doing here?" demanded Lottie.

"I'm a hostage."

"Sarah," hissed Agnes, "what's a hostage?"

Juliet stepped into the room. The girls formed a circle around David, who stood stiffly, a folded sheet of foolscap in his hand. "David Smithson is our guest, and I expect you to treat him as such."

"Smithson," mused Sarah. "Are you perchance related to the sheriff of Easter Ross?"

Her sisters stared, gape-mouthed. As one, they stepped back.

David stood taller. "Yes. Or I should say 'aye' since I'm in a Scottish home. The sheriff is my father."

Agnes stepped forward, her fists upraised. "He's a foosty scunner. We hate him."

David blinked in obvious confusion. "Why?"

"Because he's a ruffian," said Lottie. "He outlaws good Scottish folks."

"And our papa hates him," Mary put in.

David surveyed them. "Your father?"

Lottie traced one of her eyebrows. "The duke of Ross."

He looked pleadingly at Juliet.

"That's enough, young ladies," she said. "I told you to stay in your room. Whose idea was it to disobey me?"

Four heads bowed, but none of the girls spoke.

"Off to bed with you."

Lottie stuck her nose in the air. "We'd better put away the good silver."

"Lottie!"

She led the troupe out of the room, their outraged murmurs trailing after them.

David stared at the floor, one slippered foot covering the other. "Are they always so forthright?" he asked.

One moment he seemed so mature, the next a child. "The girls are quite friendly, truly they are."

He smiled uncertainly and handed over the letter. "That girl doesn't like me. I wouldn't have stolen the silver."

Juliet wanted to hug him. "Of course you wouldn't. Your father would arrest you."

"Oh, he'd never do—" He halted, then laughed. "You were making a jest. How kind of you."

"Lottie is sometimes impertinent, but she didn't mean to hurt your feelings."

Smiling, he smoothed his hair. "I'm sure you're right."

"I intend to visit your parents tomorrow."

"My father went to Dingwall. He won't be home for a week or so. But Mother will be most glad to see you."

Juliet settled him into a guest room, then returned to the duke's bedside.

Under the influence of laudanum, the duke slept soundly, but during the early hours of the morning he grew fitful, pulling the cold towel from his face and calling out her name.

"I'm here, Lachlan." She pried his fist free of the blanket and twined her fingers with his. He slumbered peacefully again.

As the pearly light of dawn seeped into the room, she gazed at his hand, so tightly wound with hers. Pale, feminine skin contrasted sharply with sun-browned strength. She'd seen gentleness in this hand—a hand that had wiped the tears from his daughters' faces, a hand that had stroked their heads in slumber.

Her mind savored the image of her hand in his, and her heart cataloged the love and security the picture implied. She carefully tucked it away amid a gallery of memories of Scotland.

Warm tears rolled down her cheeks. His hand squeezed hers. Startled, she looked up and found him watching her.

Against the purplish bruises that masked his face, his eyes shone a vivid, glassy blue. The ice pack had brought down the swelling, but days would pass before his nose returned to normal. An image from Virginia came to mind. She smiled.

"What's so funny?" he whispered.

"You look like a raccoon."

He pulled her toward him. "What's a raccoon?"

Feeling as weak as a kitten fresh from the womb, she allowed him to pull her against his side. "A furry animal with markings like a black mask over his eyes and rings on his tail."

His hand roamed her back, her arm.

Familiar feelings of security, of longing, stirred to life.

"You haven't checked my tail."

She chuckled, and decided that if she should ever marry, her husband would have to have a sense of humor. "Nor do I intend to. How do you feel?"

"Like I was trampled by a herd of Highland cattle."

"You should sleep."

His hand slipped around her waist. "First tell me why you were crying."

She dredged up the safest answer. "I was worried about you."

Lachlan sent her a calculating gaze. "Did you worry so over Mabry?"

"It wasn't necessary. He doesn't have enemies who blacken his eyes."

"What did he say when you told him you wanted to come to Scotland?"

A lie leapt to her tongue, but she couldn't speak it. "He wished me well on my journey."

Lachlan hugged her, then grunted in pain. "Tell me again about Virginia."

She spoke of the long days of harvest and of the celebration that followed. When his hand stilled and his chest rose and fell, she eased from the bed. She donned a plain woolen dress, fetched David's letter, and let herself out the back door.

The time had come for her to take action and settle this ridiculous feud.

Chapter 16

Crisp air, ripe with the promise of spring, surrounded her. To the south, the formal gardens looked like a lad after his first barbering. Beds of yellow and red tulips, and snow white crocuses splashed the land with color. Shoots of heather and gorse pierced the freshly tilled ground. The herb garden, planted in the shape of a cinquefoil, was covered with worn blankets that kept the frost from the tender plants during the cool nights.

To the east, the sun climbed over a bank of clouds that resembled great sheets of white slate. According to the duke, summer was on its way, but Juliet wouldn't be here to see it. Sadness tugged at her. She hastened her steps and rounded the corner that led to the circular drive. A herd of sheep grazed on the front lawn.

She turned to look back at the house. And saw David Smithson framed in the window of the guest chamber. He smiled and waved.

She smiled, too, and lifted her hand. Then she began the half-mile walk to the other end of the cobblestone street.

Situated on hills at either end of Clan Row, Rosshaven and the home of the sheriff of Easter Ross faced each other. The sheriff's sprawling mansion had once been home to the laird of Clan MacLeod. No one in the duke's household had dared venture to the other end of the street. Until last night, when the duke had kidnapped David.

As she descended the hill, Juliet passed cottages, the

doors decorated with dried heather, the yards featuring budding rowan trees. Maids in woolen dresses and Scottish bonnets, milk pails or baskets in hand, scurried from house to stables.

But as she started the upward climb to her destination, the houses took on a distinctly English flavor. Most were surrounded by hedgerows and boxwoods and beds of blooming pansies. Maids in cotton frocks with starched mobcaps and aprons wielded brooms. None paused in their labors, but all watched Juliet's progress.

Differences abounded here. How could a governess from Virginia serve as messenger between two men from such divergent cultures? Apprehension at the meeting to come gnawed at her stomach.

At the top of the hill, she stopped and blinked in disbelief, for before her lay an unlikely sight: a field of tobacco plants. Only half of the sowed seeds had sprouted. The shoots were stunted from lack of moisture and sunlight, the leaves withered by the Highland frost. What had made the sheriff think he could grow such a crop here?

Puzzled, Juliet marched to the servants' entrance and reached for the bell.

"Hello," said a voice behind her. "May I help you?"

Turning, Juliet spied a tiny, dark-haired woman emerging from the stable, an egg basket in her hand. Beneath a woolen shawl, she wore a robe, which parted to reveal the advanced condition of her pregnancy.

"Hello. I'm Juliet White. I'd like to see Lady Bridget."

A smile of curiosity brought a gaminelike quality to the woman's delicate features. "I'm Bridget Smithson, and you're neither Scottish nor English."

Juliet curtsied, saying, "No, milady. I'm from Virginia, but I'm employed by the duke of Ross."

Lady Bridget came forward, her gait graceful in spite of her condition. Pretty red lips curled into an easy smile. "How is Lachlan?"

Shocked, Juliet said, "You know His Grace?"

Laughter shimmered in her eyes. "Aye. We were playmates as children, although I'm older by two years."

"Impossible." The word flew from Juliet's lips. Aghast

at having spoken so frankly, she said, "Forgive me. It's just that you look so much younger."

"And aren't you sweet to say so. Come, Juliet White, let's go inside and have tea . . . before the children wake."

Juliet shored up her courage and withdrew the letter. "His Grace kidnapped your son last night. I'm dreadfully sorry, but you mustn't worry. David's well and in good spirits."

Bridget glanced up at the second-floor windows. "I wondered why he was still abed. He usually rises with the sun." Slipping a fingernail under the seal, she opened the letter and began to read. Motherly love wreathed her features.

When her hostess tucked the letter into her pocket, Juliet said, "His Grace would never hurt the boy."

Lady Bridget's shoulders rose and fell. "I know. I suppose it's best, but I'd hoped Neville would see reason before the feud came to this. He's so stubborn." She waved a hand toward the field. "He even refuses to help me with the tobacco."

"I'm surprised you'd try to grow it here."

" 'Twas a mistake." Scorn laced her words. "My father's brand of humor. In his will, he left Neville nothing but a wagonload of seeds, but didn't bother to tell us what kind. I should have foreseen the trick, but I kept hoping Papa would soften his heart. He never liked Neville." Ruefully, she added, "Most Scots don't."

"You could plow under the plants."

"And let my father have his jest? Oh, nay. I'll harvest a crop from this bletherin tobacco if it kills me."

Baffled, Juliet followed the agile woman up a flight of stone steps and into a formal solar. Lady Bridget was not at all what Juliet had expected. "I don't understand. You're not angry about the kidnapping? I thought you'd be frantic."

"I'm too near my time to be frantic. Please sit down." She indicated a glass-topped table surrounded by harp chairs. In a corner sat a brimming toy box and a child-size table covered with slate boards and a miniature tea service.

A uniformed maid entered. Lady Bridget handed over the basket and said, "Fetch three changes of clothing for Master David and his good suit. Find his boots and Sunday shoes, too. Put them in my tapestry traveling bag and set it by the front door. And have Dorcas bring us tea and scones."

Lady Bridget eased into a chair and smoothed her skirts. "There. Now we can get acquainted."

"You intend to let His Grace keep David?" Juliet asked.

"He must," Lady Bridget said, sighing. " 'Tis the only way to get Neville to see reason."

Juliet noticed the burr in Lady Bridget's speech. "You're Scottish."

"Aye. My father was Gibson MacLeod, the earl of Tain."

"Sarah told me about his death. I'm so sorry."

"Don't be sorry. Gibson MacLeod was a cruel, stubborn Scot." She tilted her head inquisitively. "Who is Sarah?"

"One of the duke's four daughters."

"So it's true." She clasped her hands. "Henrietta wrote as much in the *Crier*, but I thought it rumor. She does flower up her stories. How wonderful for him. I also read that you're handfasted to him."

Juliet wiped a smudge from the glass tabletop. "That was a mistake."

"In the reporting or the doing?"

"Both. You have other children?" She hurried on, "Please tell me about them."

Lady Bridget gave Juliet a sly grin, but didn't pursue the matter. For the next hour they exchanged stories of children. Juliet learned that the sheriff and Lady Bridget had five children. David, the eldest, a boy, six, and another, five, followed by two girls, four and three.

"When do you expect the new babe?"

Lady Bridget patted her stomach. "On May Day."

Cogburn would arrive before then, and Juliet would be on her way home. Dread tugged at her heart. If only she could stay in Scotland. If only she could be a wife like Lady Bridget, secure in her position and loved by her husband and children. If only she were free to marry the duke and be a mother to his girls.

During the next week Juliet often visited Lady Bridget. She told herself concern for the boy was the reason, but she listened, all rapt attention, as Bridget revealed the sad story of the childhood of Lachlan MacKenzie, a boy ripped from his home by war, stripped of his lands and titles. An orphan, he'd made his wealth in trade and shipping. Seven years ago he'd persuaded King George to return what the English had taken.

Juliet resisted the duke's formal invitation to resume their intimate relationship. He coaxed and courted, cajoled and connived, but she managed to evade him. Her heart couldn't withstand any more pain.

Neville returned from Dingwall. He blustered threats of revenge but refused to negotiate with the duke for David's release. The Scots in Easter Ross applauded His Grace; the English, astonished that a peer of the realm would resort to barbaric kidnapping, grumbled their profound disapproval.

All of Easter Ross, and especially Tain, became a caldron of discontent. Any day it would boil over.

Scots and English quarreled in the streets and the taverns. When Juliet questioned the duke, he proudly said, "At least they're talking."

Henrietta announced in her column that the Thistle and Badger Tavern had added rum and shepherd's pie to the menu to accommodate the influx of English customers. Henrietta didn't report that a stool had taken flight through the window of said tavern. The tense situation couldn't go on much longer.

Juliet walked into the duke's study and placed a bulky package on his desk. "Lady Bridget sent you this."

He glanced at the brown-wrapped package, but didn't seem curious about the contents. He reared back in the chair, his eyebrows lifted in question. "Visiting her again?"

She had come to loathe that bland, handsome stare. Like a tether, the strain between them grew taut. "Yes."

"Did you see Neville?"

Preoccupied with the mysterious package, Juliet said, "No. He just arrived this morning. He's meeting with the mayor."

"What's on that canny mind of yours, Juliet?"

He knew her so well, yet he didn't know the truth. "Do you know where the sheriff got those tobacco seeds?"

"I don't particularly care."

She told him about the earl's bequest to Neville, about Lady Bridget's determination to protect her husband's pride.

The duke reached for the brass paperweight and rolled it in his hand. He seemed miles away, his brow furrowed. At length he smiled and said, "What's in the package?"

"I wouldn't know. I don't open other people's packages."

"Open that one."

Hearing a dare in the command, she yanked on the string, wishing she were yanking on his braids instead. How could he be so obstinate? How could she love him so?

The wrapping fell open. So did her mouth, for inside lay a magnificent robe of forest green velvet, richly covered with thistles embroidered in golden thread.

His chair hit the floor. "Sweet Saint Andrew, Bridget has done it now."

"What does it mean?"

"Trouble. 'Tis the ceremonial robe of the Order of the Thistle, Scotland's highest badge of chivalry."

"Is it yours?"

A droll chuckle emerged from his lips. "You don't think I deserve it?"

His flippancy fired her temper. "Scotland's idea of chivalry is no concern of mine."

He leaned across the desk and traced one of the thistles. "Nor is it mine at the moment. The robe belonged to my father and to his father before him, and so forth, back to James the Fifth."

Wistfulness dragged at Juliet; she didn't even know

her parents' names. Trailing her hand over the exquisite garment, she said, "How did Lady Bridget get it?"

"My mother gave it to her for safekeeping, because she was convinced I'd one day win back the title," he said tonelessly.

Just before the English hanged her from the chandelier, Juliet thought sadly. "Will you wear it?"

He looked her up and down. "I'd rather see you in it. Wearing nothing else."

Lately she felt alone, adrift. She'd lost her purpose here, and her principles, too. It would be so easy to yield to him, to build one more memory. One more heartache. Virginia and ten years of indenture awaited. On a shaky breath, she said, "No."

"A poor response from the woman who consented to become my mistress. Have your menses come?"

Appalled that he would broach such a delicate subject, Juliet said, "That's none of your concern."

He folded his arms over his chest, but the casual pose belied the intensity in his eyes. "Oh, I think it is. Answer me. Have they?"

"No."

As casually as if he were asking her choice of wines, he said, "Are your breasts tender?"

She marched to the door. "I will not discuss this with you."

In an instant, he loomed behind her. "Then I'll see for myself." His hands closed over her breasts. Pulling her against his chest, he whispered in her ear, "Tell me, Juliet." One hand slipped lower and caressed her belly. "Do you nurture our child here? Will you blossom with a lad or a lassie?"

Heartsick and aching to have him hold her, kiss her once more, she turned in his arms. And fell victim to the full force of his seductive power. He could easily propel her into sweet insanity and distract her from her purpose.

"Tell me," he said in a tone that could as well have meant "Love me."

"I'm not always . . . predictable." Embarrassed, she

flushed, but his tender, encouraging smile urged her on. "I'm not like other women."

Need shone in his eyes, and unable to resist him any longer, she gave him a smile of surrender. His lips moved a breath away from hers. "Nay, lassie. You're like no other woman."

He crushed her to him, and for a moment her breasts did feel tender, but she knew the cause—it was that familiar pull of his masculinity, that urge to be joined with him, to hear him say she made him feel like a great golden eagle soaring above the clouds.

His tongue darted into her mouth, and she gave herself up to his ardor, returned his passion. Craving the feel of his hair in her hands, his cheeks beneath her palms, she caressed him, lingering at a favorite spot below his ear before moving on to the sensitive skin covering his ribs.

"Oh, Juliet." He cupped her hips and pulled her against the trunks of his legs. "I ache for you. Come back to my bed."

Her heart pounded like a tom-tom, and a sigh of contentment rose in her throat. She didn't carry his child; she couldn't dare dream of having a part of him to love forever. He could control his passions and ensure that she didn't conceive; he'd done so before. Could she risk loving him more than she did now?

At the sound of tramping feet and giggling children, she stepped back. Studying her hands, she said, "You promised to take David riding, and I promised the girls they could practice with their bows and arrows."

"Tonight," he vowed. "First we'll make love in the bath, then before the fire." Grinning like the rake he was, he added, "After that, we'll use our imagination."

She was saved a reply when a knock sounded at the door. Would that she could save her breaking heart so easily.

Later she stood on the rear lawn with Jamie and the girls. One hundred child-paces away stood the new archery target that featured a drawing of Neville Smithson wearing horns and missing his front teeth.

Mary let an arrow fly. It slammed into the target and pierced the comical Neville between the eyes.

"Sarah," said Mary, "it's your turn to fetch the arrows."

Sarah, blond braids streaming behind her, dashed toward the target.

Idly, Juliet searched the horizon for a party of horsemen. The duke had ridden out with David and a dozen soldiers. A ploy, he'd said, to show the English citizens that Neville's son was unharmed and enjoying himself.

Sarah yelled, "I can only find eleven arrows."

Mary motioned for her to keep searching. "Look farther that way. Lottie tried to hit the boats in the harbor."

"Did not."

"Did so."

Sarah darted behind the target and dropped out of sight over the hill. A moment later a terrified scream rent the air. Jamie took off like a streak. Juliet picked up her skirts and ran as fast as she could. Her mind filled with visions of Sarah tumbling down the bracken-covered hill, her body bloody and broken. Behind Juliet scampered Agnes, Lottie, and Mary.

"Look!" screamed Agnes. "It's the sheriff, and he's got Sarah!"

Juliet saw him then. Mounted on a galloping horse and thundering down the hill, he held a screaming Sarah face down on the saddle, her arms and legs flailing. Jamie leapt patches of dead bracken in an attempt to catch the fleeing horse. "Stop you bletherin bastard!" he yelled.

Bitter hatred engulfed Juliet. How dare these men use gentle Sarah as a pawn in their silly game!

"Shoot him, Mary," said Agnes.

An arrow whizzed past Juliet. To her surprise and delight, it pierced the sheriff's shoulder. But the shot had little power at such a distance. He brushed off the arrow as if it were a mosquito and dug his heels into the horse's flanks.

"Hoots, Mary!" Agnes squealed, jumping up and

down. "You shot the foosty sheriff. I'll get my pony. You ride behind me and shoot the bugger again."

Mary started gathering the fallen arrows. Agnes ran for the stables.

"Come back here this instant, Agnes MacKenzie," Juliet said. "Stop that, Mary. You're not going anywhere."

"But, Mistress White . . ." Agnes wailed.

"You'd never catch up to him." Burning with helpless anger, Juliet watched the sheriff ride away with Sarah.

"Oh, Mistress White," wailed Lottie, "what will happen to her?"

Juliet's mind whirled. Lady Bridget would care for the girl—if the sheriff took Sarah home. Surely he would.

Jamie dragged himself up the hill. Panting and flushed, he held his heaving sides.

"Find His Grace at once," Juliet said.

"Aye," he grumbled, heading for the stables. "And there'll be hell to pay."

Juliet ordered the girls inside. She paced the foyer until she heard horses' hooves on the drive. Shaking with anger, she marched to the front door and threw it open. And came face to face with the forbidding figure of the duke of Ross.

Nostrils flaring, his brows arched, his mouth set in a hard line, he glared at her. "So, Juliet White," he snapped, "you've managed to lose another of my children."

"Me?" Dumbfounded, she let her instincts take over. She drew back her arm and slapped him. "This wretched business is all your fault."

He grabbed her wrist and dragged her into the study.

"Let me go!" She tried to pull away, but his hand gripped her like a steel manacle.

He shoved her into a chair and stood over her. "Whose idea was it to help Neville kidnap Sarah, yours or Bridget's? Or did the three of you cook up this scheme together?"

Blind fury seized Juliet. "Why, you miserable cur!" She stood up. "How dare you accuse me?"

He pushed her back down.

"What are you doing? What are you talking about? He took Sarah." Her voice broke and she couldn't stop the tears. "He snatched her up like a sack of meal. She was screaming. And all you can do is rave about bargaining." Knotting her fists, she raised them to her mouth. Her teeth sank into her knuckles, but still she couldn't get herself under control.

"Whose idea was it?" he demanded.

"Go to the devil." But even as she spoke the angry words, an idea came to mind. Lady Bridget hadn't been upset about David's kidnapping. Lady Bridget had sworn to save her husband's pride. Lady Bridget was a Highlander, same as Lachlan. Lady Bridget knew the duke and her husband would not come to terms, so she was trying to force them, to put them on equal footing.

As menacing as a deadly snake ready to strike, the duke said, "Do you know what you've done, Juliet?" Whirling, he slammed his fist through a carved oak screen. The wood splintered. "Blessed Christ, woman! I had Neville right where I wanted him. He had to bargain with me."

Words failed Juliet.

"Why did you send Sarah to fetch the arrows?"

"Fetching arrows is part of archery. If it weren't for you and your absurd feud, we could live here in safety."

"Why Sarah, damn you? And why can't you ever tell me the truth?"

Squeezing her eyes shut, Juliet calmly said, "He would have kidnapped any of the four."

"Either you don't understand or you're as cruel as—"

"Understand?" she shouted. The absurdity of his statement hit her like a blow. "Does anyone in this stupid, backward country understand anything? Why are we arguing? Go get her!"

He plopped into the chair beside her. "I can't."

The next morning the upstairs maid slipped a note into Juliet's hand. Even before she opened it, she knew who'd written it. Love squeezed her heart as she read Sarah's childish words.

Dear Mistress White,

You mustn't worry about me, as I am perfectly
well. The sheriff didn't hurt me. After I quit screaming, I was very brave, just like David when Papa
took him. The lady Bridget said you should be
proud of me. I miss you and Papa and Lottie and
Agnes and Mary. Lady Bridget says I can come
home as soon as Papa and the sheriff stuff away
their pride and speak to each other. I play with the
other children here, and read books from the sheriff's library.

Tell Papa I love him. I love you, too. I'm glad
you're handfasted. You'll be my mama soon.

Your loving pupil,
Miss Sarah Suisan MacKenzie

At the bottom of the neatly penned letter was a note
from Lady Bridget asking Juliet to keep the letter a
secret, especially from the duke. That way the men
might come to an agreement sooner.

Juliet smiled and put the letter with Lillian's. So the
sheriff's wife had indeed engineered the kidnapping.
Juliet just hoped the sheriff wasn't as mad at Lady
Bridget as the duke was at Juliet. She must do something to end the feud. But what?

For the next week the duke dogged Juliet's heels, one
day an apology on his lips, the next day an accusation.
Frustrated and hurt, she refused to listen or to speak to
him. His three daughters, and sometimes David, ferried
oral messages to her, which she ignored. She tried to
come up with a plan to aid Lady Bridget in her effort
to bring peace between the duke and the sheriff. But
nothing feasible came to mind.

The pens of Flora MacKenzie and Henrietta Worthingham flew. For the first time in its existence, the *Tain
Crier* hit the streets daily. It was one thing, the lady
journalists said, to capture a strapping lad, but quite
another to abscond with a sweet-faced lass who'd served
tea to most of the prominent citizens and curtsied prettily to all of them.

English and Scot alike rose to Sarah's defense. Boxes of scones and shortbread, jugs of milk and cider, appeared on the sheriff's doorstep. Not to be outdone, the English citizens sent baskets of fruit and cherry tarts by the dozen, pretty polls and china tea sets.

The duke made an event of buying David a fine, swift mare with, according to Henrietta, a mouth like butter and the disposition of a lamb. Every morning the duke and his hostage rode boldly through the streets of Tain.

Sarah never made an appearance.

The sheriff issued a statement saying that the girl was as healthy as her mulish father.

Flora MacKenzie dared him to prove it.

The mayor demanded he produce Sarah. Neville refused. The mayor and the leading businessmen, both English and Scots, came to console His Grace of Ross. A case of liquor later, they'd managed the task and gotten the duke dead drunk in the process.

Although a kidnapper himself, the duke of Ross suddenly became the injured party.

Without their sister, Mary, Lottie, and Agnes turned into wayward, whining souls. They ate little and slept less.

By the beginning of the second week, Juliet knew what she had to do. She penned a note to Lady Bridget and sent the maid Lucy to deliver it.

Once the duke left for his morning ride and Cook left for market, Juliet ordered each of the girls to pack a bag.

"Where are we going?" demanded a petulant Lottie.

"You'll see."

In ten minutes, their bags packed, the girls appeared downstairs. Like a goose with her goslings, Juliet led the way down the hill. From the opposite direction came Lady Bridget, her brood skipping along behind her. Curious faces, belonging to both English and Scots, appeared at windows. Murmuring crowds congregated on the street.

Juliet stopped and ordered the girls to march in single file. Lady Bridget did the same with her children. As they passed each other, Lady Bridget chuckled and said, "Lachey will come home to a surprise, won't he?"

A maid answered Juliet's knock on the door of the sheriff's home. Juliet strolled inside and told the girls to follow. The sheriff appeared and stood staring at her, a map roll in his hand. He looked haggard, his fair hair in disarray, dark circles under his eyes.

"What's the meaning of this?" he demanded.

As if she hadn't a care in the world, Juliet began removing her gloves. "It's quite simple, sir. Since you insist on keeping Sarah, you'll have to keep us all."

The sheriff of Easter Ross looked as if a snake had crawled up his leg.

Lottie, Mary, and Agnes, bless them, didn't say a word.

Sarah skipped into the room. "Oh, Mistress White!" she exclaimed, her eyes as large as tea saucers. "And Agnes, Mary, Lottie!" She rushed forward and embraced her sisters and Juliet.

"White?" Like the clanging of a bell, the sheriff's voice boomed through the foyer.

Four small bodies huddled close to Juliet. Anticipation knotted her stomach, for if her suspicions were correct, he had known Lillian. "Yes. My name is Juliet White, and I'm from Virginia."

"Bloody bones!" His archangelic face froze in surprise. The map crumpled in his hand.

"Don't you hurt her," said Agnes, "or my sister will shoot you again."

Mary brandished her bow. He didn't take his eyes off Juliet.

For the first time since leaving Kinbairn Castle, Juliet sensed that her goal was within reach. But would Smithson tell her what she needed to know?

Neville's surprise turned to cool disdain. "Take yourselves to the nursery," he said to the duke's children. "I'd like to speak with Mistress White. Alone." Pivoting on his heel, he slapped the rolled map against his thigh and strolled through an open door.

The girls didn't budge.

Lottie's haughty gaze was fixed on the stairs. "I insist on having a room to myself."

"Mistress White!" bellowed the sheriff. "I'm waiting."

"Go," said Juliet. "And behave yourselves."

Hope and fear in her heart, Juliet walked into his study.

Chapter 17

Eager to see Juliet and his daughters and find out what all the commotion was about, Lachlan kicked his mount to a canter. Sheep scattered on the lawn. Beside him, David flapped his elbows, urging the dainty mare to keep pace. Side by side, they mounted the hill to Rosshaven Castle.

A breeze from Dornoch Firth rustled the noontime air and cooled Lachlan's brow. Summer would be along soon, a glorious time in the Highlands. He missed the peace and tranquillity of Kinbairn. He missed peace and tranquillity in general.

And he missed Sarah.

A fierce pain twisted his gut. Unassuming, sweethearted Sarah had become a pawn in a game of vengeance. She was well cared for by Bridget, the mayor and Henrietta Worthingham had assured him of that. But Lachlan worried that Sarah might not understand why she'd been kidnapped. She could recite the Acts of Parliament, but, God love her, she couldn't comprehend the problems in Easter Ross.

He drew rein. "Take the horses to the stable, David."

"Of course, Your Grace." David craned his neck to look back toward town. "Uh . . . . may I ask you something, sir?"

Amused at the lad's intuitiveness, Lachlan said, "Certainly, David."

"Why was everyone staring at us today?"

Lachlan scanned the street. Maids swept the stoops,

a task that should have been completed hours ago. Groups of people dotted the yards. What were they doing? "I wondered about that myself."

David scratched his head. "It's very strange. Mrs. MacKenzie, the collier's wife, snickered at me. And look"—he pointed to the house across the street—"those people never open their drapes. And look there. See Lady Crossbridge and Mrs. MacKenzie-the-music-teacher? They haven't spoken in years."

"Most likely they've made up their quarrels. That, or they have little else to occupy them. I don't think anyone intended to be cruel to you."

David sat straight in the saddle, the reins held loosely in his hands. "I'm sure they wouldn't, sir. Shall I tell the stable master to give the horses oats? They've had a hard ride and deserve a bit of pampering."

In more than appearance, Neville had left his mark on the lad, for David was as intelligent as his father. "Aye, but don't tarry. Lottie will be setting the table."

"Aye, sir. She's awfully persnickety about table manners and such."

Lachlan dismounted and passed over the reins. Had one woman closed Neville's brilliant mind to the people and the culture of Scotland? Short of revealing the damning past, what could Lachlan do to open it? "Who the devil knows," he grumbled, letting himself in the front door.

He stepped into chaos.

Each of the banisters hosted a hooting lad. A pair of lassies sat beneath the chandelier and played tug with a worn blanket. In the center of the mayhem stood a very pregnant, very familiar woman.

"Bridget?"

Spreading her arms, she raised her eyes to the chandelier. "Welcome home to Easter Ross, Lachey. Or should I say, Your Grace?"

A sense of foreboding prickled his skin. "Lachlan will be fine, Bridget."

Shrieks bounced off the stone walls of the foyer. "It's the duke of Ross! Run for your life!" shouted the elder of the lads. In unison he and his counterpart slid down the banisters and dove behind Bridget's skirt. The terrified lassies, stiff with fear, screwed up their faces and began to wail.

Struck dumb, Lachlan leaned against the door.

"Mary Catherine! Margaret Ann!" Bridget admonished, *Haud yer wheesht!* He's not a monster."

"Oh, yes he is," said the elder lad, peeking around her skirt. "He hangs bairns from the castle walls until their skin rots off. Then he feeds their bones to the badgers."

"That's quite enough, Robert." She turned to the younger lad. "Edward, stand up."

In a pitiful voice, the lad said, "No. I'm afraid of badgers. I want to go home."

They sounded like his lassies speaking of Neville. The younger lass buried her face in the blanket. Her head was covered with a mop of black ringlets, reminiscent of the child Bridget had been, the child who had been his friend. In spite of his anger, Lachlan felt his heart soften.

Bridget patted her younger son on the head. "We can't go home just yet."

An ugly suspicion took root in Lachlan's mind. Perhaps this homecoming was the reason behind the curious stares and the sudden camaraderie in Easter Ross. He pushed away from the wall. "Where's Juliet?"

Bridget gave him a sassy smile. "Guess."

"And my children?"

Bridget twisted her wedding band.

Like summer lightning on the moon-dark moors, the answer flashed in his mind and sparked his ire: Juliet had taken his lassies to Neville. Everyone in town knew of the exchange.

Why had he trusted her again? Why had he forgotten her quest in Scotland? Was she now cozying up to Neville, using her clever wiles to wheedle the truth from him?

But Neville didn't know the truth.

"Now, Lachey," said Bridget, "you always did squinch up your face like that when you were angry. 'Twas part my idea, part hers."

He stepped forward. The bairns yelped. Sweet Saint Ninian, these bairns were as frightened of him as his lassies were of Neville. "You listen to me, Bridget Mac-Leod. I'm not some ignorant farmer too stupid to see through the tricks cooked up by a couple of meddling women."

Her chin jutted out. "Don't you be putting words in my mouth, Lachlan MacKenzie. And I'm Bridget Smith-son now, and I never said you were stupid. You did." She folded her hands over her stomach. "I don't cook, either."

"Does Neville know you're here?"

A halo couldn't have made her look more innocent. "I'm sure he does by now."

"Christ!" Lachlan spat. "Why couldn't you have married a Scotsman eleven years ago?"

Calmly she said, "Because I didn't fall in love with a Scotsman eleven years ago."

Disgruntled, he said, "Well, I wish you had. 'Twould've saved me a bushel of trouble."

Hands on her hips, she stepped forward. The two lads moved with her. "Don't you be blaming me. There's more than a bushel of your clansmen in Easter Ross who wouldn't be happy if Bonnie Prince Charlie himself sat on the throne. Oh, the pranks they can pull."

Thinking of Conall MacKenzie, Lachlan silently agreed.

"Did you know," she said in a caustic tone, "that on Hogmanay last, the MacKenzies of Invergordon, after drinking the alehouse dry, offered to sweep the stoops of the English citizens?"

" 'Tis a fine custom, Bridget, sweeping out the bad luck."

"Not if you dip the brooms in manure!"

When would the petty rivalry stop? "If your husband would come down off his damned English pedestal and treat them like people, they wouldn't do such things."

Sadly she said, "He's tried, Lachey. I swear he has. They want a Scot to speak for them. They want you. Won't you try to come to terms with Neville?"

"He loathes me."

"But you were great friends at court. What happened?"

"I don't know," he said honestly.

"I think you do."

"Leave it, Bridget."

The lad Robert bounded up the stairs and straddled the banister. Lachlan dashed after him. He snatched up the boy and held him at eye level. The boy went stiff. Lachlan said, "We do not play on the banisters. You could fall and break your neck. Do you understand?"

Color drained from the boy's face. Lowering his voice, Lachlan said, "We do, however, have many safe things for children here. Like picnics on the kitchen floor. Would you like that?"

Robert gulped and nodded. Lachlan put him down.

"Mother!" a surprised David said from the doorway.

A light of sheer joy shone in Bridget's eyes. She went to him, the lad Edward still hanging on to her skirt. Chattering excitedly, the other bairns formed a circle around their eldest sibling.

Lachlan breathed a sigh of relief. If his suspicions were correct, he couldn't talk to Bridget about the problem between him and Neville. Only her husband could.

"I have a horse, Mother," David said. "A mare of my very own, and His Grace says I'll make an excellent rider once I find my seat, which I'm certain will be soon, for I practice ever so hard."

"Aren't you the smart one, lad?" Bridget said, checking his ears, examining his hands.

A knot of envy lodged in Lachlan's throat. He wanted his family back. He felt adrift without his lassies, without Juliet. But he wouldn't pine for her, for once Neville realized who she was and told her his version of a seven-year-old tale, she'd never forgive Lachlan. Only the truth would change her mind. But even if he dared reveal the truth, she probably wouldn't believe him. And it broke his heart to think she'd believe the worst of him.

Her hands on the lad's shoulders, Bridget said, "Take the others to the kitchen. I'd like to speak to His Grace."

Like bairns after the tinker, they followed David from the room. Lachlan held his breath.

"Thank you for buying him the horse and teaching him to ride," she said.

"Neville should have done it."

She clucked her tongue. "Funny, he said the same thing about you and that telescope he bought for Sarah."

Stark terror clutched Lachlan. "He had no right."

"Why not? What's the difference between you riding with David and Neville stargazing with Sarah?"

The answer to that was no one's business but Lachlan MacKenzie's.

Her dark eyes grew sad. "Juliet said you'd see reason. She's perfect for you, you know. Stop growling. You're just too stupid to admit you love her."

"I thought we'd settled the matter of who's stupid and who's not."

"You disappoint me, Lachlan. Juliet and I only wanted to help."

Help, he thought ruefully. He'd have ten kinds of trouble if he didn't get Juliet and his lassies home soon.

"If you truly want to help, Bridget, then tell me how I can make the English accept the Scots."

She arched her brow.

"And vice versa," he grudgingly added.

She took his arm and started down the hall. "I thought you'd never ask."

Juliet clasped her hands to keep them still and waited for the sheriff of Easter Ross to speak. The smell of tobacco and the feel of tightly leashed anger hung in the air. In jerky motions, he unrolled the crushed map and began smoothing out the wrinkles.

Although impeccably dressed in a waistcoat and knee breeches of cocoa brown wool, he looked ragged around the edges. His white cravat threatened to tumble free of its intricate tie, and the lace cuffs of his fancy silk shirt had lost their crispness. Thanks to the kink in his nose and his frayed temper, he now looked more like a downfallen angel than an upstanding choirboy.

"You're Lillian's sister?"

Juliet gasped, and her heart threatened to crack. No

one had ever asked her that question. The Mabrys had never seen Lillian.

He slammed a box over the map to hold it flat. "Don't bother denying it."

Years of bottled-up sorrow and frustration erupted. Knowing she teetered on the verge of tears, she shielded her torment with boldness. "I have no intention of denying it."

Casually he picked up his pipe and tapped out the ashes. "How is dear Lillian?"

Of course he wouldn't know about Lillian's death. The duke had hidden her away at that ancient hospice in Edinburgh, where she'd stay for eternity. "My sister is dead."

The pipe hit the floor. His blue gaze pierced Juliet. "When?"

As if reciting a hard-learned lesson, she said, "The twentieth day of June, seventeen sixty-two."

He snatched up the pipe and peered into its scrimshaw bowl. His hand shook. "So long ago? I'm sorry. I didn't know. I thought— Well, never mind. My condolences to you."

No one had ever told her that, either. No one had bothered with the feelings of an orphaned child. Suddenly Juliet felt like that lonely little girl. "The last time I saw her I was a child. Please tell me about my sister. What was she like?"

"His Grace knew her better than I," he said bitterly.

Neville Smithson had cared about Lillian. Juliet liked him for that. "The duke and I don't discuss my sister."

Neville chuckled. "No, I don't suppose so. A rake of his caliber probably doesn't even recall the face of one woman among hundreds. Poor Lillian."

He said the name so casually, Juliet found the will to trust him, to satisfy an abandoned child's curiosity. "Do I favor her?"

His gaze snapped to her. He studied her face for so long that Juliet half regretted asking the question.

A sad smile gave him a boyish look. "No, you don't. You're taller, thinner. Lillian was—" He rubbed the broken bridge of his nose. "She had a childlike quality about her. She was gay, never troubled with tomorrow. Not, I think, so sensible as you."

"Where did you meet her?"

"At court in London. She was a companion to a titled lady."

Happiness flooded Juliet. Lillian had accomplished much more than she'd set out to do. She'd lived a charmed life at the English court. "Tell me more."

He glanced at the lantern clock. "It's late, Juliet. I've assizes tomorrow, and we have loads of time to discuss Lillian."

He spoke with such fondness that Juliet thought she might break down. For years she imagined meeting Lillian's Scottish friends, hearing about the happy times, the times before the duke of Ross. Suddenly Juliet hated him.

Bolstered, she said, "Lillian died giving birth to the duke's child—a girl."

His mouth curled in a sneer. "Which one?"

"I don't know."

"Ah. And you've fallen in love with him. Don't deny it. I've seen that expression often enough."

She wasn't sure anymore.

He took her silence for agreement. "I wish you luck, Juliet White. More luck than your sister had."

In her heart, Juliet knew she'd need it.

On Monday morning the sheriff hired a beribboned cart and a prancing white horse. His coachman squired the girls to their favorite tea shop. By Monday afternoon the duke had engaged an open carriage and four matched grays. Jamie drove the sheriff's children to MacKenzie's Mercantile where they spent a generous allowance. That evening the duke attended the theater with the Meltons and was seen arm in arm with their daughter, Miss Felicity. Juliet cried herself to sleep.

On Tuesday the sheriff himself took Juliet and the girls to Pickwell's Dining Club. When Sarah requested broonie, Mr. Pickwell fetched the dessert from MacLeod's Bakery. An hour later the duke and Lady Bridget and her children strolled into MacKenzie's Fish

House. For dessert, Mr. MacKenzie offered marzipan candy from Covington's Confectionery. That evening the duke was the guest of honor at a musicale attended by so many eligible young ladies that the *Tain Crier* had to add a page to list all of the names. Juliet used the paper for kindling.

On Wednesday the carriages met on Thistle Road. The children waved to one another. The duke nodded curtly to the sheriff. Juliet witnessed the spontaneous greeting. So did Lady Bridget, for she winked at Juliet. The paper went unread that evening.

On Thursday the duke treated David and his brothers to a round of golf. The sheriff presided over the town council, which degenerated into an arguing match. Still wearing his sporting clothes and Highland bonnet, the duke strolled in and took the seat reserved for the over-lord. Six hours later he and the sheriff shared a tankard at the Thistle and Badger Tavern. A reliable source swore that the duke paid considerable attention to a bar-maid named Ellen and even left her half a crown for her trouble. Juliet tossed the paper down the privy shaft.

On Friday the duke took his hostages to the fortune-teller in the city of Easter Loggie. When questioned about the exuberant welcome she'd offered His Grace of Ross, the sultry Gypsy confessed to being a former mistress of the duke. Henrietta went on to report that the sheriff waved a greeting to the duke and the peer of the realm returned the salute. At last a reconciliation between the two most stubborn men in Scotland seemed possible. Juliet buried the paper in the compost pile.

Who would yield the other's children first? The duke or the sheriff?

Speculation ran wild.

English pubs and Scottish alehouses posted odds and took bets. Constables were hired to direct cross traffic on Thistle Road and to see the drunken patrons home.

On Saturday the two men and their "wards," as the women and children were now called, met at the Chil-dren's Circus in Tain. An amused Juliet looked on as four armored knights on caparisoned steeds offered rides to the duke's daughters. Giggling, their faces aglow with excitement, their cheeks pink from too much sun, the girls waved to the crowd. Lottie tossed rose petals. The air sang with the thrill of spring.

A fifth mounted knight approached Juliet. The visor hid his face, but his dark blue eyes gave him away.

The duke of Ross.

"Come, fair maiden." He extended a gauntleted hand.

Armor rattled as he leaned toward her, his powerful thighs restraining the prancing horse. "You want to," he coaxed.

God help her, she did. Knowing she shouldn't, certain she'd be sorry, Juliet raised her arms and allowed him to lift her onto the saddle.

His arm circled her waist and brought her snug against his breastplate. The cool steel of his visor touched her cheek. "Miss me?"

Miffed at her own weakness, she said, "As much as I miss the dung of Mr. Mabry's cows."

He guided the horse away from the crowded fair-grounds and into the quiet forest. "You don't mean that. Tell the truth, Juliet. You feel empty without me."

"How dare you say such a thing while you court every eligible female in Easter Ross?"

"Jealous?"

Of course she was. "You can sire four illegitimate sons for all I care."

"Duck!" He crouched over her. Juliet grabbed the horse's mane. A low branch loomed ahead. It whizzed past her and slapped his helmet.

He reined in the steed, set Juliet on the ground, then dismounted. "I'd rather get a legitimate son from you."

He'd say anything, rake that he was. But she knew him too well. "That's unfortunate, for I'm unavailable."

He drew off the helmet. His hair flowed past his shoulders. "You're handfasted to me."

"That's a farce and you know it."

"Neville is poisoning your mind against me. Don't you see that?"

Longing tugged at her. She couldn't fall victim to him again. "Take me back."

"Ah, lassie." He took her in his arms. Putting his lips close to hers, he said, "I was hoping you'd say that."

He'd gotten it all wrong. She opened her mouth to tell him so, but the feel of his lips on hers was so right that she couldn't find the will to argue. With a steel-encased hand, he cradled her head. With an expert touch, he summoned her desire. Delicious visions came to mind, visions of him loving her, him swearing she made him feel like a king. Oh, God, she longed to be his queen.

"I wondered," boomed the voice of Neville Smithson, "when the stag would come to rut."

Juliet froze, but her lover continued as if he hadn't heard. Mortified that someone had witnessed her wanton behavior, she drew away. And saw the sheriff mounted on a white horse.

The duke pulled her back. "Give me your tongue," he whispered. "Nay?" Innocence wreathed his face. Louder, he said, "Then perhaps I should wield my claymore and rid us of this intruder. Would that please you, Juliet?"

She glanced over her shoulder. Would the sheriff back down? The hard set to his jaw told her no. Experience told her the duke wouldn't consider yielding.

What could she do?

"Juliet . . . ?" beckoned the duke.

Her spine went limp at the tenderness in his voice. Over the buzz of desire that rang in her head, she heard the sheriff move his mount closer. She had to do something.

She scooped up the helmet. "Put this on."

The duke complied, but raised the visor. "Ask me to bring you Rome, my sweet, and 'twill be yours."

Taking a deep breath and praying for the best, she reached for the duke's visor and slammed it shut. "There, brave knight." To cover his muffled curses, she shouted, "You've received your reward."

Choked laughter erupted behind the visor. "Clever wench."

ompliment gave her courage, and stirred emo-
e refused to define. Turning to Neville, she said,

"Good day, my lord high sheriff. Will you ride with us?"

He sat back in the saddle, a smile quirking his lips. "Lead the way."

The duke touched his helmet in salute, then lifted Juliet into the saddle. Holding her close, he guided the horse to the fairgrounds. Once there, he seemed reluctant to let her go.

His parting whisper, "Come back to my bed, Juliet," singed her ears and warmed her heart.

Early the next week the sheriff took the girls sailing on Cromarty Firth. Afterward Juliet put them to bed and retired to her adjoining room. Unable to sleep, she sat in a chair in a corner and stared into the darkness.

The shutters flew open. Moonlight poured into the room. She jumped to her feet in time to see a pair of very familiar legs touch the carpeted floor. With the stealth and agility of a Shawnee brave, he eased through the window and crept toward the bed.

The duke of Ross.

Excitement fluttered in her stomach.

He'd come for her.

Buoyed by joy, she went to him. Silver light shone on his beloved face, accentuating his regal nose and elegant cheekbones.

"Don't scream," he whispered, clutching her arm.

Scream? She wanted to shout her happiness to the heavens.

He'd come for her.

"Is Mary all right?"

Euphoria plummeted. Juliet felt like a soiled rag, discarded now that its purpose was served. He hadn't come for her; he'd come to check on his children. "They're all fine."

"But Neville took Mary sailing today."

Struggling for aloofness, Juliet said, "And you think she might be sick."

He surveyed the room. "She always gets sick on the sea."

"Not this time." Juliet pulled away.

"Where are you going?"

"To fetch my robe."

His eyes raked her, from the neckline of her gown to the toes of her slippers. "Expecting Neville?"

As if he'd hit her with his fist, she reeled. "Get out."

"Not before I deliver a message. Cogburn Pitt arrived today. He's most anxious to see you."

Did the duke know why Cogburn had come? She had expected him, but news of his arrival brought her no joy. She would have to leave Scotland now. She'd have to leave the children she adored and the man she distrusted. "Where is Cogburn?"

"In the library at Rosshaven, visiting with Ian."

"Will you give him a message?"

"Aye, if you tell me something, Juliet White." He stalked her into the corner. "Have you lain with Neville?"

He caught her arm before she could slap him. "That's none of your business."

"Oh, yes it is. You're handfasted to me."

"Handfasted. That's your heathen custom. Not mine. I want nothing to do with you."

He sucked in his breath. "Then you *have* lain with Neville. Tell me this, Juliet. Do you enjoy raising your skirts for both of us? Do you wallow beneath him and dig your nails into his back, too? Ah, still modest, I see. Tell me this, had you planned to go so far to steal Lillian's child?"

Her pounding heart grew silent. Her mind wailed with rage. "How did you find out?"

"Lottie brought me the letter."

"When?"

"Before we left Kinbairn."

Words came tumbling out: "You knew all along who I was. You lay with me. And you knew. You spoke of the future. And you knew. You made me love you. And you knew." She clutched his shirt. "Which one is my niece?"

"You'll never learn the answer to that."

"Oh, yes I will. I read Scottish now. I'll go back to Kinbairn. I'll look in the Books of the MacKenzies."

"You won't find the page you want. I burned it."

"How could you?"

"Shush." His hand covered her mouth.

Her teeth sank into his flesh.

"Ouch!"

"Tell me."

"Never."

The door swung open. Neville stood on the threshold, a lamp in one hand, a pistol in the other. "Rutting again?"

Without thinking, Lachlan stepped between Juliet and the gun. Neville's friendly overtures had been an act. He had no intention of forgetting the past and making peace. And Juliet was no better than her selfish, whoring sister. Lachlan cursed himself for a naive, chivalrous fool. "Angry because I got here before you, Neville?"

"A novel twist, don't you think?" He jerked the gun toward the hall. "You're under arrest, Your Grace."

Lachlan glanced over his shoulder. Juliet's face had gone pasty white, her eyes blank. Why had he said such a hurtful thing? Because his world had gone tapsal-teerie and he had only one way to right it. But by choosing that path, he ran the risk of losing her forever. In despair, he reached for her.

She recoiled.

"No more of that," said Neville. "Juliet, are you well?"

Her eyes drifted to Neville. As if dazed, she nodded, walked to the chair, and sat.

"Please excuse us, Juliet," Neville said.

Ignoring the gun at his back, Lachlan led the way down the hall. As a child, he'd come here often, and although twenty-five years had passed, he easily found his way to the study that had once belonged to Gibson MacLeod.

Neville seated himself behind his desk and put down the gun. With his thumb and forefinger, he traced his bent nose. "Shall I wake the clergyman? Or will tomorrow do?"

Satisfaction rippled through Lachlan. "The clergy? So you've finally decided to bargain."

Neville smiled the smile that had once sent duchesses

into a swoon. "To uphold the king's law. Do you deny that you seduced Juliet White?"

"I don't answer to you."

"No?" He spun the pistol on the table. The metal whirled on the desk. "Juliet is unwed and under my roof. As sheriff, it is my duty to see justice done. You compromised her." He stopped the spinning gun, the barrel pointed precisely at Lachlan's chest. "You'll marry her."

"When badgers sing!" Rage pumping through his veins, Lachlan shot to his feet. "I'd just come into the room. I was fully dressed."

Neville picked up the gun. "Sit down. And don't forget that I know you better than most. I saw you at court."

Annoyed, Lachlan said, "That's just a wheen o' blethers. I've changed." Thanks to Juliet, he was a different man.

"Bah!" spat Neville. "It's a blessing I entered Juliet's room when I did."

"Who's to say *you* haven't been up her skirts?"

As calm as a good Christian on Sunday, Neville said, "My word as a gentleman. Seducing sisters is your specialty, not mine."

Here it comes, thought Lachlan. "I don't ken what you're talking about."

"Lillian."

Lachlan tried not to flinch. As always, Neville didn't mince words. "Think you I seduced her?"

"I know you did, and thanks to Juliet, I also know Lillian died bearing your child."

Lachlan had expected as much. But being blamed for a crime he hadn't committed rankled his pride. "You hate me for taking in your discarded woman, don't you? It fair makes your common blood boil."

"By damn, yes," Neville said, sneering.

"Is it the only reason you hate me?"

"It's enough, you thick-headed Scotsman. Lillian was mine."

Be reasonable, Lachlan told himself. The strife in Easter Ross had ground to a halt and would stay that way only if he made a lasting peace with Neville. But first, they must put away the past. Lachlan said, "Put down that gun and tell me why you never tried to find Lillian."

The pistol hit the table. "I don't share women with you."

"What could you have offered Lillian? You were wed to Bridget at the time."

A twitch marred the smooth plane of Neville's jaw. He shot to his feet and walked to the window. Drawing back the drapes, he peered into the night. "I offered her my protection and a house in London. Even a bastard is entitled to a mistress."

Lachlan thought of his four lassies and the careless people who called them bastards. "I'm sorry I called you a bastard. Your father's sin is not yours. I know that now."

Neville's shoulders slumped. "Thank you."

Lachlan propped his feet on the desk. "What did Lillian have to say to your noble offer of protection?"

"She pouted those pretty lips and said she wanted marriage."

Lillian's version had been vastly different. She had sworn she was tired of Neville, that he was a poor lover and tight with his coin. "Was it then you told her you were already wed and had a son?"

He nodded and turned around. "She started throwing things and yelling that that was fine because she wanted a richer man. She found one, I see. A newly instated, unattached, and very wealthy duke who wouldn't make an honest woman of her. But he will her sister. Get your boots off my desk."

"Sorry." Lachlan sat straight in the chair. "This wealthy duke wants his woman and his lassies back. And a lasting peace in Easter Ross."

Neville stared at the gun. "You said as much in the tavern and again in Easter Loggie."

"I meant it. Lillian's dead and buried. Can't we leave her to rest in peace?"

Neville shoved his chair so hard it tipped over. "You seduced her. She was my mistress. You made me look the fool."

Seizing the opening, Lachlan said, "I swear, on the souls of my kin who died at Culloden Moor, that I did not seduce Lillian White. I never lay with her. I did nothing to blacken your name."

The solemn pledge had the desired effect on Neville. "God help me, for I believe you." He sounded very much like the man Lachlan had once known, a man who had sworn to uphold the law.

Neville righted the chair. "How do you propose we solve our *mutual* problems here in Easter Ross?"

He needed Lachlan's help. Like a gambler playing an ace on his opponent's king, Lachlan said, "A betrothal might put us on the path."

"Not on your life. You'll marry Juliet straightaway or go to jail as any criminal in my district would."

"I won't force her, Neville. The lass must come to me of her own free will."

"Do you love her?"

"Oh, aye. Twice I've proposed marriage, but she'll nae agree."

A troubled frown creased Neville's brow. "She thinks you seduced Lillian."

"Aye, she does. 'Tis the reason she won't have me."

"Then why did you bring up a betrothal?"

" 'Twasn't me I was speaking of. 'Twas David and one of my lassies. He's a fine laddie. I'd be proud to call him son."

Neville's mouth went slack. He stared in disbelief. "Such a marriage would unite our families and ensure peace between Scots and English in Easter Ross."

Hiding a smile, Lachlan said, "Aye, 'twill. I'll petition the king to name David the earl of Tain."

His face a picture of doubt, Neville chewed his lip. "Why would you do that?"

"Because you and I were friends once. I think we can be again. Besides, an earldom is David's birthright from his grandfather. I'll make it so."

"Gibson MacLeod was a cruel old man."

"Aye, he was, but David favors you."

Neville shook his head and smiled ruefully. "Don't waste your pretty compliments on me, MacKenzie. I know you." He extended his hand in friendship. "Sarah, then. She'll become David's wife."

Lachlan's stomach lurched. "Nay."

Neville leaned forward, his mouth set in a determined line. "She's perfect for him. They're both bright. They're both handsome children. David talks too much on occasion, but he's—"

"Her brother."

"—never rude or cruel. They like each other. Both have told me so. The MacKenzies like him . . . all the Scots like him, and the English adore Sarah—er, what's that you said?"

"He's her brother."

Neville's face paled. "You lie."

Lachlan crossed his legs. "I've no reason to lie about such a thing, Neville. She's Lillian's lassie. By you. Not me."

Neville wilted into the chair. "But, how . . . ?"

Lachlan laughed. "You of all people shouldn't be needing a dissertation on that."

"How did you get the child? And when?"

"The king made you sheriff on the condition that you'd reconcile with Bridget. You left London. Lillian came to me for help. I gave her passage money to Virginia. Six months later I received word that she had died in Edinburgh."

"You could have told me." He leaned back and stared at the stuccoed ceiling. "If you knew she was carrying my child . . ."

"What would you have done? Brought the mite home to Bridget? You needed to patch up your marriage and be a father to young David." Lachlan blew out his breath. "Wonderful as your wife is, I don't think she would've welcomed Sarah. I couldn't bear the thought of the lassie in an orphanage. I'd already fetched Lottie, Agnes, and Mary. Fatherhood agreed with me."

"I don't know what to say."

"You must give me your word you'll never tell her. 'Twould make her life seem a lie."

"I agree. Living with the curse of bastardy is hard enough for a child."

Would Neville ever overcome his bitterness? Lachlan didn't know, but he intended to help. "You haven't done so badly."

Neville gazed around the room. "No, I suppose I haven't. Who else knows about Sarah?"

"No one."

"You have my word. I'll never tell Sarah."

Lachlan felt as if a weight had been lifted from his shoulders. He held out his hand. " 'Tis best for the lass."

Neville rubbed his forehead. "Sarah," he repeated as if her name were a revelation. "I don't know whether to shoot you, thank you, or arrest you."

"If you throw me in jail, the MacKenzies will revolt, savages that they are and all."

Neville made a hissing sound. "Since when have they needed an excuse to revolt?"

"They speak so well of you. They fair praise your name."

Neville laughed, took Lachlan's hand, and shook it. "And the badgers will sing a song about that, too, I'll wager." He plopped into the chair. "Lottie will make David a fine wife."

"Aye, she will. You'll send her and her sisters home tomorrow?"

"No. I'll bring them myself." Neville grew serious. "Will you tell me the names of the women who bore Lottie and Agnes?"

Sensing that the information could seal their friendship, Lachlan said, "Lottie's mother is Alice Marlborough."

Neville sputtered, "My God, Lottie's a descendant of Charles the Second."

Warmth filled Lachlan. "Aye, and she fair acts the queen, doesn't she? I hope her MacKenzie blood and her fine husband prevail."

Shaking his head, Neville said, "And Agnes?"

Lachlan chuckled. "Bianca Campbell."

Neville groaned. "You bagged Argyll's niece?"

"Aye, but she was a pretty fair bagger herself."

"You've been in some fine beds, MacKenzie."

Emptiness plagued Lachlan. "Mine's lonely now, though."

Neville's expression grew kind. "What will you do about Juliet?"

Lachlan sighed, too weary to fight the futility that gnawed at him. "I don't know. She came to Scotland to fetch the child and return to Virginia."

"She fell in love with you. I have the power to force the marriage."

"The lassie's too stubborn to force, and she blames me for Lillian's death."

"Tell her the truth," Neville said. "She wants desperately to learn about Lillian. She often asks."

"What have you told her?"

Neville shrugged. "That Lillian was companion to a titled lady. I couldn't tell her the truth."

"Neither will I. And 'tis not my place to tell her who sired Sarah."

"It's mine."

"Aye, 'tis. And I would have Juliet know only fond memories of Lillian."

Smiling sadly, Neville said, "Like the time she gifted me with a braying ass. My Lilly was a great one for a jest."

"I'm glad you remember her that way. There's no point in revealing any of her other amorous escapades at court."

"I can manage that. I was, after all, her last *escapade*."

Lillian had bedded dozens of men before Neville. Her reputation was legend. But Juliet needn't know that.

Neville got to his feet. "I'll talk to Juliet, but since you have Henrietta Worthingham under your thumb, you send word of the betrothal."

Distracted, Lachlan nodded.

"I'm curious," said Neville. "How did you win the English over?"

Lachlan pushed out of the chair. "The same way you'll win over the Scots. I'll help you."

Neville laughed. "Who would have thought I'd ever be your pupil, MacKenzie?"

Chapter 18

Juliet folded her woolen dress and placed it in her traveling bag. Her hands no longer shook. Her stomach no longer roiled. Even when she recalled the duke's angry words, she didn't cringe in horror. Like a hot blade searing a wound, his accusation had numbed her pain and sealed her heart. She knew what she must do.

Virginia and her future awaited. She would sail on the next ship with Cogburn. For the most part her plans would remain the same. Happiness with the Mabry family awaited her. Fulfillment was hers for the taking.

She hefted the bag to the floor and picked up her shawl. Only one more task remained. Quietly she walked into the hall. She heard voices; the duke's and the sheriff's. What could be taking them so long? And why weren't they shouting?

She paid them no mind; she'd already invested too much time in their quarrel. It wasn't her concern. She had her own life to live.

Carefully she opened the door to the room where the girls slept. One lamp, the wick turned low, illuminated the room. As she gazed at their sleeping forms, love blossomed in her breast.

Mary lay on her side, her face to the light. No longer a chubby, vulnerable child, she would seek out her own answers to life's questions.

In the next bed lay Agnes, flat on her back, her face turned boldly to the world. She would make life give her what she wanted, and she would run over anyone who stood in her way.

On tiptoe, Juliet moved on to timid, trusting Sarah. As picturesque as an angel, she slept on her stomach, her cheek resting on hands, which were folded as if in prayer. The future would be kind to this gentle girl; her father would make it so.

Oh, but he'd need all his patience and love for the last of his lassies. And as she stood beside the sleeping Lottie, Juliet wondered what the future held for this clever and queenly girl.

What kind of husbands would the duke find for his lassies? Fine ones, she imagined, for where his children were concerned, he was a man to be praised.

She stepped back and surveyed the last three girls. One of them was Lillian's child. But Juliet no longer cared which one. She loved them all. She would never forget them. And if she credited herself with any part of their growth, it was the loyalty they now showed to each other.

Good-bye, sweet lassies. Lang mae yer lum reek.

Footsteps sounded behind her. But Juliet wasn't alarmed. She didn't belong in Scotland. No one here could frighten or threaten her. Not now.

Feeling oddly detached, she turned. The sheriff of Easter Ross stood in the doorway. Concern knitted his brow. She'd come to like this Englishman, and if the duke of Ross would but try, he could renew his friendship with Neville Smithson. They were so similar—both fiercely loyal fathers, both stubborn, demanding men.

He moved aside. She closed the door and walked to her room.

He followed. "You're leaving."

Ignoring the tightness in her throat, she said, "Yes."

"I thought you loved Lachlan MacKenzie. He wants you. He'll fetch you back."

Juliet thought of the indenture paper she'd signed and of the protection the document now offered. "No, he won't. He'll find himself a proper duchess or go back to wenching."

"He can be very persuasive."

Hearing admiration in his voice, Juliet said, "Then you've come to an agreement with him?"

"Yes, thanks to you."

"I'm very glad for you both, and for the people of Easter Ross."

"Why won't you stay, Juliet?"

"I can't."

"Because of his association with Lillian?"

So, the duke and Neville had spoken of her. "Enough has been said about my sister and the past. I want only to go home to Virginia."

"Do you . . . ah"—he pointed to her bag—"have all of your things? I mean, surely you've left something." Smiling, he added, "Women always do."

Only my heart and my sister's child. "I have everything I need."

"The Bristol packet doesn't sail until daybreak. You can't stay alone at the docks until then."

She thought of Cogburn, his ready smile, his complaints about the cold. "I won't be alone."

"Nevertheless, please come downstairs with me. I'd like to talk to you."

She felt drained and out of place, ready to go home. "About what?"

He took her arm and guided her to the stairs. "I have a story to tell you about a prideful bastard from King's Arms Yard in London, and his follies at the English court."

An hour later Juliet stepped through the kitchen door of Rosshaven. Warmth and happiness surrounded her. With all her heart she wished she could stay here and grow old with the duke of Ross. But such was not the fate of a poor bond servant from Virginia.

"Good luck," Neville whispered.

She turned and waved, too grateful to speak, too excited to dally. Pulling off her shoes, she tiptoed through the kitchen. Voices drifted from the library. She stopped and put her ear to the door. And smiled when she heard Cogburn's voice.

". . . wretchedly cold country. Now, Virginia, there's a place to warm your bones."

"Heathens and criminals," spat Ian. "An' horse races a quarter mile long. Who ever heard of such a thing?"

Torn between exuberance and sadness, Juliet moved on. Things would work out. She'd leave Scotland with a clear conscience and unsullied memories of Lillian.

Lachlan hadn't seduced Lillian. Concern for the child

had kept him silent. Concern for the child had made him strike out with cruel words. Her heart, so broken and bruised a while ago, now thrummed with resigned contentment. She could tell him good-bye. She could even tell him the truth.

And she would love him once more before she did. She'd leave Scotland with the taste of his lips on hers. With that in mind, she made her way to his study.

He lay slumped in a wing chair facing the fireplace. Glow from the remaining coals cast a golden light on his beloved features. Shirtless and slumbering peacefully, he looked every inch the mighty Highland lord. He'd braided his hair, donned his doeskin breeches and family amulets.

Smiling in soul-deep satisfaction at what was to come, she quietly added logs to the fire. Then she took off her clothes and donned the ceremonial robe. Weighing at least a stone and dragging the floor, the garment was perfect for Lachlan. The sleek satin lining caressed her skin and fostered memories of his hands and his lips. A shiver coursed through her.

Kneeling before him, she rested her head on his knee.

He stirred, but didn't wake.

With her fingernail, she traced the inside seam of his breeches. His eyelids drifted open, revealing sapphire blue eyes that glittered with awareness. His gaze took in the family robe, her upswept hair, her hand on his leg.

She basked in his silent, sensual appraisal.

"Do you like the robe?" he asked, reaching for the golden cord tied in a bow at her neck.

Anticipation brought a smile to her lips. "Not as much as I like you."

Grinning a rakish grin, he pulled on the cord and said, "What part of me do you like best?"

Untied, the heavy robe slipped below her shoulders. With his index finger, he mapped her collarbone. Pleasure skittered over her bare skin, and her eyes drifted shut. "I like your honor, your good heart, and perhaps your nose."

"My nose?" he choked out.

Laughter bubbled inside her. "Don't tell me other women haven't mentioned your nose."

"Not," he said blithely, "at a moment like this."

Swamped by sentimentality and raw desire, she said, "It is a special moment, isn't it?"

His hands stilled and his expression grew serious. "Why is it special to you, Juliet?"

"Because Neville told me that he sired Lillian's child. I'm sorry I accused you wrongly."

He sat back in the chair and stared into the fire. "So now you can give yourself to me without guilt. Or are you atoning?"

Something was wrong. He should welcome her. He should say his rakish words and make her laugh. "I'm doing neither."

He strummed his fingers on the arm of the chair. His expression told her nothing about his thoughts. "Did he tell you which child?"

"No."

He faced her again. Flames from the now roaring fire danced in his eyes. "But you came here to get the child and take her back to Virginia. Have you changed your mind?"

She couldn't lie to this Lachlan MacKenzie; his expression was too honest, too open. "Partly."

"That isn't much of an explanation, Juliet."

The fire crackled and warmed her back. She didn't know how to manage this grave-hearted Lachlan MacKenzie. Where was the rogue? "I must return to Virginia, but I can't take a child from the father who loves her. I thought I could. But I can't."

He folded his arms over his naked chest. Muscles bunched in his arms; sinews in his neck grew taut. "So I'm to be treated to one final night in your arms before you flitter off with Cogburn Pitt?"

She crumpled inside. Tears clogged her throat. He sounded so very cold, looked so very angry. "It's all I have to give you, Lachlan."

He grasped her shoulders. "Why, Juliet? Why won't you stay with me?"

Her head fell back. Warm tears rolled down her cheeks. "Because I gave my word."

"To whom?"

"The Mabrys."

In that instant she glimpsed a vulnerable man behind the mighty Highland lord. "What about me? You gave yourself to me."

"Yes, and I won't forget you."

"How can your pledge to a family half a world away mean more to you than we do? We love you."

How could a wealthy Scottish duke understand the life of a poor bond servant? "It's not a matter of loving them more than I love you and your children. Please try to understand."

"Bless Saint Ninian, I am trying. Write to the Mabrys. Hell, *I'll* write to them and tell them you're not coming back. If that's not enough, I'll have the king send them a bletherin royal writ."

Misery carved a hole in her heart. "I can't. In exchange for money to come here, I indentured myself to the Mabrys for ten more years. I'm legally bound to return."

His eyes grew wide with shock. "You traded ten years of your life for the chance to find Lillian's child?"

"Ten years wasn't so much, not to me. I didn't know Lillian had a child until I arrived in Scotland. Then I had to find her. I couldn't let her be mistreated. I wanted to love her."

"You do, Juliet. Only a wee bit more than I, but that's because I've known her longer. Shall I tell you which one she is?"

She laid two fingers across his mouth. "No. I love them all the same."

"But it's what you came for. You want to know."

She shook her head. "I know all that I need to know. Lillian's child is safe with her wonderful father."

On a fake grumble, he said, "I'll be a better husband, I trow. How much money did the Mabrys give you?"

"Five hundred pounds."

"I'll pay five million pounds if that's what it takes to keep you. Cogburn can deliver the message and the money for your indenture. Will you stay, Juliet? Will you be my love?"

The words filled her, surrounded her, healing the wound that had been her heart. Happiness lay before her in the form of a man and his love. She thought about the years to come. She would bear his children; she'd wake up at his side every morning. He'd tease her; she would give as good as she got. Feeling brave and joyous, she said, "Aye, Lachlan, I'll love you always, if you'll do one more thing."

He tapped her nose. "I can think of a dozen more things, but most of them require a feather bed. Two of them, however, could be accomplished nicely in this chair."

Suppressing a smile, she said, "Will you marry me legally?"

He tilted his head to one side, causing a braid to dance about his shoulder. His expressive eyes glowed with mischief. "And hear you promise to obey me? Oh, aye, Duchess. I'll wed with you today."

She felt shy and insecure. "I don't know how to be a duchess."

He smiled and eased off the chair. Facing her, his hand on his heart, he said, " 'Twill take much training and patience and sacrifice on my part. But I shall endure."

She covered his hand with hers. "Will you forgive me for deceiving you?"

He chewed his lip and tried to appear stern. "Forgive you? Perhaps I will, my love. But 'twill take much loving and understanding and sacrifice on your part."

Breathless with anticipation, she said, "Where shall I begin?"

Grinning her favorite rakish grin, he said, "Taking off that robe would be a good start."

Filled with amused affection, she slipped the robe from her shoulders, and as the symbol of Scotland's highest order of chivalry pooled around her, she embraced the man who'd earned it.